Books by
Barbara Spencer

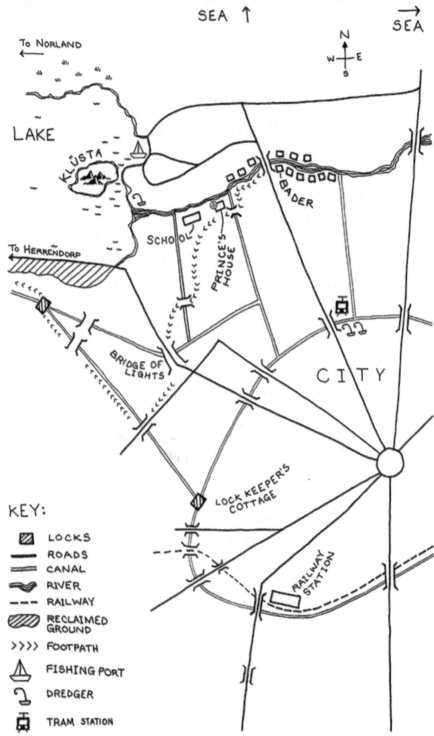

Canals and walkways of the old city

They set out in the dead of night. Not the witching hour between twelve and one, when ghouls and warlocks roam, but the hour between three and four, when souls depart their bodies and even monsters sleep.

The men have not slept. Gathering together early, they have sat out the hours in a low-beamed room lit by rushes and lanterns, supping at pale gold Jenever and beer that smells strongly of hops, in an effort to keep both demons and fear at bay. Another night and their drinking will lead to merriment and song with an accordion ringing out. Tonight, only a dull confused muttering breaks the silent air.

Around the hostelry, stinking of poverty and superstition cluster close-knit houses, their streets made not of stone but of water. Women wait too, in dark rooms lit only by candles – no one sleeping. Some are big with child. Others, the young and beautiful and innocent, are held captive, screaming into the implacable faces of the elderly to be let free, to be allowed to run ... to warn.

Outside, clinging to tiny islands of stone on which houses perch, lurks the detritus of the fishermen; lobster pots and broken nets, oars resting against a wall, small skiffs tied up to the bank or upturned. Boats, their sails neatly furled, await the approach of early dawn before venturing out to sea.

Nothing moves in the darkness except fleetingly: a rat scurrying along a gutter pursued by the looming shadow of a cat. Silence falls and with it the sound of death.

1

Leaving my books scattered about the lawn, I wandered down to the tiny beachhead, the afternoon sun layering sheets of steel across the surface of the lake. To the east, not far as the crow flies, a few kilometres only, lies a tiny fishing harbour and on days when the sky rises higher and higher, it felt so close you might imagine if you stretched out your hand you would touch it. Today only a tall-masted ship is tied up at the dockside, the tip of its masts lost in the blue wash of the sky. And nearby, staring at me balefully like a hungry black toad – Klüsta – the island of a thousand rumours.

I dreamed about it again last night. Until I came here to college and stumbled upon the lakeshore, I knew it only as a black shadow lapped by waves in which I saw figures moving. I imagined my brother Pieter to be among them. That might well have been wishful thinking for the island is no longer inhabited except by birds.

There was a village there once. Even that is difficult to imagine for the rocky outcrop lies cocooned within a mesh of turbulent water. Sometimes when out walking I'd overhear fishermen boasting about their escape from the dreaded Devil's

Hand, a little line of five rocks on the island's foreshore, its
stormy waters greedily anticipating their next meal of wood
and hemp. They'd swap stories as they tidied their nets checking
them for holes, about how the current around Klüsta was set
fast that day, dragging them onto the rocks, and only a belief
in the Almighty gave them strength enough to escape.

'For goodness sake, Maidy, what is it with you and water?'

Startled, my pen hand jerked leaving a nasty smudge. Ruth
was strolling across the grass, her corn-coloured hair swept into
an elegant chignon. I wondered which magazine she'd copied
it from – and when? She'd been wearing it loose at lunchtime.
Behind her, the college building gleamed pale against its
background of dark fir trees. Embellished with pillars and
porticos, and flanked by wide angled steps, it reminded me
of the vulgar opulence of a sultan's palace, its fancy cupola
tall enough to block the afternoon sun which threatened my
writing with its gleaming spirals of light.

'You told me you were planning to work. Haven't you a
story to write?'

I picked my way across the pebble bank onto grass, careful
to avoid stepping on a cluster of daisies, their cheerful faces
capable of brightening even the gloomiest of days. 'I have and
I was,' I laughed a shade self-consciously. 'Only last night I had
this dream—'

'Tell me later.' Ruth cut across my words, her attention
fastened on the swing doors. It didn't bother me, well used
to my remarks brushing past her unnoticed like the wings of
a moth. 'It's more important to find Jules before he leaves for
home.'

I glanced down at my watch. 'No one's out yet – it's still a
few minutes to the bell. How did you manage it?'

'I simply bat my eyelids and look feeble.' Ruth smiled
and a dimple tugged at the corner of her cheek. 'Works like a

charm. You know what it's like when the bell goes – a stampede with everyone rushing to get out first. Ugh!' She shuddered dramatically, 'I can't bear it. All those unwashed bodies. No, thank you!'

'Honestly, Ruth, however will you cope when you're a doctor?'

'Don't worry, I'll be a brilliant doctor, you'll see. Besides, patients are always washed before the doctor sees them.'

'So why Jules? I thought it was Frederick.'

'Frederick! He's no use, he's languages.' Ruth flipped her hand, dismissing him. He was last week's companion. 'I need Jules.'

'Why him in particular?' I persisted, adding more cautiously, 'He's not … dare I say it, really your type.'

'Who is, in this god-forsaken place?' Nonchalantly, she swivelled her long fingers in a circle. 'However, in this instance, Jules is perfect for the job. I was reading a magazine in anatomy and wasn't paying attention when Professor Blaize announced our anatomy assignment.' She giggled. 'Luckily, Jules was.'

I began to pack my books away. 'You mean he's clever.'

'The cleverest.'

She bent down as if to help, picking up my journal that was lying open on the grass, its pages fluttering back and forth in the breeze. I'd never used it as a diary, writing dull lines about even duller events; instead, I filled its pages with memories of childhood and scraps of stories. Of little interest to anyone except me, for whom they were precious jewels that needed guarding against pickpockets and burglars. I'd hate for anyone to read them and scoff – especially my best friend. I waited, my hand stretched out, palm upwards.

'Remind me to read your stories some time. I promise not to laugh.'

'That's just it. You would, and I'd be mortified.'

'How many stories have you actually written?'

'Possibly a thousand and one like Scheherazade.'

'And finished? *How many?*'

'Honestly, Ruth,' I said, trying to sound serious and failing miserably. 'You know perfectly well the answer to that. I am more like one of the sultan's hapless wives who were executed next morning. I promise this one is different. It *has* to be finished. Professor Dulmes gave us the work three weeks ago and I've hardly started it yet.'

'Is he that tall skinny man who talks with a plum in his mouth?'

'He does not,' I protested indignantly. 'He speaks beautifully, using all the right words in *all* the right places, *and* he's read every book in the world.'

'So what *are* you going to write about?'

I hesitated, aware of her reaction. 'I thought perhaps my soldier,' I ventured after a long pause.

Slamming my journal shut, she thrust it deep inside my bag as if wanting to obliterate every word on its pages. 'Not that beastly man – I forbid it.'

'I can't think of anything else,' I sighed. 'I'm not like you, Ruth, I've never been abroad. I've never even been out of the city.'

'So make it up.' Metaphorically, Ruth stamped her foot. She used to do it for real when we were little. Once she understood it wasn't ladylike, she never did it again. 'That's what real writers do,' she snapped. 'What about the stories you told me about pirates and princes? You can use one of those.'

You don't argue with Ruth, still I tried. 'They're fairy stories. I've grown past that stage in my life. Besides, I'm supposed to write about something real and that's the only thing I can come up with.'

The bell broke into the silence of the afternoon.

Dragging me onto my feet, she tucked her arm through mine. It isn't difficult to do, I don't weigh much. The afternoon sunlight extended our shadows across the smooth green turf; Ruth's was almost half a head taller … an elegant goddess.

Why couldn't I think of some other word to describe her? If I was ever to become a writer, I needed an armoury of descriptive words at my fingertips. I stared at the ground, trying to dredge up a word that might do her justice. Ruth wasn't simply beautiful; she was glorious … like sunshine after a thunderstorm.

We've been best friends since childhood. She was pretty even then, despite being thin and dirty, and wearing ragged clothes. And she knew it. Later, in our childhood games, it was always Ruth who played the part of the princess and I her faithful lackey. And, naturally, it was Ruth who decided we should go to college. I'd never given it a thought, expecting to look for a job after I left school. But Ruth had set her mind on it and her father, Meneer Endelbaum, was only too happy to agree.

I had felt nervous about asking Pappy and had delayed until the very last moment. 'You have to come with me,' she had admonished on a daily basis, as each time my answer to her question was an embarrassed, 'Not yet.'

'You live in one another's pockets,' Pappy had teased when I finally plucked up courage.

Maybe I could fit into Ruth's pocket for I remained a little squiddy thing; tall enough perhaps, but slight and finely built, with a mane of dark hair that tumbled in an unruly mass down my back whenever dampness crept into the air. Very different from my brother and sister; a comfortable plumpness clothes Berthe's limbs, leaving them rounded and shapely, and Hans will resemble Pappy one day, short and stocky, although now he possesses the slight form and energy of youth.

Ruth would never fit in anyone's pocket. With a figure like the hourglass of sand that sits on our mantelshelf, her skin is flawless and lightly touched with sun, as if she inhabits a distant land in which the sun shines every day.

She stared around the forecourt as it rapidly filled with scurrying figures anxious to get home, as busy as an ants' nest that had just been stepped on. 'Jules?' Her clear bell-like tones floated through the bellowed cadences of departing students. Ruth rarely shouts, she had no need to. The majority of students are boys, their antennas permanently slanted in her direction. She is Queen Bee around whom every drone unwittingly and inescapably gathers.

He glanced up, the skin of his face invaded by acne, leaving a pockmarked map of tissue. It made him self-conscious and, in the canteen, he usually hid behind a book. Seeing Ruth smile at him, a spasm of nerves raked his Adam's apple. He swallowed and it moved convulsively. 'Me?' He pointed his finger at his chest bone.

'Of course!' She carolled, and waved her hand at the bicycles stacked higgledy-piggledy on the gravelled forecourt. 'Somewhere among that little lot is my bike. Be an absolute sweetheart and find it for me.'

It's weird how quickly the eye becomes accustomed to beauty. Most days, I never noticed; this was Ruth, my friend from next door. That day, though, she was wearing slacks and somehow, the loose folds accentuated every plane and angle of her body. Picking up a pleat of cream fabric, she gently wafted it back and forth. 'I don't want to get these dirty, they are new on.'

Eyes flew in her direction. I read in them shock at the flaunting of tradition but mostly, envy and desire.

'Ruth, at least tell him where it is. We could be here for ages,' I whispered from behind my hand. Parking was a nightmare, except it was bicycles that caused the traffic jams, not cars. 'I need to get home. Remember, I've got a story to write.'

'Nonsense. Just imagine how heroic he will feel when he does find it.'

I should have known better. Of course Jules knew where Ruth's bicycle was, so did probably ninety per cent of the other boys. A moment later, he had separated her sparkling green machine from the stack and, leaving his own on the ground with its back-wheel spinning, had wheeled it across the yard, rather like an adoring puppy fetching a slipper for its master.

'May I ride back to the city with you and ...' He hesitated long enough to take a shot at my name, his voice uncertain. 'Margaret?'

'Magrit,' Ruth reminded him.

That's my name, Magrit. Magrit Bader.

Maidy ... little unmarried one ... that came later.

With dozens of bicycles, evening time resembled the biggest funeral procession in the world, and a great cortege of soberly clad students poured down the driveway onto the highway, which swept across the southern shores of the lake. Built high on an embankment, the road floated like a magical stairway, the north shore of the lake so far distant it merged into the horizon. On maps, this vast tract of water is described as an inland sea, although its waters were fresh rather than salt and whenever gales whipped the ocean into a wild frenzy, fishermen sailed their boats upriver from the sea and worked the lake. Setting out at dawn, they were returned by early afternoon, their baskets overflowing with eel and crayfish, freshwater clams and oysters.

In the distance, a square-rigged schooner headed out across the lake, its sails little more than a dark stain upon the water. Moving fast, sunlight has gilded the ripples in its wake with wisps of gold and silver, reminding me of the pirate ships that dominated my childhood fantasies. With their black sails billowing and guns run out, they would hurtle into battle against a fat-bodied merchantman. Sometimes, in bad weather, when waves crashed against the shore, I still caught the thunderous concussion of wood against wood as their hulls collided. With the white sails of the merchantman clinging

7

like a damsel in distress, they'd split open toppling its polished spars into a blood-red sea.

I let Jules ride alongside Ruth, and trailed behind. He wouldn't have thanked me for trampling on his precious taste of paradise. Besides, I needed to think about my story. To Ruth, the very idea of my making friends with the enemy was abhorrent, writing about it even worse. Yet in the past three weeks, I had wasted page after page searching for a story that never existed. What had I ever done besides go to school? Perhaps that's why I was so eager for my birthday. In a few days I would be sixteen and I'd been thinking of little else for weeks, hoping beyond hope everything would change and, at long last, I'd get to experience something worth writing about.

In our ancient community of fishermen and lace-makers, a sixteenth birthday is akin to that of a mountaineer, who, after years of struggle, finally reaches the summit of the highest peak in the world. I had never seen a mountain, except in books. Our land was flat, our mountains the proverbial molehill and only in clouds that build over open water were peaks and escarpments to be seen. Even so, I could easily imagine the euphoria climbers must feel on discovering a new world stretched out below them. A sixteenth birthday is on a level with that – at least it is for girls. Overnight, we become adults, eligible to be courted and to marry. Even Mother was married before she was seventeen. More importantly, we are permitted to put up our hair and I had already asked if I might get rid of my plaits. I hated my hair. I wanted to cut it and feel the breeze on my neck, but that would be sacrilegious and Mother would have been so angry. Even with so small a change, she had pursed her lips, smoothing the heavy tresses back from my face. 'You have my hair,' she said, but didn't say no.

Ruth had already reached this milestone. Her birthday is in March, the same as Berthe, when winds still ripped down the waterways; although, for her, becoming sixteen made little difference; all the privileges about to be bestowed on me she acquired ages ago.

It was more than ten kilometres to the outskirts of the city, although an easy ride and all too quickly over – for Jules at least. We hit a main road and the long line of cyclists slowed, waiting for a row of cars to pass before turning out. Up ahead stood the Bridge of Lights, a busy crossroads for both canal and road, and here the bicycles scattered like birds chased by a predator, students heading to their homes in different parts of the city. Originally named *Liberation,* the bridge had been destroyed in the war and rebuilt in haste, although there was never enough money to paint its iron girders. At sunset, whenever the metal caught the rays of sun, its glowed so brightly fishermen said it was visible out at sea.

'If you want a boy to like you, talk about his job, his hobbies, and mention food a lot,' Ruth said as Jules, waving an enthusiastic farewell, headed along a different pathway home.

'However do you know that?'

'My dear child, I read.'

'Darling Ruth, *I read*; you skim through magazines.'

'I may, on occasion, pick up a magazine but which of us is the more worldly?' She used a lofty tone. When we were children, it was done to keep me in my place and had become a habit.

Our wheels hit the cobbles at the edges of the little enclave where we live and automatically we slowed and dismounted, walking our bikes along the canal, where every seat was occupied by old men and even older women, enjoying the sunshine, their black garments reminding me of a flock of crows in a ploughed field.

'I was thinking about the story you've got to write,' Ruth said as we crossed the helmeted bridge heading for the river way. Here, the daily noises of the city, with its trams and motorcars, were drowned out by the loud cry of a fisherman calling the

9

weight and price of the fish to a gaggle of housewives, patiently waiting to purchase their dinner.

I grimaced in protest. 'You were talking bones.'

'I can talk and think,' Ruth dismissed my objection. 'Besides, with boys, I rarely listen.'

'Yet you always seem so attentive.'

'Years of practice. You really have to think of something else while they're droning on and on. It's so boring, I'd go mad. I was thinking, you should write about Pieter.'

Automatically, even though I was pushing and not riding my bike, my hand reached for the brake. My bike and my thoughts lurched to a stop in tandem, my route home lost amongst a collage of painful memories.

'You have never mentioned his name,' I said. 'Not once in six years. *Why now?*'

'Because it is six years.' Ruth frowned, her dark eyebrows a straight arrow of determination. I knew she plucked them. 'And because I have put aside my dreams of marrying him.'

'Your dreams? Ruth ... we were children.'

'He would have waited.' Again, that metaphorical stamp of the foot.

'I thought ...'

'Well, you thought wrong. I only ever wanted to marry Pieter.'

I pictured my brother, his face as vividly alive as the changing patterns in the sky, recognising truth in her words. As in the song about the moon, Ruth also knew her worth.

'So I will be like you, Maidy, and never marry, and we will be friends forever.'

I flinched at the use of my nickname and took a step back, my mind whirling painfully. My thirteenth birthday, why did I join in the lies and tell them the mirror was a blank?

'Think of it as a catharsis.'

'Catharsis!' My voice sounded raw and painful in my ears. '*That* word didn't come from a magazine.'

Overhead a seagull cried out, its plaintive call cutting deep into the soul. I shivered, suddenly cold.

What had Ruth called it? A healing?

Maybe she was right.

Maybe that's what I should write about; the year the swans came, and my brother, Pieter, vanished.

Book 1

Memories of Childhood

2

In the market, cardsharps ply their trade and trick you with the speed of their hands in *Find the Lady*, or they pull a card from your sleeve that you'd swear they wrapped in a handkerchief moments before. Memories are like that. You believe them to be one thing and your parents and siblings remember them as another.

Of the early years, I remember little, and many of those memories are artificial, innocently supplied by Pappy when he sat me on his knee before bedtime to tell me a story. Finishing with the closing of the book, his stories would drift into things that happened when I was a baby, planting tales of love and delight in my head. Only the stories Berthe tells are designed to scare. She is four years older and happily torments me until I dread to sleep alone, and creep into her bed seeking warmth and comfort. Then she confesses, laughing at my white face, that she made up the story because her feet were cold, and in truth, she remembers little of the war, except for the sound of the invaders' boots on the roadway outside.

I am told they came at dawn. People stayed in their homes with their curtains drawn, yet still the sound of marching feet ransacked the silence, unending, unendurable, day after day, until even the sun ran away and hid behind the dark clouds of war. And in the dead of night, people ran away too. Deserting homes that had given them shelter through storm and tempest, to place their trust in a rickety old barge or sailing yacht that had never slipped its mooring in twenty years, praying it would carry them to safety. And in the early dawn, when the boots began thudding across the cobbles, hundreds of houses were left with their front doors open, almost as a gesture of welcome.

'Our neighbour, Meneer Endelbaum,' Pieter tells us, 'he scuttled his family out of the city even as the heavy boots of the enemy echoed on the bridges. And for five long years, he was never able to laugh. Do you know who taught him how to laugh again?'

Of course; I have heard the story many times.

'After the invaders eventually left, they crept back to the city, ragged and hungry. Do you remember meeting Ruth?' I nod eagerly, for Ruth happens to be my very best friend, although the day we first met her voice was stilted and hesitant as she pronounced words of friendship foreign to her ears.

'Mother fed them and, afterwards, Pappy hustled Meneer Endelbaum off to the town hall, signing over the documents to the house he'd kept safely for five long years.' Pieter pauses dramatically in the same place every time he tells the story.

I wait for him to start up again, acquainted with every word and every gesture; a good story; a story that can be relied upon to send me to sleep with happy dreams, banishing the monsters that lurk under the stairs or in the cupboard.

'Pappy led Meneer Endelbaum out into the backyard and dug up the daffodil bulbs that were waiting for spring to burst into life. In a box, buried deep under the earth, were the diamonds entrusted to him long years before. Then Meneer Endelbaum laughed. "I am like the story of the Sleeping

Beauty; my laugh has slept for five years." And he grabs Pappy and waltzes him round and round, shouting with joy.'

That bit always makes Ruth and me giggle. We perch on top of the big bed, with its goose down quilt, our bare toes wriggling in delight at the idea of old people dancing; for at eight or nine years of age, you always think of your parents as old. In reality, neither is much above forty.

I gaze at them almost eight years later, and Pappy has grown old. He says the invaders made him that way. It's not true – it was losing my brother.

But I don't want to think of that now – that story is still waiting in the wings. Today, I am looking forward to Berthe's birthday. My sister will be thirteen in a few days and her present from Pappy will be her very own mirror. Pappy say it's a long-standing tradition in our family, the mirror part of a daughter's dowry. 'And if the birthday girl looks carefully enough,' he whispers to Berthe, 'making sure she sees no other living soul first, she will discover the face of the man she will one day marry.'

We live in city of bridges, where the river flows from west to east and the canals from east to west and from north to south. Crisscrossed by roads, whose pathways are abruptly halted whenever they meet up with water, the little waterways that are home to us are very different from the sprawling masses of the new city, with its docks and railway, smart shops and tall buildings. Here, our walkways are cobbled and every bridge is different.

We still have wooden bridges. As they become rotten and insecure, they are replaced by stone or cast out of iron ore, with intricately patterned railings. Brought down the canal by barge from a forge on the outskirts of the city, they are seared into place with sparks from a welding iron.

I have my own special bridge, and I run along the pathway

from school anxious to reach it. It is the only thing I can do better than Ruth and I run fast, my satchel bouncing on my back, keeping time with my feet. The March weather is blustery, undecided if it should bring winter to a close or, like the first day of April, continue to fool us, and the waterways are grey and bad-tempered, angry with a wind that steals droplets of moisture from its surface, tossing them recklessly into the air like a mischievous puppy.

'Wait for me! Wait for me!' She wails.

Yet no matter how far she is behind me, or how breathless she sounds or, indeed, how much I love my friend, my feet cannot stop. I hear them flap-flapping against the cobbles, never ceasing until I reach the exact centre of my bridge.

It's a tiny walkway, its stones so old no one living can remember a time when it didn't exist, not even Grandpappy, who once told me he was as old as Methuselah. Below me stands a miniature castle, as tall and slender as the goblet of wine Pappy pours for my mother at dinner time, its windows and doors tinted green. Strips of paint have peeled away and they curl into tight whirls, leaving the wood bare in places, and its brickwork is cracked like skin that has drunk too heartily of the sun's rays. A strip of garden, no bigger than the pinafore our cook wears, brushes the edge of the canal and is filled to bursting with pots of flowers. A rare sight in our city of stone, where there are few trees and even fewer flowers. Later there will be scarlet anemones and tulips. Today, though, it is the turn of the snowdrops. Brought out from under the eaves to enjoy the brightness of the day, their white buds are fringed green to match the doors and windows.

Out of breath, Ruth, clasping her right side, acts out a scene of grim agony, in the forlorn hope that I might feel ashamed for leaving her behind. Only, you can't feel sorry for someone who happens to be the most beautiful person you have ever seen, with skin as soft as peaches ripening in the sun and a mane of hair burnished with precious metals.

'Is he there, your prince?'

I shake my head. 'No.'

'Tell me again. Please, Magrit, tell me again. Tell me about the prince.'

My chest is pressed against the stones of the balustrade and I can't take a deep breath, but it's enough. 'He is tall and ...'

'Dark?'

'Not today. Today, he is wondrously fair, and a gardener.'

'A gardener! Gardeners are dirty and I don't like dirty people.' Her lip quivers with dismay.

'Ruth, he's really a prince.' I hastily add the words, fearful of losing my audience. 'At the end of the story, he will be dressed in silk and satin like the princess.' She nods, comforted. 'Only long, long ago he was cursed by an evil magician ...'

'Why?'

'Because he stole a flower from the magician's garden. Now, he's forced to work in a garden filled with winter, where there are no flowers or leaves, until a beautiful princess ...'

'Which is me.'

I hear the reluctance in my voice, because today the princess is dressed all in silver, her sandals made from the silken thread of a spider's web, and I want to wear them.

Clothes always play a part in my stories; they are important to my friend. When her family returned to the city, they had nothing and there is nothing to be bought either, our factories bombed and its machinery smashed. The same as every other housewife, Mevrouw Endelbaum is forced to scour the markets in search of cloth to make garments suitable for Ruth to wear, prettying them with strips of lace or ribbon from a gown worn by a lady in a bygone age. One time, she discovered a man's dinner jacket, nearly new. No one asks how it came to be there, not after so many years of war, and our school isn't bothered about it being black rather than navy blue, grateful to have any of their pupils decently clad in a city suffering disease and starvation.

'So, what do you want for your birthday?' I ask Ruth, hurrying the final words of my story in which the prince and princess live happily ever after.

'A new dress and some party shoes ... and a party. I've never had a party.'

'You had a party six months ago.'

Ruth blows out her lip in a pout. Even that doesn't make her ugly. 'That wasn't for me. That was for my parents, to celebrate our return. I want a real birthday party with our friends from school and I want your brother, Pieter, to come.'

I know if she asks Pieter will say yes, for Ruth is special. No one ever says no to her.

Leaving my bridge to its silent musing, Ruth and I break into a run and chase down the narrow street, its close-set buildings leaning over us with a smile. On one side, where stones have subsided and stand awkwardly to attention like a row of one-legged soldiers, is Bloch's Patisserie. For the longest while, they have sold only bread and scones, the butter and sugar needed for cakes a rarity. When I ask, Pappy tells me the same family had owned it for two centuries. 'Sadly, they disappeared, as did so many people. Another lady owns it these days. Alas,' his eyes twinkle at me, dispelling the tragedy of the story, 'she has yet to learn how to cook.'

Opposite is a wondrous old bookstore that burrows like a mole through the walls of houses on either side. A bell rings out when you open the door, although there's never anyone there, only spiders and cobwebs that hide under its low, black beams. Even the books are dusty, except for those in the window in their bright paper jackets.

Our old city is tiny and, despite its twists and turns, if you keep the afternoon sun on your back you end up at the river. Tidal, its mud-filled banks resemble the bowl of a teaspoon, curving round, and its walkways are patterned and dressed in fancy costumes made from broken cobble and smooth stone. You pass a jeweller that sells watches and mends them again if they go wrong, and a tiny coffee shop that sells beer. In summer, its metal tables perch unevenly on the cobblestones and customers use beer mats folded over, wedging them under the legs to stop them wobbling. Nearby sits a flower seller. Tucked into a corner of the bridge, she exchanges her seat for one by a warm stove only when icy winds begin to invade the river bank. Once spring pokes its head up, she is back, surrounded by a vast swirling skirt of flowers that spill their perfume into the air.

This is the bridge my soldier guarded. Painted white, it swings open for tall ships when they order it. He's there the morning I first start school, with Berthe walking beside me, carefully holding my hand. Placing his rifle against the wall, he holds back the traffic with one hand, waving the group of schoolchildren across with the other. Berthe refuses to speak to the soldier, Mother told us not to and she always obeys. I am not yet five and rarely remember my mother's instructions, busily drinking in the delights of the old city with its hidden corners, where the fairy folk of my imagination live.

Then one day, the invaders march out of our land as they marched in. This time, I am big enough to watch although I am not allowed outside, even when I plead I want to say goodbye to my soldier. I run to my bedroom, peeking through the curtains, and see him just for a second. He stares every which way, scrutinising even the shadows in the alleyway and the drawn curtains of our house, wanting to say goodbye to the child who has befriended him in a city in which he is the enemy. Even though I hear tell of the cruelty handed out when they stole our land and our lives, my soldier isn't cruel. He is gentle, exactly as Pappy would have been if forced to wear a uniform and carry a gun.

Our house stands on the far side of this bridge. The end one in a long line of houses, that run down the side of the canal on its journey around the city, like an obedient dog keeping step with its master. Ruth and her family live next door and they are much richer than us, although their house could fit into one of Pappy's coat pockets. As grave and elegant as Mevrouw Endelbaum, it is tall and very narrow, with a façade of rose-pink and grey bricks, and stairs so steep only a child's foot can fit them. Since the age of ten, Ruth's toes have overlapped their edges, and she points them sideways so as not to trip.

As we run towards the bridge, it is our neighbour's house I notice first. Covering the tiny shop window is a dainty awning made from rose-pink fabric. The shape of a half-umbrella, it has frilled edges with the word *Endelbaum* printed on them. It's new, only a few months old and very different from the awning that sprawls across the front of Pappy's shop. Old and sagging, with its white canvas stained green by rainwater, it resembles a fat old man about to eat his dinner, a dirty napkin spread across his lap. Seated next to him is a long thin giant in a pink frilly apron.

'It's the perfect house for us,' Meneer Endelbaum says. He is not as tall as his wife, and his hair is snow white. 'You can fit my diamonds into a sock but not your father's mirrors, eh Magrit,' he says with a twinkle in his eye, and chucks me under the chin.

I think it strange that Meneer Endelbaum should say mirrors and not children because Mother and Pappy have four children who fill the house right up.

'I have my Ruth,' Meneer Endelbaum says, when I tell him God was mean not to give him more children. 'She is all the children in the world rolled into one. Why would I want more?'

Pappy tells me when I ask, that Meneer Endelbaum wanted a big family, only God didn't grant that blessing. 'Instead, he gave them life. That is the best gift of all.'

I didn't know what he meant then. I do now.

3

When I reach our house, if it is raining or the shop is empty
of customers, I open the shop door and tiptoe silently in.
Mevrouw Kleissler always catches me. The walls and floor
of the shop are adorned with mirrors and their shimmering
images never fail to arrest my feet. At first, they display only
the reflection of a scrawny schoolgirl, a pathetic waif in a grey
flannel coat way too short for her, her long skinny legs encased
in woollen stockings, with a knitted bonnet over her ears. My
coat was once Berthe's, my gymslip too. Mother has unpicked
it and turned the fabric inside out so the shiny pieces on the
back are hidden. In the blink of an eye, the image transforms
into a beautiful princess dressed in a gown of silk, with glass
slippers on her feet that trip daintily up the stairway.

'Magrit,' Mevrouw Kleissler smiles her reprimand. 'Who
are you today?'

'Cinderella, and I'm off to the ball.' Forgetting she is there,
I point my toes and raise the hem of my dress over the steps. I
look up. My prince is waiting.

Today, though, the shop is busy, and I run down the street
towards an unassuming little doorway. Painted brown, it is

furnished with a brass bell push and door knocker. Recently the Burghers who rule our tiny community have given it a number, so that it will recognise its place among other houses in the street. Opening on to a hallway covered in green linoleum, steps corkscrew down into the basement workshop where the mirrors are made. Pappy calls it his *atelier*, insisting his work is equally as skilled as any of the great masters whose paintings hang in the museum.

I head out into the yard where Pieter is overseeing the loading of mirrors into a horse-drawn cart, packing them into long wooden crates like coffins. I wave, and he comes to sit for a moment on the back steps.

'Which way did you come today?'

Pieter sits beside me, listening to adventures in which I fight dragons and sail over crystal blue seas. The distance is our little joke – my path from school expanded into a journey crossing continents and worlds. Only when I have reached a satisfactory conclusion will he get to his feet stretching, 'Let's go home.'

'Can I tell you a secret?' I lean my head against his shoulder.

'What?'

'Mother doesn't like birthdays.'

Gently, he smooths back my hair. 'Sometimes grown people don't like birthdays. Especially women.'

'Why?'

'Because they fear getting older.'

'It's not that.' I screw up my face in disgust; I am never getting old. 'Mother is looking forward so much to Berthe's birthday. We are having a special dinner with all her favourite dishes. Mevrouw Kleissler is invited and Meneer and Mevrouw Endelbaum ...'

'We are all excited about Berthe's birthday, Magrit,' Pieter says, giving me a hug. 'Thirteen is a very special age for a girl, almost as important as sixteen. So what is it?'

'Mother fears that something is waiting up ahead and each birthday – yours especially – brings it a little closer.'

Pieter's glance is troubled. Maybe he is wondering if I have lived too long in my fantasy world and can no longer separate truth from fiction.

He goes back to work and I chase upstairs to the first-floor landing, a busy thoroughfare of doors and staircases around which our lives revolve. Our living room is large and comfortable, and little changed from when Pappy's parents were alive. Leading off it is the kitchen. My fantasy world has no place there, despite a range that stays warm even when snow and ice linger in the street. I visit to do my chores and leave again quickly. This is Mother's kingdom. She is stricter than Pappy and, in truth, I am a little afraid of her. Maybe because she never talks about her life; very different from Pappy, who boasts of hiding under the bridge until after the school bell has rung, wanting to spend the day helping fishermen unload their catch to earn a cent or two.

I ask Pieter if she has any brothers and sisters. He shrugs. 'Who knows?'

She is like a new book, a story hidden behind its uncut pages. All I can say for certain is that she is superstitious and dislikes birthdays, and on festive days more than any other she is sad, her dark eyes full of pain and unshed tears.

Up and up I go. Berthe and I have our bedrooms on the third floor where ceilings slope down to the floor and only the interior walls are vertical. Eagerly, I run to the window, dropping my bag to the ground, and stare down into the salt-lashed sail of a barque on the river. A seagull brushes my window sill, ignoring my face moments away. They have no cares, no worries, only the joy and freedom of the wind.

On the breeze I catch a strange sound. At first, I imagine it's the bellows our workmen use to make the furnace burn brighter. Gradually it alters, becoming almost metallic, discordant, resembling the squeak of a door or a loose spar on a cutter that swings back and forth tracing the pattern of the wind. Below me on the street, doors open and women run out onto the stoop, peering upwards. Huge birds are flying across the city, heading west, their plumage as white as freshly fallen snow, their long necks stretched over the rooftops. A glint of late afternoon sunshine breaks through the clouds, painting the tips of their wings gold, all except for their leader. Coal black, this swan dismisses sunshine from its feathers as easily as a duck dismisses water.

'In every stage of your life,' Pappy once told me, 'there will be moments that drive a wedge into your heart. Memories that no time can eliminate.'

'And what are those, Pappy?'

He lays his chisel on the work bench, sitting me on his knee. 'The day I married your mother, and the day your brother was born.'

'Why not when I was born?' I tug at Pappy's sleeve, impatient to be told my birth was also a memory too valuable to hide away.

'By the time you were born, I was saying – please God, not another mouth to feed.'

I run on down the stairs, my feet clattering on the wooden treads, eager to tell. Below ground, it is different again. In the distance, the furnace roars out a constant command for food. Pappy says it's really a giant who bellows with pain because he has corns on his toes and his boots hurt. 'Nevertheless, he is a kindly giant who keeps our house warm in winter.' I have often asked Pappy if I can meet this giant. I am never allowed. He is responsible for melting the metal to coat the back of the mirrors and Pappy says it is dangerous work that only a giant can do.

On the walls of Pappy's workshop lies the history of his family. Suppliers of ornamental mirrors since the seventeenth century, when Pappy's ancestor was chosen by the Prince of Orange to make mirrors for his salon of dance, so he could admire his perfect elegance and neatly turned ankle with every step he took.

'What a vain peacock,' I protest when Pappy tells me the story.

'Magrit,' Pappy chides, his wrinkles crinkling like stars at the corner of his eyes. 'Without a world of peacocks, we would be sitting in the streets begging for the clothes on our back.'

Pappy delights in telling the story of how, aged ten, he was apprenticed to an artist who beat and starved him in a garret facing north. Then, aged thirteen, he was apprenticed to a cabinet maker, who beat and starved him in a cellar facing south. Pappy stories remind me of skeins of fine coloured wool that have become tangled, equally impossible to sort into truth and fiction. Only when he is painting an intricate design on glass is he serious, for then he needs his hand to be steady, his glance keen. Whatever is asked of him he ignores until the delicate set of brushstrokes is completed and all danger passed.

Mother's voice drifts up to meet me as I chase down the twisting staircase to the basement. 'I am convinced you do this on purpose, Pappy,' she says sharply. 'I have waited fifteen minutes for a reply as to what you wish to eat for dinner.'

'My beautiful Margaret, if I could have kept you longer, I would.' Pappy is wiping his hands on a cloth smelling of turpentine. 'Is it not better to waste fifteen minutes and save two months? For that is the time it has taken to decorate this piece. What do you think, Pieter?'

'Sorry, Pappy, I'm on Mother's side today.'

Pieter gets to his feet helping Pappy move the newly decorated mirror to a safer spot. He left school at fourteen. Mother says he was anxious to do so, announcing his intention on his very first day there. When the teacher called out, 'Does anyone know what they wish to be when they grow up,' most of the children kept silent over-awed by their new surroundings. Not my brother. Up went his hand. 'I want to make mirrors like my Pappy.'

His apprenticeship will last seven years and by time he is twenty-one, he will be a master craftsman, earning a man's wage. Even now he is well on his way, his fingers nimble and his sight accurate, quick to learn the skill of silvering a mirror to keep it from tarnishing for twenty years – the lifetime guarantee offered by Baders, for our mirrors aren't cheap.

They are very close, he and Pappy. And I love them both very much.

'See, it is finished, Margaret, and I will eat whatever you choose to serve.' Pappy blows her a kiss. 'And what do you wish for your birthday mirror, Magrit?'

'Pappy,' Mother frowns. 'Magrit has more than four years to think about such nonsense. It is Berthe you should be thinking of.'

'My dear, her present is already complete.'

He points to the corner of the room where a cloth-covered mirror stands. Taller than me, its face is carefully screened from curious eyes and it is bound with string to deter curious fingers. My feet break into a shuffle, too excited to remain stationary.

'Did you Mother,' I say. 'Did you see Pappy in the mirror?'

'Of course! He was so very handsome, with eyes so large and wistful, they quite melted my heart away.'

I stare at Pappy, his cheeks tinged pink. 'Are you sure it was Pappy? He has a big nose.'

Pappy roars and gathers me onto his lap. 'It is an undisputed fact,' he says, in a voice as dignified as our pastor when he's reading the notices in church, 'that noses begin to grow in step with failing eyesight. If my nose had remained as small as it was when I met your mother, where would I perch my spectacles? They would fall off.'

He points to the wall where patterns are arranged in a line of decorative arrowheads, each one cut from the corner piece of a mirror. 'So which is your favourite?'

On the wall are lace fans, embroidered with hearts and a universe of gold and silver stars. Purple dragons bow down to a knight who has feathers on his helm and a red cross on his white tunic, and there are waterfalls of green, and gold mermaids. Flowers too, shy and timid, and fairies with wings of gossamer that hide behind their silken petals, and clumps of blue heather bells as light as thistledown.

Remembering the swans, I point to a section of painted wood where two swans are floating in a mirrored pool of water, tiny blue birds flying overhead. Bader mirrors are never plain gilt; their edges carry scenes of countryside woods, flowers and birds, the feathers in their outstretched wings as delicate as a spider's web.

They say children see everything; nothing escapes their innocent gaze. Suddenly pale, my mother places her hand on the wall as if to hold herself upright. She glances with concern at my brother, who, ignoring the conversation, is cutting out an intricate pattern in wood with a jig saw.

'When did you see swans, child, or is it Pappy's drawing you like so much?' she says, her voice as sharp as the edges of the saw Pieter is using. Pappy has his back to us, cleaning his brushes, and doesn't hear.

'I saw them through the window,' I boast, wanting her to be pleased that I had chosen something real, not something from a picture book. 'They were so beautiful, especially the black one.'

I catch her savage intake of breath. Her attention fixes on the window, except there are none in the basement. Above our heads, circles of milky-white glass form gratings in the pavement floor, which ring out under the footsteps of people hurrying past.

'Mother, I'm sorry.' I feel my mouth twist up.

She drags her eyes away from the wall and I notice her face bruised, as if she's been struck. Pappy stretches out a paint-streaked hand, his gaze concerned and anxious. She stares down at Pieter, who is frowning down at his work, his long, fair hair flopping down almost over his eyes. Reaching out, she gently brushes it away, her touch as soft as the down on a duck's breast. He glances up then, his smile warm and mischievous. Had it been Hans, he'd have jerked his head away, impatient of any show of affection. Not Pieter. Instinct tells him that for Mother, he will always be a small boy.

She says quite mildly, 'For something that is to be with you all your life, Magrit, why not choose more wisely. When you are as old as your grandmother is now, it will remind you of being a little girl.'

I want to say: *The swans will remind me, for I have never seen anything more beautiful, their feathers were like polished silk.*

But I am only little. I hold my tongue and nod when she tells Pappy that fairies are for me, creatures of joy unlike swans that are vicious and cruel.

That night, my dream-filled sleep takes me to the shores of a lake. In the distance, floating on the water is a village, a bell tower standing proud over its rooftops. No more than fishermen's hovels, their roofs of painted tin are patched and worn. Pencil-slim passageways burrow between them, little wider than the rat-runs that pepper the banks of our city canals. Close by, paddling on the water, are the swans I had seen that day; strong birds, their wing span taller than the tallest of men. They swim up, taking food from my outstretched hand, and speak their thanks.

Half-asleep, with my dream still washing over me, I awake, hearing the voices of my parents raised in anger. Alarmed, I tiptoe down the stairs, their voices growing louder with every step.

'Why didn't you tell me? How could you let me go on believing … all these years?'

Mother's voice, full of tears, breaks in, pleading, 'How could I tell you? How could I tell any man?'

'We went through so much, Margaret, to be free.' Pappy's voice, like the thunder that rumbles over the city in summer storms, is not designed to damage. Nevertheless, I can sense anguish tearing him apart. 'You cannot let it happen. Not to my child … I cannot believe you deceived me. He is my own flesh, no different from the others.' Pappy groans and I feel his pain. 'Why did we ever return?'

'It would have made no difference. There is no hiding or running. Not from this.'

'Then you beg! Plead! Anything! Even your life.'

Shivering, I creep back upstairs and, opening the door to Berthe's room, crawl into her bed, my tears soaking the front of my nightdress. I don't understand the words being shouted into the air, yet little as I am, I sense lightning fork down through the middle of our house, splitting it in two.

The following morning, Pappy, his eyes ringed with lack of sleep, tells us that Mother has had to go out and will be back in time for dinner.

*

No more is said about Mother leaving us for the day and, clouded by time, I cannot remember if she did return that same night. Perhaps it is more than one. I remember she was there for Berthe's special birthday, her face smiling as if someone out of sight is pulling the strings. No one observes this apart from me and Pappy, especially not Berthe who, for days, has been the centre of attention. But then to Pappy, Mother is his life. Like the sun, she is the centre of his universe, time slowing to a crawl in her absence.

4

Other memories crowd my mind and like a tub filled with water, a flood of jumbled recollections cascade over the rim. A few bully their way into my attention demanding to be heard, as clear as if they had happened yesterday.

My tenth birthday cries out for attention first. After six long weeks of waiting, with Ruth lording it over me with tales of her party and her new clothes imported from Paris, I have at last reached the plateau on which she is standing. I love birthdays, when presents are left unopened until the day's work is ended, and the family is taking its ease. People who open their gifts at breakfast forego hours of suspense and expectation. All day long, you are able to feast your eyes on tantalising packages wrapped in brown paper and string, your fingers aquiver with anticipation, wondering what's in them and trying to guess. By dinner, you are almost bursting with excitement. Even then, you have to wait a little longer, aware Mother will be serving your favourite meal and you are allowed a second helping because it is your birthday.

Mother has made me a new dress. Wrapped in white tissue paper, and tied with a thread of gold embroidery silk,

I carefully smooth out the creases in the flimsy paper to use again. Tucked and flounced, I recognise the smocking on the bodice as something she has worked on over the winter.

I cannot say for certain if I have ever possessed anything new before that day. With four children to clothe and feed, and with business in the doldrums, Mother is hard pressed even to find outfits suitable for church on a Sunday. I mostly wear clothes whose hems have been shortened or lengthened with a strip of bias binding, clothes that Berthe has grown out of – even her shoes. Hans wears Pieter's cast-offs while Mother spends her evenings unpicking cloth and turning it to use again. The invaders are long gone, yet it still continues to be shelter and warmth that people crave. Pappy tells us the woollen mills and cotton factories have been rebuilt and are gradually starting up again.

'Such is the need for clothing, perhaps it would be more sensible if clothiers spent their time in church on their knees, begging Jesus to turn five bolts of cloth into a quantity sufficient for the entire city.'

Mother is shocked by his irreverent suggestion and shows her displeasure by plucking savagely at a row of stitches on the jacket she's unpicking.

I hold up my dress, swishing the skirt, copying the way Ruth flirted with her new clothes. 'How splendid,' Pappy says. 'There is one condition.' I hold my breath. 'You cannot grow for at least two years.'

I wrap my arms around his neck, saying softly, 'I promise.'

'Silly,' Mother says smiling up at Pappy. 'Have you seen the hem I have put on it?'

Of course Pappy has. He sat at Mother's side while she was making it.

'Here, child, I made this for you.' He hands me a small package, his hands still sensitive enough to draw dancing fairies on its plain white wrapping paper, despite the swollen knuckles on his right hand. Trembling with excitement, I carefully unpeel the wrapping paper. Inside is a tiny oval hand-mirror, a trellis of gold clinging to its edges as if it has come straight from fairyland.

'Pappy, why didn't you tell me you were going to make something for Magrit's birthday,' Hans grumbles. 'I could have painted her a picture and used my pocket money to buy a new pencil.'

'Don't be so mean, Hans.' Berthe offers me a neatly wrapped parcel, one that is soft and squashy and totally mysterious, sealing the gift with a kiss. 'From both of us,' she says. At fourteen, Berthe has almost stopped growing, whereas Hans has not yet begun and remains a skinny, truculent schoolboy, jealous of everything outside himself. When I open the package, hair ribbons tumble out and a rainbow of colour spills onto the table.

'I have something for you, too.' Pieter gets to his feet to close the window, a chill wind blowing in off the river onto Mother's shoulders. During the day, the river plays host to a bustling scene of creaking spars and screeching seagulls that dive-bomb boats in search of a stray titbit. In summer, when the windows are left open, only in the evening is it possible to talk without shouting. 'Perhaps not as useful as hair ribbons or as splendid as the gift of a mirror or a dress.' He passes over an oddly shaped package, its newspaper wrapping stiff and bulky where it has been doubled over. 'I found it in the market and thought you might like it.'

Inside is a music box, its wood unpainted and the mirror in its lid cracked. 'It's not new,' Pieter apologises. 'Watch.'

He winds the key and the ballerina, in her frothy white tutu, climbs gracefully to her feet and dances to music that still rings true.

*

Of all my memories, only one remains a fiery beacon, the flames of consequence reaching up to the sky, each detail indelibly etched as if Hans had used a pencil to draw in the lines – Pieter's sixteenth birthday.

We all know Pieter is my mother's favourite. Like breathing, it is something we never question. He is tall and graceful with a lurking gleam of contentment, and his eyes are full of mischief, yet mischief designed to give pleasure, not pain. As for Mother, his birthday is always special, and the day begins with polishing the living room furniture.

Hans and I have been sent down to the yard to beat carpets and curtains, the latter made of heavy velvet festooned with long, gold tassels. I love our sitting room with its high ceiling – but not its curtains. They crowd the windows, leaving the room sombre even on a sunny day, and those nearest the dining table are kept drawn to stop the wood fading. Carved from mahogany that came by ship from some far distant land more than a century ago, it bears a rich deep lustre from constant polishing.

I ask Mother if I may set the table for dinner.

'No. You'll only break something, Magrit,' she warns. 'When you've finished the carpets, you can fetch my best lace tablecloth from its drawer in the study.'

Hans and I don't hurry, aware it will take the maids at least an hour to clean the big windows and polish the dining table and chairs. There are other tables too; a little clutch that dance attendance on the settees and armchairs, as if they are the underlings of the prince Pappy is always talking about. Their polished tops wear a covering of carpet patterned in red that echoes the colour of the flock wallpaper. Where sunlight has lingered, this has faded to rose. Nevertheless, it has stood the test of time well.

Hans pegs the little squares of carpet on the clothes line and we tackle these first. I soon stop exhausted.

'What are we going to buy Pieter?' he calls. Although he's

not much taller, Hans is very much the stronger. In his hands, the carpet beater resounds hollowly and I see the dust of the past year, afraid of his flailing arm, fly into the air.

'Perhaps a book on famous artists.' I pile the squares that are finished neatly by the back door.

'I'd like a book for my birthday too. When I leave school, I want to go to college …'

I frown. 'Aren't you going to work with Pappy?'

'No! I don't want to make mirrors.'

'Why not? What do you want to do?'

'I told you,' he speaks impatiently, his voice gruff. 'I want to go to college and become a famous artist, the same as those men whose pictures hang in the museum.'

'Does Pappy know?'

'No, and don't you go telling him either.'

'I promise. What about Pieter's present? Mevrouw Kleissler gave me a little money for my birthday and Berthe will help.'

He swings his arm … thud … and the carpet jumps into the air. 'All right, we'll go this afternoon. I'll ask Pappy for an advance on my pocket money.'

'How many weeks is that?'

Hans explodes into laughter, instantly vanquishing the belligerence of a moment before. '*Six!* Pappy says I will have to sweep the workshop floor every night for ten years to pay it off.'

Berthe doesn't come with us, preferring to spend the afternoon with friends as amiable and placid as she is. Even with her contribution, we don't have enough money to buy new, and the book we choose is second-hand. Like much of the stock in that dusty old shop, the owner has purchased it for a few cents from some starving family. Yet Monet's pictures are new to Hans, and I feel certain Pieter will cherish the book as did the family who once owned it. As I lift it from the pile, its pages fly open and a glorious procession of pink and white water lilies flood out. Among the pages is a handmade bookmark. A child has tried to copy the flowers on one side. On the other, it has printed in childish scrawl: *Papa with dearest love.*

Pieter's face shines with delight and he grabs Hans in a bear hug, letting him go only to wrap his arms around Berthe and me.

Had I known it to be the last time; would I have clasped him closer and held on to him?

At dinner Pieter sits on Mother's right-hand side, while Hans sits next to Pappy at the far end of the table. I am opposite, with Mevrouw Kleissler, Ruth and her parents, and Berthe, somewhere in between.

'Berthe has made Pieter's birthday cake. I have been saving eggs and butter for a month.' Mother confides in Mevrouw Endelbaum. Ruth's mother suffers from poor health, and she has been telling Mother how badly she sleeps. 'My eldest daughter is very different from my youngest,' Mother complains, happy to have an audience. 'Magrit is so dilatory whereas Berthe is the opposite; both competent and surprisingly skilful. I am sure our dessert will be quite delicious.'

'Margaret,' Pappy says overhearing, 'there is a gap of four years between our girls. Doubtless Magrit will one day prove equally as efficient. Berthe, since you made Pieter's cake, I think it only fair to let you bring it in. If we give the job to Hans, we will not see him again until he has eaten every crumb.'

'Indeed,' Mother frowns. She disapproves when Pappy sides with me.

'Hans get the lights,' he says.

The glow from the candles casts flickering shadows on to the wall. Mother stares at them with alarm as if they are uninvited guests, and I see her face pinched and shuttered when Pieter's first attempt to blow them out removes only ten. She doesn't approve of birthday candles, believing bad luck must follow if you fail to blow them out in a single breath. Meneer Endelbaum gave them to us. He bought too many for Ruth's cake and doesn't want to waste them.

All too soon, the celebrations are over and I am sent off to bed. Happy though. We wear our best clothes as we do our best manners, always remembering to say *please* and *thank you* – if only for the one night. And everyone is gay, laughing at Pappy's jokes, relaxed after a glass or two of wine; the air vibrating with mirth, drowning out the horns of fishermen impatiently clearing a pathway to the sea.

It is late when I wake needing a glass of water. Unused to cake, it has left me thirsty. I open my bedroom door and hear Pieter scream out. Like the blade of a knife thudding deep into my chest, it tears through the darkness of the stairwell. Again and again, the scream echoes, panicking the air into violent movement. The blackness swirls out of control and I stop my ears with my fists, scrunched up on the ground in a tight ball.

'*Make it stop, make it stop!*' he pleads, his voice as high-pitched as a girl's.

Mother's voice, breathless with pain, '*He promised.*' Then more calmly, as if she has dragged her emotions together as a beggar clasps rags around his body. 'Check on the children. They must not see this.'

I watch Pappy come to the head of the staircase. His head is cocked, listening to the silence. He does not see me tucked into the shadow of the wall, my arms wrapped over my head to block out the sound. 'We're safe. They're still sleeping.'

Behind his calm voice, I can hear Pieter whimpering like a cur stamped on by a pair of hob-nailed boots. 'Please make it stop. *Oh God, please make it stop.*'

And the agony in Pappy's voice, 'Noooo!'

Then Mother. 'I'll get my cloak.'

I see her shadow, foreshortened by distance, huddled over as if in pain.

Then nothing, except for the door to the yard closing softly.

We are told Mother and Pieter have gone away. But when she returns, she is alone.

5

As the gentle tide that washes marks from the sand, time brings a lessening of our grief. Although so many lies are told about that night, conversations started and never finished, after a time no one can bear to hear more, and, by silent consent, the name Pieter vanishes from our vocabulary. It doesn't stop the lies though, nor the changes to our family that accompany them. Ruth cries, her distress so visible and heart-rending, I am forced to conceal mine, and grow up silent and watchful. Mother and Pappy change the most. Although the loss of Pieter brings them closer together, it also pushes them further apart, each guarding thoughts too painful to share. Even the festive season, on the fifth of December, is diminished by his absence; only three pairs of clogs now at the door instead of four, wiping away the jollity of the day as easily as winter snow wipes footprints from our pavements.

I am guilty of lying too, and perhaps my lie is the greatest of them all.

The eve of my thirteenth birthday.

Mother has scrubbed the house from top to toe – only that's not quite true for we still have maids to do the heavy work. She stands in the middle of the room, directing brooms into secret corners where spiders gather and grow fat on flies that have blundered into their web. Not the whole house either. Pappy refuses to let anyone clean his workshop and our maids rarely venture into the rooms under the gable. That has become our job, Berthe's and mine.

'Magrit, you are not to peek.' Berthe slams the door in my face and I wonder what she has bought that needs hiding. I giggle and skip down the wide wooden stairs, and down again, and yet again and again to the atelier. I hold my breath and all the shushings and whisperings, doors locked to stop me peeking, withdraw into the distance. There, in the middle of the floor, draped in the same grey overcoat that had clothed Berthe's gift, stands a long, thin object. I know what it is; an elegant swing mirror, its glass bevelled for extra depth. My birthday gift. Although I have grown in the four years since Berthe's birthday, it is still taller than me.

Excited, I feel as light as gossamer. Through the glass grating above my head, I glimpse the bright shape of the moon, a thin crescent of light on its upward journey into a distant sky. Had I been outside, excitement would have floated me up into the air to grasp at its silvery beams. Tomorrow morning, I will see the man I am going to marry for the very first time. The words reverberate through my head: *Before you see or speak to any living person, if you gaze into the mirror, you will find reflected there the face of the man who will one day become your husband.*

It has happened that way for my mother and for every woman in our family, for hundreds and hundreds of years, ever since mirrors were first invented. Now, it will be my turn.

By the time Pappy quits work for the night, the sky is already darkening. He and Hans carry my present up the four flights from the workshop, Pappy grumbling all the way. 'If I get a bad back, who will earn the crusts to feed you? We should hoist furniture up the outside of the house like civilised people. Hans, remind me to call a workman to fix a hook into the gable first thing in the morning.'

My brother is a good workman and I often hear Pappy praising his skill; it is rare for him to complain.

I wake early. Pappy and Hans have left the mirror facing the window, its narrow shape a roadmap of my future. In a moment, all will be revealed and I will see my husband. I feel sorry for Hans then. Boys have few traditions, except the right to smoke a pipe at sixteen. I can stare as long as I want and memorise every molecule of my husband's face until I know it as well as I know my own.

Ruth scoffs when I tell her. I argue it is little different from the rings Meneer Endelbaum crafts in his shop. Ladies gather in the street under the rose-pink awning, almost drooling in their eagerness to possess the fine diamonds that were once the prerogative of only the very rich. I had reached thirteen cushioned in a world of mirrors. Like diamonds, sunlight is refracted into a kaleidoscope of colours that herald a glorious future. How could it be so different? For me, there remains only one mystery – I might know who I am to marry, but not when. My fingers tremble and I say a little prayer, the words vanishing from my memory even as I say them, concentrating on the grey overcoat and willing myself to remove it.

It falls to the ground with an abruptness that startles and, for a moment, I cannot steel myself to move. Gradually, I raise my head. At first, all I see is the frame of the glass then fairies begin to dance, their gossamer wings seeking a leaf to light upon, the tips of their toes skimming the web of a spider. Dragonflies with diaphanous wings join in the chase, dipping down to sip at a pool of nectar, in a joyous cavalcade of greens and blue, shards of sunlight falling on them bright as golden dew.

In the topmost section of the mirror, I see the May sky shining in a riotous celebration of spring. I am tempted then to run to the window, to look down into the water, aware the sky will be reflected there also and anxious to see what patterns it is making.

A part of me still wishes I had.

I see my face plain and serious, my hair dark and my fringe cut so straight Mother could well have used a ruler. I am wearing a blue pinafore dress. New for Christmas, I have chosen to wear it as a compliment to the sky. I had thought it beautiful until that moment. My eyes the colour of violets clash like twin souls in purgatory, my cheeks washed out above the solemn blue of the cloth. Below its hem, my skinny legs in their white ankle socks remind me of the matches Pappy uses to light his pipe.

I stare and stare. So far in my life I have believed three things. Pappy loves me, I am never going to die, and I will marry a prince. I knew it would happen because I prayed to God every night and the pastor says, if we pray long and hard enough God will answer our prayers. Now, it is only two things. Who would ever wish to marry me? I think of Ruth with hair the colour of corn silk and skin of golden amber.

Dredging the depths of the mirror with eyes forlorn and heartbroken, I wait for something to appear. Even a plain man … not a prince. It will be satisfactory and I will make him a good wife.

All at once, the sky outside darkens and a cloud wipes away the sunshine, its reflection spreading a cloak of black across the face of the mirror. A wind must have got up, for suddenly the cloud is rent into strips of darkness that transforms into shadowy figures, a dozen or more, hunched and bent low. Beyond them, I see dark swirling water.

Alarmed, I take a step backwards, my gaze still riveted, and unable to break free from the menace emanating from the glass. Then, in the depths of the mirror, something stirs. In the top corner, where a wide strip of bevelling forms an angle with the glass, I spot the tip of a black wing. At first, I believe it to be a flaw in the glass. Maybe a fraction of light has become distorted in contradiction to the rest. It grows steadily and I recognise the wing as belonging to a swan.

They have visited only that one time, the year of Berthe's special birthday. A few stayed, straying along the canals in search of food. One day, dawdling home from school, I came across some boys beating at a swan with long sticks. Without thinking, I ran down the bank, hitting out wildly with my fists and shouting loudly until they laughed and ran away. It was only a young bird, its feathers streaked brown, darkening to black. Clumsily getting to its feet, it stroked its beak along its wing tip trying to restore some order to his feathers. I saw then it was hurt, its wing jutting awkwardly. I stretched out my hand and, for the briefest of moments, it allowed me to stroke its head. 'I'm sorry, I can't mend your wing, but please go away. It's not safe.' I whisper. As if memorising my face, I felt its stare piercing yet somehow all-knowing, omniscient. Waddling lopsidedly into the water, it paddled down the canal, its graceful neck swinging round from time to time as if to check I was still watching.

Gradually, the dark cloud disappears beyond the edges of the mirror, swept away by the swan's wing and I realise that, in truth, the cloud has passed over the river and into the streets beyond. All at once, the sun returns and there is nothing in the mirror except my white face.

Berthe hammers on the door. 'Come on, Magrit, we're going to be late for church.'

When Pappy asks, I admit I have seen nothing.

'Nothing? Impossible! Surely, you must have seen a beautiful young girl with a smile as tremulous as quick-silver and eyes as shy as violets.'

I shake my head and give a painful half-smile, tears pressed up against my eyelids. I want to tell him the truth but I am concerned he might laugh. I bite my lip to stop the words coming out. That's when I make up the lie.

'It didn't work, Pappy. I expect I caught sight of someone's reflection in the water and the magic was ruined.'

'But that is all to the good,' Pappy roars. I sense huge relief, almost exuberance.

I know Pappy's grumbling about carrying the mirror upstairs to be a façade. Pieter worked with him on Berthe's mirror and the memory will have been painful. I realise also that his constant praise for Hans is an apology, a reassurance that he loves his second son equally and would mourn his passing too.

Pappy pulls me onto his knee as if I am still a baby, hugging me tightly. 'I will celebrate this day like no other because I need never dread you leaving home, like Berthe. You will stay with me for ever, eh Maidy?'

I have not heard the word before, but it soon becomes my name. Even then I could have spoken out, but nervous and unsure what the images in the mirror might mean, I hold my peace and leave the lie alone.

Book 2

The Return of the Swans

6

The early-morning air nipped my shoulder and I ran to my cupboard to get my shawl. Grandmother made it out of oddments of coloured wool, crocheted into small squares and sewn together. She'd sit in a chair by the window, her fingers busy, so accustomed to the pattern she rarely needed to look down at her work. Instead, she watched the world go past. If something caught her eye, her head would tilt like a bird's, and the fingers grasping a strand of wool against her crochet needle would hover unmoving, until a barge laden with coal had passed down the waterway or a couple of women had finished their gossiping and disappeared inside their house, closing the front door. The shawl grew in tiny steps over a number of winters and was given to me after her death. She never wore it; it lay in her drawer, my name already pinned to it. I kept the little square of paper pressed into the pages of my journal. Her writing was ill-formed. With her family about her, she had no need to pick up a pen. She left Berthe the lace tablecloths that had been made for her bottom drawer and never used. Something in the demeanour of her granddaughters must have made her think that Berthe would be in need of a dowry one day, and I only a shawl.

I flew back to the window, throwing off my painful thoughts even as I wrapped the shawl around my shoulders. Only one day in every year is this special and I couldn't afford to waste a single moment.

Below, a car had stopped in the middle of the street, a couple of cyclists stationary alongside, balanced on one leg, and I guessed the bridge was about to open. Standing on tip-toe, I craned my head. In the distance, I spotted the three-masted schooner I had seen at the lake. In the early morning sunlight, with its tall sails washed with gold, it looked as imperious as an emperor out for an early morning stroll.

Barges patrolled this stretch of the waterway all day long, too low in stature for the bridge to bother with them, while fishing vessels skilfully sloped their mast and sails to pass underneath. It was a rare sight for the bridge to open, and it was happening on my birthday.

Eagerly, I watched as the operator climbed leisurely into his glass wheelhouse on the far side of the river. Abruptly, the two halves of the bridge shuddered as if in protest at being ordered to move. Then, like hands extending a blessing, they began to separate rising up until they were rigidly upright. I imagined them to be soldiers standing to attention, saluting the emperor yacht as it passed between them, and clapped my hands in delight.

Figures on deck waved their thanks to the keeper before swinging round to trim a sail, seeking wind for a smooth passage seaward. A dozen pairs of eyes followed their progress. Only the women, already up and scrubbing clean their doorsteps on the riverbank opposite, ignored this delightful spectacle.

A moment later, even they got to their feet as the air slowly filled with the creak of heavy wings, beating the wind into submission. It reminded me of the breathy sounds our church organ makes as it gathers strength to sound out the hymn we are going to sing. Beyond the schooner, heading along the wide sweep of river, came a flock of birds. Like a mirroring cloud, the unblemished white of their wings surpassed even that of the sails. In an elegant vee-shape they pursued their leaders, two black swans, swooping down over the tall masts to greet the white canvas as one of their own.

At school, we had been taught their appearance was considered a presage of evil. The superstition remained and swans were greeted with both ribaldry and disquiet, as were black cats and walking under ladders. I considered them beautiful and doubted anything so lovely could be evil.

I had waited every year for the past six to see them again. Now, like a surprise birthday present, they were here. Out of the corner of my eye, I saw one of the women shake her fist. Another picked up her bucket and ran back into the house, leaving her step dirty. The rest watched hands on hips, their heads strained back, until the sound of wings had faded into the silence of the sky.

I heard Ruth call and peered out. She was standing on the walkway by the bridge. 'Aren't they magnificent?'

'What are you doing up?'

'Happy sixteenth birthday, first.'

A workman, waiting for the bridge to reopen, glanced up. Catching sight of me leaning out of the window, he grinned and called out, 'Sixteen, eh? I'll have to come courting.'

I blushed and wrapped my shawl more tightly, conscious of my hair cascading loose down my back, freed from its plaits while I slept.

'You're too late,' Ruth called. He swung round. I knew he wouldn't look up again. 'She's already spoken for by a prince.'

'And you?'

'I'm spoken for too.'

'Pity.' The bridge dropped into place and he spurred his bicycle into movement, waving back at Ruth.

'Why so early?'

'Because we have to get to college early and I forgot to tell you.'

'Why?' I craned a little further.

'I'll explain on the way.'

Ruth was wearing a green twinset over a dark-green dirndl skirt, the steel clasp of her wide, waspy belt reminding me of the two halves of the bridge swinging into place. She often wore it for college. She said it was her least flattering item of clothing. It wasn't. The folds of her skirt swayed as she moved, the wide belt emphasising the tiny circumference of her waist, her hips blossoming seductively beneath it.

So different from me; I had emerged from the chrysalis of youth little changed, my eyes wide, their questioning gaze intensified. No matter how much I stared in the mirror, I found no answers. As a butterfly, I was a disappointment. Flat-chested with long legs and long narrow feet, I was as dark as my mother although with eyes of violet rather than brown, my limbs angular and coltish. Not so Ruth. Her promise of spring had melted into a magical summer. Breath stopped when she walked past, flowers lifted their heads in awe at the softness of her skin and its perfume. I was incapable of deciding whether I envied more her legs bronzed by the sun or her breasts, their proud outline rebuking my pathetic offerings on a daily basis.

'What's the rush,' Pappy said from behind his newspaper as I flew downstairs. I kissed him fleetingly on the cheek, loving the clean smell of soap and water that clung to his skin. 'It may be your birthday. Nevertheless, there's still ample time to tidy your bedroom, although perhaps not enough to make it messy again.'

Hans and Berthe laughed; not unkind mirth edged with malice but the soft, indulgent tones of affection from older siblings towards a younger sister.

'And enough time to get going on a diary.' Mother got to her feet, handing me a neatly wrapped parcel. Of course

I knew what it was. She did it every year, a new journal for my writing. Strange, while Pappy aged with the loss of Pieter, Mother had grown more beautiful, the sadness in her dark eyes claiming people's attention wherever she went. Since Pieter left, Pappy had become like the old grandfather clock on the landing. He ticked on but had no heart for it.

'All famous writers start with a diary,' Mother added as I thanked her.

So many changes … we used to hold back on festive ideas and gifts till Pappy and Pieter had finished work. These days, no one is interested in a celebration that lasts all evening and is remembered all year. Instead of a family dinner, we go to the theatre or to a concert. That night, it was the theatre – a play by the English playwright, William Shakespeare. Only the three of us: Mother, Pappy and I. Hans and Berthe preferred to stay at home.

I poured myself a cup of coffee, carrying it to the table.

Hans leapt to his feet, pulling out a chair for me. Twirling an imaginary moustache, he draped his napkin over his arm, bowing politely. 'What would Madam wish to eat? We have some new cheese or perhaps a little sausage?' He pointed at the dresser, where Berthe had arranged plates of cold meat and cheese.

'Stop being silly,' I exclaimed, amused by his teasing. 'You know perfectly well I prefer rolls and honey, especially when they're fresh. The honey is special too,' I picked up the jar and waved it under his nose. 'It's my present to myself. I bought it from the bee-lady in the market. Anyway, now I'm grown up, I can serve myself.'

'That's a long speech,' Hans winked at Pappy. 'It must be your birthday. Here.'

Picking up the tongs, he placed a bread roll on my plate, a hint of warmth still radiating from it. Larger than the norm, the baker had fashioned an elegant bow out of dough, sprinkling it with brown sugar crystals.

'Oh, Hans, you didn't …?'

'No! I promise. Meneer Bork reminded *me* about your birthday. He said to tell you he'd ordered the sun especially.'

Hans waved a casual arm at the window, rays of sun already spreading their light across the dark depths of the river. 'Pappy, however old is he? He told me he remembered you as a small child; that time when Uncle …' Hans hesitated. Pieter had been named after Pappy's brother who'd been killed in the war. 'When your older brother pushed you into the canal to teach you how to swim.'

'I remember that too. I nearly drowned. Meneer Bork had to jump in after me.'

I knew the story, Pappy sprinkling outrageous embellishments as lavishly as the brown sugar crystals on my bread roll. 'Why are you up so early, Berthe?'

'You're only going to be sixteen once, Maidy,' Berthe replied cheerfully. 'Besides, I want to dress the shop window. It gets so dirty with all that scaffolding.'

'You have scaffolding inside the shop, Berthe?' Pappy twinkled up at her.

'No, Pappy … it's in the street, as well you know,' she replied in her usual placid fashion. I loved my sister even though we shared nothing in common, Berthe as stately and gracious as the yacht I had seen that morning. 'Besides, it's not the renovations, it's the children. I love them dearly and when I'm married, I shall have a bushel. There's always a row of them, their faces pressed up against the glass trying to decide which of the chocolate figures to choose. And they have such sticky fingers. That reminds me.' She fished in her bag, which she'd left on the back of her chair, pulling out two foil-wrapped figurines. 'A little extra birthday gift; I thought you and Ruth might like them.'

Hearing Ruth call from the bottom of the stairs, I stuffed the last of my roll into my mouth, and got to my feet. I had already nailed my colours to the flag and brushed my hair into a ponytail, to mark the importance of this day. On seeing me, Pappy had raised his eyes from his newspaper and nodded, his attention focussed on Mother. I watched her mouth tighten but she said nothing.

It was done. I was sixteen.

I ran downstairs, wondering what Ruth had in mind. Obviously something special because Ruth loved her bed; getting up was the hardest thing she did all day.

I hurried out to the river walkway where I'd left my bicycle. In summer we rarely bother to put them in the yard, often using them in the evening when the sun forgot to set and lingered way past bedtime. I peered round in alarm.

'What?' Ruth bent down to open the padlock on her bike.

'My bicycle, it's gone!' I exclaimed in panic.

She giggled and pointed to a brand-new machine with gears, its silhouette elegant and sleek, a neatly woven basket attached to its handlebars.

'Mine?'

I stared up into the faces of my family peering down from our sitting-room window.

'Oh, Pappy,' I exclaimed.

'It's from all of us,' he called, wrapping his arm around Mother's shoulders.

My birthday gift wore a sparkly blue overcoat and possessed a cushioned seat, which promised a smooth ride even on bumpy roads. After a preliminary skirmish with the new brakes – which almost tipped me headfirst into the water, much to the delight of Hans, who had stayed watching from the window – we set out. Despite its streamlining, Pappy had obviously taken great care to choose well and it was easy enough to ride. After a few cursory wobbles on its thin tyres, I felt confident enough to speed up, although I missed the familiar clanking of Mother's old bike. Whenever I rode fast, or as fast as its creaking joints would allow, the noise blurred into a continuous rasping, like an old and valued friend whose irritating mannerisms fade into the background until they are no longer there.

It had rained in the night, washing the streets clean, and my tyres swished through puddles, the sun hadn't yet got around to drying up. Ruth kept overtaking before dropping back again, undecided whether to lead or follow, little different from a mischievous puppy bouncing round its owner. Wobbling over the cobbles, I crossly told her so. Fortunately, we encountered few other people as we cut through the narrow walkways, dismounting only to navigate my bridge. It had become smaller as we had grown bigger, its walls flaking away under harsh winter winds, although doubtless it would still be there in a hundred years.

'I keep wondering if I should catch you when you fall off,' she replied laughing, 'or clear the way, in case you bump into someone.'

'As if I am likely to do either.'

Below my elbows there were faint indentations in the stone. I wanted to believe I had made them, leaning over to see into the water. Except at age five, I had fumbled my toes against the wall, hoisting myself up on my elbows to catch a glimpse of the canal below. Even at eight, I had needed to stand on tiptoe. Now, I leaned comfortably.

If Ruth had hoped writing about Pieter would appease the angry gods, she was wrong. It reopened wounds that I thought long healed and I had not found the courage to write his story for the world to read. I had completed my homework assignment with a tale from my childhood, describing my prince's garden.

Sadly, my prince had turned out to be a little old man who loved his garden. He was there now, pottering about, tending his pots of flowers. He looked up and I waved. I wanted to ask if he remembered the little girl, her feet scrabbling for a purchase on the rough wall.

Ducks were paddling below, circling a tiny stretch of water as if it contained something precious that needed guarding, the water lapping lazily against the stones of the bridge. As a child, I had seen palaces of light in these same depths, imagining mermaids and mermen playing among the reeds. In truth, there was probably little at the bottom except mud, or perhaps the occasional bicycle, its owner too drunk to negotiate the bridge. Nevertheless, very occasionally, when the sun hung low in the sky, throwing its long shadows across the front of a building, I still caught a glimpse of those handsome film actors who had once accompanied me to school, leaping from their celluloid screen to rescue a beautiful maiden, her black hair flowing down to the tips of her toes and dynamite wrapped around her feet.

We cycled on, not saying much. Like the ducks upended in the canal, I was wallowing in the glorious sensation of being grown up.

'Oh dear!' I stopped dead and pointed to the Bridge of Lights. By now people were heading into work, dozens of bicycles flocking across the bridge. A figure was leaning against its metal joists, his bicycle parked next to him. 'Jules is waiting for you.' Even at this distance, I could see he'd made a special effort, his hair neatly slicked back and wearing a different jacket. It looked new.

'*Jules?* Bother!' Ruth hurriedly braked. In my head, I heard the angry stamp of her feet and felt a bubble of mirth hastily swallowed back down. It served her right for crowding my bicycle and making me nervous.

'I won't have a stupid boy spoiling my surprise.'

'Poor Jules,' I said.

'Why do you always feel sorry for them, Maidy, and never for me?' she rebuked. 'It's me who has to put up with them, remember.'

'It's you who encourages them,' I retorted, concerned about the word *surprise*. Ruth's generosity might be unfettered, but it always made me slightly uncomfortable because it could never be reciprocated. With three children and a business only now starting to become profitable again, Pappy didn't possess the wealth of Meneer Endelbaum, who had bestowed on his only child obscene amounts of money even from an early age. Besides, the gifts she lavished on me seemed purely a reflection of her own taste: books from risqué authors I'd never dare read and instantly got rid of, rings for fingers that Mother would insist remained unadorned. For my fifteenth birthday, she had given me a silk petticoat, its deep fringe of black lace both too fine and too revealing for me ever to wear.

'I don't. You know I don't.' Ruth's voice rang out plaintively and a passing cyclist slowed and gave me a glare.

'Do you need assistance?'

'No,' she replied merrily and waved him on. 'I'm fine, thank you.'

Ruth cannot understand that a pearl of greeting dropping from her lips is enough; her smile, a little too much.

'So how do we get to college? You told me you wanted to be early.'

She giggled, her good humour restored, 'Only because of your surprise. Come on, we'll use the old road.' Placing her weight on her pedals, her bike glided into motion equally as obedient as her swains. 'I promise you, I was only being polite and if Jules is stupid enough to believe otherwise, he can wait all morning and get a demerit for all I care.'

Cutting across the road behind a tram, she dived into a narrow lane running parallel to the canal. The area surrounding the bridge had been badly damaged during the invasion, as was the main port on the east coast, which was flattened. Modern apartments stood there now, with the new seaport sited further south. It was the sight of all this rebuilding, so prosaic and dull, that drove Hans out at night, anxious to record the grace and elegance of a past in which houses were as decorative as a painting. He complained the modern city, with its mishmash of colours and styles, looked little better than the rug in his bedroom made from rags.

Once out of view of the bridge and the looming presence of Jules, Ruth cut back to the canal road, heading for the nearest lock where we could cross. Narrow barges huddled against the towpath. With bricks and mortar so costly, they'd been turned into family homes and their black paintwork glistened with glossy tulips and blousy peonies in shades that had no existence outside an artist's palette.

Pappy had once taken me to visit a family, to demonstrate exactly how spacious and comfortable their accommodation was. 'However, I wouldn't suggest you move in, Maidy,' he had teased. 'They'd throw you overboard for being untidy.' Inside had rivalled outside for neatness, with narrow bunk beds along each side, covered by curtains suspended on a polished brass rail. A tiny wood stove, with its iron sides picked out in green, and its chimney stack poking through the cabin roof, provided heat for a family of eight, with a single hotplate to cook on.

Under the warm sunshine, we walked our bikes across the broad, black beams of the lock. Below our feet, water trickled through its closed slats and, nearby, children were playing a noisy game of tag, racing barefoot across the row of barges moored heel to toe. Pausing for a moment, they shielded their eyes from the brightness and waved. I waved back.

'I must remember to tell Hans,' I pointed to a little row of poplars set back from the towpath, thinking what a lovely picture they made. Our museums hold a galaxy of such scenes. Planted with spindly precision, behind them a low-lying farmhouse nestled into the dip; its whitewashed walls glistening in the sunlight with traces of grey smoke seeping into the blue of the sky from its chimney. 'It must be awful to be stuck inside on such a beautiful day. It's made for artists.'

'Honestly, Maidy,' Ruth said sweetly. 'What am I going to do with you, always thinking of other people? It's your birthday, remember. Today is all about you. Come on.'

7

Old Lake Road curved round in a natural horseshoe although, despite its name, we were nowhere near water. Rarely used, it was in good repair and, with a burst of enthusiasm, I began to free-wheel its slight slope, my legs in their white ankle socks and sandals stretched out in a paroxysm of joy. As usual, I was wearing a navy-blue skirt, topped by a white blouse and navy cardigan, my customary uniform, a raincoat folded on top of my basket. Ruth often lent me magazines, scolding that I would never get a beau until I stopped looking so dowdy. Their pages were filled with exquisite young women wearing gowns from Paris, with elegant shoes on their feet. Sadly, beautiful clothes were the same as my daydreams of becoming a princess: unlikely to happen. Mother considered college an extension of school and supplied clothes little different.

A passing cyclist swung round, smiling at me. He raised a hand in salute and cycled on. It was a glorious day. The breeze ruffled my hair with a caressing touch and the morning sun kissed my neck with a thousand good wishes for my birthday. I felt excited and happy. It so often rained on my birthday and I wanted to call out, 'I don't need a present today – the sunshine is gift enough.' I kept quiet. Once Ruth made up her mind, whatever it was I had to go along with it. That's what you do for best friends.

Several kilometres distant, standing tall over the land like some great basilica of remembrance, loomed the mound on which the highway was built. Together with our college building, it had been constructed by the conquering army, spilling the blood of our people as heedlessly as a profligate farmer scatters corn seed, with little concern as to quantity. Throughout one endless winter, men, women, and children dragged earth in buckets, raising the embankment higher and higher, the invaders wanting a fast road to pleasure as well as one to protect their western border. Now, as if a memorial to the dead, the land salvaged from the depths of the lake was awash with buttercups and among them, a flock of sheep contentedly roamed. There were no trees, and I worried Jules might catch sight of us as he cycled along the highway and guess it had been done on purpose to avoid him.

Crossing over the highway, the horseshoe lane eventually converged with the lake on the far side of the college. However, unless you were well acquainted with the area, it would have been easy enough to ride past, a wall of willow stems blocking all view of the water. Sometimes in summer, students slipped out of the grounds to laze on its tiny beach, occasionally dipping a toe, although it was rare for anyone to swim before July, its shallows frozen for months on end in winter.

Ruth pulled to a halt and got off. 'This will do. You can use the trees as a dressing room.'

'A dressing room?' I echoed nervously.

'I'll do your hair.' She ignored my question. 'Don't worry, I won't suggest make-up.'

'That's a relief.' I laughed weakly, hopelessly in the dark.

'Look what I've got you.' Excitedly, she pulled some

coloured fabric from the bag nestling on top of her books and held it up. 'Trousers like mine. *Happy Birthday.*'

'But Ruth ... we're not even the same size,' I protested half-heartedly. I stared enviously at the pinky-mauve folds, my voice drooping like the pale green strands brushing against my shoulder.

'Honestly, Maidy, do give me credit for *some* sense. Of course they're your size ... and the colour's perfect.'

It was. I had never seen such a colour and guessed it had to be expensive. 'But Pappy and Mother ...'

'They're not going to see you out here and you can change back before you cycle home. I bought you a matching twin-set too.' She held it out, a short-sleeved jumper, its cardigan a shade darker.

It was so perfect and yet so bold ... it simply wasn't me. I wore navy-blue with my hair in plaits.

Ruth hastily checked her watch. 'You have five minutes. I hope you're wearing clean underwear, it would be a shame to ruin the effect with tatty old stuff.'

'I always wear decent underwear,' I giggled. 'Mother said it was essential in case I was ever run over and taken to hospital.'

Ruth was right. My parents weren't here. Feeling almost wanton, I hurried into the trees tugging at my hair ribbon, excitement speeding my movements. If I was ever to do anything adventurous, it ought to be on my special day. I remembered my impatience of earlier and felt ashamed. How unkind to think Ruth was anything other than generous. I didn't deserve such a wonderful friend.

I emerged from the trees, my discarded clothes folded over my arm, feeling my legs caressed by the soft fabric as if by a lingering hand, and was alarmed to see Ruth's smile ebb away.

'Don't they suit me?'

I was met with a shrug of indifference and knew straight away I'd done something wrong. 'Leave your hair out, you can wear it like mine today if you want,' she said withdrawing her offer to dress it for me. 'Tomorrow you can go back to your drab little life and your ponytail.'

I gasped, the jibe stabbing as hard as a knife. Nearby, I heard voices and turned towards them so she wouldn't notice the sudden blurring of my eyes. I reached up and parted the tendrils of willow. Swimming into shore were four boys.

'Ruth,' I called, forgetting my hurt. 'Over there!'

'Oh my … it must be freezing. Are they mad? *Oh!*'

Her hand flew to her mouth to cover her surprise as they swam into the shallows and stood up.

In theory I knew what boys looked like, our biology teacher had told us in our final year of school, although I had never seen a boy or girl naked. We are a prudish people. Even with Ruth, my best friend, I'd been grateful for a private corner in which to change.

There were four of them. I felt my eyes drawn to one in particular, his skin the colour of my morning cup of coffee, his hair darkly glistening with bubbles of water trapped in its curls. When he moved, a shaft of refracted light clothed his head in a halo.

He dived back under the surface, his feet kicking spray high into the air, his back a graceful arc, as long and supple as the streamlined shape of a seal. With a roar, he pulled the others down with him and they tumbled back into the water in a bright blaze of energy. No different from gambolling puppies, they rolled over and over, a jumble of light and dark, their legs and arms wrapped tightly. One tried to swim to freedom and was caught by the dark boy, vanishing under the water in a torrent of spray and foam. They stood up laughing, their arms draped across each other's shoulders, bending over to catch their breath.

I knew I should move but I couldn't. I had never seen anything quite so glorious. Like the gentle slope of our land, the elegant plane of their shoulders swept down to their buttocks, their spine a narrow river running between. My brain flashed a picture of Jules with his pallid skin and spots and I chased it away again. These boys were beautiful, their limbs bronzed, easily rivalling the great works of art that had flooded the museums once the city was free. I found myself eager to touch them, to run my hand down the length of muscle from thigh to knee. Each one was the same, yet very different; the muscles of the dark-skinned boy well-developed, his arms and legs solid and smoothly rounded. The tallest of the four was majestic, having broad shoulders tapering to narrow hips. He wore his hair long, its mid-brown lengths tipped with sunlight like a golden diadem. The third and fourth resembled mismatched clothes; the shortest with a long trunk and shorter legs, heavy at the thigh, his face was vividly alive as if the world was a great joke. His lips were firm and full, his mouth tilted in a perennial smile, and I found myself smiling with him. He called out, pointing to something way out over the lake, his friends bellowing their appreciation of his wit, and I knew I had guessed right in thinking him the joker of the pack. The last was fair, his hair almost white in the sunlight, his back and chest smooth above long, long legs.

I felt Ruth tug my arm. 'We're going to be late,' she hissed, her stage whisper designed for my ears alone. 'It'll be us that will get the demerit if we don't hurry.'

We weren't late, and as we rode the last hundred metres up through the grounds to the college forecourt, Jules was waiting. He dropped his bike carelessly to the ground, like rubbish he couldn't be bothered to put in a bin, and sped over.

'I waited for you by the bridge.'

His manner had also changed, acquiring an air of confidence, chasing the belief that Ruth was interested in him.

'Oh sorry,' Ruth's tone was off-hand almost brusque. Jules had served his purpose; she had moved on to someone new.

One of the boys at the lake, perhaps? Logic dictated if they were swimming close to college, they had to be students. I tried not to let it bother me. Sad thoughts belonged to another day, not this one. 'Maidy wanted to use the old road by the lake. You know how she drools over scenery.'

I could see she was still upset with me, her words disparaging, meant to sting.

'Maidy? I thought …' Jules floundered trying to recall my name. 'Isn't your name …?'

'Magrit, yes.' I helped him out.

'Oh, Maidy, I'm so, *so* sorry.' Ruth put out a hand to Jules, her smile only for him. It must have felt like being struck by a thousand volts of electricity. I was astonished not to see him sway on his feet. 'It's her nickname. I mean fancy calling anyone *little spinster*, no wonder she hates it.'

Surprisingly, I didn't. Pappy had told me it meant *little unmarried lady*. 'The word carries a far sweeter ring to it than Magrit, with its hard 'g'. We named you after your grandmother. It suited her, she was hard as nails; you remind me of the bread rolls we love so much, with a soft crust.'

'Dearest Jules, promise me you won't say anything.'

'I promise.' Jules switched his gaze, focussing his attention on me, his smile intense and admiring. 'You do look nice, Marg … I mean, Magrit.'

Ruth flinched. Her hand darted out touching his sleeve. 'Jules, are you going to walk me to class?'

He turned away but the expression said it all. He'd won first prize.

I stayed where I was in the middle of the forecourt. Ruth usually made a point of telling me her programme for the day, arranging when we would meet up. She'd obviously forgotten. I expected her to remember any moment, calling the information over her shoulder, making fun of her absentmindedness. Everyone was staring. Perhaps I did appear ridiculous and she had felt too embarrassed to tell me. Self-consciously, I tried to tie up my hair, fumbling nervously with the ends of the ribbon.

'Birthday?' A girl called, directing her voice at me.

'Yes!' I said, surprised. Even girls who had shared our school days sang to a new tune once they went to college, throwing off childhood alliances as easily as mud from their shoes. Here, they herded into groups or they divided into boyfriend and girlfriend, rarely bothering with those outside their immediate circle, unless necessity dictated. This was neither.

'You look ...' she shrugged and came over, 'I would never dare wear trousers. My mother would kill me. But on you ...'

'What?' My words came out on an anxious breath.

'Let's just say you bowled Jules over – and the rest.' She drew a horizontal line across the air with her finger, indicating the crowd of students slowly heading through the swing doors, their heads continuing to flick back in our direction. I heard the bell ring. 'That's why Ruth took him away.'

I shook my head. 'Impossible.'

'Okay, don't believe me. You should wear those colours more often, they really suit you. By the way, I'm Kirsten.'

'Yes, I know. Thank you.'

'For what?'

It was a strange feeling, chatting with some girl other than Ruth – nice, all part of this new experience of being sixteen. 'Out there, I felt like a fish dumped in a tank full of sharks.' I glanced past her, noticing four figures strolling down the drive towards us. I recognised them instantly, even wearing clothes. I giggled, remembering a joke I'd once heard from Hans. 'Are they new?' I pointed.

'Definitely! And ... *gor-geous!*'

Pappy had said, with the exception of Mother, the beauty of our country belonged to its men, who resembled finely bred racehorses. 'Our women are more like ponies, comely and rotund when young.' Kirsten reminded me of that pony, with its barrel shape after feasting on the fresh grass of the meadow where it lived, its jacket healthy and its eyes bright. She wasn't beautiful but possessed a friendly, open face.

She waved her hand and ran off. 'I'm going to be late,' she called over her shoulder.

I was late too. I stared helplessly across the forecourt, searching for a place to leave my bicycle. Jules had obviously found somewhere to park Ruth's, although he'd left his own on the ground. I didn't want to do that to my beautiful new gift.

'May I help?' The voice was low and music rang through it. It was the dark boy. Up close, his skin had more the colour of chocolate while his face exhibited the classic beauty of a Greek statue; his nose long and elegant, forming a tee shape with his eyebrows, which were thick and straight. Only his eyes contradicted the music in his voice, like an unsightly smudge on a precious work of art. Dark as midnight, they pierced my clothes as if I had been the one cavorting naked in the lake. I felt uncomfortable and kept my gaze steady, pretending not to understand the message in his eyes, reading in it only the helping hand his words had promised.

Without waiting for an answer, he took the handlebars of my bike walking it round the corner of the building. 'Students rarely see beyond the end of their nose.' He pointed to a narrow stretch of wall between two buildings, quite empty of bikes.

'Did you cycle in?' I said somewhat tactlessly. My voice sounded nervous to my ears and I coughed to clear my throat.

He seemed amused, 'Not exactly.'

Remembering, I felt my face flare and hastily ducked my head searching through the contents of the basket, my spare clothes folded neatly on top of my books. 'Thank you, I must go.' Carefully directing my smile at his knees, I grabbed my books and darted off, furiously condemning my stupidity.

Behind me, as if echoing my embarrassment, the sun vanished behind a cloud. I felt its dark shadow and walked faster.

When the bell rang for lunch, I felt too agitated to eat. In any case, I hated the hurly-burly of the canteen. It was a battleground, both in noise and confusion, with too few seats and too many students. Unless you were prepared to use elbows and knees, you mostly ate standing up.

I had chosen to study history and literature. History – because I wanted to understand what motivated one country to invade another; and literature – because of my writing. Many of the more celebrated European writers were still banned from the book shelves of our college library because of their country's affiliation in the recent conflict and, this term, among other things, we were reading a translation of *War and Peace* by the Russian writer, Leo Tolstoy.

None of the four boys were in my group. I guessed them to be older; all four seemingly confident in their own masculinity, especially the dark-skinned one. Instinctively, I had felt uneasy in his presence, sensing the power in his voice. Like the tunes of the Pied Piper, it oozed charm enough to entice girls to his side, light years away from the students I met up with daily in class. Gauche and awkward, for the most part they wore their rapidly growing bodies like prickly new clothes. With luck, the newcomers would be in years three and four, although it was unusual for students to change college so close to their final year, unless their families moved house. And that, if anything, was even rarer. For centuries, in our tiny land, people had been content to live and die in the town or village in which they'd been born.

That morning, even without images of the swimming figures playing on my mind, I had found it difficult to concentrate. For the briefest of moments I had been the centre of attention, my childhood fantasy come true. And it was Ruth who had made that possible. Throughout the long hours of the morning, my classes barely registered, staring down at my clothes, and gently smoothing the delicate nap on the soft wool, its colour the blush on Cinderella's cheek when she first met her prince.

'It's actually fuchsia,' I said out loud in reply to a question. I heard sniggering and realised the question had been, *what was the name of Napoleon's general?*

Embarrassed, I waited with bated breath for the sarcastic comment. It came.

'Magrit, as a teacher, I assumed I'd heard everything. Obviously not.' Professor de Witt's beady eyes gleamed with suppressed amusement.

'I'm sorry, sir, I wasn't listening.'

'Evidently.'

'It's my birthday,' I hastily added, hoping it would rescue me from his usual punishment for late work or inattention – a five-hundred word essay.

'Ah! Sixteen! Now, I understand.'

'Yes, sir.' I felt my cheeks burn.

'If it happens again, Magrit, at least try to say black. Since it was a very black day for our country when it was annexed, you might get away with it. Do you happen to know when we shrugged off this particular yoke? And please don't say yellow.'

I heard the titters and wanted to crawl under my seat. '1815, sir.'

'In that case you are reprieved, only because it's your birthday. Listen, all of you. This week,' he stretched out an arm, wagging a finger in mock ferocity. At least my blunder had given him an amusing story to tell, which I knew he would delight in embroidering. 'I wish you to investigate why the annexation took place, and the reasons it broke down. Dismissed. And a happy birthday, Magrit.'

Even if I had been hungry, I wouldn't have dared to show my face in the canteen after that. Until something equally amusing came along, my gaffe would be the principal subject of gossip among the student body. I hurried off down the corridor to the library, aware Ruth would check there first if she wanted my company. A vast gallery of a room, its height spanned two floors, with tall windows on one side. For five years, it had played host to officers of the invading army who held weekly dances, an orchestra of local musicians seated on a dais where the librarian now had her desk.

It wasn't busy but I wasn't alone. In the bay I'd come to think of as my own was one of the youths – the fair one. He wore glasses and was dressed in brown slacks and a cream shirt, with sandals but no socks. Instinctively I peered down at my feet wishing I'd removed my ankle socks, hoping the hem of my trousers would hide my oversight.

'Am I invading your space?'

It seemed an odd question until I realised I had walked straight towards him, looking neither left nor right, and ignoring all the empty seats.

'Oh, no ...' I glanced wildly, blushing. 'Oh!'

He laughed. 'I am in your seat,' and got to his feet.

He was taller and older, though not by much, a year or two. 'I was researching myths and legends.' He saw me pause. 'Is this your book, too?'

It was. I felt the flush in my cheeks deepen with shame and confusion. I couldn't say so – not now. I hastily sat down, pulling a copy of *War and Peace* out of my bag.

He pointed across the room. 'Doesn't he belong over there with the other Russian writers?' His tone was warm and contained hidden laughter. 'By the way, my name is Jaan,' he said, and stretched his hand across the table to shake mine.

It was an oddly formal gesture, one that belonged to our parents, and regarded by students as hopelessly old-fashioned. We raise a hand in greeting. I grasped the hand he held out and felt the skin of his palm soft from his swim earlier.

'I am in your seat *and* reading your book. Not bad for a first day,' he said ruefully. His hand dropped mine. Reaching up, he raked his fingers through his still damp hair.

My embarrassment evaporated and I laughed.

'I'm Maidy.' I stopped, realising what I'd said. At college, everyone called me Magrit. He didn't comment by so much as a raised eyebrow; possibly he wasn't aware of the term. 'And, yes, it is the book I'm using.' I sat down opposite him. 'Still, there has to be a thousand books in this library.' I tried to copy the lightness of his tone. 'I can easily find something else to read.'

'What interests you?'

'Everything,' I admitted, no longer feeling shy. I tip-toed my fingers through the air pretending to take in all the shelves, 'I only hope I live long enough to read them all.'

A shadow crossed his brow, gone next minute. I noticed his eyes behind his glasses, filled with a gentleness that was so familiar whenever Pappy smiled at us. Deep blue, they were slightly misty behind the lenses, reminding me of an early autumn morning.

'No, I meant in this section.'

'Oh! Perhaps Roman and Greek gods.'

'Why?'

His expression displayed none of the brashness of his friend and I felt encouraged. 'Because they weren't perfect. No different from us. They usually made a mess of things and an even bigger mess when they tried to set it right. Although, for the gods, it mostly panned out in the end.'

'Not always.' I caught a shade of bitterness at odds with the sunshine of his smile, and his mouth twisted ruefully.

'It doesn't matter though, does it?' I found myself wanting to reassure him. 'We all know they didn't exist. They were simply stories invented by people to explain the world around them.'

'So why do you bother with them?'

'I never thought.'

'So think now.'

'I want to be a writer.' I said, thinking how comfortable he was to talk to, conscious I had never spoken of my ambition except to my own family. Inside my head, it sounded so boastful. 'Theirs was such a magical world; it's easy to get lost in it. My life is very ...' I stopped. To admit to *dull* would be to betray my family, especially Pappy who was totally content with his life. No – not quite. Pappy's life would have been complete if Pieter hadn't gone. 'Predictable,' I managed.

'Like shutters closed against the sun.' Jaan's words came out on a whisper.

Startled, I wondered how he had guessed what I meant from my confused rambling. He was staring out of the window, its view across the open water of the lake, and again I caught a suggestion of anger. It was gone next moment. 'The outside of the shutters isn't always worth seeing.' He took off his glasses and rubbed his eyes.

'I still want to see it,' I burst out impetuously. 'I want to stow away on a sailing ship as boys do, and see new lands and eat strange foods.' Jaan shifted the direction of his gaze and I read nostalgia in his half-smile. Keeping his head bent, he picked up his glasses, fiddling with the side pieces, clicking them open and shut. 'Yesterday, I passed a ship recently come into port and heard its crew speaking in a foreign language. They seemed tired and the ship's paintwork was dulled with brine, its deck a sea of canvas ripped and tattered so I knew they must have travelled a great distance ... '

'And you felt a tingle down your spine imagining the wonders they had seen and envying them.'

'Yes,' I exclaimed. 'How—'

'Jaan?'

In one smooth movement Jaan was on his feet, his reaction

71

that of a startled deer espying a hunter. I sensed both tension and an almost physical removal ... as if he had leapt bodily to the far side of the room. I spotted a boy walking towards us, the one I'd nicknamed the joker. 'May I introduce Maidy, she's a student here,' he said, his manner formal, the complete opposite of a moment before. 'We were talking books.'

'Were you?' The dark eyebrows rose several times, his mouth pursed, its corners lapsing into a mischievous grin. 'I'm Waldger and you're needed, Jaan. Nice to meet you, Maidy. May I say ...' he bowed formally, 'this college boasts the most beautiful women. I have just seen a goddess, with eyes so dark they reminded me of moonlight on water and hair like ...' He flew his eyes round the library and a doleful expression flooded his face. 'I can't think of a word extravagant enough. I promise it's not *dusty old books*.'

'Burnished gold, if you mean Ruth.' It was an easy guess. I had seen that stunned expression many times before.

'You know her? What bliss. Will you introduce me?'

'Waldger!'

I heard the warning. Waldger blinked and took a step back. 'Ignore me. I get carried away sometimes. Good to meet you, Maidy. Come along, you.'

Grabbing Jaan by the arm, he towed him forcibly towards the door. I waited, a smile perched ready, but Jaan didn't look back.

8

At the end of the day, I hurried into the cloakroom to change, unwilling to risk my green-clad dressing-room with its floating walls in case, however unlikely, some of the other students decided on a swim.

I needn't have bothered. The brightness had faded with clouds banked thickly over the lake, the horizon a layered belt of grey and brown. I've always loved clouds. I thought of God as an artist, like Pappy, the skies his drawing board, decorating them with sketches of inlets dozing in sun-soaked seas, and magical beasts with horns and spiked tails.

As I went down the steps into the forecourt, I spotted Jules hovering on the driveway. He was ducked down behind a rhododendron bush, its adolescent green buds hinting at a promise of beauty to come, fiddling with the back wheel on his bike. Of course, there was nothing wrong with it, the ploy so obvious even the most gullible would see through it. He was waiting for Ruth. Most times, it was mornings when they gathered. As she cycled into view, her admirers joined her for a final triumphant cavalcade. Ruth called it a pantomime of infatuation, although for the boys concerned, it was deadly serious. At sixteen and seventeen, few possessed the confidence to ask her for a date.

Ruth was talking with the new students and smiling up at Waldger, her long lashes slightly lowered.

A week after my thirteenth birthday, Meneer Endelbaum had ordered a mirror for Ruth. She asked for music and Pappy had drawn golden notes, crochets and quavers, dotting them up and down the sides of the frame, as delicate as those shafts of sunlight on the canals I once mistook for mermaids. It has become her best friend. I have told her time and time again she'd make the perfect film star. 'You must spend hours practising in your mirror to tilt your profile like that.'

Ruth greeted my appearance with a wave, her displeasure of the morning vanished. I wondered if perhaps she had misjudged the generosity of her gift and had regretted giving away something so very beautiful and costly. I threw it out as undeserving. Cost was never an issue with Ruth and she had beauty enough to spare, she had no need of the bit she'd passed on to me.

I collected my bike and, as Jules was doing, hovered at a distance, pretending to arrange my books and clothes. Jaan was there. I noticed his fingers move as if to acknowledge me. Then the reception doors clattered open and the dark boy strolled out.

Unrestrained, every girl's eye flew to him and stayed. He knew it and had expected it although, as he made his way across the courtyard, there was no unseemly swagger. He had no need, his walk as graceful and lithe as a panther's. As if the door's opening had been a signal, boys not yet left for home drew themselves to their full height, becoming as alert and edgy as beasts that sense a rogue male in their territory. Fingers of angry air began to invade the forecourt and warnings, like arrows loosed from a bow, were hurled at his feet. There was anxiety, too, in the posturing of the girls. They fingered the hair curling behind their ears and smoothed their skirts over their hips, in recognition of something never experienced before … and wanting it. Vying with each other to attract.

Against my will, I felt my eyes lift, tracing his steps.

Immediately his friends, conscious of his approach, cut their conversation with Ruth.

I heard Jaan say, 'Here's Zande now.'

Ruth glanced up, her eyes widening into speculation, almost greedy in its intensity, hastily transformed into a smiling welcome.

'This is Ruth.' Waldger introduced her.

Zande paused for a long moment, eyeing Ruth casually out of the corner of his eye. Then, almost dismissively, he angled his head away. 'Tristan?'

A moment before, the tall, brown-haired boy had been involved in conversation with Ruth. Now I saw him a few paces away, clear air all round him. Up close, his high cheekbones and beaky nose gave him the profile of a Roman emperor. From beneath a deep forehead, eyes of an unfathomable grey studied Zande, their expression wary.

'I asked about the basketball team,' the dark boy said. 'They've agreed to give you a trial next week.'

I was observing Ruth. Being ignored was something outside her experience. She was used to being the centre of attention and I was intrigued by her reaction. It riled. Her head came up, taking Zande's dismissal as a challenge, and I felt a sudden disquiet. These were no naïve boys who allowed their feelings to be overturned by a mocking or derisory remark. These were young men with all the power that young men possess.

Turning her back on him, she launched once again into the animated conversation of a moment ago, as if it had never been interrupted. Slowly, Zande ran his eyes over Ruth, taking in the hour-glass figure and lingering over it. Abruptly, in a gesture redolent of tossing away something of little or no worth, he spun on his heel and began inspecting the girls still loitering in the courtyard, on the off-chance of attracting his attention.

As if he had given permission, Tristan and Waldger seemed to relax, their voices ringing out loudly. Only Jaan stayed silent. I wondered then about his friendship with Waldger, his reaction on seeing him in the doorway. Occasionally in school, girls hinted dark secrets about boys liking only boys. I saw Waldger's attention drift downwards, fastening on the swell of Ruth's breasts. No, it wasn't that which had caused his anxiety.

'Haven't we met before? I can't help feeling we have.'

I jumped. I hadn't observed Zande step towards me, still curiously trying to make sense of the little scene I had witnessed. He turned his smile on me. I felt it like a tidal wave, lost and tumbling in its violence, only finding my feet on shore again as it faded and trickled back down the beach. My fingers gripped the handlebars of my bike tightly, only too aware that every atom of Ruth's being was focussed on him, her laughing conversation with the others a side-show.

'Er ... you helped me find a parking place for my bike this morning. I was wearing different clothes then,' I muttered, embarrassed.

'Not today. Besides, I would still have recognised you ... and your bike.' Zande's voice caressed my face with a delicacy I could never have imagined. I stepped back to stop myself stepping forward.

'Magrit and I live next door to one another in the old city,' Ruth called.

I caught the anger in her voice and understood she had already decided on Zande and resented my intrusion. Yet not for a moment would anyone else have guessed, her face as serenely beautiful as always.

He glanced idly over his shoulder. I expected him to step away as boys always did when they had Ruth's attention, instantly forgetting my presence. His mouth twisted, his dark eyes sparkling at some joke only he was privy to.

I had always found it difficult to disguise my feelings, my face a playing field of emotions. Now I kept a guard on it. Ruth was his real quarry. That lingering smile announced his intentions as clearly as if he had written a note. Like a mouse caught in the claws of a cat, I was to be the means of achieving it, a mere bagatelle.

I etched a nervous smile. 'Ruth, we need to go.'

'Are you running away?' Zande came close, his lips moments away from mine. In my imaginings, my prince had been as gentle as his garden of flowers. There was nothing tender about Zande. His eyes raked knowingly over my body like an invading army. This time I did step back.

Zande did too. He snapped back on his heels. '*You!*' His expression changed, the allure of a moment before wiped off, surprise uppermost in his voice.

I felt my face flare, wondering if he'd seen me changing behind the willow stems. Unexpectedly, his dark eyes focussed me, lost and helpless, the violence of a moment before gone and I was out of my depth, the shore a long way off.

I dragged my gaze away, staring down at my bike, desperate to be back on dry land, to feel calm and in control of my feelings, not tumbled by such conflicting emotions.

'Oh my goodness, Magrit,' Ruth called. 'Have you seen the time? You're right, we must fly.' Her best smile was reserved for Waldger. Quickly mounting her bike, she set its wheels in motion and headed off down the drive, swinging round to wave back at them. Then, as if it was an afterthought, she swept her gaze across Zande confirming her challenge.

9

I was grateful to Jules for waiting and said so. 'We are going to the theatre tonight.'

The road was easily wide enough for three to ride abreast, even with an occasional car overtaking. Now, in the face of Ruth's silence, it was Jules and I that talked. In anyone else, I would have believed them to be sulking, her friendly overtures that morning a thing of the past. I excused her, deciding she was probably tired. We had started early and it had been an eventful day. I felt drained and hollow inside, exhausted by emotions I had never before encountered, as if someone had taken a serving spoon and scooped out my insides. I didn't know what to think about Zande. The moment I'd thought myself safe, my feelings back on solid ground where I could rely on them, he had thrown that look of appeal, his violence dissolved into the soft twilight of entreaty, and I had found myself lost and floundering again.

Across the shining water, the last traces of sun fluttered like a butterfly trying to escape the encircling clouds. The surface of the lake remained empty, deserted, and sadly I realised that my celluloid pirate, the long-standing companion of my dreams, had been chased away by senses newly born and never before experienced. My beautiful day had become buried under feelings that had little to do with happiness and love. In the space of a few minutes, the innocent images that had accompanied my feet throughout the long years of adolescence were gone for good, consigned to a drawer labelled childhood.

'Are you going to the theatre as well, Ruth?' Jules asked with his most encouraging smile. Only that morning, she had joked with him. Now, she never bothered to reply.

I felt ashamed for her, conscious Jules would be trawling through every word he'd uttered since they first met, seeking the one in which his fault lay. However naïve he was, he didn't deserve to be crushed underfoot like a bug. 'No,' my laugh sounded contrived. 'Just my parents and me. It's Shakespeare.' I added, 'Othello.'

'Isn't he that foreign writer?'

'Yes. And the most famous.'

'What's it about?' He darted a hopeful smile at Ruth and was met with a wall of indifference.

What was it about? Beauty, love, jealousy and hate ... and destruction. 'Othello is the commander, a great man in war, who is destroyed by his own jealousy.'

'Does it have a happy ending? If it does, I might ask my parents to take me. My mother won't watch anything that's sad. She says she lived through too much of it in the war.'

'It's only a play; it's not real.'

Jules grimaced. 'Makes no difference to that generation. So what happens?'

'Tragically he murders his wife, the one person he really loves. Then, learning she was innocent all along, stabs himself.'

'Saving the state the cost of a trial. Good man.'

I was astonished by his almost droll expression, totally unexpected and bravely done. I considered him with new eyes, seeing past the camouflage of ugly blemishes, and guessed if he was going to mourn Ruth he would do so in private.

I waved goodbye at the bridge. He wouldn't be there next morning. He knew there was no point.

'That was unkind, Ruth.' I tried to stop the words but couldn't.

'He invited himself.' I imagined her feet hitting the ground in temper. 'When did I once ask him to join me?'

I didn't remind her.

Pushing our bikes along the canal, we walked quickly and in silence. There was a brooding quality to the air and our footsteps echoed hollowly as we crossed the helmeted bridge. I watched a couple of seagulls take wing, heading for open water. There was a storm brewing and they knew it.

As always when we argued, I had begun to feel a sense of remorse. Ruth had given me a wondrous birthday. It was not her fault strangers had come to the school. 'What did you think of the new students?' I asked, wanting to provide her with an opening.

'Not much.' Her voice sounded coldly polite, as if I was an unwelcome visitor, and I guessed she was still smarting from my comment about Jules.

'That's impossible.' I kept my tone easy. 'You can't say *not much*. Seeing them without clothes was altogether too much.'

Ruth giggled and I knew we were all right again.

'Ruth,' I burst out impulsively. 'Why don't you send the clothes back? I've only worn them once; they'll never know.'

She hesitated. 'The trousers were a dreadful mistake; they really didn't suit you. If you want, I'll exchange them for a different size and wear them myself. It would be a pity to waste them. You can keep the twinset, you'll find it useful.'

'That's perfect.'

It wasn't. The slacks had suited me very well indeed. Kirsten had been right, and I had met up with glances of admiration all day. I camouflaged a shrug of resignation. If I was to escape this sense of guilt, draping my shoulders like a fox-fur stole, this was the price I had to pay. I pulled the bag from my basket and passed it over, leaving the twin-set behind on top of my books.

'What about you?' It was a polite enquiry.

'I'll ask Mother if I can have a new skirt.'

'That would be much better.'

Ruth began fiddling with a strand of hair, nervously threading it through her fingers, a gesture that belonged to girls uncertain of their place in the world – not Ruth. 'Which of the boys did you like?'

Before I had time to answer …

'I liked Waldger. He's enchanting, *so* funny. Or perhaps Tristan. They say he's an outstanding athlete.'

'Not Zande?' I couldn't resist.

'I hated him. Bombastic, swaggering … he's convinced every girl fancies him. I thought *you* one of them.' Her brows drew together in a frown and her mouth twisted. Yet another gesture I'd not seen before, her armoury of emotions schooled and honed to perfection.

'He was only being polite,' I said hurriedly, aware Zande was behind these unchartered movements. 'He thought we might have met before, only he was mistaken.'

'Is that all?' Ruth's brow cleared. 'I doubt if someone as sophisticated as Zande would have remembered, even if you had met before; a schoolgirl in dreary navy with her hair in plaits.' Her voice teased yet I knew she was deadly serious. Naively, I had imagined her displeasure the result of over-generosity, believing her gift too valuable. How could I have been so gullible? For the briefest of moments, I had borrowed the attention that was hers by right, and she didn't like it one bit.

I hadn't imagined the day could get any worse. From a

beautiful sunrise, thunder clouds had ripped my birthday to shreds. As if mocking me, I felt a drop of rain and pushed my bike harder.

*

By the time we reached our house, it was raining sharply and the temperature had dropped. I ran down the streets towards the tobacconist's shop where Hans bought his newspaper, heading for the double gates into our yard. The building had once belonged to our family as had a number of buildings on the river. Grandfather had sold it and now the little window overlooking the street displayed pipes and tobacco, instead of the traditional green plant.

Pappy smoked a briar and I liked that one best. He said it came from the root of a bush, probably older than he was, its rough grainy finish reminding me of Pappy's worn face, although Meerschaum pipes were the most popular. Starting off life pure white, over time, they became stained brown with tobacco smoke. The shop also sold Peterson pipes, with silver waistbands and long polished stems that reminded me of soldiers on parade, and tiny corn pipes that were cheap to buy and popular among young men, starting out on a career of pipe smoking.

I pushed open the narrow door in the gates. A crack of lightning streaked through the sky as if the god of heaven, Zeus himself, was angry, and sheets of ice-cold rain hit the pavement, chased by thunder. Lifting my bike over its high sill, I ran it across the yard into the shelter of the outbuildings. Gloomy and cavernous even on a sunny day, under a lowering sky they were as dark as midnight.

'Ruth? Come and have some tea with us,' I called in a spirit of reconciliation. Leaning my bike against the wall, I added, by way of enticement, 'Berthe's made a cake.'

Ruth hesitated.

'She's decorated it with sixteen chocolate elves.'

In her own way, my sister was as much an artist as either Pappy or Hans, her cakes and puddings as skilful as a beautiful painting, and most probably took as many hours to create.

'In which case I'd love to.' Wrapping her jacket round her books, Ruth brushed drops of rain off her skirt, its green folds clinging to her thighs. 'I'll just run home and change first; I must look a dreadful sight. And I can't stay long, I've got another test to revise for.'

The back door was unlatched and I chased in. I didn't bother to go into the shop and greet Mevrouw Kleissler. My clothes were damp and Mother would only fuss, insisting I'd catch cold if I didn't change. I could hear her upstairs chatting to Pappy in the sitting room and wondered if he'd left work early to get ready for the theatre. Another voice joined in the conversation and I heard laughter.

For a moment, I didn't recognise it; then I did. Not Hans, his voice was a light tenor with a slight bark to it like an over-excited spaniel. This was the voice I recalled only in my dreams and had not heard for six years.

My brother Pieter.

10

I sat down on the top step, my legs suddenly too weak to hold me upright. The secret I'd kept all these years pounded at my temples, demanding to be heard. Once again, I experienced the terror of that night, so potent still, in my mind I heard Pieter cry out.

Cautiously, I got to my feet, my hand on the door knob. For a moment I felt reluctant to open it. Pieter was gone. Where, no one had ever said. This was someone who sounded the same; it had to be. I was mistaken.

But I wasn't.

He was sitting in his old chair as I'd last seen him on the night of his birthday, scarcely older than I remembered.

'Look who's here.' Pappy got to his feet and came over to the door, tucking his arm through mine, welcoming me in. 'You remember, Maidy, Pieter.'

'Maidy? I remember Magrit, a little skinny child who loved reading.'

My head whirled with a thousand questions. I floundered about, unable to put them into words, like a book thief who dithers in front of a shelf of rare volumes, unsure which to steal first. I found my voice, saying awkwardly, 'I became Maidy because I failed to see anything in the mirror on my special birthday.'

'Pappy, you're so wicked! Maidy, I promise, it's a fable.'

I sensed Pieter clutching at my words as a drowning man would reach for a life belt or a piece of driftwood. 'Pappy borrowed it from one of the stories that Hans Anderson wrote; the one about the Emperor's New Clothes.'

I remembered the story. The book of fairy tales Pieter used to read to me still sat on the bottom shelf of my bookcase. It had bright pictures on the cover. In the story, tricksters sold the king a suit of clothes that didn't exist, assuring him that only the great and good could ever see them. It had taken the innocence of a small child to show him up as being naked.

Memories of my brother's laughter, the warmth of his smile, slowly crept back into focus; those Pieter was exhibiting for my benefit simply an artifice, replicas of the genuine article. Like a blind beggar, he was feeling his way through this first encounter – and needed help. My questions had to wait.

'Berthe saw the man she's going to marry, she told me so,' I offered him my gift. 'And Pappy, you told us that for hundreds of years every woman in our family has been given a mirror as part of her dowry.'

Pappy chuckled and the strain in his voice eased out of sight. 'That bit's certainly true. The women of our family have always received a mirror on their thirteenth birthday.' He rubbed his chin ruefully. 'Maybe I did embroider the tale rather too much. Perhaps the tradition was fine as it was. As for Berthe – your sister's a goose.'

'Mother?'

'I did see Pappy.' My mother sat by Pieter, his hand in hers, her air one of great joy now her child was safely back where he belonged. For the first time ever, she allied herself with me, offering up her memories as a sacrifice on the altar of our discomfort. 'I was fourteen, perhaps a little older. It was my first visit to the city. I wandered about and found myself staring into a shop window, marvelling at the images. I had never seen myself in a mirror. This young man came up behind me and I saw him in the glass for the first time.'

'So you see, Maidy,' Pappy beamed his thanks, 'you are wise beyond your years. You saw nothing except your reflection and said so.'

I laughed with him, partly with relief that the first awkward moments were behind us, hoping conversation might now flow more easily, and partly with gratitude. The day of my thirteenth birthday, I had sensed something stirring in the heart of the mirror and had never again plucked up courage to stare into its depths, despite the dancing fairies that beckoned so joyfully. Pushed up against the wall, I used it as a clothes-horse, snatching a fleeting glance as I hurried past. Maybe, at long last, I could accept those dark shadows as nothing more ominous than wisps of cloud that had wandered across the sun.

I heard the shop bell chime and Mevrouw Kleissler's, 'Good afternoon, Ruth. The family are upstairs. Do go up.'

Ruth drifted into the room. Her long hair was damp and clung tightly, the rain changing its strands of gold into copper. She had changed into a dress of palest green, with long sleeves, its skirt full and floating. She reminded me of a creature of water, a naiad, as ethereal and delicate as the nymphs that haunted the waterways of my childhood.

She gasped. 'Pieter!'

I saw Pieter glance once and not look away. I had seen the identical expression earlier that day, on the face of Tristan, staring silently down at Ruth while she was talking to Waldger.

11

'I've been travelling, Ruth.' Pieter said in reply to Ruth's breathless enquiry: where have you been all these years?

'Exploring countries with names I'd never heard before. To reach them, we crossed oceans so vast the sun rose, set, and rose again before we found land. The first time we did it, despite all scientific evidence to the contrary, I honestly believed we would tumble off the end of the world. There, we encountered seas with waves taller than any of the ships that sail down our river; monsters that ate ships for breakfast and spat out their bones, leaving indigestible spars of wood and tangled ropes behind.'

I kept still, scarcely breathing, listening to stories about a world I could only dream of.

'Gradually, as we headed south, night and day swapped places, until daylight was the longer both in winter and summer.'

I remembered Pieter as being quiet, filling the silence with his merry smile while he considered a reply to your words. Now, the speed of his speech made me wonder if he was trying to spill out every last detail before nightfall. I reminded myself that he would be feeling awkward. After so many years, we were all of us strangers. Like his voice, slightly different from my memory of it, crisscrossed with dark and earthy overtones. Music still rang through it and – something else too – a hesitation, as if the words he was speaking had lain unused in some dark cupboard.

'There were islands that grew out of a turquoise sea …' He smiled shyly at Ruth, 'I can see you in a dress of that colour, it would suit you very well.'

'Are you saying,' Ruth smoothed her skirt over her knees, 'this doesn't?'

'No … I …'

Ruth stretched out a hand, touching him lightly on the arm. 'I'm teasing, Pieter. In the future, turquoise will be my very favourite colour. Please go on.'

Pieter peered down at his arm as if it was laced with rich jewels. 'I …I … I'm sorry, I have forgotten what …'

'You were saying that you loved the islands … *with their turquoise seas.*'

'Although there was danger even in such gentle waters.'

I wondered if he had meant to say those exact words, with their underlying message that she might be dangerous too.

'I've seen both sharks and killer whales basking in those seas. In the end, I preferred the mountains with peaks so high they were lost among the clouds.'

Outwardly, he appeared little different from the day of his sixteenth birthday, when he had insisted his cake should be cut into equal portions. If an unexpected guest had arrived or Lars, the foreman, was working late, Pieter would have given away his own slice rather than let someone else do without. Nonetheless, my overall impression was of someone stronger than the willowy youth who had shared our life, his muscles powerful and clearly defined, although his hair still flopped over his forehead, his cheeks fresh and his beard light, his smile amused and playful. Only when you unexpectedly met his gaze was it noticeable how much he had changed. The eyes that opened onto the world were full of experience, not all of it good.

And the smile he kept flashing towards Ruth ... that was new, too, and very different. As children, whilst teasing me and pulling my pigtails, he would listen to her talk, a contented smile lurking at the corners of his mouth. In that he'd not changed, metaphorically tugging at the strands of my hair, exclaiming every few minutes, 'How can Maidy be so tall, so grown-up, so serious,' his tone implying that perhaps I wasn't grown-up after all and remained that silly child, light-years younger than Ruth. 'I taught you how to walk and to read. Such a baby you were, always falling down. I believed you a ... changeling.' Again that slight hesitation. 'A fairy, because you were so different from the rest of us. A dark-haired, serious fairy.' He slid his smile slowly across the table at Ruth, his fingers edging it in her direction, his blue eyes hesitant, uncertain how she would respond.

He needn't have worried. She responded with gaiety and enchantment, her eyes flashing up to his face whenever he spoke of lands dozing in sunshine. This was a side of Ruth we seldom saw. I knew she found my lack of sophistication boring. She had travelled beyond the confines of our country, while I hadn't even left the city; my knowledge of the world second-hand. She showered Pieter with attention, her eyes saying what her speech couldn't – that never before had anyone proved so interesting.

I watched her fingers pluck at the strands of carpet on the little table top, instantly falling still again, a sparkling glance at Pappy or Pieter her only movement. I envied her stillness, her limbs falling into a natural elegance. My body, like my face, was a betrayer of my deepest feelings, my limbs content to be silent only while I slept. I remembered Ruth boasting that she often let her thoughts stray, while boys ploughed endlessly long furrows on subjects in which she had little or no interest. I wondered how she could possibly think about something else and be so charming. If that's what she was doing now, you could never tell.

'Weren't you afraid of being shipwrecked?' I burst out, surprised Mother had remained silent, allowing tales of danger to her first born pass without comment.

'Never,' he said. 'We were all experienced voyagers.'

Berthe's footsteps sounded on the stairs. The shop where she worked closed at five and she was always home by six, you could set the clock by her. Like Pappy, she hated straying from what was known and loved.

Her scream at the sight of Pieter echoed so loudly that Mevrouw Kleissler heard it in the shop and came running upstairs. Berthe burst into noisy tears and Mevrouw Kleissler, remembering how often she had wished her husband back from the dead, joined her. For a long moment, chaos pinned order into a corner, then Pappy took charge.

'Pieter has been travelling, Mevrouw Kleissler, and will be with us for a few months,' he said firmly, attempting to quieten the two hysterical women. 'You will see him tomorrow and the day after,' Pappy reassured the elderly woman and sent her, still sniffing into her handkerchief, back downstairs, telling her to get along home, before closing the door on her fading footsteps.

Berthe wrapped her arms around Pieter, and a fresh paroxysm of crying wracked her frame. 'I thought you were dead and Mother and Pappy daren't tell us.'

Pieter patted her back awkwardly. Again Pappy rescued him, pulling out a chair for Berthe to sit down, untwining the arms from Pieter's neck, wrapped as tightly as bindweed that chokes its host plant to death.

Outside, the rain continued heavily, the early evening

light swallowed up by a dark overcoat of water-soaked clouds. Pappy switched on the standard lamp, its long, beaded tassels clattering raucously in the breeze from the window. He leaned over to close it. With a gesture of his hand, Pieter stopped him. 'I'm not used to enclosed spaces.'

His fingers gripped the arms of his chair and I wondered if he was already regretting his decision to return, discovering his old life to be as close-confined and claustrophobic as the dark mahogany furniture and velvet hangings made our sitting room.

'Tell me everything you've done,' Berthe ordered, wiping away her tears. 'I don't believe it; you've scarcely changed at all. Did Mother tell you, I'm engaged to be married?'

She burst into a long-winded description of her fiancé and their arrangements for the wedding. Pieter listened intently, sharing an amused glance with Pappy. Berthe hadn't changed, her imagination confined to a tiny pool of thoughts and feelings, uninterested in exploring further. She was content with what she had and desired nothing more. If you wanted surprises, you wouldn't find them in Berthe.

'So why did you leave us so abruptly, I cried for weeks,' Berthe said to a room full of silence that came from breath held, fearing the reply. 'You didn't even say goodbye and not even a letter in all this time.'

'Come, Berthe. Let Pieter get a foot in the house before bombarding him with questions,' Pappy broke in.

'I work for a lord, a prince; an impatient man who hates to be kept waiting.' Pieter stretched his hand towards Mother as if asking permission to speak. I caught her slight nod giving it and wondered if they'd practised that lie together before trying it on us. I wondered also, what the real truth was. 'He wanted to set sail that night. I had to leave or miss my chance of seeing the world.'

'Who is this lord? Are we going to meet him?' Berthe's

curiosity poked its head tentatively a little way out of its shell like a reluctant tortoise. 'If you invite him to dinner, I'll cook.'

'Maidy, have you noticed the time? We've talked so long, we've missed the theatre.' Mother got to her feet, cutting across Berthe's question.

'You were going to the theatre, Pappy? I can't believe you'd get dressed up and go to the theatre.'

It was a joke from our childhood that Pieter's memory had touched upon, like a forgotten Christmas cracker spilling its haul of sweets, and the awkwardness of the moment vanished. Mother's constant complaint had always been that Pappy was happiest in his work clothes. Whatever the weather, he wore a comfortable pair of trousers made baggy from sitting all day painting. In winter, he wore a heavy-knit pullover over his shirt and a navy jacket thick enough to withstand the icy winds that lurked in the yard, waiting for him to emerge and oversee the loading of a mirror.

'It was only Shakespeare,' Ruth trilled, as melodious as any songbird, 'nothing of any real importance.'

Mother glanced over at Pappy, her expression that of a cat eating from a bowl of cream. 'Pieter, are you hungry? Ruth, *do stay for dinner*. After-all you're part of the family. Berthe, come and help, there's a good girl. We'll serve Maidy's cake for pudding.' Pieter made to get up. 'No, you're a guest ... *Oh, how silly!*'

Pieter grinned at her and the awkward moment was gone. 'No, I'm not, Mother. I'm back and I want to stay.'

There was a noisy kafuffle as someone tripped on the stairs. I heard Hans call out, 'Berthe, you home?' The door into the hall opened and Hans stuck his head round.

'What on earth's happened, Maidy?' Leaving the door half-open, he bent down to take off his outdoor shoes, slapping water off the sleeves of his jacket. 'Weren't you supposed to be going to the theatre?'

He noticed Ruth first and smiled warmly. Then he saw Pieter.

As if unbelieving, he took a step backwards. I don't know why, but I felt a need to hold my breath. Then he was across the room, enfolding his brother in a bear hug. Mother and Pappy smiled. I did too, with relief. For six years Hans had played the older brother, the pretender to the throne. Now the rightful heir was back from the dead.

As if the arrival of Hans was some sort of signal, I got up to lay the table. Mother and Berthe vanished into the kitchen, emerging after a short while with a platter of chicken legs, the table already furnished with potatoes quietly steaming in their jackets. Pappy got to his feet to open a bottle of wine, leaving Ruth, Pieter and Hans chatting about childhood adventures.

Our traditional drink is Jenever, a type of gin made from juniper berries. The men of our family have always taken a glass with their dinner and Pappy was no different, a firm believer in celebrating the end of a good day's work. When the boys were little, Pappy warned them he used it as paint stripper, wanting to prevent them indulging in the fierce liquor before they could cope with it. Mother refused to touch it and because he loved Mother more, Pappy bought her wine. Now, he made a great show of filling seven glasses. It was the first indication that I was truly grown-up.

I sipped at it, trying to identify the taste and Pappy laughed when I said I could taste greengage and vanilla.

'If you were in France, they'd offer you a job on the spot.'

After dinner, Mother and Pappy always sat by the fire while Berthe and I cleared the table. Tonight, though, she remained at the table close to Pieter. He sat in his old chair, Mother quietly moving it back from the table whenever we had guests.

Among people whose livelihood comes from the sea, there exists a belief that sons and husbands lost to the waves could only reappear if a place at the table is kept open for them. We had always accepted Mother's superstitions without knowing why. Her talking about how she and Pappy had first met was like a glimpse into a rare book and, incredibly, of all the superstitions to dominate her being, one had been justified. Once again, her family was complete; Pieter on her right, Berthe to her left, Hans and I flanking Pappy. Guests had always been placed somewhere in between. Tonight, though, it was Ruth who sat next to Pieter, while I brought in an extra chair from the study.

If one of our great artists, Vermeer or Rembrandt, had set the scene to canvas, it would have shown a family group sitting comfortably around a table, lit by the warmth of lamplight, and his brush strokes would have created only the joy of reunion. Pappy's smile was jubilant, the glance he shared with Mother full of relief that his son was home. Berthe had already forgotten her questions in the delight of having her family whole again. And Ruth was a part of it all, smiling to cue, her eyes demurely accepting Pieter's cautious advances. Only Hans remained watchful, his demeanour as edgy as that of a caged bird, and I wondered if he shared my doubts. Pieter's return was something I had longed for, wanting to make our family whole again. Sadly, like my prince, that dream no longer existed except in my imagination. In six years, the deep crater his absence had left had been filled in and was no longer there.

After Ruth had said goodnight and gone home, Pieter became increasingly restless, fidgeting with his spoon, twisting it over and over, his hands roving haphazardly as if they were migrating birds waiting for a signal to take to the air, his eyes darting constantly to the open window wanting to follow them.

Silence fell and to break it, I got to my feet kissing Pappy goodnight. Pieter stood up with his arms held out as if to embrace me. He pulled back and I sensed he wasn't quite sure of his place in the household.

'I need my bed,' I said. 'It's been an eventful day.'

I felt exhausted, and in need of quiet and solitude.

Conversation had flowed steadily all evening, Pieter asking the questions that any person who had not visited for the longest while might ask. Yet, nothing of any importance had been said. That took place in Pieter's painful expression whenever he believed he was unobserved and Mother's and Pappy's possessive posture, that of birds protecting their young.

'I forgot it was your birthday, Maidy.'

'It doesn't matter,' I said lightly. 'Your being here is present enough. Besides, in a few weeks, we can celebrate yours. You'll be how old, twenty-two? That's old.'

I heard anger in his tone. 'Not yet, it isn't. I still have a few good years left.'

*

I couldn't sleep. Wrapping myself in my shawl, I pulled out my journal, wanting to record the events of the day while they were fresh in my mind, and hoped my words would strike the page honestly. I had always found it difficult to commit my feelings to paper, and my journal was full of crossings-out. Paragraphs rewritten again and again, never quite reaching the perfection I wanted from them. Words for me were a living entity; resembling one thing in thought; in print, even the simplest phrase was capable of taking on a meaning very different from the one intended.

I wrote about Pieter's homecoming and also of Jaan, with whom I had sensed a tentative flowering. Next moment, the hand held out in friendship had been snatched away and his offer of friendship, like a seedling succumbing to frost, had shrivelled away.

And Zande? In a single, smouldering glance, he had exposed my fantasies as the foolish ramblings of a child. The memory of his presence, so close I could almost feel the warmth of his breath, still made me uncomfortable. Hurriedly, I stood up and, drawing close to the open window, leaned out. The night sky remained dark and sullen. It had rained again and the pavements streamed with water, rivulets trickling down the bank in a raft of miniature waterfalls. Zande would demand a high price for his friendship and only a foolish girl would pay it. I tried to close my ears to his voice, hearing his words as soft and delicate as a day-old chick; aware most girls would think it a price worth paying.

Footsteps echoed across the walkway and I saw Pieter. He leaned over the rail by the bridge, staring down at the water. Ducks were nesting under the bank, their home of mud and reeds backed up against one of the concrete pillars on which the bridge rested. I caught a faint indignant quack and a splash as his shadow fell over their nest.

I was about to call out when Mother appeared. Pieter tucked his arm through hers and she leaned her head against his shoulder. I saw then he was very much the taller. They talked softly for a moment or two, while I watched the darkness intensify and wondered if another storm was on its way. Mother reached out, her hand clinging to Pieter's. He shook it off and took off across the bridge, her hand trailing emptily after him.

12

Sunlight woke me. May through July are months in which darkness takes a holiday, gifting our country long days filled with warmth and light. Yet the brevity of the darkness, so magical at first, quickly becomes bothersome and we hang summer curtains of thick cotton at the bedroom windows, dyed dark green to block out the light. The maids had already washed and ironed our curtains, leaving a neat pile on my bedroom chair. I always delayed hanging mine till the very last moment, reluctant to miss a minute of spring, although now I was mindful, if I didn't want to feel perpetually tired, I would shortly need to use them.

Wrapping my shawl around my shoulders, I tried to recapture the holiday mood of my birthday. The rain of the previous night had left a chill in the air, the wind in a capricious mood, scuffling scraps of paper along the canal bank. It caught at a discarded newspaper tossing it high into the air before draping the glass crown of a lamppost in a paper skirt. A car trundled past followed by two bicycles, the workmen in their brown overalls deep in conversation. From across the river, I caught the metallic clank of a bucket and spotted the usual coterie of kneeling figures. I rarely saw their faces, only the swaying of their hips clothed in black as they scrubbed energetically back and forth, their ambition little higher than their front doorstep, desiring it to be the whitest in the street. A little way off, a housewife crossed to the water's edge and shook dust from a doormat. The family of ducks was also awake, mother duck marshalling her little ones along the waterway in search of breakfast, their diminutive webbed feet paddling furiously to keep up with her stately progress. She reminded me of the elegant sailing ship I had seen the day before.

When I got down, Pieter was already at the breakfast table talking closely with Pappy. For a moment, I saw him as a stranger, someone I'd never seen before, as if by accident I'd picked up Pappy's glasses and they had distorted my vision, leaving it blurred. He appeared fresh and wide awake as from a good night's sleep, and I wondered how long he'd stayed out. Pappy positively glowed, beaming out his pride and love for the world to see.

I went to the kitchen to get some coffee. Surprisingly, my sleep hadn't been invaded by bad dreams – or at least nothing that had stayed in my subconscious long enough to trouble it. However, the puzzlement that had dominated my waking thoughts remained, leaving me tired and a little jaded.

'Pappy's filling me in on all the changes,' Pieter called. 'Mother always baked bread herself. Now, I gather, Hans gets it from the bakery.'

'How did you sleep, your first night back in your old bed?' I said.

I wanted to ask Pieter where he'd been so late. Not even bars in the new city that serve cheap liquor stayed open much after eleven. As a child, bursting with curiosity, I would have demanded he answer my questions. I was no longer a child.

'Like a top, the moment my head hit the pillow. However,

I did find it somewhat strange to experience a bed that didn't rock.'

'Did you always sleep aboard?' I placed the pot of fresh coffee on the dining table, a thick layer of carpet under the tablecloth to protect its polish from the heat.

He shrugged. 'We journeyed the length and breadth of the world, Maidy.' I felt pleased he had adopted my new name so easily. He picked up his cup. 'May I walk with you to college? I feel a need to become reacquainted with my new, grown-up sister.'

I wanted to get to know him too. Over time, my memories had played me false and I no longer trusted them. 'I don't walk to college, Pieter, I ride. It's more than twelve kilometres from here.'

The street door slammed shut and I heard Hans' feet on the stairs. He came in, a basket dangling from his wrist, a cloth tucked across the top to keep the bread warm. Removing a pair of tongs from a basket of cutlery on the sideboard, he lifted the oval-shaped rolls onto our plates, serving Pappy first. The warm smell of bread triggered a rush of saliva.

'I hope you bought enough, I'm starving.'

Hans grinned at me and left the covered basket within reach. 'I calculated three for Pieter and Pappy, and six for you.'

Hans knew perfectly well while six rolls might be eaten by him, I rarely, if ever, managed more than two, however hungry I said I was. Pappy complained I ate like a bird. I tore into my roll, dipping its end into my coffee.

'Where is your college?' Pieter said.

'Herrendorp.'

'Why so far, why not in the city?'

Hans sat down and opened his newspaper. Reaching over, he helped himself to some smoked sausage. 'Because, when the conquerors finally quit our land, they left behind a ready-made building on the edge of the lake, and the Burghers decided it would be sensible to try and find a use for it.'

'That's true, Pieter,' Pappy refilled his coffee cup. 'You were probably too young to remember, but the land across the southern tip of the lake was confiscated.' His tone was accusing. I remembered him telling me that the majority of our citizens, who had survived those dark days of conquest, thought the building should have been demolished. 'When the occupying army found they needed a road, they simply took more land. The authorities are trying to trace its original owners. Perhaps that's why—'

He broke off, hearing Mother's step on the stairs. She was chatting to Berthe. They were always last up. Mother blamed her hair, plaiting it afresh every morning, while Berthe, even when we were little, refused to stand in a queue for the bathroom, staying in bed until everyone had finished.

Pieter got to his feet, kissing Mother warmly on the cheek. Berthe too. Overnight, he had obviously decided he did belong. Yet, demonstrations of affection were the act of a stranger. Maybe Pieter had not objected when Mother ran her fingers through his hair, something that made Hans cringe away in embarrassment, nevertheless he rarely offered a kiss. None of us did, apart from me. I hugged and kissed Pappy, sensing in him, even from a child, an open and warm heart.

'In which case, I'll walk with you as far as the edge of the city.'

'May I come up?' Ruth called from the stairs.

Pieter tumbled his chair backwards, quickly catching it before it fell.

She was wearing her cream trousers, a cardigan draped around her shoulders and the sun of the previous day had kissed the skin of her arms. Hans frowned, burying his head in his newspaper.

'I was asking Maidy's permission to walk with you to the bridge,' Pieter's voice rang with the hesitant uncertainty of the night before.

'I hope she said yes,' Ruth carolled and launched a smile that no one, not even Helen of Troy, could have matched.

Finishing my breakfast, I chased back upstairs to collect my school bag. Anxious to avoid running up and down two flights every time I forgot a piece of homework, I usually left it in the study, where I kept my books. In the excitement of Pieter's homecoming, I had forgotten and taken it up with me. By the time I opened the door to the yard, Pieter had unearthed our bicycles from the garage, and he and Ruth were waiting by the open gate, a line of cars drifting past on the street.

'Ruth says you're studying literature and history,' Pieter called as I closed the back door.

'Did she also tell you she is going to become a doctor?'

'Of course. But eight years!' Pieter frowned. 'Why so long?'

'Because there's a lot to learn,' Ruth flashed, 'Even then, I'll only be twenty-four.'

'Yes, but I'll be thirty.'

I felt a sudden frisson, as if he had been about to elaborate on his statement and changed his mind.

Pushing Ruth's machine, he crossed the road into the narrow walkway by the river; Ruth walking alongside. The tide was out, leaving a narrow culvert of water between mudflats pitted with the tiny clawed feet of waders. It was early and there were few people in the streets. Bars and shops wouldn't open until later, even the tempting glitter of watches in the jeweller's window remained hidden behind thick wooden shutters. A brisk breeze funnelled down the river, slapping water against the concrete pylons of the bridge. Faintly, in the distance, I caught the irritating whine of an outboard motor like the buzz of a mosquito. Fading away, silence fell, and I sensed the city holding its breath before bursting into life. It was immediately broken into by the echo of our footsteps; Pieter's and Ruth's slow and languorous, mine lighter with more urgency.

Without hesitation, almost as if it was routine, something

he had done only yesterday or the day before, Pieter turned his back on the river and strolled down a narrow walkway, between two rows of houses. There, the warm smell of baking bread greeted us. It surged through the open doorway of Meneer Bork's shop, creating a flood of saliva in the mouth. Pieter stopped and sniffed. 'I missed that,' he said, his tone light; nothing there to explain the flash of pain I had seen when he acknowledged he would be thirty to Ruth's twenty-four.

'Do you remember the broken guttering?' Reaching up, he fingered the stretch of pristine guttering above our heads. 'Such a pity they mended it. Best spot in the city for icicles.' He caught my eye and gave an amused grimace. 'Remember Hans telling you that Jack Frost had left his long fingers behind, and you believed him.'

'I remember sucking the juice out of them as we walked to school and blowing on our hands to warm them,' I retorted. Of course I remembered. But then I'd had six years in which to recall every event I had ever shared with my brother.

'On Saturdays, Ruth, Mother used to send us to buy the bread,' Pieter explained, intently examining the guttering as if the story he was relating had been inscribed on it. 'There was always a queue and to amuse ourselves, we took it in turns to pick out a tune on the ice organ, asking people in the queue behind to guess what it was.'

'How sweet.' Ruth began fidgeting with her watch, twisting it round and round on her wrist, the diamonds on its face sparkling whenever light caught them. 'Pieter, we do have a college to go to – sometime today.'

Of course; these were our memories, Ruth had played no part in them.

'You could skip school and show me the city instead. There must have been so many changes.'

'I can't, Pieter, not today.' Ruth touched his hand with the tip of her fingers, letting them linger for a second longer than necessary, softening her refusal. The fingers on his other hand moved and I knew he wanted to cover her hand with his. 'Another day and I'd love it.'

A moment later and he had stopped again, captivated by the bright paper jackets in the window of the old bookshop. It hadn't changed much. A little shabbier perhaps, leaning forward as old people tend to do; the days were long gone when everything was second-hand. Glowing with excitement, his eyes traced their titles like a man starved for knowledge, and I wondered if they didn't have books at sea.

'The book you gave me for my sixteenth birthday, is it still about?'

'The one about Monet? Of course! I keep it on a shelf in my room. I was going to tell you that I'd started a collection of postcards ...'

'Pieter, do you remember Bloch's Patisserie and that awful bread they sold. I swear there was sawdust in it. Papa said he found rat droppings once.' Ruth pointed across the street. The patisserie had recently changed hands, its tragic history fading from memory as quickly as had ration books and hand-made gifts wrapped in brown paper and string. A few months ago, a shop selling cards and fancy gifts had opened in a street near our house.

Turning his back on the bookshop, Pieter swept his eyes over Ruth, examining her as intently as he had examined the paper-covered volumes a moment before. 'You obviously only look and never touch,' he complimented.

Ruth's mouth twisted. This was a game she played well. 'I promise you, Maidy and I would live on cake if we could. Your sister, Berthe, she's so amazing. I can't even make my own breakfast. She never follows a recipe, but seems to know by instinct what goes with what. Her cakes are always mouth-watering.'

'How could you tell, Ruth, you only had a small slice?'

'Pieter,' she cocked her head flirtatiously, gazing up out of the corner of her eyes. 'Were you watching me?'

'Mother tried to teach me to cook,' I broke in, 'she gave up after Pappy told her if he wanted to eat burnt offerings he would have become a fireman. After that she left me to my books.'

I expected Pieter to laugh, as Hans and I had done. He didn't so much as comment, his attention focussed on Ruth. I lapsed into silence understanding my brother's offer had been little more than a ruse to be with Ruth. All the questions left unanswered from the night before would stay that way. Disappointed, I left him and Ruth to chat together and neither noticed my silence.

It was usually a twenty-minute walk to the edge of the city, but with Pieter stopping every few metres to exclaim about something different or new, it took forty and by the time we emerged from the cobbled passageways onto the smooth pavement of the city streets, I felt both cold and a little downhearted. Ahead of us, the bridge stood stark and bare, its side trusses littered with bolts, their domed heads mimicking the position of draft-pieces on a board. Early morning, when college students gathered, its pavements were thronged with bikes, the air resounding with their noisy chattering. The scene always reminded me of the starlings that gathered each autumn on the telephone wires, ready to fly south and escape the onset of winter. All at once, with a universal nod of acceptance, bicycles would be mounted and the flock of students departed.

'Oh, heavens, we are late,' Ruth exclaimed, seeing the pavements empty apart from pedestrians on their way to work. Mounting her bike, she pushed off into the traffic leaving me to follow. 'If I get a demerit,' she called over her shoulder, 'you can buy me flowers as a punishment.'

'She's joking.' I said, noticing the Pieter's sudden concern. Still, demerit or no, I felt certain flowers would be waiting for Ruth when she arrived home. I pushed off more slowly, wobbling slightly until I got my balance, still slightly nervous of the trams and cars that zoomed past on both sides, filling the air with noise.

'Isn't it wonderful,' Ruth burst out, waving to Pieter for a second time. She indicated right, cycling down a short stretch of road towards the highway that bordered the lakeshore. I didn't risk waving, the thin tyres of my new bike requiring all my attention. Below us, the lake seemed to be asleep, diminutive rivulets as of exhaled breath trickling across the shoreline. 'Having him back,' she chatted on. 'I can't believe it and exactly the same … it's totally perfect. What a handsome couple we make.'

I thought her joking, aware Ruth's enthusiasms rarely lasted more than a moment or two. Like a bee flitting from flower to flower, she stayed with boys barely long enough to remember their name, before flying away again. Then I spotted her hurt expression. Her childhood dream had seemingly been resurrected and had already taken flight.

'I shouldn't have laughed.'

'No, you shouldn't, Maidy. I never laughed when you wittered on about your pirates and princes. They were silly … and imaginary. Pieter is real. And so lovely, I can't believe he's back after all this time. How happy we're all going to be, now he's home.'

Saying nothing further, Ruth pounded her pedals and after five minutes or so, the ribbon of cyclists came into view on the highway ahead. We caught up as they swerved into the college driveway. Here tall spruce formed a shadowy tunnel, made darker still by evergreen shrubs planted on both sides, the dark green of their leaves still drab and forlorn after the long winter.

'Did you ever finish your story?'

'Yes, and I got it in on time which was miraculous for me.' I grimaced, my droll tone acknowledging the difference between us. Ruth's work was always flawlessly presented and on schedule, if not submitted early. 'In the end, I didn't write about Pieter's disappearance; I couldn't. Good thing, as it happens. I wrote about my bridge instead.'

She wasn't listening, her attention elsewhere, diligently sorting through the groups of gossiping students. Dismounting, she walked her machine round the corner, leaving it where I had left mine the day before. I caught the muttered words as she checked the dwindling crowd again, 'He isn't here,' and caught a look of dejection … almost distress.

I wanted to ask who, except I knew perfectly well, because I'd also been hoping to see Zande. Maybe my first instinct had been correct and Ruth was his real quarry, nevertheless, all the common sense in the world couldn't prevent a tiny flame sparking into life at the thought he might be there. But not Ruth – that made no sense, none at all, especially after her avowal about liking only Pieter.

'Who, Ruth?' I reached out, hoping I was wrong and she'd set my mind at rest.

She didn't reply, busying herself with her books, the thick volumes she needed for biology and physiology filling the wicker basket on her bicycle. The bell rang for class and before I could ask anything further she was gone, leaving my question unanswered.

13

There was never any need to get up early on a Saturday, and I took my coffee back to my room. I leaned on my window sill to drink it, my nose pressed up against the glass, as always my attention drawn to the long sweep of houses on the opposite bank. Built in the same century as our house, they were very different. Tall and thin with an almost vulgar display of coloured tiles and fancy brickwork, they reminded me of a wealthy dowager, who wears her best wig every day and bedecks herself in jewels and furbelows to take the dog for a walk.

In my imagination, I knew everyone who had ever lived in those houses and gone adventuring with most of them: the blond-haired deckhand, who first romanced a kitchen maid before carrying her off in his boat to explore far distant lands; the orphaned child plucked from the snow who, after many scrapes and mishaps, grew up to be so beautiful she married the prince who owned the house. Together, they lived happily ever after, cared for by an army of servants who ensured their new princess never soiled her hands, cleaning shoes and silver or brushing the yard. All the jobs Mother made me do and which I loathed. At night, the current residents left their lighted windows uncovered and they glittered like fairy lights strung between trees.

'No one dared defy the enemy while they lived among us,' Pappy replied when I asked why people left their curtains open at night. 'The day they finally left, that evening every light in the city was switched on and people danced in the streets.'

Very faintly, I heard my name being called. I peeked out spotting Ruth by the lamppost. Pieter was with her.

I pushed open the window and waved. 'What's going on? It's not like you to be out of bed this early on a Saturday.'

She called up. 'I've left a message with Hans; he'll explain. See you later.'

I watched them walk across the bridge and disappear into the streets beyond. Two halves of a pair, they were both tall and with a matching stride. Last night when we cycled home, Pieter had been out in the yard waiting for Ruth, issuing an invitation to dine with us again. She'd been so delighted to see him and it was such a happy evening, by the time we said goodnight, I had decided the confusion at college that morning was nothing more than my imagination working overtime.

It was gone eleven before I'd bathed and dressed. No one was about, Berthe was at work and Mother in her room, and the sitting room was deserted, its big sash windows tightly closed.

Leaving my coat and bag in the hallway, I chased down to the basement. Pappy and Hans were standing by the big table in the workroom, where designs for new mirrors were sketched out on paper. The foreman was with them, a smile on his face, listening as Hans stubbornly tossed out Pappy's ideas as *old-hat*. I think it was the phrase Hans used as much as the sentiment that amused Lars, and I remembered he had worked with Pieter also.

'Whenever I come down to the workroom, you and Pappy are having a row.'

Hans glowered. 'It's not a row, if it's anything it's an argument. Today, it's only a difference of opinion.'

'Your difference of opinion is somebody else's row,' I retorted mischievously.

Pappy patted Hans affectionately on the shoulder. 'For six years, I've had to put up with your brother disputing my experience. On occasions, I've even asked myself which is the master and which the apprentice.'

'Only because …' Hans stopped and, just as suddenly, grinned. 'Oh, well, you've heard it all before.'

I had, whenever Hans got drunk and landed in my bedroom, needing to talk.

'Ruth left me a message?'

Hans screwed up his nose, exactly as Pappy did when he was on the verge of saying something outrageous. 'They've caught the ferry over to Norland and won't be back until late. Ruth has suggested you take your poor hard-working brother to the cinema instead of her. It's all right for some people,' he grumbled. 'I wanted to ask her out on the lake last summer except I *never* get a Saturday off.'

'I gather you had something planned,' Pappy said, noticing my disappointment.

'We'd planned to go window shopping, Pappy, and to see the new musical,' I explained. 'I've already arranged with Mevrouw Kleissler to dust the mirrors next week instead of today.'

'That's why Ruth suggested me as a substitute.' Hans cocked his head to one side, frowning in imitation of Mother when she was displeased. 'Only you can forget shops. I'm not traipsing round them.' He grinned. 'Not unless you cross my palm with silver.'

'Not a chance. And if you are going with me to the cinema,

I refuse point blank to watch a musical.' I frowned at him. 'Last time, you told me that men dancing were sissies.'

Hans held the door open. 'Can we go to the old place then? It's got good memories.'

'Honestly, Hans, they closed that down ages ago. Shows how observant you are.'

'I loved that cinema.'

'It was a wretched place,' I retorted, although I too remembered it fondly. It's where I had first encountered pirates with black-curling mustachios, watching, my breathing silenced, as they swung with death-defying arrogance over shark-infested seas. 'Remember, the bucket seats that slammed down into place. And the film breaking down …'

'Always in the most exciting place. That's where I learned to whistle,' Hans added.

'I remember,' I said sternly. 'My ears are still ringing.'

'Hmm, so where is this new cinema?'

'It's not exactly new; it's been open a year. It's behind the railway station. Haven't you seen it?'

'To be honest, I don't go that way much.' He shifted awkwardly from foot to foot. 'I hate the buildings in that part of the city, they're so ugly. If I go there at all, it's to drink at the old inn on the canal bridge. At least that's genuinely old, not some pseudo structure built yesterday. I readily confess on the way there, all I'm thinking of is that first sip of beer. On the way back …' He squinted over his shoulder at Pappy who was talking to Lars, lowering his voice to a whisper. 'I am forced keep my eyes peeled on the kerb to make sure I don't trip …'

'*Hans!* If for one moment I believed you to be serious …'

'What?'

'I'd make you pay for our tickets.'

I ran upstairs laughing.

'Maidy, if you're passing the tobacconist on your travels,'

Pappy called after me, 'will you get me some tobacco? There's some money in my jacket pocket.'

Still buttoning my coat, I hurried down the road to buy Pappy his tobacco before I forgot. On Mother's list, forgetfulness is only one of my many crimes.

Hans wouldn't finish work for at least another hour, so I wandered on past the tram terminus, hidden away behind its nest of fir trees, a trail of discarded needles ringing their trunks. A raucous clanging came from the dredgers at work on the canal and I crossed over the road to watch for a while. Perched on specially weighted barges, claw-footed buckets hoisted the grit-laden silt from the canal bed, a stream of muddy water pouring out as they rose into the air. Their long spindly arms pecking at the water reminded me of storks pursuing a fish. Nearby, a line of trucks waited on the tow path to drive the rich harvest to areas where water was eating into the land.

It wasn't a day for sightseeing, the wind biting off the open stretch of water and I hoped Ruth had been sensible enough to wear something warm, rather than simply fashionable. It would be bitter out on the lake.

Hastening back across the road, I ducked into the shelter of the little walkway, the parade of houses with their tall chimneys forming a sturdy bulwark against the vagaries of weather – both hot and cold. In summer, their thick stone walls were slow to heat up, yet in winter, snow both fell more lightly and disappeared more quickly than anywhere else.

My thoughts, as had my dreams the night before, still hovered around Pieter. Although conversation and laughter roamed non-stop all evening, I had gone to bed unsatisfied, as if I had been ravenously hungry and permitted only scraps to eat. Once again, there was far more left unsaid than said. That first night, in all innocence, Berthe had asked the question: if Pieter had been working abroad why hadn't he written? Letters regularly travelled from the farthest corners of the world, postcards too. Ruth had sent me a card from Paris. Maybe it had taken longer than a week and she was home before it reached me, but Pieter had had six years in which to get in touch.

Yesterday, I had resented Ruth's frivolous chatter which had prevented me asking questions. After thinking it over, now I felt almost grateful. Whatever the answer to Berthe's question, no one departed a family they loved so abruptly unless they were taken away – as had happened to our citizens when the invaders ordered it.

I caught the ringing of a bicycle bell and quickly drew to one side, my shoulders brushing against a downstairs window. Not a metre away, two children were busily searching out pieces for a jigsaw puzzle. Seeing my shadow cross the window, they waved and smiled as if, in that moment, I was a member of their family and they were welcoming me home. Hans often set up his easel in this passageway, never bored with sketching its tall chimneys. He told me when the lights came on at night, the little street was transformed into the sparkling segments of a caterpillar.

I wandered on, the long row emptying into the lane that ran past our old primary school. Backing onto a canal, the authorities had erected spiked railings at that end of the playground, to stop boys climbing over and falling in. I'd been happy to leave, my dilatory nature a frequent victim of the harsh treatment meted out by its teachers. Surprisingly, today though, only gentle reminiscences came to mind; the day we carved our initials on the underside of a bench in the playground. It was the year Pieter finished school and Berthe had helped me carve the letters MB, leaving Hans to ink in the cuts.

I tried the gate, hoping to find it unlocked. It wasn't, although I felt certain our clumsy signatures would still exist; even the scratches on the school's front door made by a dog hadn't been painted over. That was the great charm of our little enclave, nothing ever changed and everything had its proper place; so different from the new city in which waterways metamorphosed into walkways overnight and bombsites were transformed into apartments, surrounded by flowerbeds whose occupants were already in bloom.

Directly behind the school stood a little row of alms houses; awkward little buildings that had their front doors opening directly onto the canal. I stood for a moment staring down at the water rushing past. They must have opened the lock gates upstream to clear storm water from the fields. Most likely, it would take all day for the spate to lessen.

'I wouldn't fancy living there,' someone called out. 'When the water is as high as this, their occupants are frequently stranded.'

I didn't need to look round. For the past two nights Zande's voice had echoed through my dreams; only now its dissonant base tones had been replaced by a light-hearted dance step.

'It's Magrit, isn't it? How extraordinary! Great minds do think alike, after all.'

He was crouched on the edge of the canal, the collar of his navy donkey jacket turned up against the wind. Seeing me hesitate, he stood up, his long legs taking the steps up to the road two at a time.

'I was just thinking about you. So where's your beautiful companion today?' He glanced along the street, searching. 'No matter.' He smiled down at me, his eyes as welcoming as a long-lost friend, nothing overly familiar in them at all, and I began to wonder if I had dreamt our previous encounter. 'Is this your favourite spot too?'

'Er ... not really.' I felt a fluttering in my chest and hoped my voice didn't sound as jumpy on the outside as it did on the inside. 'It's rather drab.' I pointed to the bank, where mud and grass saturated by last night's rain lay in a sorrowful heap. 'I can think of prettier ...'

'Oh, but it isn't,' Zande cut across me. His light tenor rang with enthusiasm, the seductive tones that had so disturbed me gone, as if washed away by the storm. 'Come with me and I'll show you. *Quick*, before the sun goes.'

Before I had time even to take a much-needed breath, he had grabbed my hand and was running back down the steps, dragging me with him. The palm of his hand felt smooth, a stranger to manual labour, the knuckles rounded like gentle slopes rising out of an earth-covered plain. I felt my pulse speed up.

'I appreciate the ground is wet, but you have to sit down otherwise you won't see it.'

'You want me to sit down?' I heard the incredulity in my voice.

His laughter was rich and full of life. 'Yes, please.'

All of a sudden, I wished I wasn't wearing white ankle socks and my old brown skirt. I sat down hurriedly, tucking my feet under me. Letting go my hand, he touched his finger-tips to the back of my neck. I felt them warm and soft, the opposite of Pappy whose fingers were calloused and marked with hard ridges from working a wood plane. Surprised I looked up, encountering the brilliance of his eyes, and then quickly down again, unsure of my breath.

'And you need to bend right down. Like this.' He leaned sideways resting his shoulder on the ground, his chin almost level with the water. 'Hold on a moment. *Wait for the sun.*'

Copying him, I stared down the long stretch of water towards the little alms houses, a string of tiny bridges, with decorative iron handrails, linking them to the street. I wondered what he could possibly see in water that swept past dull and uncaring. All at once, the sun broke through. Lit by the sun, the iron work of the bridge was immediately transformed into a hollow tree-trunk, myriad shades of light and shadow darting across the restless water. It swayed back and forth against the

114

iron stanchions of the little bridges, like a dancer in a sequin gown, pestering her partner to take to the floor.

'Why, it's …'

'Extraordinary?'

I couldn't take my eyes away, fastened on the ripples as they slid into the bank splintering into a thousand gleaming droplets.

The sun vanished and so did the vision. Reluctantly, I sat up again.

'The human condition can be so restrictive,' Zande said, his lower half still reclining on the bank. I found it impossible to withdraw my gaze, marvelling that any person, man or boy, could be so elegant; the lines of his body blending seamlessly. 'We stand in our eyrie high above the earth and miss out on a great deal of beauty.'

'However did you discover it?'

He sighed. 'Stranger things than this have happened to me.' Then as if relenting being so enigmatic, 'I enjoy unearthing the unusual.'

'My brother insists the only way to see a church is to lie on the floor.'

His mouth twisted in a grin. 'I did that in the basilica in the city until I was informed it's not allowed.' He shrugged. 'Authority figures are so hidebound by their own importance. I'm pretty sure the gods, if they exist at all, wouldn't bother about people lying down in their house.'

I gurgled with amusement. 'You know the city well?'

He sat back up, his head still facing the water, directing his words at the canal. 'I was here before, yes. That's when I discovered this place, although it didn't have quite such a pleasant ending.' Ruefully, he rubbed at his arm.

'I used to walk along here, on my way to and from school …'

'Yes.'

I wanted to ask if that's what he'd done – used the walkway as a shortcut – except I doubted it was from our school, I would have remembered. At that moment, he swung round. His mouth twisted in a smile and my question ceased to be important.

It was impossible to believe this was the same person; he could so easily have been a doppelgänger, someone I'd never met before, except for his eyes. I was reminded of the moon that controlled the tides. His eyes were the same, they called to you; the microscopic specs of hazel within their dark surround as compelling as magnets.

I gazed at the sky, hoping its magic would be repeated. Without the sun, the little bridges were once again plain and ordinary, no longer special or magical. 'And there's me thinking I knew every stick and stone in this city.' I laughed awkwardly. 'I'm always boasting I could find my way home blindfolded. Silly, isn't it?'

'*Very!* I'd guarantee you'd end up falling in, whether the river or a canal, I couldn't say. Whichever it was, you'd get wet.'

I chanced looking up. He was casually watching the flood of water, his head half-turned. That's when I saw him change. Not physically … no. His form still resembled that of a Greek god, much in demand by artists and sculptors. It was more as if all the light had been sucked from him, leaving only a hollow shell.

He got to his feet in one graceful movement and held out his hand, helping me up. I felt his hand soft as a calf-skin glove, his long fingers tapering into the smooth filbert-shape of his nails.

'I'd ask you for a coffee, except I have to go, I'm meeting a girl.' He chuckled at my startled expression. 'Isn't that what gossips at college are saying of me, that I spend all my time trying to seduce girls? I promise; it's only ninety per cent of my time. It was obviously lunchtime when I met up with you.'

116

It was a cruel jest, implying that I wasn't pretty enough to seduce, his voice once again mocking. I sensed a door shutting, leaving me on the outside. Yet, deep down, I couldn't bring myself to believe he meant it as an insult, rather more someone who was exiting the house and putting on their jacket because it was expected of him.

He grimaced awkwardly, the intensity of his expression almost painful. 'I like talking to you, Magrit. You don't disappoint.'

I thought that remark curious also, but he was gone before I could ask what he meant, walking fast down the main road towards the city.

14

'Tomorrow, Pieter, you must go into town and buy some new clothes.' Mother's stern voice rose up to meet me as I came downstairs, futilely brushing at the creases in my black skirt which I had left buried under a pile of books all week.

The remainder of Saturday had passed in a storm of confusion, my feelings skittering like seagulls attempting to land on a frozen river, reliving my encounter with Zande and puzzling over his mercurial changes of mood. Only our visit to the cinema had given them some respite, embattled by Indians who surrounded a wagon train; both Hans and I enjoying the film hugely. Yet the moment we emerged into sunlight, I found myself wanting to walk back to the canal to see if the little tunnel still existed or whether it was as much a figment of my imagination as the pain in Zande's voice when he said goodbye.

I kissed Pappy fleetingly on top of his head and went into the kitchen to make some fresh coffee. He was reading the newspaper and didn't notice. Mother was brushing Pieter's jacket, the stiff bristles of the clothes brush rasping against the wool cloth, and I recognised the jacket as one of Pappy's, grown too tight across his middle. Pappy had complained that the jacket had shrunk with wear, unwilling to accept that he was expanding into middle age. It fitted Pieter well enough, a faint line marking the cloth where the hem had been let down. Mother must have sat most of yesterday altering it.

'You'll be the belle of the ball in church, Pieter.' I popped my head round the door. 'Girls won't have eyes for anyone else.'

'Beau!' Pieter glanced over his shoulder, his eyes glittering with suppressed excitement. 'They are in for a disappointment then. I'm not going to church; I'm taking Ruth out.'

'It's going to be a lovely day.' Mother worked the brush down his lapels, adding, as if he were a paying guest residing with us for a few weeks, 'the city is quite beautiful at this time of the year.'

'I expected us to be going as a family today,' Berthe came into the dining room, her gloves in her hand. In her black dress, she reminded me of a stately galleon, the material swishing softly as she walked. She laid her gloves on the dresser on top of her Bible, 'To give thanks for Pieter's safe return.' She joined me in the kitchen, picking up a saucepan to warm some milk.

'Not today, Berthe. Really, Pappy do get on with your breakfast, you will make us late,' Mother chided, skirting over the issue with almost unseemly haste.

I was surprised; in my mother's view, the outward symbols of religion were of supreme importance and she had always been strict about Sunday worship. The faith of Ruth's family, with its observance of the Sabbath from sunset on a Friday evening, was something that had always sat uneasily with her.

Pappy took his fob watch from his waistcoat-pocket. 'There is time; my youngest daughter hasn't even begun eating. No doubt she will rigorously apply Sunday observance laws to her jaws and give them a day of rest also.'

I dutifully smiled at his well-worn joke, almost as much a Sunday ritual as church, only the facial expressions that accompanied it different. Today, Pappy's countenance shone with love for his family. 'My dear Maidy, looking at you today I am reminded of one of the stories Hans Anderson ...'

'Pieter,' Mother called, almost running him to the door. 'You mustn't keep Ruth waiting.'

Hans' feet sounded loudly on the upper stairs. 'Coffee, Magrit, for the love of your brother.' Yawning noisily, he stumbled into the sitting room half asleep, the buttons on his jacket askew. 'Was that Pieter? Where's he off to?'

'Maidy, dear, bring your mother some fresh coffee,' Pappy called, pushing her half-empty cup across the table, 'hers has gone cold.' Mother sank into a chair and he took her hand, gently kissing it as if in apology.

I brought a fresh cup from the kitchen and sat down to drink mine, finding the hot liquid very welcome. I hadn't much appetite but dutifully took a roll, aware Mother's sharp gaze would note if I didn't eat and she would comment. I had woken to dreams of Zande playing loudly in my head. Although they had quickly absconded, leaving nothing behind except a vague sense of disquiet, my appetite had gone with them.

Berthe and Hans were chatting together, unaware of the tensions swirling round the room. Surprisingly for siblings, they had little in common apart from shared memories, their conversations relapsing into well-worn and repetitive themes at mealtimes. That day, it was the fund to repair our church organ.

I picked up the honey, carefully cataloguing this moment alongside all the other awkward silences since Pieter's arrival. The homecoming of the prodigal son should have been a time for rejoicing, not clumsy speech directed along pathways not meant for it. Pappy was the most straightforward person I had ever met, very different from Mother. Even at age sixteen, I had little clue as to her real character. Now I sensed in Pappy a holding back, a curbing of his tongue, for which my brother's return was responsible.

Monday morning only served to reinforce this feeling. Pieter once again hijacked our morning walk through the old streets, chatting almost exclusively to Ruth. If it had been anyone else, it wouldn't have bothered me, so used to the off-hand behaviour of boys once they set eyes on Ruth; still, it should have been different with Pieter. He was my brother and it was from our house he vanished. Surely, he possessed some spark of curiosity as to how we had spent the years of his absence? Although, to be fair, our entire history was as drab as our streets on a rain-soaked day and of as little consequence; for what had we done in the intervening years? Mourned his absence? We had all done that.

When Professor Dulmes kept me back at the end of class, I wasn't surprised, whirling in and out of attention all morning.

Our literature course embraced writers of the nineteenth century or earlier, Professor Dulmes insisting the twentieth was far too modern. 'Literature,' he informed us in our first session with him, 'is like fine brandy. It should be left untouched for several decades to mature.'

Student lore had him pegged as a foreigner who lived alone and spent his free time in the cinema watching French and American films. I admired him as a teacher, his knowledge of literature immense, although he possessed a strange manner as if life was something he must apologise for. He was also a brilliant linguist and totally at home in our language, confidently sidestepping the slip-shod vowels and colloquialisms of our student population. According to gossip, he had been forced to work as an interpreter for the invaders and after they left, had stood trial for collaboration. Despite being found not guilty, he was no longer welcome in his own country.

'I'm sorry, professor,' I apologised before he could get a word in, 'if I was inattentive.'

The door shut behind the shouted conversations in the corridor, reducing them to a whisper, little louder than the sound of a motor engine on a distant road.

'My dear child, I have twenty-five other students – quite enough to keep me busy.' His pince nez glistened in the light, almost as bright as the pomade he wore on his dark hair, which he combed straight back. 'I read your story last evening and was surprised and delighted by the description and emotion that a simple bridge can conjure up. It was very well written.'

His words took me by surprise. 'You liked it?'

'Very much. Your best piece of work by far. Perhaps I should ask you to write about bridges every week.' Professor Dulmes didn't make jokes, although he was attempting one now. He handed me back my sheets of paper, nodding in a pleased fashion all the while. 'Run along.'

I had no idea why teachers said this when our corridors were plastered with warnings – *Don't run.*

I headed to the library in the hope of finding Ruth, wanting to share my delight. My successes were negligible compared with hers; nevertheless, she always awarded them generous praise. I pushed open the door. On both sides of the room, low stacks of shelving created secluded bays, making the library a popular spot for trysts and private meetings. In the second bay along, the one I had come to think of as my own, I spotted the top of Jaan's head.

A buzz of soft whispering broke into the air, stealing the librarian's concentration away from her work. Like a train blowing off steam she glanced up, her finger on her lips. 'Shush, no talking.'

As if it had been a signal, Jaan looked up. Seeing me search for a spare seat at one of the other tables, he beckoned.

I know I hesitated.

He got to his feet and came over. 'Please.'

Taking my arm, he drew me back to where he was

working, the long table awash with books, mostly bound in leather, their titles tooled in gold leaf faded with age. 'I'm glad I caught you. I wanted to say sorry for ignoring you.'

I clutched my bag to my chest, somehow expecting the obvious excuse … that he hadn't recognised me.

'Call it what you will.' He stood by my side, twirling his glasses in his fingers, his blue eyes contrite. 'First-day nerves, perhaps. Still, that's no excuse after sitting in your seat and hogging your book.' He pointed to the chairs left haphazardly askew by departing students. 'Please stay.'

It was a good apology. I tried to keep my tone formal, delighted that our little kernel of friendship hadn't been eradicated as I had thought. Friends were rare. I failed miserably; relief making me bold enough to tease.

'Am I to warn you not to do it again?'

I caught the faintest of sighs. 'Certainty is not one of my talents,' he said, matching his tone with mine. 'You look happy?'

'I am. I was searching for Ruth. Have you seen her?'

'I left her talking to Tristan.'

'Not Zande?' I blurted out.

'Why Zande?'

I shrugged, as if my words were unimportant. 'I think she likes him.'

He sighed impatiently. His eyes appeared tired, rimmed by faint purple bruises as if he'd been working a while. 'That will do her no good at all. In any case, he's gone off with Waldger. They have business in the city.' His expression cleared, the deep blue of his eyes focussing directly on me. 'I may not be Ruth, but please tell me your news. From where I am sitting, you have grown two metres overnight.'

I laughed, aware I'd been staring at his face. It was a good face, the plains of his cheeks long, his jaw angular.

'My professor actually enjoyed my story.'

He pulled out a chair. 'Sit. I am all ears.'

'It's nothing. A little story, that's all.'

'Go on.'

'You surely can't be interested?' I protested.

As he had the day before, he placed his glasses in the spine of a book to mark his place. The volume was old, its leather jacket worn thin and fraying at the edges, its print close set on flimsy pages, little thicker than tissue paper.

'You're short-sighted?'

'Tit-for-tat, Maidy, I said some stupid things the other day. And, no, I am long-sighted. To read, I need glasses.' Placing his arm on the page to keep his book from closing, he held out his glasses for me to try. I did.

'Your face resembles a squashed marrow,' I remarked flippantly, hastily handing them back.

'How strange, yours looks fine from here.' He grinned at me, dropping them casually back in the book.

I noticed then how he smiled with his eyes. I had read in one of Ruth's text books that technically speaking, eyes cannot smile, it's the muscles contracting around the eyeball that change its shape and angle. The book was wrong. His did.

He was so different, the edgy nervousness of the day before gone. Better dressed than the average student, his blue, cable-stich pullover was new and he had on grey slacks; shoes and socks too, in deference to a drop in temperature, yet, still no tie. His shirt was open at the neck, exposing a smooth hollow at the base of his throat.

'Shall we start again? Tell me about your story?'

'It's about a bridge; the smallest and the oldest in the city.' We had spoken only once before yet I felt as relaxed with him as if he were a member of my own family. 'I believed in fairies as a small child … Don't laugh,' I said crossly and Jaan quickly camouflaged his grin with a cough. 'If you saw my bridge, you might be tempted to believe in them too. Below it, perched on the canal bank as if the wind had blown it there, is a tiny house. Something a pixie might live in. It has a miniscule balcony, just large enough for pots of flowers to shelter under.' I hesitated. 'It must sound silly ...'

'No, I promise, it doesn't. Go on.'

'Mermaids featured in my story rather a lot ... and pirates and princes.'

'Princes?'

'Don't you know that all little girls fall in love with a prince?'

'Do they?' he shrugged. 'I didn't have a sister. I was an only child.'

'You're not from this part of the country, are you?'

He seemed startled. 'Why do you say that?'

'It's your accent.'

'I have an *accent?*'

'Only a little one. Your 'a's are broader.'

'I might say your 'a's are narrower. But yes, I'm from the south.'

'Don't they have colleges there?'

Immediately, I sensed his discomfort at the question, haphazardly flicking over a couple of pages. 'This suits our purpose,' he answered shortly and got to his feet. He replaced his glasses in their case, slipping them into the breast pocket of his jacket, the pages of his book ruffling back and forth as if unable to make up their mind what to do next. 'I need to go.' He paused, then, as if regretting his haste, 'Do you spend every lunch hour in the library?'

'Mostly,' I hesitated, concerned that I'd ruined our burgeoning friendship by probing too deeply. 'I'm sorry.' My words startled him, and he eyed me warily. 'Sometimes, I ask too many questions,' I elaborated.

'Oh, that.' He seemed relieved. 'No, I really have to go. I'm meeting the others in town. I only slipped in to make my apology for yesterday.'

'A bit of a long apology.'

He laughed. It was cheerful and carefree; the shadow that had clouded his brow a moment before wiped away.

'Pass me the books down will you, and I'll put them away.'

Crouching down, he slipped the volume he'd been using back onto the shelf.

I handed down the others, glancing briefly at their titles. They were all about Greek deities, except one volume about mortals who'd been cursed by them.

He stood back up, brushing imaginary dust off the knees of his trousers with one hand. 'Why did you tell me your name was Maidy? It's Magrit isn't it?'

I said confidently, 'Friends call me Maidy.'

He nodded. 'Thank you for that. Will I see you tomorrow?'

*

I was late leaving class at the end of the day and as I pushed open the door to the courtyard, I heard Ruth, her voice as unmistakable as warm honey. She was talking with Tristan, his height alone making him stand out from the crowd; except there wasn't a crowd, most of the students had already left.

I was only ten minutes late getting out, but at the end of the day no one hung around and the tail-end of the wheeled procession was already clearing the drive. Behind the chattering cyclists the grounds stood empty, a vast open space of concrete and gravel rendered insignificant under its daily invasion of bicycles and feet.

Ruth saw me and waved. Tristan didn't stir; his attention riveted on her.

Collecting my bike, I stowed my books away and walked it across the courtyard, continuing to heap blessings on Professor Dulmes. For girls as clever and glamorous as Ruth, words of admiration often passed unnoticed. For shy and plain girls, they represented something of rare value, like a jewelled casket, to be cherished and hidden away, only to be remembered and brought out when life became complicated and full of trouble, falling apart around them.

I couldn't hear what Tristan and Ruth were talking about, except to recognise it wasn't about much. This was one of Ruth's greatest skills, changing ordinary crumbs of gossip into fine wine. She lifted her chin, flirting coquettishly with her eyes, a habit she had copied from Hollywood films with their mannered but exotic heroines.

I didn't pay much attention, so used to her flirtatious ways with boys. She loved the power her beauty gave her, much like a tropical flower that attracts insects in swarms before devouring them. It never bothered the flower – it didn't bother Ruth, either.

Maybe in hindsight I had over-reacted over Jules. In a way Ruth was correct; she'd not asked him to become infatuated with her. For students, falling in love with Ruth was considered a coming of age, almost a rite of passage. It never amounted to much; it might have if Ruth had shown the slightest interest, scoffing at the doleful countenance of her swains. Even I found it difficult to take their elaborate gestures of grief seriously. After a few days moping about, they were usually recovered enough to pay attention to other girls, ones that might already fancy them.

Tristan's laugh rang out and I saw his stance taut, and a muscle in his cheek flicked restlessly. I took a small step back, alarmed by the passion in his gaze, all-consuming as if he had been allowed a glimpse of heaven. Only in fiction had I ever come across the phrase: *built of the stuff tragedies are made from.* This was not fiction. But Tristan would still take heartbreak far too seriously.

'Ruth, we need to hurry.' I broke in nervously, hoping to curtail the tête-à-tête before it did any permanent damage. 'It's going to rain.'

'You go on home, Magrit,' she replied in an offhand manner. 'Tristan's trying to convince me he's going to play football.' She angled her face towards him, 'In this weather too.' Tristan had been nursing Ruth's bike, and his thumb moved restlessly, caressing the chrome of the handlebars. He quivered at her words as if from a physical blow. 'I mean … look at it.' She pointed in the direction of the shoreline, black clouds resembling the steaming flanks of wild horses homing into view above the trees, their leaves touched by darkness.

For me, the little scene didn't ring true. I felt as if I was observing an actor on a stage rehearsing his lines, and I picked up on Ruth's line of sight resting on a point beyond Tristan's shoulder.

'You'll get wet,' I tried again, aware if there was anything Ruth hated it was rain.

It made no difference.

'Tristan will get wet. I intend staying under shelter. Besides, I've got a jacket. See you later.'

Dismissing me, she glanced at her watch, its diamond encrusted hands and crystal face recording each minute of every hour. Meneer Endelbaum had imported it from Switzerland for her sixteenth birthday. Tristan's grey eyes followed the movement of her arm, as if jealous even of the silver chain circling her slender wrist, and I felt unease like a cold draught on my back.

15

By the time I reached the highway, it was spitting with rain and I stopped under a tree to put on my coat. Beneath the deep slope of the embankment, the lake lay unmoving, a carapace of heavy mist pressing down on it, raindrops pitting its surface in a fusillade of tiny cannonballs. I cycled fast. If I still had my old bike, I would have been drenched, the wind picking up as the rain swept in, blowing fume-covered waves onto shore. Even so, I was grateful when the silhouette of the bridge finally came into sight, momentum carrying me across the canal and into the main road, its surface glistening darkly in the storm. The buildings gave some shelter and I raced on towards the centre of the city, where pedestrians, only their feet and legs visible under a black umbrella, scurried along the pavements like a posse of black beetles.

Earlier, there must have been a collection or a delivery because the yard gates remained open, pushed back on their hinges. I swerved in, anxious to get out of the rain, and dumped my bike against the wall of the garage. Seeing the workshop doors ajar, I tucked my books under my arm and raced down the ramp. Two of Pappy's workmen were sat in the doorway putting the finishing touches to a mirror. After Pappy completed the painting, the wood surround is given several coats of fine varnish. This is toxic, and the workshop doors were left open to dissipate its fumes.

Shaking the water from my coat, I inspected it eagerly, finding the warm glow of the furnace comforting after such a bitter wind. Pappy had drawn a family of ducks, with their permanently supercilious expressions, mirroring the birds that bustled up and down the waterway. Across the top, seagulls soared in and out of billowing clouds, dive-bombing their water-bound enemy. It was so realistic, you could almost hear their indignant squawk each time a morsel of bread was lost to the greedy gulls. It was beautiful yet funny and I burst into laughter.

Lars rested his brush. 'That's what I said to the master. I told him no one would take the mirror seriously.'

'Who chose it?' I enquired impetuously. 'I bet a plain woman because it was expensive.'

It had to be; each of the ducks individually drawn and very different from its fellow, their wing feathers tipped with gold leaf that reflected light from the furnace.

Lars wiped his hands on a cloth, a strong smell of turpentine pervading the workroom. A big man, he had lost a leg in the invasion, and his peg leg made him roll from side to side like a sailor in rough seas. Pappy said he was a good and honest workman. 'Your father said she chose the ducks, and he applied their expressions.'

'What happens if she brings it back?' I brushed my shoulders to rid them of rain. I had retied my hair in a tight knot when I put on my jacket but it still felt damp. I bent down to remove my shoes. The steps up to the ground floor were painted rather than carpeted and Mother always worried that someone might slip if they got wet.

'She won't. She's too rich to get the joke.'

I remembered Pappy saying that an excess of money often blinded people to ordinary living. 'Rich people rarely get jokes. Even if they do, they cannot believe the joke might be against them. They live on a different planet from the rest of us.'

I headed upstairs, hanging my coat on the rack. Hearing a murmur of voices, I pushed open the living room door. Pieter was deep in conversation with Mother and Pappy. He appeared comfortable as if he was finally home, yet to me his presence in the sitting room still felt awkward and I knew it would take time. All the same, I felt ashamed as if I'd somehow snubbed him.

Pieter got to his feet, smiling gaily, 'Where's Ruth?'

It was habit that made me prevaricate. I shouldn't have done it. He was my brother and my first loyalty was to him. I should have admitted that Ruth had stayed behind because of some boy.

I don't know why I didn't.

'She had an extra class.'

A puff of warm air touched the back of my neck. I spun round. Of course, it was Hans; he'd crept upstairs unobserved as he often did as a child, playing tag among the numerous staircases in our house. He was so light on his feet when he wanted, he was always able to tag Berthe or me before we could run away. He winked and pushed the door open wide for me to enter first.

'I expected Pappy to have you working by now, Pieter,' he called. 'After all, you've been on holiday for six years while I've been learning how to paint ducks.' His voice may have sounded light and teasing, but his face implied something different. I noticed Mother's anxious expression and saw Pieter's knuckles whiten where they gripped the table edge.

I crossed to the window, stooping down to give Pappy a hug. 'I thought Pappy always did the painting,' I said lightly, recalling Hans' youthful rages.

131

Pappy chuckled and the tension vanished. 'Not this time, Maidy, I only sketched in the outlines, Hans did all the work. I decided to take a few days' holiday and spend it with my son.'

I tapped Pieter on the arm, pulling at his sleeve to get his attention. 'You really must see this new mirror before it's packed up. It's quite wonderful; Hans has done a brilliant job and it's so comical. Pappy's drawn one of the ducks fighting off a seagull. I wish I'd chosen them for my mirror.' I recalled how I had wanted swans. It was Mother who had insisted on fairies.

'And we have been working,' Pieter added peaceably, spotting Hans' hurt expression. Pappy never took holidays. 'I spent the day sketching. Not as good as you, Hans. Pappy says you're an amazing artist. I was showing him some of the patterns I saw in the East.' He shuffled some pieces of paper. 'Come and join us.'

'Ruth not here?' Hans stared purposefully at the door as if undecided whether to accept Pieter's invitation or not.

'She doesn't live here, Hans,' I rebuked.

'Pretty much she does,' he retorted. 'Six nights out of seven. Isn't that right, Pappy?'

'Have you been counting?' Pappy twinkled up at him.

He shrugged and dropped into the chair opposite. 'May I see?'

I listened for an edge to his voice. It was okay. He picked up the top drawing, the paper covered with swirling shapes. I knew Hans would favour the symmetry of their lines, so similar to the pantiles on the palace roof. I was right, it caught his interest immediately. He pulled a pencil from his top pocket and began tracing its curves and angles.

I followed Mother into the kitchen. As a child, I had tried to avoid it, hating to be given chores that interrupted my daydreaming. In reality, it was a homely place, dominated by a black-leaded range, with a line of bright copper pans hanging down from hooks. That was one of the tasks I hated the most, polishing copper and silver with a cloth that quickly became gritty, staining the tips of your fingers grey-blue. The range wasn't new, nothing in our kitchen was apart from the refrigerator, and even that was four years old. Against the wall stood the dresser my great-grandfather had built as a wedding gift for his daughter, my grandmother. Its carved oak shelves were filled with blue and white pottery and, over time, bits and pieces had been broken. Although Mother had replaced them, the patina on the old dishes was crazed with fine lines, making them appear mismatched against the bright clarity of the new. Hans was always rearranging them, complaining that certain pieces should never sit side by side because they didn't get on and argued all the time.

Mother felt my skirt. 'It's damp. Remind me to buy you a proper waterproof, the same as fishermen wear.' Recalling their ugly yellow oil skins, I groaned silently, wondering not for the first time why Mother seemed so determined to make me look like a drab. 'Go and change, there's a good girl. How long will Ruth be?'

'Ruth? Why?'

'Pieter said he asked her for dinner.'

'Tonight? She told me you'd invited the whole family next week.'

'Also Mevrouw Kleissler; she's longing to have a chat with Pieter.' Mother bent down and opened the door of the oven to check on the progress of dinner. Steam billowed from an earthenware pot and I smelled beef and onions, laced with carrots and tomatoes. Like the furnace in the basement, the stove was coal-fired. One of the men cleaned it every morning, carrying the ash away before bringing up enough coal in a bucket to last all day, leaving Hans or Pappy to bank it down at night.

'You said she was held up at college?' Mother didn't wait

for my reply. 'You know Pappy has always thought of Ruth as a daughter.'

'What are you going to serve?' I quickly changed the subject.

'This evening?' Mother said, mishearing.

'No, next week. Judging by the scent of tomato and herbs, tonight you've made us a stew. I'm glad, it's horrid out.'

'I've done broad beans and potatoes as well.' Mother filled the heavy kettle with water and placed it on the iron plate to boil. 'Perhaps we might treat ourselves to some smoked eel and I will buy a joint of beef, since our neighbours are not allowed pork. I'll ask Berthe if she will make an apple cake and buy cream on her way home.'

It was rare for Mother and me to talk. It was Berthe that shared her love of home and cooking. Sadly for us, ever since the day I plucked up courage to ask Pappy if I might go to college, our conversations had become mostly question and answer. Tonight, it felt as if she'd been wearing one of grandmother's whalebone corsets for the past six years and had finally decided to leave it off.

The kitchen door opened and Hans stuck his head in, his face as dark and shuttered as it used to be when we were little, and he had suffered a trouncing at the hands of his elder brother. 'How long till dinner?'

'When Ruth gets here.' Mother began arranging the kitchen cloths over the metal bar on the front of the range. 'Why?'

'Storm's gone. I'm going for a breath of fresh air. I was painting ducks all day. You coming, Maidy?' I caught his impatient tone.

Forgetting my damp skirt, I grabbed my coat and ran after him. He was already halfway down the stairs.

'I had to get out.'

Hans pulled the street door shut behind us. Recently, Pappy had installed a long cable between the bell push and first-floor landing. Now, if someone rang the bell, Mother could open the door from the landing and not spend her day running up and down stairs every time a tradesman called.

I tucked my arm in his. 'I know, I saw.'

'Do you see everything, Maidy, with your writer's eye?'

Hans squeezed my arm, and I understood he meant the words as a compliment. I didn't deserve them. Until two days ago, I had believed in fairies. Then, like the eruption of a volcano, the veil had been ripped from my sight, with events assuming a clarity I had never imagined possible. I felt tempted to confide that my new, grown-up status had gone even further than putting up my hair, but I feared his probing. How could I admit that a pair of arrogant black eyes had stripped away my misconceptions, leaving me as naked as Zande's imagination had made me, and banishing my naivety as quickly and easily as Pappy stripped old paint from wood?

'I know you felt angry.'

I felt his shrug through the thick fabric of his winter jacket. 'What's going to happen to me, now Pieter is back?'

'I don't understand.'

'I've completed almost five years of my apprenticeship. Do I have to give it all up because Pieter is taking up his again? Pappy hasn't enough work for us both. He won't let his workmen go; they've been with him too long. Longer than either of his sons.'

'He won't do that.' I tried to sound convincing. 'Not Pappy.'

'Won't he? I've sketched this city from one end to the other and not once has he asked to see any of the patterns I've created.' I caught his jealous tone. 'Pieter is back a couple of days and already Pappy is thinking of a new range of hand mirrors based on his ideas.'

He stopped and leaned over the balustrade of the bridge, staring into its black depths as if it was a book of the future and he was reading from it. The wind had changed direction, clearing away the last of the rain and diminishing to a gentle breeze that tip-toed across its surface. Daylight had been banished by the storm and, in the glow of the lamplight, ripples etched with gold imitated the work Hans had done that day. I listened for the familiar tap-tap-tapping of rope and steel against wood, the stays and shrouds that raise and lower the sails of a boat vibrating in the breeze. At night when the breeze lessened, the gentle sounds lulled me to sleep.

'I think you should be glad.' My response surprised my brother. He lifted his head, staring at me. 'You've always wanted to paint. In a year or two, maybe less now with Pieter here, you'll be free to travel to those sun-drenched lands you're always dreaming of.' I squeezed his arm. 'Remember hiding in my room, afraid Mother would find out you'd been drinking? Telling me how you wanted to become a real artist and discover colour in the sun-kissed shores of the south?' I remembered thinking at the time that Hans had probably discovered the word *sun-kissed* in the bottom of his tankard. 'Pieter's coming back will give you that chance.'

Hans wriggled his shoulders. 'I'm not sure I want to go away now.'

I was tired, my thinking dulled, and for a moment I didn't grasp what Hans meant. Couldn't he see that his dream was at last within touching distance? He didn't need to complete his apprenticeship with Pappy. He could work somewhere else for the final few years. Once qualified, there was nothing to stop him earning a living anywhere, especially now Pieter was home. He was correct. There wasn't enough work for an extra person and, in an excess of fairness, Pappy would put the loyalty of his workmen before his sons.

A picture of Jules, with his pitted skin, begging to be noticed, crept unbidden into my mind.

Oh, Hans, not you too!

A dark shape scurried across the road. Automatically, I flinched back and clutched him, both my feet up on tiptoe.

'You silly!' He tucked his arm through mine, sensing my fear. 'It's only a rat. Do you remember me putting one in your bed? It was the only time Pappy ever thrashed me.' He patted my hand. 'I still don't see why all the fuss. It was dead, after all.'

When I was little, I used to kick my brother, the only way I could retaliate against his strength. I had an urge to do that now. 'You deserved it, too. You were a holy terror. For months afterwards, I couldn't get into bed without checking first.'

Hans chortled. 'I guess I wanted to be like Pieter and stand out. I never did. I was always short and stocky with a snub nose. Still, I wasn't the only one to get into trouble. Mother hit you once, remember? The night you broke curfew and slipped out to see the ducklings hatch on the canal. Pappy found you tucked under the stones of that little bridge.'

I shivered, remembering. I had understood enough to get off the street when the siren sounded, yet remained too young to appreciate I was putting Pappy's life at risk, searching for me.

'Come on. You're cold. A brisk walk to the canal bridge then home for dinner. I could do with a beer. Shame you're still too young to drink, I should have brought Berthe,' he teased.

Ahead of us, dark silhouettes of tall houses lined both sides of the waterway, their lights creating puddles of warmth over the ground. It was cold, though not the heavy dragging cold of winter that left you gasping for breath; this was a cold that your limbs could easily combat by walking briskly, a cold that left you invigorated and freshened, eager for more.

'She'd never let you go near a bar, Berthe doesn't approve of such places.'

'Don't you pity Yoav?'

'No.' I pictured Berthe's fiancé. Tall and very thin, his wrists protruded from his sleeves as if, by mistake, he'd picked up a jacket belonging to a stranger. He worked as a bookkeeper by day, and was studying at night to take his accountancy examination. He and Berthe rarely met up more than once or twice a week. 'She'll make him a good wife.'

'She'll feed him to death.'

On impulse I burst out, 'What should girls look for in a boy?'

'Maidy!' Hans sounded shocked.

I giggled at the startled horror in his voice. 'I'm sixteen,' I quoted, 'old enough to be courted.'

'I gather you've met someone?'

I hesitated. 'There were some new boys at college. I liked one of them, he seemed very … approachable.'

'*Approachable!* That's sounds like some stuffed shirt.'

I nudged him with my elbow, 'Friendly, then. Is that better?' What had I thought about Jaan? That he might become a friend? Perhaps, eventually, more than a friend? I remembered the touch of Zande's hand grasping mine and shrugged the thought away. 'It doesn't matter. You see,' I hesitated, 'Ruth bought me something new to wear for my birthday. It made me feel different somehow – truly grown up.' I brushed my hand dismissively down my skirt, its colour one with the evening sky, conscious of a desire to wear clothes that mirrored the spring. 'I detest navy blue.'

Hans burst into noisy laughter, trumpeting both in joy and temper. 'Perhaps now Pieter's home, Pappy will give you money to buy something new.'

I considered his remark odd but didn't comment. 'You didn't answer my question.'

'I didn't think you serious. Besides, how do I know what girls want?' I heard the bitter tone creep back into his voice.

'So, what do boys wish for?'

'Beauty, elegance, charm. Someone you need to take care of.'

He had described Ruth, except she didn't need looking after. Ruth had been in full control of her life and her surroundings from the moment she stepped back on shore at eight years of age.

Berthe was laying the table when we got back. Mother, as if she'd been watching for our return, bustled in, placing the stew pot on the table. Pappy was sitting by the fire with Pieter and Ruth, lamplight shading their faces. Ruth had changed into an ankle-length wool dress that matched the soft gold of the lamp, its skirt cut on the bias. I noticed Pieter was having difficulty keeping his eyes off her.

Hans also; his expression solid with shock and awakening. He concentrated his attention on her fingers lightly tapping Pieter on the arm, as if providing a musical accompaniment to her words – exactly as she had acted with Tristan.

I wanted to promise him it meant nothing, that she did it to everyone; except I was no longer certain of anything.

Hans caught my eye. I shook my head, warning him not to ruin the evening for our parents and he nodded in understanding.

'Good walk?' Pieter nodded a cautious greeting. He would have remembered Hans' ungovernable temper. No doubt he imagined his shuttered expression was due to Pappy's unintentional slight over the patterns.

I answered for my brother, saying casually, 'The wind's dropping. It's nice out. With a bit of luck, there'll be a moon later.'

Dinner had finished, and Berthe and I were washing up when I overheard Pieter asking Ruth to go for a walk. And her response, 'I thought you'd never ask.'

Berthe, as the eldest, always chose to wash, leaving me the more arduous task of wiping the pots and putting them away. Ruth had gone upstairs to the bathroom. There was a WC next to the kitchen, a tiny cupboard of a place that had been installed for our grandparents. Both Ruth and I preferred the bathroom on the second floor, with its walls lined with mirrors from Pappy's workshop.

Hearing her feet on the stairs, I opened the door to the corridor, teacloth in hand. Hans was waiting at the bottom, staring up at Ruth, his expression admiring. Unlike the staircase in Ruth's house, the treads on our stairs were wide and shallow, leaving plenty of room to pass. Only Mother's superstition stopped us, convinced bad luck must follow if you crossed on stairs. As children, she had despaired whenever staircases played a part in our games, nervous we would fall and break our necks and bear out her fears. But as youngsters, our feet were fast and sure, never slipping.

From the sitting room came the sound of laughter, Pappy's chuckle leading the way. Ruth's glance flicked away and Hans headed up to his bedroom without speaking.

I burst out. 'Ruth, *please* don't play with Pieter's feelings.'

She stared at me blankly. 'What on earth are you talking about?'

'Tristan,' I said, not wanting to betray Hans.

She batted her hand at me as if swatting a fly. 'Oh, that. It's nothing. I was being polite, that's all.'

'It's not nothing,' I stormed. I recalled the intensity of Tristan's expression and the misery in my brother's. Couldn't she see how different they were from the dolls of our childhood, that she could leave in a corner until she wanted to play with them again?

I saw her astonishment. I was rarely, if ever, angry – and never with her. She might get impatient with me; that was different. 'We're not children anymore, Ruth, acting out our games. Can't you see how it affects them?' I fumed, 'it's not fair.'

'Oh, for goodness sake, Magrit,' she snapped out my name. 'You're so naïve. That's what you're supposed to do when you go to college, make friends with other students. Something *you're* obviously quite incapable of doing.'

She had only ever lunged at me once before. Foolishly, I had asked about her life, trying to keep one step ahead of the enveloping hordes. Six weeks is a huge gap when you are little, and Ruth was both taller and stronger than me. Even when she arrived on our doorstep, a little scarecrow of a girl, her eyes made larger by hunger and her hair cut short and plagued with lice, the back of her ankles ribbed with dirt, she was still the taller. She had grabbed hold of my wrist and twisted it in a Chinese burn. 'What are you talking about?' she had hissed. 'Nothing ever happened and if you want to stay friends, you will remember that. My family were always rich, with clothes and food in abundance.'

I never asked again.

'*Stop nagging at me.* You know perfectly well I only like Pieter. He's the one for me.'

'You talking about me?' Pieter opened the door from the sitting room and came out, shrugging on his jacket.

'And if I was, would you be pleased?' As quickly as a chameleon changes its coat, Ruth's voice took on warmth and a gurgle of laughter.

'Can't think of anything I'd like more.' Pieter lifted her coat off its peg, helping her into it. He took her hand. 'No gloves?'

'I won't need them if you're there.'

I scuttled back into the kitchen, my head buzzing, and slammed a saucepan down on the sideboard, making the pottery rattle.

Berthe gazed at my red face. 'Don't you want Ruth and Pieter to get together? It would make Mother and Pappy so happy.'

Wringing out the dishcloth, she hung it over a tap to dry while I finished putting the pots away.

'But only if she loves him.'

'That goes without saying, Maidy. Of course she will love him. Everyone loves Pieter.'

I wandered back into the sitting room and picked up my books, meaning to take them into the study and do some work. Perhaps Ruth was right. After all, she had travelled; I hadn't. She knew far better than me what the world expected.

Mother was sewing, a lamp shining down on her piece of work, leaving its edges in shadow. Pappy was making a pretence of reading the newspaper, his eyes skirting round the room. He appeared to be counting his blessings.

'Pappy.' I took a deep breath, remembering what Hans had said. 'I wondered if I might buy something new to wear for college. After all, I am sixteen. That's considered grown up, even in our community.'

I didn't mean it to come out as a challenge.

'Ruth bought me a twinset for my birthday and I wanted to find something to wear with it.' I felt my face burn and hoped the lamplight was too dark to betray me. I never lied to Pappy. I hurried on. 'It was so generous of her.'

'As your birthday evening should have ended in a visit to the theatre, and I managed to escape that particular form of torture ...' Pappy raised his eyebrows comically.

'Pappy, I realise you only go to the theatre to please Maidy and me ... but surely not torture.'

He beamed. 'My dearest Margaret, torture doesn't even come close.'

Berthe was right. How happy Pieter's return had made him. The entire evening, whenever he got a word in, Pappy had told jokes, his voice plumbing the depths of despair as if the words he was reeling off were of deadly import, rather than the forerunner of continued merriment.

'However ...' He pulled out his wallet, passing me some money, the thick paper crackling like electricity.

I had bitterly regretted giving back my gift, reproaching

myself for being oversensitive. A new outfit meant little or nothing to Ruth, Meneer Endelbaum could afford to buy her a new outfit every week if he wanted. Yet for me ... those trousers has been the most precious garment I'd ever owned, the cloth soft yet light, promising warmth even on the coldest of days. I might even have summoned the courage to flout convention had it not been for Pappy. I would have hated to deceive him, however outdated his ideas. Even if I managed to appease my conscience, they would still have needed to remain hidden in my cupboard and left unworn, unless I changed in the college toilets, my outdoor changing room far too risky. What if I was discovered in my underwear by four naked students? I broke into giggles at the very idea. Then Zande's face pushed its way to the foreground of my thoughts and I hurriedly closed them off. His scrutiny that first day had been way too familiar; it didn't need further encouragement.

I heard Pappy say, 'Nothing outlandish! Take Ruth, she has perfect taste.'

16

I slept badly and was late getting up. Anxious about Hans, I had planned to stay awake until his return, immediately dropping into a deep sleep and waking again a few minutes later to the sound of footsteps. Sleepily, I listened. The echo of feet on stone vanished, dulling as they sped across the wooden slats of the bridge.

I heard Mother and Pappy's footsteps heavy on the stairs, as if their thoughts had lead in them. Yet the late night didn't show on my brother's face when we met up at the breakfast table and Pappy seemed his usual cheerful self. Only Hans appeared tired and jaded.

To an outsider it was a typical family gathering, with Pieter and Hans arguing cheerfully across the table as they used to do. Berthe was chatting with Mother about her wedding, while Pappy read the newspaper. Then Ruth's footsteps sounded on the stairs and everything changed. Pieter shuffled his chair back, impatiently waiting for the door to open to welcome her in. Mother, as if she had been listening out, swung round, smiling warmly. I saw Hans watching Pieter, his expression no longer relaxed but shuttered and suspicious. Only Berthe ignored Ruth's entrance. She carried on talking, cheerfully unaware of the currents scudding around the room.

Ruth was still angry with me. I recognised the signs straight away, although for anyone not accustomed to her moods, all they would see was enchantment and a desire to please.

Her gaze brushed past me. 'Good morning Pappy, good morning Mevrouw Bader. Pieter?'

As delicate as a moth's wing, she touched his shoulder and his hand flew up to grasp it.

I saw Mother smile.

Abruptly Hans jumped to his feet and, leaving his breakfast half-eaten, went downstairs. I stared purposefully at Pappy hoping he'd noticed. He hadn't, his attention resting on his eldest son. In one of my nature books I had read about the common cuckoo. We never hear them in the city. Last summer, cycling to and from college, I had become used to their mocking call. They lay a single egg in another bird's nest and toss out the young already there.

'Darling Maidy, you aren't wearing my gift.' Ruth sat down in the seat left empty by Hans. She placed her hand on Pappy's arm, her smile a little too contrived. Small children do that to gain attention. 'It was so silly of me. I bought Maidy a twinset and some trousers, the same as mine, for her birthday. Quite rightly, she decided the trousers weren't for her, even though she looked wonderful in them.'

I held my breath. Even as a child, Ruth was rarely spiteful. When it did occur, her actions were always well considered. This time, she'd had a whole night to brood on my words.

'Magrit, you didn't wear trousers for college.' Mother always used my birth name to emphasise displeasure. 'Think of the scandal it will create if our friends hear of it.'

'Mevrouw Bader, don't be angry. It was *all* my fault. You know me ...' Ruth's smile lit up the room. 'I am such a scatterbrain and she did give them back.'

'Perhaps you will go with Maidy and buy her something suitable, I gave her some money.' Pappy poured gentle oil over my troubled waters.

'I'd *love* to. Maidy, we can after college tomorrow. I know exactly what will suit you. And I promise, Pappy, it will be perfectly appropriate for a well-brought-up lady.'

She twinkled up at Pappy and he chuckled. Even Mother's brow cleared, although I knew she would speak to me privately later.

'I'm getting more coffee, Ruth,' Pieter picked up his cup, 'May I bring you a cup?'

She touched his arm. 'Not this morning, Pieter. I just flew in to tell Maidy ...' Ruth checked her watch. 'Oh, heavens, I must run, I have a test. Pieter, if you want to walk across town with me, we have to go now. You can test me on the way.' A frown flew across the table containing the message ... *not you*. 'Maidy, don't rush. I'll see you at lunchtime.'

Blowing me a kiss, Ruth headed out of the room. 'Do hurry, Pieter.' Gulping down his coffee, Pieter wiped his mouth on his napkin and raced after her.

I wasn't bothered about Ruth being angry. That would pass and perhaps I had deserved it, aware how much she hated criticism. I was more concerned that neither Mother nor Pappy had noticed how prickly Hans was becoming.

They were talking about Mevrouw Endelbaum becoming ill again. I didn't stop to listen. Quickly buttering a roll, I filled it to bursting with slices of sausage, mindful I had changed sides and hating myself for it. As a child, I had always been on Pieter's side. Hans was the big bad brother who had bullied me and called me a pest. Casually covering the roll with a napkin, I tucked it out of sight in my bag and ran downstairs after Hans.

He was stoking the boiler, riddling hot ashes into a metal tray; the coals within its iron mouth glowing red and spilling their heat into the room. Seeing me burst in, he stood up, wiping his hands down the back of his overalls. He didn't need to do this particular job. Hendrik, who'd been an employee of Baders even before Pappy joined the company, would have done it willingly enough. He had never shown any interest in the artistic side to the business, content to do menial jobs, sweeping up glass shavings or packing a shipment of mirrors in straw. It was Hans who had insisted he must play his proper part as an apprentice.

'You'll be hungry by lunchtime.' I said, giving Hans the little package of food.

He blinked, rubbing the back of his hand over his eyes, and I saw a smudged tear.

I was shocked. Last night I had reckoned it to be simple infatuation, no different from Ruth's swains at college, who wore their heartbreak on their sleeves. Something Hans would quickly come to terms with and let go – as I had my daydreams.

The other afternoon, when we parted at the bridge, Jules had said something very strange. Ruth had ridden on and didn't hear. I had stopped to wish him well, adding, 'I hope you'll be okay,' and had read in his acknowledgement resolve.

'According to the medical profession, you can recover from heartbreak in six days or let it ruin your life for six years. I am hoping for the former.'

For Hans, it would be six years. Jules had only known Ruth less than a year, Hans practically all his life.

'I wish ...'

'So do I, Maidy. Don't worry, as long as you feed me freshly buttered rolls ...' He rummaged up a grin. Like blinds at the windows, he was closing his feelings down, hiding them in a place where they couldn't be damaged still further. I wanted to weep for him.

Lars wandered in and wished me good morning. If he was surprised to find me there, he didn't show it. 'Meneer Bader told us Pieter was home. It will be good to have him back.'

No one had mentioned if Pieter was intending to stay and take up his apprenticeship again, although Pappy must have confided something to Hendrik and Lars. Understanding their concern, he would have wanted to offer reassurance their jobs were safe. I was glad. Both were good men and both had families.

Waving a goodbye, I ran across the yard to get my bike. As little children we had played here too, covering our old clothes with garments that Mother had put out for the rag and bone man, and wearing mismatched boots on our feet, too big or too small and already scuffed and worn. Aware I was late, I didn't bother with the walkways, cycling straight down the street towards the city centre. We seldom went this way. With traffic heading into the city increasing year on year, Mother always worried that a careless driver might tip us off. It was further than the walkways that cut a diagonal path through the city streets although, if traffic was light, it took less time. Having done the journey once, I now felt quietly confident about riding single-handed whenever I needed to indicate.

When I reached the bridge, I was surprised to find Kirsten among its gossiping residents and pulled to a halt alongside her. 'Never seen you here before.'

'This is me trying to get in early for a change. I'm usually scampering up the drive as the bell goes.' She gave me a cheerful grin. 'I've got one demerit this term already. To be truthful, I was intending to go in with Jules and slept through the alarm.'

'You know him?'

'We went through primary together; he lives in the next street. He thinks you're nice.'

As if a klaxon had sounded for the start of a race, students began to mount their bikes and calling a final word over their shoulders, the long line headed out into the traffic. Kirsten and I followed, riding at the back of the column.

'Did you get to meet the new students?' Kirsten said, adding before I had a chance to answer, 'I gather Ruth did, and was her usual charming self.'

'Which question do you want me to answer first?' I signalled right, following the cyclist in front of me and accelerated down the slight incline towards the lakeside highway.

Our pace wasn't particularly fast. Once we had turned off the main city route onto the highway, conversation broke out again; the air ringing with long names and Latin phrases, a veritable feast of learning. I'd been surprised how seriously most took their studies. When we went for our interview, Pappy confided that many students would have lost parents or close family members in the war, and for them, the cost of a college education would have exerted huge pressure. I watched them scuttle through their studies, exactly as I sensed Jules was doing, pushing time to the limit in a vain hope they might graduate the sooner.

'You don't need to bother,' Kirsten grinned cheekily. 'I sort of answer them myself as I go along. I heard on the grapevine you'd met Zande. He was seen talking to you. *Please note* ... I did say *he* was doing the talking.'

Startled, my head flew up, causing me to wobble unsteadily. 'What was I doing?' I replied nervously, praying no one had spotted me lounging on the ground by the canal.

'My informant said you were staring up at him transfixed as if he were a snake. I also heard he spurned Ruth. The other girls were delighted, although a few of the boys felt sympathy. Can't for the life of me think why.'

'If I remember rightly, I did manage a sentence or two.' I joked. 'I'm not so sure about Ruth.'

'What do you mean?'

'To be honest, I'm not sure what I mean ... I got the feeling Zande was play acting. He tried it with me,' I burst out, confident Kirsten wouldn't scoff. 'I think he did it to annoy Ruth ... you know ... get her attention.'

She shrugged, making her bike swerve. 'If that's what it was, it didn't work. Last thing I heard, she's taken up with Tristan. Zande has moved on also. Wish it had been in my direction.' Kirsten sighed loudly. 'Sadly, boys rarely notice clever girls. Shame really.'

'They don't notice shy ones either,' I said, recalling that Zande had begun our conversation by asking where my beautiful friend was.

As we neared the college grounds, several dozen bicycle bells burst into song as if to announce the arrival of someone important. Accelerating, the long column veered off the highway, freewheeling down the lane and onto the driveway. Slowing to a stop, Kirsten examined the mayhem of the courtyard, students rushing around like headless chickens, searching for a place to leave their bikes, the metal racks already overflowing. 'It's ridiculous,' she exclaimed, glowering. 'There's never anywhere free except the ground. You'd think the college authorities would do something about it.'

'When I first applied, they assured Pappy there would be a bus.'

Kirsten grinned suddenly. 'Told me the exact same thing; wishful thinking on their part.' She scoured the crowded courtyard, every inch of space heaving with bicycles. 'Oh, this is impossible,' she stormed.

'Come with me,' I beckoned. 'I'll find you somewhere.'

I doubled back along the path towards the sports centre, pointing triumphantly to the sandwich of brick and grass Zande had showed me, empty except for Ruth's machine.

'Heavens!' Kirsten exclaimed. 'How did you discover this? I've been here almost two years and never knew it existed.'

'Zande introduced me to it,' I said, unpacking my books.

'You told me you only managed one sentence,' she said accusingly.

I spluttered with laughter. 'I did! Boys do that to you, they
…'

'Reduce you to idiocy,' Kirsten completed my words. 'You
go away, and spend the next twenty-four hours working out all
the clever things you should have said.'

I remembered the lines I had written in my journal.

The bell echoed across the courtyard. 'Help!' Kirsten broke
into a run, shouting back over her shoulder. 'I must dash. Why
would anyone with sense stick maths way up on the third floor
and then present you with text books that weigh a ton?'

17

I saw nothing of Ruth during the day and guessed she was avoiding me. When I reached home, Mother told me Pieter and Ruth had gone out for the evening, adding the words: 'I am so pleased.'

That surprised me. After her manner on Sunday, perhaps it shouldn't. Aware of her grief at Pieter's loss, somehow I had expected her to keep him close and discourage Ruth from popping round all the time. Yet, quite the opposite was happening. Bewildered, I sensed in her a sort of impatience, as if we were late for an event and she wanted to hurry us up. Next morning, I saw that an extra place had been laid for Ruth at the breakfast table and a chair brought in from the study, unsure if it was Pieter or Mother who had organised it.

'Maidy, is it all right if I come with you, again today?' Pieter said, fetching Ruth some coffee from the kitchen.

'Pieter, you no longer need to ask Maidy's permission,' Ruth teased, smiling at me.

I was forgiven.

It was a glorious morning which Ruth matched easily. Her dress was new, bought for a visit to the theatre a month ago; the blue of the fabric rivalling the sky on a spring day, and equally as lovely. She was wearing heels too and, as she came in, Pieter's breath deserted him. Even for Ruth, this was a special effort, and I wondered why. She didn't need to impress my brother.

I walked behind; my thoughts bombarding me like the seagulls that mobbed the fishermen whenever they landed a catch of fish.

Sensing my mood, Ruth constantly spun round, tossing a smiling word over her shoulder, including me in the conversation. 'Ask, Maidy, she'll tell you. Much better than me at history, I'm such a flibbertigibbet.' A moment later, another smile, 'Maidy, don't forget we finish early today. Oh, Pieter,' her hand flew out caressing the front of his jacket. 'Can you believe they actually want us to do sports? Maidy and I have enough exercise cycling to and from college. Especially in winter. So, we have all afternoon to do Maidy's shopping. And I'm not inviting you to join us.' She peeked up at him, opening her eyes wide to soften her words.

Pieter gazed down at her, his face almost luminous with happiness. Even at a distance I could feel the pounding of his heart, bursting with feeling for her.

I was as happy for him as I was sad for Hans.

'Can't I come? I'd really love to.'

'Sorry, it's girls only.'

Her dress, with its stiff organza petticoat, swayed, almost dancing along the street as she pirouetted around, including me in their conversation.

We left Pieter at the bridge. Peculiarly Ruth seemed almost anxious to get going, awarding Pieter a cursory peck on the cheek and saying we would be late. We weren't, quite the opposite; the crowd of students not yet gathered. I squinted back over my shoulder noticing Pieter standing alone, his hand poised to wave.

The weather seemed to have settled again; the horizon

melted into a soft blue-grey haze – always a good sign. The downpour the other night had brought the grass verges to life, and they shone with a riotous pageantry of wildflowers, yet so fragile a careless boot might easily have crushed them. Only farmers approved of rain. College students, with at least ten kilometres between them and shelter, hated it and, once again, rumours were circulating that by winter, a bus would be running.

As we cycled along the lakeshore swans were feeding in the shallows, the surface garlanded with white feathery arches as they bent their long necks to retrieve some morsel of weed rooted in the mud. I spotted two tiny cygnets nestling under their mother's wing and slowed. Threatened by our presence, she hissed at us to stay away, her cold black stare menacing.

I should have heeded her warning.

The bluff on which our college building stands runs through a patch of scrubby woodland. There were no gates. There had been once. Made of iron and adorned with the shield of an all-conquering army, they'd been torn down and never replaced. A tangle of rotting branches had fallen across their cracked stone base, as if wanting to obliterate all memory of that particular evil. I swerved into the lane and braked, sensing the looming presence of Zande.

How or why I knew it was him, I had no idea. Yet I felt it as strongly as an electric shock running through my skin. He was leaning against a tree part-way down the drive; his skin, together with the soft brown of his shirt and slacks, blending gracefully into the bark of a young spruce.

Ruth, who was riding ahead of me, caught sight of him in the same moment. Braking, she dismounted and began to wheel her bicycle down the drive, smoothing her hand down over her hips in a gesture reminiscent of the girls that first day. I was shaken by the triumph in her eyes and knew, as if the words had been written in plain hand across the sky, that she'd been hoping this might happen. The dress, the shoes, the special effort … they were for Zande, not Pieter.

I had always resented Ruth's childhood declaration of love for my brother, certain it would pass. Only that morning I had finally become convinced I was mistaken and it was as genuine as the diamonds Meneer Endelbaum displayed in his shop window. Now, I didn't know what to believe.

Before I could say anything, a slight, fair-haired girl emerged from behind the tree. I recognised her as being in the year above. Elina. Fully aware Ruth was watching, Zande embraced her, swirling her around until she had her back to us. Elina put a hand to his chest as if to stop him. Ignoring it, he pulled her closer, his lips crushing, his eyes closed, lingering over that kiss.

It was intentional and blatantly intended to shock. By my side, I saw Ruth stiffen, the handlebars on her bike quivering with suppressed rage.

Without warning, Zande opened his eyes and looked straight at her, aware she was there and wanting her to see. Then he caught sight of me standing behind in the middle of the driveway. He flinched and for a moment, I imagined he was going to step away, as a child does when caught doing something reprehensible. He shrugged and bent to kiss Elina again, conscious I was watching.

And wanting me to understand.

I did, only too well.

Ruth was his real quarry. And he didn't care how many hearts he had to break to get to her – but only on his terms, not hers. Except, for some reason I couldn't quite fathom, he had no intention of involving me. If I wanted to warn Ruth that he was playing some sort of game, I could. In his arrogance, he'd already decided my warning would fall on deaf ears. He was right. After my outburst the other night, Ruth would think me jealous.

Anger flared and I quickly cycled on, painfully recalling our encounter on the canal bank. No doubt that was play-acting too, hoping I'd follow the script he'd already prepared. What part had I been programmed to play? The fool? Chosen for fleeting entertainment, aimed at bolstering an ego already set at gigantic proportions.

Once again, I didn't hear a word of my lectures, my mind ranging backwards and forwards, constantly reverting to that kiss. I tried to banish its memory, my feelings at loggerheads with logic; that's how he does it, he traps girls in his web, convincing them they are different. Yet, why bother to tell me I wasn't part of his game? Or was this yet another game, his sadistic nature finding amusement in my confusion?

Despite my anger at his bare-faced effrontery, I couldn't help but wonder how it would feel, imagining the gentleness of his lips pressed against mine.

For the first time, I envied my sister and her placid approach to life. She and Yoav might never experience the heights of passion. Berthe wasn't even aware of their existence and, even if she had been, lacked the curiosity to explore them, instinct keeping her on ground both familiar and safe.

At the end of class, Meneer de Witt, no longer finding my inattention quite so amusing now my birthday was over, requested politely I stay behind to make up for my delinquency. My task, and it was a horrid one, was a five hundred word essay defining the importance of Kronos and Ananke, the gods of time and inevitability, in relation to the conquests of Napoleon. I wrote how an ordinary soldier, bolstered by his triumphs in war, grew to believe he might become emperor of the world, the consequences of this belief among other nations, and the inevitability of his final defeat.

By the time I put down my pen, I hated history with a vengeance although, in all fairness, I deserved the punishment. Meneer de Witt wasn't a patient man at the best of times, and

I'd been lucky to escape first time round. The bell had already rung for the end of school and I ran to the staff room to leave my work.

By the time I got outside, the courtyard was deserted, the students either on their way home or at the sports centre. Behind me, the swing doors opened with a crash. I spun round on my heel, expecting to see Ruth. I'd not spoken to her since that morning and I was wanting to learn how she viewed Zande's playacting. Hopefully, she would decide he wasn't worth it and concentrate solely on Pieter, who truly cared for her.

It was Kirsten. She backed out, weighed down with an armful of books, holding the door open with her bottom.

'If you're waiting for Ruth,' she called, heading across the forecourt. 'She's with Tristan at the sports hall.'

'No! That's impossible.'

Kirsten dumped her books down in the basket attached to the front of her bike and began arranging them neatly, tucking a plastic cover over the top in case of rain. 'Why? Have I missed something? For instance, a mile-high banner saying Ruth can't date Tristan? He's safer than Zande.'

'We were going shopping,' I blurted out. 'She must have forgotten.'

Kirsten had one of those faces that are easy to read, every emotion inscribed in capital letters on its surface, like the blackboards our lecturers used to write their instructions. I read in it condemnation. I knew she didn't approve of Ruth. 'I bet you she hasn't.'

I remembered then that she was best friends with Elina, the girl we'd seen Zande kissing.

She bent down to unlock the chain on her back wheel, pulling it free. 'Go and check. I'll wait and we can cycle back together.'

Hurriedly packing my books away, I ran down the path to the sports hall. Built against a backdrop of pine and spruce, it had only been finished a year. I'd never been inside, not even for the opening ceremony. That day, Ruth had decreed a visit to the new cinema more exciting than dull speeches.

Ahead of me, double glass doors opened up into a square lobby strewn with notice boards and team photographs. Cutting through the girls changing room, I pushed open the door to the playing field. A sea of mud met my eye, the grass churned up under a forest of boots. A game of football was in progress, Ruth nowhere to be seen among its spectators. Retracing my steps, I hurried up the steps to the first-floor viewing platform, hearing the thump of a ball in the distance.

Swing doors gave onto rows of seats overlooking two basketball courts. Only one was in use; busy with running figures, their heavy breathing drowned out by the sound of the ball bouncing against a hard surface and the squeak of plimsolls as a player swivelled to take a shot.

There were few spectators, no one much interested in watching the first games of a season. Only if we did well would the seats be crowded. Even if they had been, I would have spotted Zande. He was seated a couple of rows down, his arm casually draped across the back of Elina's seat, his dark skin conspicuous against her pale flesh. She was cuddled into him, her head resting against his shoulder, her hand on his chest, the opposite of the gesture I had seen that morning, pushing him away. She seemed oblivious to the attention she was creating, the few spectators more interested in the game being played out in these seats than the one on court. These were scenes for walks by the canal at night, not broad daylight and in public – and definitely not so soon after a first meeting. From now on, girls would call her fast and boys would think it. Zande already knew that and didn't care. I recognised his triumphant smile.

Ruth was sitting next to Waldger in the row below, her shoulders braced, her body angled away from Zande. To a casual observer, the message was clear; he was no longer of any interest, she had moved on.

Jaan was there too; on the far side of Waldger, with an empty seat between them. He appeared uncomfortable, shifting restlessly on the hard surface of the wooden seat. As if their minds were connected, he and Zande swung round in the same moment and spotted me at the top of the steps.

I relaxed my face to smile at Jaan, my hand already moving to greet him. He shot a startled glance at Zande, who was on his feet shrugging off Elina's restraining hand, then Jaan looked away as if he didn't know me.

I reeled back from the rebuff as if from a painful blow, my thoughts cascading like a pack of spilt cards. No boy had ever shown the slightest interest in me. Maybe it had only been politeness and I had imagined his warm offer of friendship and exaggerated his laughter. Nevertheless, it hurt.

'Magrit!' Zande's tone was jubilant. He beckoned, his scrutiny lingering; slowly sweeping over me from top to toe. If I had hoped to come across as dowdy in my plain skirt and cardigan, I failed miserably. He looked and saw only what was beneath. So very different. Gone was the friendly smile, as if that too had been an illusion, like the jewelled cavern guarded by its little bridges.

'What a wonderful surprise. Join us. You can take Elina's seat.'

She swung round glaring. Waldger patted the empty seat beside him and nodded encouragingly. Only Jaan didn't move, once again concentrating on the game. Tristan was easy to spot, nimble and fast on his feet. Defending the basket, his height allowed him to dominate other shorter players, springing high into the air to capture a rogue ball.

I looked back to where the real action was taking place. 'No thanks.' I kept my tone polite and my feet still. The other night, I had scribbled the words in my journal: *in Zande sincerity exists like a vein of gold buried deep in a mine.* Now I considered them silly and trite. How stupid to imagine I might be the one to unearth that precious vein of metal.

'Did you forget our date to go shopping, Ruth?'

She slid round in her seat. There were a couple of boys in the row in front and their eyes slyly followed the movement of her legs, with its glimpse of suspender. 'I promised Tristan I'd watch him. It's his first match and he's nervous,' she replied, her tone cajoling. 'Let's do it tomorrow.'

'Would you allow me to accompany you? I'd be delighted and Tristan would never miss me, not if Ruth is here.' Zande placed his hand on the back of his seat. He vaulted over and was by my side – standing close, his breath soft on my cheek.

Ruth's reaction was plain enough for anyone to see; her darkling glance momentarily wishing death would strike me down. Elina's was little better, her face striving for control, shuttered and angry, her fists clenched. I felt their jealous rage merge like a twisted cord. At that moment, I hated Zande. I hated him for girls everywhere and in particular for poor Elina – content with her own little life until a god crossed her path. For that's what Zande believed himself to be; his ego on a par with the gods I had written about that day. I hated him for Ruth too. He could serve her nothing but harm.

Waldger laughed.

The ugliness of the scene ripped through me and I backed away, wanting no part.

'Why do you do this, Zande?' I flared at him.

He stepped back and the gluttonous expression in his eyes vanished, replaced by something more cautious. 'Do what?'

'Destroy everything around you.'

Not waiting for his reply, I stormed off down the steps, desperate to breathe the clean, unpolluted air of the lakeside.

18

Kirsten took one look at my face. 'Told you so.' She put a sympathetic hand on my arm. 'I've got money. Let's go to Rougiers and eat cake. Come on.'

I grabbed my bike and followed her down the drive.

The brightness of the day had already faded and a cold wind had sprung up, cloud over the lake resembling pleats of corrugated cardboard. I had brought my mac, remembering the rain of the previous night but didn't stop to put it on, wanting to get away.

'Slow down,' I called, laughing.

I wasn't laughing inside. My head throbbed and, no different from the swans milling about in the middle of the lake, my ruffled feathers needed smoothing.

The scene I had witnessed continued to play over and over. Its images clashed discordantly, as did Waldger's cruel mockery. Poor Elina, she mattered no more to Zande than toys to a spoiled child, who threw them aside when offered something new. If I had said yes, he would have accompanied me to the city, never sparing a moment's thought to the hurt he had left behind.

If I could see that, why couldn't Ruth? Her interest in

Tristan was a sham, an illusion, little more than a ruse to make Zande jealous. Waldger knew it and thought it funny. I didn't and feared for Ruth. Like gloves belonging to some errant knight, she had thrown down her challenge, unaware Zande knew the game far better than she, and had played it before. If anyone was going to get hurt, it would be Ruth.

Why? Why did she need to do this? Wasn't Pieter good enough for her any longer?

And Jaan? He had twice offered friendship before turning away and cutting me dead. That hurt even more than all the rest because it was so unexpected. Was he no different from Waldger and Zande? I hated the very idea, every instinct screaming out that I was wrong. Nevertheless, I had to face facts. He was the same as his friends, you couldn't trust any of them.

I wondered what had made them so uncaring and choked on my tears, my chest tight.

Kirsten slowed and stopped. 'Sorry, Elina's used to me riding fast. I've got brothers – both younger – and I spend my time chasing one or the other.' She patted my arm and dug into her pocket, pulling out a handkerchief. 'I keep a spare. Elina's a real waterworks. Never go with her to the cinema. She always cries. Doesn't matter if it's sad or not.'

I gulped, managing a watery smile.

'Forget it. You're not Ruth's keeper.'

'I wasn't crying about Ruth.'

'No?'

I shrugged. 'Maybe that's a part of it. We've been friends a long time.'

Kirsten pushed off, riding alongside. 'Tell me about your family.'

I was grateful. 'Pappy makes mirrors. My brothers are both older and work for him.' She wouldn't understand about Pieter vanishing for so long and I couldn't say. I felt almost ashamed; perhaps because I didn't know why.

'Of course – Baders. How silly of me not to remember. Your sister works in the chocolate shop. My little brother's current ambition in life is to marry her. He's only ten.'

She laughed; a friendly uncomplicated girl. The perfect companion for when your emotions are twisted into knots. Ruth had always set goals impossible for me to achieve. Kirsten was the opposite, content to let me be. Yet, I was still grateful she'd not witnessed the scene in the sports hall. With her simple view on life, she'd have condemned her friend's behaviour as wanton, unable to comprehend that Elina was to be pitied. Zande reminded me of the unrelenting power of the invaders. Innocence stood no chance.

The road from the bridge into the city proper was busy and, wanting to chat, we dismounted and pushed our bikes along its wide pavements. Here, every other shop served ice cream, coffee and beer. Despite a penetrating wind, on the off chance of persuading passers-by to stop and take some refreshment, staff had set out tables and chairs on the pavement. We passed a man immersed in his newspaper, a cigarette in one hand and a coffee in the other, and a couple talking softly, their heads almost touching, their feelings obviously more powerful than the blustery wind.

Rougiers was a noisy bustling place and we were lucky to find two empty spaces in the bike stand. We pushed open the door to a wall of sound as conversation roamed nonstop, augmented by the constant clink of cups and saucers. One of the main reasons for the café's popularity was its glass frontage with its panoramic view of the square. Kirsten, who obviously knew the drill, lingered in the doorway, running a friendly eye over customers seated at tables in the window, calculating who might be ready to leave first.

The room was big with lofty ceilings, a line of fans dropping down like slumbering bats. Emitting a steady humming sound, their blades whirled unceasingly in a futile attempt to clear the haze of cigarette smoke. As if some attempt had been made to brighten up the café, a series of black and white photographs had been pinned to the walls; the images badly faded where light from the window had caught them. Taken in the era when motorised trams and cars were in their infancy, they portrayed shopkeepers, the majority sporting a luxuriant moustache as a sign of their prosperity. Vanished into the ether as had horse-drawn buses and rag and bone men, they wore striped aprons and straw boaters, and leaned possessively against the entrance of their small shop, their arms folded across their chest.

'Have you never been here?' Kirsten said, observing my wide-eyed stare.

'Only once – for Ruth's birthday, the year we left school.'

I didn't elaborate further, the memory uncomfortable. Meneer Endelbaum had ordered a cake made of ice cream and I'd asked Mother if I could have one for my birthday, 'Only a little one, not big like the one Ruth had.' She had invited the entire class. 'Just for us and the Endelbaums.' It was only later I realised how selfish that sounded; Berthe would have been hurt, thinking her sisterly offering not special enough.

Out of the corner of my eye, I spotted a woman reaching for her purse and nudged Kirsten. Several other people were watching the same spot. Ignoring them, Kirsten darted across, and politely asked the woman if she was leaving. I would have felt far too embarrassed to stand at her elbow while the woman paid her bill. It didn't bother Kirsten, her attention drawn to the bustling scene outside, and sitting down even before the over-worked waitress had managed to clear the table.

The main square had grown up adjacent to the royal palace, its ancient ruby spires and turrets eye-catching against the plain grey stone of its neighbours and, even at night, the square was busy. Whenever the glass doors opened, a roar of traffic flowed in, cars circling its central reservation endlessly like fish in a tank; its flower borders, planted with yellow primulas and narcissi, providing a welcome spot of colour in an otherwise wintry scene.

'Look at that' Kirsten tapped on the glass, pointing to a couple walking past, the high collar on the woman's waist-length jacket resting snugly against her neck.

'She's wearing fur,' I gasped. Grey had been the colour of the winter and the woman's skirt of dark grey wool was long and tapering with a kick pleat, her hat black and perky with a tiny veil that hinted at hidden delights.

'I'd give my eyeteeth to wear a hat like that.' Kirsten groaned, fixing the woman with an envious stare. 'Of course, it would clash madly with what I'm wearing,' she joked wafting a nonchalant hand at her blue skirt, a heavy jumper pulled down over her hips. 'Don't you just love this place? You can sit here and see the world pass by. And that man's suit? I bet it's mohair,' she hissed, pointing to the woman's companion, walking politely on the outside of the pavement, his shoes gleaming with polish and a soft trilby on his head. 'You couldn't have a better view, not even if you were sitting in the front row of a catwalk in Paris.'

'Catwalk?'

'That's what it's called. Models walk down a raised passageway, between the chairs where the audience sit.'

The waitress bustled up and Kirsten ordered tea for us both. 'We need to go and choose our cakes.'

'What about our table?' I murmured, gazing over at the glass counter where a line of customers were waiting to be served.

'Leave your bag. Come on.'

At the counter, customers were darting back and forth, unable to decide between chocolate gateaux at one end, éclairs dripping chocolate and fresh cream in the middle, or apricot tortes and vanilla sponges, lavished with raspberries and cream, at the other end. Fingers pointed, hesitated a moment, and pointed again.

'If they were sensible,' Kirsten hissed out of the corner of her mouth, 'they'd place a selection on every table and you paid for what you ate.'

Overhearing, the assistant serving us laughed. She picked up the strawberry tartlet I'd chosen, its red berries poking through a sweet glaze. Kirsten had opted for mille-feuille, its layers of puff pastry drenched in raspberry nectar, with cream between each layer and icing on top.

'We tried that, only their bills were so huge we had complaints.'

'Whatever happened to your slacks?' Kirsten said, as we sat down again. 'They would have been perfect with this cold wind.'

'I returned them,' I admitted.

'Why? They really suited you.' She picked up her plate, twisting it to inspect her trophy from both sides.

A crocodile of children were passing the window, walking dutifully hand in hand, their attention drawn to the cake counter. The two tallest, walking at the rear of the line, both had uniforms of grey trousers and blazer a size too small. I presumed they had grown recently and had parents too poor to buy afresh before the start of a new school year. They were heading for the museum, a dull after-school treat for little children; most would be bored stiff within a few minutes, their teacher pointing out architecture that only she could see and was interested in.

I shrugged, 'Same reason as you. You said your mother would kill you.'

'I exaggerated. Even if she had agreed, I still wouldn't dare – not with my shape. They really suited you,' she admitted generously. 'I tell you what; I bet some of the seniors have a pair hidden in their bedrooms.'

'I did think of doing that,' I confessed. 'Sadly, people who live in the old city are at least a dozen years behind the times.' I twirled my finger in the air, indicating the other customers. 'My father's generation believe women belong in dresses – the longer the better.' I erupted into giggles, remembering.

'What?' Kirsten said suspiciously.

'Nothing really, just something that happened the other day. Ruth and I usually walk along the canal to get home,' I confided, 'and when it's hot, we're forced to run a gauntlet of old people sitting out on benches. They already disapprove of us for showing our legs, and not hiding them away under thick lisle stockings. The other day, when Ruth was wearing her cream trousers ... this one old biddy ...' I began to giggle again. 'I promise, she never took her eyes off Ruth, pursued her all the way along the canal. I swear she didn't even blink until we'd crossed the bridge. I told Ruth, she was being cursed,' I finished airily, the painful episode at college retreating in the congenial atmosphere of the café and Kirsten's warm friendship. 'And to watch out for ladders and paint tins.'

'But just think how sensible trousers would be on a bicycle. If there's a strong wind, I have to use one hand to hold down my skirt, otherwise passers-by will either see my petticoat or a length of bare leg covered in gooseflesh.' Kirsten grinned mischievously.

I enjoyed talking to Kirsten. She made me forget there were such things as problems and doubts.

The waitress rattled up, planting a tea pot and water jug on the table.

'You take milk?'

'Please, but not sugar.'

'You can't taste it anyway, not when you're eating cake.' Kirsten picked up the pewter tea pot, pouring out the amber-coloured liquid. 'Changing the subject, did you realise there's a science to eating cake?' She pushed the little china milk jug across the table. 'Help yourself.'

'Thanks. Go on.'

'First, you must decide which piece to try first. Are you a *go for it* sort of person?'

'How do you mean?' I said, automatically stirring my tea even though it didn't contain sugar. I almost never drank tea at home, none of us did except for Pappy. Mother served him tea every afternoon after he had finished work.

'Cakes are scrummy anyway, so they're not the best example. If you're a *go for it*, you eat the best bit first.'

'I never do that. I eat the nasty bits first, and save the best bits till last. What does that mean?'

'I guessed you were. One of my brothers is a *go for it;* the other is a *hang-back* the same as you. A conformist.'

I remembered the dress that Mother had given me for my tenth birthday, keeping it to wear on Sundays for church. 'It sounds dull.'

'No, not dull; sensible and safe.'

'And you're saying that's not dull!'

Kirsten and Elina were both fair, although Elina was by far the prettier, with an elfin face and hair to her waist. Kirsten wore hers parted in the middle with side plaits, which she wrapped across the top of her head, emphasising her broad brow. Plain and unpretentious. Yet that's often how friendships worked; no different from Ruth and me. And most times, it was the pretty one who was vulnerable, needing constant reassurance of her worth. Kirsten had her feet planted firmly on the ground. Not like Elina.

'Their characters are poles apart too,' Kirsten was saying. 'The youngest, Mikel, never thinks of the consequences of his actions; Kian never takes a step without thinking about it, in case it ends badly.'

I remembered my dreams of stowing away on a ship, aware they would stay dreams.

Kirsten paused and broke the icing on her cake. 'I wish they hadn't come.'

Although she had been talking about her brothers half a second before, I didn't ask who she meant. Silence fell as I replayed the scene in the sports hall, making no sense of its swirling undercurrents – except the obvious.

'Some of the girls are being spiteful to Elina, jealous, I expect, that he didn't pick them, and the boys have gone all weird too; so protective and chauvinistic. One of the girls in our year told her boyfriend she was going to the cinema with a friend … and he actually followed her! It's ridiculous,' Kirsten stormed. 'But they're so different from the local boys; far more worldly, almost a different species.'

'You remind me of a kettle that's about to boil over.'

'Well!' Kirsten gave me a wry grin and clattered her fork on her plate, trying to dredge up every last crumb. 'I feel so sorry for Elina. I tried to warn her. I told her he was playing some game with Ruth.'

'You don't like her do you?'

'No! *Do you?*'

'I love her.' Without thinking I trotted out my stock answer. 'I did. I mean I do. She's always been my best friend.' I didn't add that I was beginning to wonder if the friendship I'd once imagined so solid was melting away, as stars did at sunrise.

'Take no notice, I was being spiteful.' Kirsten screwed up her nose, frowning fiercely. 'But it's so *easy* for her. She's unbelievably beautiful, her family are well-off, and she's clever. Besides that, every boy in college wants to go out with her …' She met my gaze, 'And she treats you badly. Sorry, but I'm *not* apologising for that. The other girls think you're nice … only they're put off by Ruth.'

'I don't see ... she's so generous and kind. Anyone would want to be friends with her.'

Kirsten held up her hand. 'Try opening your eyes, Magrit. The other day, she saw you as a rival and spurned you. Today, she's got better fish to fry and ignores you. Who wants that sort of friend? I know I don't. Come on.' She eyed the counter covetously. 'If we stay any longer, I shall be forced to eat another cake.'

Pushing back her chair, she stood up. 'Let's go and buy those clothes. If I can't convince you with words, I can with deeds.' She saw the doubt in my face and tucked her arm through mine. 'You're not going to fall out with me for telling you the truth, are you?'

Kirsten was right. If the students had chosen another college, Ruth and I would be fine and I wouldn't now be questioning if she really was my friend. Or, indeed, if I actually knew her at all and from the outset had seen only a beautiful exterior, like the frame of an oil painting, so decorative you never noticed the blemish on the canvas inside.

'Then you and I are going to be friends. Come on.'

We wandered out into the bustle of the main street, so different from our tiny enclave with its old-fashioned shops. There was even a department store. The first time I had seen it, I believed it to be the royal palace, with dozens of windows in its red brick façade and turrets and spires of jade beautifying its roof. One year, Pappy had supplied some mirrors and, as a treat, he asked the lift operator to give Berthe and me a ride. To the wide eyes of a tiny child, its lift gates were made of golden bars and the operator had used a golden lever to whirl us up to the fourth floor and down again in record time.

We wandered past handbags, nylon stockings, and silk scarves that were stacked in shallow boxes lined with tissue paper, heading for the stairs to the first floor where clothes carried a more modest price tag. The higher you went, the more expensive clothes became. On the fourth floor they sold original designs from Paris and Italy, and fur coats made from Russian mink and sable.

'Don't you dare!' Kirsten dragged me away from a rack where black, brown, and navy were displayed. 'Navy is a killer, and with your colour eyes – so is blue. From now on you wear nothing except green ...' she began ticking the colours off on her fingers, 'turquoise, pink, purple and ... light grey.'

They had a limited range in my size and I picked out two skirts, one in grey, the other patterned in greens and turquoise, both in heavy cotton suitable for summer. The assistant said they really suited my dark colouring and immediately found a blouse and cardigan to match.

Pappy had been generous and there was some money left. Kirsten made me buy a pair of turquoise sandals, the same colour as the cardigan, with small wedge heels and peep-toes.

'To be worn *without* socks,' she insisted, nodding her head at the assistant when she asked if we wanted the box. It was so easy with Kirsten; shopping was quick and painless, the very opposite of a shopping trip with Ruth, who demanded to try on every pair of shoes in the shop then bought nothing.

'If I ask Mother first, will you come and have tea with us, next week,' I said as we parted, Kirsten heading in the opposite direction, towards the railway station. Her father had worked for the railway all his life, even during the years of the occupation. Now, he held a good position as a senior engine driver, his small house overlooking the main line. Kirsten told me she wanted to work for them too, which is why she had opted to go on to college.

'Most likely by next week, I will be rescuing Elina from her broken heart.'

'You're not serious?'

Kirsten stopped dead and the woman walking behind bumped into her, treading on her heel.

'*Ouch, that hurt!*' She glared at the woman already half way down the street. 'Magrit, do you *really* see him staying with her?'

I didn't! She had nothing to offer a god except herself. Kirsten was right. Even that wouldn't hold him.

19

I was in bed reading when I heard footsteps in the street. It was almost eleven so it had to be Hans. Once shops closed, the only other person likely to be about was the tobacconist from next door. He lived alone, his family the men who frequented a nearby inn. He also had fought in the army and lost a leg, his gait unmistakable. Hans walked with steps that were firm, edging into a run, full of energy and life. Tonight, they sounded uneven, halting. I knew he drank, never much, as an apprentice he didn't earn much, and guessed he was seeking a crutch, to dull the pain of Pieter taking what he cared for most. I wondered if Pappy realised, although he'd said nothing and if I had spoken out, he would have considered it unchristian.

'Pieter was lost for six years,' I could hear his voice softly rebuking me. 'Remember your Bible, Luke chapter 15, verse 7. "I tell you that even so there will be more joy in heaven over one sinner who repents, than over ninety-nine righteous people who need no repentance."'

I'd been unable to settle, my pillow hard, finding it impossible to get comfortable. Even my nightdress conspired against me, riding up around my thighs. A plague of feelings pounded my brain, mostly to do with Zande. An elegant enigma, he wandered through my mind at will, whispering his soft words until I rammed the pillow over my head in frustration. Eventually giving up on sleep, I pulled out a copy of Othello. Professor Dulmes read Shakespeare in its original form; I needed a translation and still found it difficult going, its themes of jealousy and hate disturbing.

I had tried and had failed dismally to stay angry with Zande. It seemed to me that history was peppered with men prepared to destroy the world for a beautiful woman. He was no different. The only bit I didn't understand was how I featured in it. Why, despite his casual behaviour, I was still lured by the gentle touch of his fingers, the appeal in his eyes? He reminded me of a forest fire – tantalising but dangerous. I was safer with someone like Jaan. Yet even he had rejected me, obviously thinking I was too dull and ordinary after all.

Hans tapped on my door. Before I had time to call out, he had opened it and come in. 'Did I miss anything?' I smelled beer on his breath.

'Hans! Please.'

'Why? Drinking helps.'

'Mother and Pappy would be so upset if they knew. Surely, you don't resent Pieter coming back. He's our brother.'

'No. I don't. What I do resent is losing Ruth and my job.'

He slid down against the wall, buckling his knees against his chest. I climbed out of bed and sat down beside him, leaning my head on his shoulder as I used to do with Pieter when I was a little girl. I didn't want to tell Hans that Ruth had never been his to lose.

'It was fun on Saturday; perhaps we can go out again soon. You can show me your city, the bits you admire. Maybe that old inn, the one that used to be a lockkeeper's cottage.'

Hans wasn't listening. Head bent, his eyes raked the ground, his hands clasped together, his thumbs revolving restlessly.

I waited patiently. This was the Hans I'd known all my life. Truculent, even tempestuous as a child, in the early days of his apprenticeship he had tried Pappy's patience sorely. Many a time, Pappy had complained to Mother that he could do nothing with him. 'That boy will be the death of me.' But Hans had grown up, learned to curb his temper, hiding his disappointments for the sake of the family. Nevertheless, he still felt them deeply.

'Where do you think Pieter's been all this time?' he burst out, after the longest while.

I was astonished to discover that Hans shared my thoughts. Everything Pieter had told us, descriptions of mountainous seas, tropical islands, ancient treasures, they could all have been found in the pages of an encyclopaedia.

'I'm not sure.' I rubbed his arm gently, demonstrating my concern.

'I wondered ...'

'What?'

'The business of the window, being shut in ... Perhaps he was in prison and Mother and Pappy are too ashamed to tell us.' Hans got to his feet, lurching slightly and put out a hand to steady himself. 'I've got to go. I've got work in the morning.'

'Oh Hans!'

He opened my bedroom door and stood there, his head bent.

I waited.

'Sss ... funny. I wanted him back more than anything. I thought we'd be so happy, as we were before he went. Only we're not.'

He went out then and closed the door.

I stayed curled up on the floor thinking back to the photographs taken every year in November, ready for the celebration of St Nicholas Eve. Only one had my uncle in it, Pappy's brother, with me as a baby on Mother's lap.

There were several with grandfather and grandmother, and two with grandmother on her own. The pictures taken after Pieter vanished always had a gap in them. However hard the photographer worked to arrange us, an empty space appeared among the smiling faces. Now I wondered if the weight of Pieter's presence might once again skew it.

Pulling out my journal, I flicked back over the entries for the past ten days. I had made a conscious decision to set to paper only the day to day happenings and no longer try to understand or record my feelings. I had failed miserably, unable to keep them under control, my emotions writing themselves into print.

I opened the entry for my birthday, adding the words: *this was the last time we were all truly happy.*

A moment later, I crossed out *happy*, replacing it with the word *content*. Happiness is rare, as fleeting as the tiny flakes of snow that herald the first storms of winter. Contentment lasts longer, and with a family I loved and who loved me, there had been true contentment. Now Mother, Pappy, and Pieter were deliriously happy, Berthe was content and Hans was neither.

*

I was about to climb back into bed when I heard footsteps on the road. Believing Hans to have gone out again, I ran over to the window meaning to tell him not to be so silly, that it would take time to adjust to Pieter's return as it had his departure, and he must be patient.

It wasn't Hans. It was Pieter.

He leant over the rail, his head bowed, staring into the water for the longest while. A light shone out from the Endelbaum house, creating a shiver of fleeting brightness on its dark surface. I couldn't see his face; it was the slump of his shoulders that gave away his despair. Yet what could be so troubling? He was home with the family whom he loved and who loved him, and he had found a girlfriend. As if making up his mind about something, he pushed up on his arms, bracing them against the rail. Swivelling on his heel, he glanced up at the light shining from Ruth's fourth-floor bedroom window. Blowing it a kiss, he took off across the bridge.

I checked my watch. It said 11.45.

20

I came downstairs next morning to discover Pieter already there, clear-eyed as if he had slept eight hours. He was chatting with Pappy and Hans about some new machinery, which cut glass more effectively than our old hand cutter that had been in use for generations. This was something Hans was familiar with, and I felt pleased for him. He appeared pale and worn, and the alcohol had left dark bruises under his eyes. But more cheerful too, secure in his knowledge, and I guessed that had been Pappy's intention.

'What about the range of hand mirrors we were discussing the other day. Could it cut the glass for those?'

'I tried it out yesterday morning, Pieter. The cut is so clean, polishing its edges will be kept to a minimum. Only, I am not sure of the size? How large should hand mirrors be? Maidy, what do you think?' Hans asked me.

It was breezy outside and the curtains stirred, their tasselled fringes flapping against the open windows like a muffled drum beating out a call to arms. It was chilly too. I had gooseflesh on my arms but no one got up to close the window.

I sat down next to him. 'About what?'

'What size mirror you would like on your dressing table?'

'Ask Ruth. I am happy with the one Pappy gave me.'

'Hand mirrors are notoriously difficult to make,' Pappy mused.

'Why is that, Pappy?'

He cleared his throat with a sip of coffee. 'With only basic machinery, cutting on an oval, or a shape of any kind, is tricky, especially if the diameter is small. Unless you're very experienced, you will end up with a distortion rather than an exact image. That's why Baders have always kept away from them.'

'But Pappy, you made one for Maidy.'

'I forgot about that, Hans.' He raised his head. 'So I did.' Pappy didn't smile; he beamed out his contentment with life. 'Is it useful?'

I couldn't admit that for years it had been my most faithful friend, even though I could only inspect a fraction of my head at a time. Last evening, when I tried on my new clothes, I had dragged my swing mirror from its corner and spent the next half hour preening, loving my sandals with bare feet. Then I had sat down on the floor in my finery, studying the fairies Pappy had painted for me, in awe of the magic he held in his fingers, capable of capturing a sparkle of sunlight in a spider's web on which a fairy was dancing.

I'd been careful to place the mirror with its back to the window, fearing even at dusk a repeat of those same dark images. The flaw hadn't vanished; it was still there in the topmost corner, a little larger than before. It still resembled black feathers, although I had been relieved to discover it no longer held me in its thrall. Pappy's explanation had taken that away, like a poisonous snake that becomes harmless once its deadly fangs are removed, and I now felt comfortable in its presence.

'The best gift ever,' I burst out. 'I use it every single day. And my music box, do you remember, Pieter?'

'That old thing! I only paid a few cents for it. At the time, I felt ashamed I couldn't afford to get you something better. If you want, I'll buy you a new one.'

'Pieter, don't you remember? Even as a child, Maidy preferred old toys to new,' Pappy reminded gently. 'We need to borrow your mirror for a day. May we?'

My face must have radiated shock. I had seen Hans testing mirrors, shattering them to pieces. 'Not if Hans is going to break it.'

Hans grinned at me.

Pappy chortled. 'It will be given back to you in one piece. I only want to see if the reflection has become distorted. How old were you, Maidy, when I made it? I can't remember.'

'Neither can I.'

I feigned ignorance, not wanting to spoil breakfast by allowing memories to sit down with us. Those years of tragedy needed no reminder.

'Mm.' He tapped the table thoughtfully. 'I can see a problem looming. We daren't use a traditional gilt surround, it would make it too heavy.'

I remembered other breakfasts with Pappy talking aloud the problems of his work. If we wanted to join in, we could. He would listen seriously, considering our words, including us all in the life of our family business.

'We are going ahead though, Pappy, aren't we?' Pieter said anxiously. 'You said yourself we needed new markets.'

'Pappy's not about to go back on his word, Pieter,' Hans interjected. 'Have you forgotten? This is what he does ... talks out the problems.' He grinned slyly at Pappy, 'Says it gets rid of all the woolly bits in his brain.'

'I'll go and get it.' I chased back upstairs to my bedroom, delight in the normalcy of the conversation speeding my steps. All this week, my sleep had been broken by concern for one or the other of my brothers. I so hoped the strain was gone for good. As children, despite their arguing, and the resentment Hans had felt at being the younger sibling, whenever danger threatened, the two of them had always stood shoulder to shoulder. At school, if one had a bloody nose most probably the other would be sporting a black eye. Pappy never asked what happened to the boys they fought.

I loved my bedroom with its wide sweeping walls, curved and rounded as the hull of a long boat. My bed ran down its middle, the only spot where I might stand up straight, with my arms outstretched, and not touch the ceiling. I had swathed its whitewashed walls in coloured pieces of fabric I'd found in the market. When the summer sun caught at the side window, they gleamed like flags of the countries I wanted to visit.

Berthe's room backed onto our neighbour's and only in midsummer did the sun rays reach round far enough to shine through her window. I had never understood why she chose it. Maybe it was slightly the bigger, although not by much, certainly not enough to renounce sunshine. At the back of the house were two more rooms, the mirror image of ours, where we stored winter bedding and summer curtains.

Berthe and I also had matching sets of furniture, chests, and armoires, which Grandfather had carved from a length of ash. Rarely used for furniture, it was a pretty wood, tinging grey in sunlight as if bleached by salt air. To stop it staining, Pappy had covered both chests with a thick layer of glass, cut flush with the edges of the wood. With electricity failing so often, we always kept candles and matches by our bedside, and the glass was mired with traces of wax. Next to my reading lamp stood the little music box Pieter had given me, crowded with memories. I felt grateful to Pappy for warning Pieter not to think of replacing it; if he had, its memories would have gone too.

Snatching up my hand mirror, I ran back downstairs, sealing the loan with a reproving kiss. 'If you break it, Pappy, you'll have to make me another.' Hearing Mother and Berthe on the stairs, I picked up my cup and vanished into the kitchen to get some fresh coffee, the dregs in my cup cold.

I heard Mother laugh and craned around the kitchen door to see why. Pappy was peering into my little mirror, slanting it to catch the light and tilting his head, his mouth twisted and his eyebrows raised, the same as women often do when they apply makeup.

'What did I tell you?' He pointed triumphantly, passing the mirror to Hans and then Pieter. I watched them preen, their faces angled first one way and then another, as if they were birds intrigued by their reflection, and I joined Berthe and Mother in the general merriment.

'Pappy, if I'd guessed you wanted to admire yourself in a mirror, I'd have bought you one for your birthday.'

'Margaret,' Pappy exclaimed. He pushed back his chair and struggled to his feet. Over the years, sitting had given him stiff knees and, first thing in the morning, you could see pain in his face when he stood up. 'No wonder I married you.' He raised Mother's hand to his lips, kissing it gently. We'd seen the gesture a million times, reaffirming his love for her. 'You have brains enough for all of us.' She blushed prettily and the moment was over.

'Hans … Pieter.' Pappy sat down again, leaving Mother to take her place beside Pieter. I noticed she had taken to wearing a shawl round her shoulders. 'That is your job for the day.'

'Pappy?' she exclaimed.

'My dear, you have given me a most splendid idea. We will send our sons together out into the big city.' Pappy's tone was intentionally dramatic. He only did it to make us laugh, loving us as much as we loved him. As I went to sit down, I dropped a kiss on his head, aware I'd misjudged him and he had also felt the strain of the past days. Reaching up, he gently patted my hand. 'To see for themselves,' he continued, 'exactly how slapdash the products of our competitors are. In the meantime,' his tone changed becoming serious again, 'I will talk to Lars about what sort of backing to use. We might try mercury.'

'No Pappy. It's no longer in use,' Mother exclaimed, 'and with good reason.'

'My dear, my ancestors used it safely for hundreds of years.' Pappy rubbed his hand over his freshly shaved chin.

I was never allowed into the furnace room as a child, Pappy fearing my inquisitive fingers might cause an accident, although Pappy and Hans had talked about it often enough so I knew the process. Pappy had always preferred mercury and still occasionally used it, saying how it always gave a pure reflection without shadows or distortions. Unfortunately, the metal was highly toxic and needed careful handling.

I picked up my little mirror from the table. The oval was too small to take a bevel, another skill Pieter would have to learn when he took up his apprenticeship again. Delighted with my gift, I had seen only the delicate tracery of its metal surround, never bothering with the quality of it, using the mirror simply to check my hair or the collar on my blouse. Immediately, I noticed what Pappy and my brothers had already seen. At its tip lay a faint blue shadow. The mirror had been backed with silver so that it was safe for a child to use; yet, in some ways, silver proved even more difficult to handle than mercury. Glass and silver couldn't bond without the addition of a chemical adhesive. Years of patient work were needed to learn this particular skill – the reason why apprenticeships were so long. The slightest irregularity, a patch left thinly coated or a microscopic blemish, and blue shadows rapidly emerged through the glass as tarnish formed.

'If we use silver, at least we are certain it will be safe. I'm positive no other firm is as skilful when it comes to silver backings. We are still the only company that offers a guarantee of twenty years.'

'Large mirrors, yes, Hans. Using silver on something so small and intricate ... Besides, it will make them expensive. We might try aluminium ... I never have.' Pappy shook his head doubtfully.

I finished my breakfast, content to let the conversation roam around me, aware I was slowly becoming used to seeing Pieter in his old place. They continued to chat, their voices arguing a point, their gestures friendly, all embracing; Mother and Berthe smiling too, their heads together. It was how it had always been and I wanted it to continue. I hated the tension and its secrets.

Then the door in the yard clicked open and the picture vanished. That morning, Ruth had chosen another new outfit, a divided skirt in light green. Twinned with a blouse, over it she wore a tan corduroy jacket with leather buttons. With her dark eyes and amber-coloured hair, it was a perfect match. Her clip-on earrings sparkled in the early light, as did her eyes when she kissed Pappy, reaching out with her hand to greet Pieter.

'You look wonderful,' he said, rising to his feet and pulling out a chair for her to sit down. 'May I get you some coffee?'

'Please. No more than a thimble-full.' She slid her hand across the breakfast cloth as an accompaniment to her words. 'Mevrouw Bader, may Pieter use one of the dinner cups? They're so very pretty.'

'Of course, my dear.'

'I heard you all laughing as I came in. What's going on?'

'It's Pappy and Pieter,' Mother smiled at her fondly. 'They were discussing a new range of mirrors.'

It may only have been a few days, nevertheless, I was aware Mother had set her mind on Pieter and Ruth marrying – as clearly as if she had written out wedding invitations and left the card on the mantelshelf for us to read. I'd overheard her consulting with Ruth on arrangements for the dinner to celebrate Pieter's homecoming, to which the Endelbaums and

Mevrouw Kleissler had been invited. At the time I'd thought it strange. Our neighbours had been present at every celebration since they returned to the city – it was nothing special for them to eat with us. Then I realised she was nervous, wanting to impress, to present us as a suitable family, and for Meneer and Mevrouw Endelbaum to approve of Pieter as a prospective son-in-law.

Carrying the delicate china carefully, Pieter placed the tiny cup in front of Ruth. As he sat down, she skimmed her fingers lightly across the back of his hand in thanks. 'I have never been into the workshop. Will you show me round, Pieter? I'd love to see it. Oh, I forgot!' She jumped to her feet, placing her bag on the table and pushing her coffee cup aside. 'Maidy, don't you just love my new outfit. And isn't this jacket the most glorious colour? Autumn leaves they call it, and my culottes are absolutely the latest thing from Paris. And terribly proper.'

Not waiting for a reply, she twirled on the spot, the hem of her skirt flaring out. 'Pappy ... I know you didn't approve of my trousers.' She peeped sideways at him. 'You may have said they were charming but I saw your face; it was all scrunched up, like this.' She scowled fiercely, her eyebrows almost resting on top of her long lashes.

Automatically, I joined in the laughter. Only Hans was silent. Head bent, he toyed with the cheese on his plate, cutting it into miniscule strips, his smile as automatic as his gesture – and equally as meaningless.

'Maidy, would you mind if I ride with Ruth to college?' Pieter called across the table. 'Hans, perhaps you and I can meet up in the city later on. It will be good to be together again.'

Panic flooded into Ruth's face and I caught the spark of entreaty she flashed at me across the table. It wasn't all right and she needed my help to make it so.

'I don't think you've ever been out that way, have you,

Pieter?' Pappy asked before I could speak. 'I remember it was out of bounds during the war. When we were little, my brother and I often cut school on a summer's day to spend it by the lake. I regret to say we stole bread and cheese from the larder ...' He glanced light-heartedly at Mother, aware she disapproved of any form of stealing, even food. 'That and perhaps an apple or two kept us going till evening. It's a pretty place. A nice ride, by all accounts.'

I kept quiet, mindful that Ruth would go along with the change of plan rather than offend Pappy. No different from our neighbour's cat that regularly curled up on our doorstep, rather than the dirty mat outside the tobacconist's shop, Ruth needed my family in her life; her own too sick and careworn to give her joy. The love she held for Pappy was totally genuine, perhaps the most genuine thing about her.

I had only once felt sorry for Ruth, when Meneer Endelbaum confided to Pappy their flight and eventual capture by the invaders. They had survived but the aftermath had proved as permanent as a wine stain, and impossible to eradicate. Pappy told me there'd been another child; it had died at birth and was never mentioned.

I picked up a roll and quickly buttered it, meaning to eat it later. Before, it would have earned me a rebuke, an insistence that I sat and ate my breakfast properly. Now, Mother didn't even notice.

'I'll walk down with you.' Hans got to his feet and pulled out his fob-watch, his expression full of jealous anger. 'I'm late for work, anyway.'

I bit my lip but kept quiet until Hans had closed the sitting room door. I felt uncomfortable, sensing the placid river on which our family sailed once again disturbed and angry, as water is whenever lock gates are first opened. 'Hans?'

'Not another lecture,' he glowered at me and waved me ahead of him down the stairs.

I ignored him. 'Hans, I'm on your side.' My fist pounded his chest lightly in confirmation of my words. 'It's not fair if you let your feeling for Ruth destroy your love for Pieter. He's not to blame.'

'I know.' He straightened his shoulders, heading on down the back stairs in front of me. Twisting the knob, he pulled open the yard door. Below our feet, the furnace was roaring out its demand for food. 'What you said before, Maidy, it makes sense.' His grin was twisted and I realised how much he was hurting inside. 'I might go away for the summer. If Pieter and Ruth …'

'You really love her, don't you?'

I watched his fists clench hard as if struck by a sudden pain. 'I've always loved her. I realise she's never thought of me that way, I was only ever a brother to her. I still hoped that one day … she might. Then Pieter came back into our lives. What chance did I ever have against his good looks and charm?' He shrugged. 'All I've got is the memory of those summer evenings, the three of us riding along the canals … they were like heaven.'

I remembered our bikes swishing silently along the towpath towards the coast, the summer air warm and fresh, not stifling as it was in the close-knit streets of the old city. All around us sea grass whispered its secrets, while a gentle breeze ruffled our hair. The moon soared overhead, joyously sharing its light with a million stars. A delicate globe of silver that changed Ruth into Diana, the huntress; poor Hans, he would have needed the strength of Hercules to escape falling in love.

I crossed the yard, feeling the wind brisk on my face, the sun already bright. I'd locked my bicycle away in the garage, not wanting to tempt fate. I could find no more words, so I waved and took off down the street, thinking what a mess it all was.

Poor Hans; he and Tristan were a fine pair … and I could

help neither of them. Before anyone had been aware of my presence in the sports hall, I had watched Tristan. Conscious of Ruth in the stands he had been acting out a courtship ritual, augmenting his natural skill with energy and purpose, the alpha male showing off to attract a female, instantly becoming the most effective player on the court.

It was early, the roads empty. I kept to the main road, leaving the pathways to Pieter and Ruth. As a tram passed by, its iron wheels grating noisily against the tracks, I caught the eye of one of its passengers – a boy about my own age. He raised his eyebrows approvingly. I suddenly remembered I was sixteen, dressed in new clothes, with a whole new world opening up. I shook off my dark thoughts and smiled back.

21

I caught up with Jules at the bridge and we cycled along the highway together. The road was quiet, with only an occasional car swishing past. We didn't talk much. When we did, bless him, he didn't once mention Ruth, although when he first spotted me, I read in his eyes the expectation I might be the bearer of good tidings.

'What's over there?' He pointed out over the lake, the silhouette of a fishing boat dipping in and out of sight in the early morning haze.

'You mean Klüsta?'

'Not there! I meant the other side of the lake. I've often seen boats heading in that direction and wondered.'

'Oh!' I felt instant relief, even a casual reference capable of awakening the dark shadows of my dream. 'That's Norland.'

'Norland? Never heard of it.'

'Yes, you have. I bet you eat something from there every week. We do.'

I was surprised to see Jules grin. He'd always seemed so serious before, yet when he relaxed even his blotches became less visible. 'I'm not much interested in food. My mother's always threatening to mince up my text books and serve them on toast, because I've usually got my head in a book – even at mealtimes.' He stopped his bike and got off, shielding his eyes from the glare. 'I can't see anything.'

I slowed to a halt beside him. 'I promise you, it's there. Very few people know of it because the people keep to themselves and only ever visit the city to sell their produce.'

'Produce?'

'Butter and cheese. I love their soft cheese, especially when it's spread on new rolls warm from the bakers. They also make a hard cheese, and sometimes we use that to make cheese on toast. Ask your Mother and look in the larder,' I said confidently. 'The label is yellow with a windmill and a cow on it.'

'Is there a road?'

I pointed west towards the bluff on which our college stood. 'Only as far as the western edges of the lake. Beyond that, it's little more than a track and rarely used, especially in winter because it floods. Besides, it's quicker by boat. There's a ferry service now on a Saturday. My brother and Ru ... a friend went.' I eyed Jules quickly from under my lashes, relieved to find he'd not picked up on my gaffe, his attention drawn to the fringes of the lake as if seeking out the road I had mentioned. 'He got talking to an old man who had apparently never left the village; never even listened to a radio. When the city offered to install electricity, the elders refused, saying they preferred water power.'

Jules whistled his astonishment. 'It sounds fascinating. Would you go with me if I went?'

I hesitated. 'In the holiday, perhaps, when we have more time.' I tried not to sound doubtful. It wasn't anyone's business except my own that I never crossed the bridge, nervous even of the little streets that bordered the harbour. My knowledge of the ferry service was second-hand, supplied by Hans who often went there to sketch the fishing boats. For my birthday one year, he'd given me one of his sketches, making a frame for it in the workroom downstairs. Delicately drawn, the quaint old houses fronting the dockside were a fitting portrayal of a bygone age. I'd hung it in the study explaining that the walls of my bedroom were far too crowded. In truth, I was a little scared that its pencil image might trigger my memory of those dark shadows.

We rode on, chatting in a desultory fashion about the day ahead. I felt completely at ease with him, although I recognised for most girls he would seem too serious, obsessed with his plans for a future that included his becoming a world-famous doctor.

Swans were feeding in the shallows, a group of thirty or more. A few had strayed onto the canals, sharing their breakfast with the ducks, and I wondered if the swan I'd once rescued was among them.

'I've never been this early,' I exclaimed as we cycled up the long driveway. The spring warmth had swollen the camellia buds on the bushes. In another few weeks, their dull green leaves would erupt into a carnival of colour. Ahead, the school yard sported a solitary bicycle, parked next to the car belonging to the director. Even our professors cycled.

'It's worth it to get a parking place.' Jules pushed his bike into the rack by the main door. 'I usually work – it's peaceful.' He raised his hand. 'See you soon.'

I felt too restless to work and wandered across the lawn, heading for the lake. Here, there was nothing except clear air and wide sweeping borders, where narcissi bloomed in spring and dahlias in autumn. Just after I started my studies here, we had a really hot spell, and Professor Dulmes allowed us to carry our work into the shade of the willows by the lakeside, their long fronds casting green shadows onto the pages of our books. Meneer Hendricks, the porter, once showed me an album of photographs that had been discovered when the building was stripped. Family groups with women and children enjoying a picnic in the summer sunshine. Meneer Hendricks is old. Few of our staff were young; it was the young men who were killed in the war.

I sat down on a bench close to the water. It was not long after eight, the air fresh and the sun warm on my back. My thoughts were once more sifting through the changes Pieter's arrival had made to the even tenor of our lives, rather as if an earthquake had struck in the night, creating a subtle shift in the alignment of our house.

'I behaved badly, yesterday. I'm sorry.'

I jumped. I didn't need to turn around, although I did. I knew his voice, as gentle and caressing as the first strands of sunlight after a long winter.

It was a false impression. I'd read an article about the breaking in of wild horses, how young stallions kicked and bucked until exhausted, even using their teeth to defend themselves. That was Zande; beautiful yet untamed, and as wild as any stallion. Anyone with any sense would keep well away from his flailing hooves. I knew I should find an excuse to leave, only I couldn't move … Something stronger than caution and good sense held me in its grip.

His hair was wet; he'd been swimming.

'But the water's so cold,' I burst out without thinking.

'I hope you haven't been peeking?' he said, his eyes glittering with suppressed amusement.

My brain stopped and I found myself gaping like a fish, unable to think of anything to say. I blushed, coming out with, 'Why?' which was somewhat foolish of me.

He didn't reply for a moment, idly examining the tiny beach. Where winter storms had washed away the soil, clumps of willow roots lay exposed, brown and clumsy looking. 'It's nice out here,' he commented, letting me off the hook. 'Am I forgiven?'

'It's not *my* forgiveness you need,' I said tartly. 'It's Elina's. How can you be so cruel?'

He shrugged. 'She's a girl – of no importance.'

'What a horrid thing to say. Girls have feelings.'

'Do they?' He cocked his head as if debating the question, an amused smile on his lips.

It was a truly beautiful smile, at one edge a tiny mocking twist that made you want to stroke it away with your finger and smooth it out.

'They are acquisitive and greedy, certainly.' He saw my frown. 'Do you even know what I mean?'

I did, and considered acquisitive an odd choice of word to use. Possessive would have been more suitable. 'And Ruth?'

'Ah, yes, the divine Ruth.' He slowly shook his head from side to side as if seriously debating my words. 'A chap would consider himself very fortunate to be with her. She's very special.'

Maybe I shouldn't have asked the question if I hadn't wanted to hear the answer.

'Yet, so very foolish. I have played this game many more times than she has.'

I was startled, shocked even, to hear my own thoughts being repeated back to me.

Zande fell silent, studying the ground at his feet. Lifting his head, 'And I *always* win.' The tiny mocking twist reappeared fleetingly at the corner of his mouth. 'You have a nasty habit of making me want to speak the truth, Magrit.' He said the words quite simply and I believed him.

'By the by, we did meet before,' Zande continued, nothing in his voice now except friendship and maybe a certain curiosity, as if I puzzled him.

'I don't remember.' I kept my gaze focussed on the rivulets, watching them break into a kaleidoscope of sparkling colour as they washed across the pebbles on the shoreline.

'You were angry then, too.' He squatted down on his haunches by my side, his dark curly head on a level with my arm. 'Why did you tell me your name was Magrit – it's Maidy, isn't it?' He plucked idly at a daisy, inspecting its tiny petals closely.

'Maidy is only a nickname for friends.'

'May I be a friend?'

The words were softly spoken and, once again, they sounded sincere. You could never doubt. I felt my breath desert me.

I had scribbled out that facile statement in my journal, *in Zande, sincerity exists like a vein of gold buried deep in a mine,* replacing it with the words: *beauty and sincerity do not necessarily walk hand in hand.* I had added a large full stop for emphasis, convinced I would never be taken in again. Yet, once again, I found myself lost and floundering, undecided which way the shore lay. I felt myself lean in ... and caught the warning bell. Ruth. It tolled in my head and I leaned away. 'You can trust friends.'

'Not always, Magrit.'

I caught the bitterness, a silenced cry of pain as if he had been dealt a vicious blow. I wondered then what it was that made him punish the world. My eyes searched for his and I read in them a terrible yearning. It vanished, replaced by an emptiness, an absence of hope, and I understood why he pulled wings off butterflies.

I held out my hand in the formal gesture that Jaan had used. 'I will be your friend, nothing more.'

I did not add: *But don't play your games with me. I am not Elina or Ruth.*

'I won't,' he said, replying to my unspoken question. He took my hand and shook it, rubbing his thumb gently over the hollow between the base of my thumb and forefinger. There was a long silence. I found myself unable to move, overcome by a feeling of languor as if the morning air had wrapped me in its velvet arms.

He stood up, his expression once again inscrutable. I felt him hesitate and knew his next words were designed to hurt. Exactly as he had done at the canal.

'However, I make no promises as to my behaviour with others.' He tossed the daisy into my lap and swung away.

On impulse, I called after him. 'How old are you?'

He stopped. I saw the muscles in his back stiffen. 'How old do you think I am?'

'Nineteen, perhaps twenty.'

'That's sounds about right. Why?' He stepped back towards me, regarding me curiously.

'You're too young to be so disillusioned. You must have a very poor opinion of our sex,' I protested, keeping a sharp edge to my tone. I needed it for protection, like a sword.

'I adore girls.' He saluted the air. 'I just don't trust them. They leech the life out of you.'

He saw my bewilderment and relented. 'Boys are straightforward. Where there is desire, they follow it. Girls cannot accept that. They complicate matters becoming clingy … needy … disgusting. And if they come across something better – they trample you in the mud.'

The final words were flung into the air as a challenge.

'You're following the wrong career. You should have been an actor,' I said calmly.

He burst into laughter, startling a sandpiper that had been diligently scouring the shore. It flew off.

'Oh Maidy … Maidy, Maidy! Why did I never find you before?'

In the distance, bicycle bells were ringing out. Out of the corner of my eye, I noticed Waldger approach across the lawn. Like Zande, his hair was wet, although he looked as he always did … cheerful and kindly. It was a false image. I wondered if the four boys had become friends because they shared something in common; all of them cruel. I remembered

195

then the toadstools I had once found, gloriously decorative, their beautiful exterior camouflaging the poison beneath. I dismissed the thought as unfair. I had no idea what made Zande behave so badly. Whatever it was, it must have been a deadly blow. I knew nothing about Tristan either; it was unjust to include him. I put it down to the hurt I felt whenever I thought of Jaan.

Waldger waved. I saw him glance first at Zande and then at me, his gaze speculative. 'Pastures new?'

Zande draped an arm nonchalantly across his friend's shoulders. 'Magrit? No, she was busily cutting me down to size.' He gave a bow and, with an oddly sensitive smile, spun Waldger around, heading back towards the college forecourt. 'So what was so important that you had to interrupt my tryst with a fair young lady?'

His voice faded away and I was alone. I stared down at the daisy in my lap and gently raised it to my lips before pressing it in my book. He'd asked for forgiveness. That I could grant easily. Even love, if he'd asked for it.

But he hadn't.

I had to go. Literature was beckoning. I pulled out my journal, writing in it: *I know what Zande meant by greed. Poor Elina – she fell headfirst into that trap. He showed her the stars and she wanted the sun.* Then I closed away the pages, fastening them tightly with an elastic binder, and went to my class.

22

That was the moment I made a decision to opt out of worrying about who liked whom, and whether Ruth was two-timing Pieter or not. When I bumped into Kirsten at lunchtime on the Friday, I greeted her with delight. She had changed her hair style – copying mine – and was wearing it in a ponytail. She looked nice.

'I'm starving and need lunch. Join me, why don't you?'

'You can never get a seat,' I protested half-heartedly.

'I'll get you one, that's one of my best subjects – finding seats. Come on.' Kirsten linked her arm in mine, giving me little choice but to match my steps with hers. A few students raised their heads as we entered the refectory, and I heard a muttered: 'Why is Magrit not with Ruth? Have they fallen out?' I had to guess at the whispered response: *It's over that new boy, the dark one. I saw them quarrelling in the sports hall.*

Kirsten pinched my arm. 'Take no notice. Earlier they were going on about Elina. I wanted to slap them.'

'Where *is* Ruth?' The dining hall reminded me of a battleground, the clash of metal cooking pots marginally outdoing the thunderous conversation, which was another reason for not eating there.

Kirsten grabbed a tray. 'She's with Tristan, probably in the sports hall. Haven't a clue what she sees in him.'

I raised my eyebrows.

'Beyond his obvious good looks and amazing physique, I mean.' She gave me a cheeky grin. 'Rumour has it that he's monosyllabic unless he's talking about sports.' She twisted round, pointing to the menu on the counter. 'Open sandwich or cooked? They have dumplings and stew today – that's pretty good, too.' She caught my look of astonishment. What?' She laughed. 'I love food and refuse to give it up to have a figure like yours.'

'I'm straight up and down.'

She nudged me with her elbow. 'The crookedest straight up and down I've ever seen. So … which is it to be?'

I gurgled with laughter, delighted with the compliment. Pappy once told me my laugh reminded him of waking to a sunny May morning and hearing bird song. I wondered where; certainly not in our city. Here we have mostly seagulls. Hans, who was listening, asked if Pappy meant a corncrake. I had read somewhere that a corncrake was dull and rather ordinary. Pappy frowned and laughed at the same time. He wrapped his arm around me, berating Hans for teasing his sister.

'I'll have an open sandwich, please. If I eat a heavy meal at lunchtime, I will want to sleep, and I have an afternoon of history,' I chatted to the woman serving us.

'Since I have two brothers who are absolute devils and drive me mad, I'll have dumplings. And if I fall asleep, too bad.'

The assistant smiled sympathetically. I guessed she had sons and knew first-hand how much energy they had.

'Follow me.' Kirsten announced grandly, grabbing apples and glasses of water from the next counter and piling them on her tray. Making her way straight through the tables, she headed for the swing doors at the far side of the refectory. In the time I had been at college, I'd not visited this part of the building. It belonged to the economics faculty; each of the faculties jealously guarding their allotted space. She pushed open the door of an empty lecture room, tiers of bench seats facing a blackboard.

'I promised you a table.' She waved her arm airily. 'Take your pick.'

A single window opened onto the sports field with its backdrop of woods. A game of football was in progress. Figures darted across the glass, disappeared for a moment before reappearing and racing back in the opposite direction.

'So why no Elina?' I said, sliding into the front row next to her.

'She's cut classes to go sailing with Zande. He gave her flowers the other evening after school. Told her he'd behaved like a heel.'

I bit hungrily into my sandwich, prawns and salad on poppy-seed bread. 'Sailing?' I muttered my mouth full.

'He has a boat.'

I hastily swallowed. 'Oh, so that's why.'

'Why what? Honestly, Magrit, you really are bad at this friendship thing. You never told me you actually shouted at him. And what does: *oh, so that's why,* mean?'

Her face said it all; pop-eyed and staring at me, the food on her plate forgotten. I didn't dare admit I'd seen the boys swimming naked, her scream would have roused the entire building. 'I was chatting to him, this morning. His hair was wet. Do you think ...' I didn't quite blush, although I hesitated.

'That Elina's gone all the way?' It was an awkward phrase to use and I considered her amazing to say it so nonchalantly. 'No, not yet.'

I took a bite of my sandwich. 'How do you know?'

'She'd tell me if she had. Besides, he hasn't dumped her.'

I flinched.

'Come on, Magrit, didn't your mother ever warn you …?'

'No! She never …'

'Not once?'

'My sister did. But … before you're married? Berthe would never speak of that. To her, it's a mortal sin.'

'You mean, *sleeping with a boy*. You can't avoid the word Magrit, you're not that prim and proper. Besides, if you eavesdrop on conversations at college, it's often about that. At least with the senior boys it is.'

'It doesn't roll off my tongue as easily as yours. Remember, I come from the old city,' I added by way of explanation.

Kirsten grinned impudently. 'You make the old city sound like a chastity belt. I promise you, it happens more often than you can possibly imagine. My mother says if you sleep with a boy before you marry him, he'll go off you. She says they want to marry virgins, yet spend all their time deflowering every girl who'll let them. Apparently, they can't help it. I'm not sure I believe her, although I'm not brave enough to try it out for myself.' Frowning down at her plate, she took a mouthful of stew, chewing thoughtfully. 'I checked the office. Apparently his family come from Klüsta …'

I jumped. The dark images of my nightmare swept across my vision. I felt a pulse pounding in my ears. '*The island?*' My voice came out as a squeak as I pointed vaguely over my shoulder.

'Magrit, what's up? You've gone white.'

'I get nightmares about that place,' I confessed, surreptitiously taking a calming breath.

'You mean when it was used as a prison?'

I grabbed her explanation as a lifeline, unable to admit my phobia had nothing to do with the invasion of our country. If only I had never looked in the mirror and seen those dark shadows creeping towards the harbour. 'Yes.'

'I'm the same. It gives me goose bumps even thinking about it. According to his application—'

'You saw it?' I broke in.

'Shush! Yes,' she whispered. 'My aunt, Dad's sister, works for the City Fathers at the Town Hall. Sometimes she brings work home.'

'And she let you?'

'What the eye doesn't see ...' Kirsten quoted. She spotted my shocked expression and scowled. 'Now don't get all prissy. Elina's my best friend and she's being led down the garden path. Of course, I needed to find out about Zande.'

'I wasn't being prissy, as you call it,' I swallowed loudly, and quickly changed the subject. 'I remember my father warning Hans: never to swim in the lake near the harbour. He said it was dangerous.'

'I can go one better than that.' Kirsten flashed her grin, instantly diverted. 'My dad told me never to go into the old city because people there were barely human.' I bit into my sandwich, grateful not to be questioned further. 'I read the letter this man ...'

'What man?'

'Van Vliet. He's the one sponsoring Zande. Apparently, he owns all the land on the southern half of the lake, including the island.' She stopped, her mouth all screwed up as if she was sucking on a lemon. 'According to the letter he wrote to the City Fathers, when the invasion happened the people took to their boats and escaped across the lake ...' Kirsten wriggled her shoulders. 'I knew it was a bird sanctuary, I never knew people once lived there. Anyway, he's offered to lease them the land on which the college stands for a peppercorn rent, provided the city agrees to his family staying permanently in the area. There'd been trouble in the past, and he wanted an assurance it wouldn't happen again.'

'Trouble ... what sort of trouble?' I asked timidly.

'Didn't say. It had to be important because it was underlined.'

'Go on.'

'That's it. He's asked for the older boys to study here every summer. Apparently, they sometimes go away in winter.'

Scraping up the last of her stew, Kirsten suddenly burst out: 'Okay, so I told my aunt a few lies. I said it was research. I don't approve of lying although I promise you it was necessary … especially if they're leaving again at the end of the summer. Elina's the sort of stupid girl who, when she hears that, will let him have his wicked way in the hope of keeping him here.'

'You mean she's in love with him?'

Kirsten snorted. 'Magrit, *honestly!* Pretty much every girl in college, including me, is madly in love with Zande. Have you ever seen anything as beautiful? I bet, if God himself came down to Earth tomorrow, he wouldn't look as good. The way Zande walks … he must have ball bearings on his feet. And have you ever noticed how he undresses you with his eyes. I found myself hoping I had clean knickers on.'

I began to giggle again. Relief, I suppose, that Zande treated every girl the same, followed by a spark of intense irritation at the realisation that I might, after all, be no different.

Except, I was.

That first day when he launched his ferocious charm, he had resembled a threshing machine harvesting wheat from a field, unwilling to let even a single stalk escape.

I had though – I had escaped. However much Kirsten tried to make me believe he treated every girl the same, he *was* different with me. He'd told me so quite plainly, that day I first saw him with Elina. He had no intention of involving me in his game of seduction.

Or of seducing me.

Yet he could so easily have made me love him. I had sensed it for the briefest of moments before he backed away and hid his real self beneath scorn and derision. He had sought me out as a child would, seeking a plaster for a cut knee, and had let me into secrets kept hidden from the world – how he despised himself for his destructive powers. He felt them like a canker. Nevertheless, he could no more stop hurting the people nearest to him, than the wheat could prevent the harvester obliterating every life form that dwelt within its strands.

But leaving?

For Pieter, maybe the removal of a rival for Ruth's affections was the best thing that could possibly happen. For me … that moment in the garden with Zande had been an unexpected and very precious gift.

I heard Kirsten say, 'So my job is to get that idiot of a girl's feet back on the ground before she winds up pregnant.'

I gasped with shock. 'You're not serious? You can't be.'

'Oh, I am. Girls do such stupid things in the name of love.'

Noticing the time, I hurriedly put my apple in my bag to eat later. 'We need to go. Here …' I fished in my bag for my purse, pulling out some coins. 'Thanks for my lunch.'

*

At the end of the day, not finding Ruth anywhere I cycled home alone. Lars and Pieter had been loading a consignment of mirrors, the familiar coffin shape of the packing cases lying in the open back of a lorry.

Securing its tailboard in place, Lars limped across the yard and pushed the gates back on their hinges, leaving Pieter to head out into the street and stop oncoming cars, directing the vehicle out onto the narrow roadway.

Closing the gates again, he slipped the bolts and with a wave of his arm, set off down the slope and disappeared into the workshop, his gammy leg thumping the ground as he walked.

Pieter took my bike and wheeled it across the yard, propping it up against the wall in the garage. 'Time for chat, or are you too busy?' he said, helping me unpack my books. 'That's going to take a while.' He pointed purposefully at the heavy volume of *War and Peace*, a bookmark poking out part way. 'I always think books as thick as that were written with but one purpose in mind.'

'What's that?' I said innocently, remembering Pieter's keen interest in the bookshop window.

'To keep you awake at night.' We strolled companionably across the yard, pausing by the back steps. 'I've scarcely seen you since I got back.'

I hitched the books more firmly under my arm. 'And whose fault is that?'

Pieter blushed, exchanging it for a friendly grin. He sat down on the top step, patting the empty space beside him. I hesitated and he grinned mischievously, 'Too fine in your new clothes to sit with your brother. Don't think I didn't notice the other day when you bought them.' He pulled out a handkerchief and spread it over the step. 'A few years ago, you wouldn't have bothered.'

'Until a few days ago, I was wearing navy blue and hating it. I never understand why Mother insists on navy blue when it's my absolutely worst colour.'

'Wasn't it the colour of your school uniform?'

'You seem to forget I'm no longer at school. I've been left almost a year now.'

Without thinking, I nudged him with my elbow, the gesture redolent of my childhood. I'd always confided my secrets this way and was surprised to discover how comfortable I was beginning to feel in his company. He was so relaxed, nothing ever seemed to disturb him. Without my being aware, his easy ways had slipped under my radar, the way a fencer uses a feint to penetrate their opponent's guard. 'Thanks for the handkerchief; this skirt has to last all year otherwise I'll be back in navy blue.' I hesitated, suddenly confiding, 'I thought perhaps I might try for a Saturday job in a shop then I can afford to buy my own clothes.'

Pieter stretched his legs, placing his feet on the bottom step. Once upon a time the four of us had camped for hours at a time outside the backdoor, my brothers involved in an argument over which game to play next.

'Would Mother and Pappy permit it?'

'I'd probably have to produce my birth certificate and point out the line where it says I'm sixteen. I am not sure if my being sixteen has actually registered with either of them yet.'

'I still think of you as a little girl. I suppose ...' he hesitated a moment, 'it's the good times we remember best. Those are the ones indelibly printed in our minds and hearts.'

Of course, Pieter had no memories of me growing up.

'Do you remember those games of tag we played?'

Pieter raised his head, peering out across the yard, his gaze alighting on the broken cobbles of the stable floor, where the rope we used to scale the fortress or the sides of a pirate ship still hung in plain view. 'Mother used to get so angry about our trekking dirt in from the street.'

'Remember Pappy putting his hands over his ears, begging us to hurry up and catch someone, otherwise he'd be deaf by evening?'

Pieter chuckled. 'If I remember rightly, it was Hans who usually won.'

Dear Hans, how he had pushed himself to win against his elder brother, yet, if asked, I knew he would swap all that for winning the game of life he and Pieter were playing. 'Only because you always let Berthe and me catch you.'

We exchanged smiles and I felt the great bond of affection that we children had shared spring to life again.

'May I ask you something?'

'Ask away.'

Pieter had been home only a short while. Even so, in that time he had grown in confidence. I was glad. It would have taken quite some courage to walk back into a family after being away six years. He must have felt so very nervous that first night. Yet, true to his real self, he had patiently set to work earning his place in the family again. How happy things would have been if Ruth wasn't there.

My thoughts screeched to a halt, ashamed of the pathway they were heading down. How could I? Ruth had been a part of our lives for as long as I could remember. You don't just dump someone because their actions make you uncomfortable. I hurried into speech, paying no heed to the pertinence of the question. 'Where do you go at night?'

Immediately, I felt ashamed, sensing Pieter's new-found confidence ebbing away, mirroring the water from the dredgers as they lifted their loads of grit into the air.

'You heard ... all the way from the top floor?'

I slipped my arm into his, unwilling to admit that after his disappearance, shadows on the stairs had taken on the shape of monsters. Night after night I had lain awake, too terrified to sleep until I had identified each creak and groan: the loud puff of air as the overhead light on the staircase switched off, the rattle of the cistern filling with water, a key grating in the lock three stories down, the soft rustle of the house sparrow as it settled down in the guttering above my head. I knew them all.

I could see Pieter battling with his reply, reluctant to give one. 'I walk. Sometimes I go to the lake and watch the dawn come up. I don't need much sleep.'

'So it was a lie about sleeping in your bed. And what you told us about travelling the world, was that a lie too?'

'No, no ... *no, Maidy!*' Pain crept into his voice. 'Every bit of that was true. It's the one thing I *can* talk about. Please.'

'What do you mean, talk about?' I leant my head against

his shoulder as I used to do, wanting to reassure him that I could be trusted with his secrets. 'It's my turn to apologise now,' I said, determined to confess my suspicions. 'I thought maybe you had taken your descriptions from an encyclopaedia. And Hans … he … I mean … we wondered if you'd been in prison?'

Pieter groaned. 'If only I had.'

I waited for him to continue; to explain and put all the mysteries to bed once and for all. He gave a long sigh and took my hand between his. They were cool and I felt the pulse in his wrist beating steadily under the tip of my finger. 'You have always seen with eyes clearer than the rest of us. I was right to call you a changeling. I appreciate you have a thousand questions. Don't ask them, because I cannot answer.'

This time his sigh was a wretched, forlorn sound that came from despair. Whatever the dark secret he shared with my parents, it was a terrible one.

'Only one more …'

'Maidy!' he groaned.

'Are you in love with Ruth?'

'I think so, and she with me.' He sounded relieved.

Immediately, I threw aside my resolve never to interfere in Ruth's life again. I grabbed his hand, beating our joined fingers up and down against the air. 'If you honestly believe I can see more clearly than you, please … *please* listen to me. You are older than her …'

'No different from Mother and Pappy.' Releasing my hand, he picked up a pebble, flicking it across the yard.

There were almost eight years between my parents, except that was very different; Mother had been content to stay at home while Pappy made mirrors. Ruth would want to travel and see the world. 'Pieter, Ruth's no different from me; she's never had a boyfriend. You're her first. It's so easy to mistake your feelings at our age. '

He shook his head, his hair flopping down over his eyes. Impatiently, he brushed it away. 'No, she is much older than you, Maidy. Besides, she had such a wretched start in life; I simply want to take care of her.'

He got to his feet. Reaching up, I pulled on his hand. I felt him flinch back as if under attack. 'No more questions.' It was sharply said, brooking no argument and once again I felt the stranger in him rise to the fore.

'It's not a question,' I persisted. 'I only wanted to tell you … ever since your birthday that year … I've been collecting postcards about Monet.' To keep Pieter's memory alive, I'd taken to collecting postcards and news clippings of Monet's paintings, the water lilies we had chosen for Pieter by far the artist's favourite subject, painting them over a hundred times. I had already filled one scrapbook. 'Would you care to see them?'

'Yes, someday when we have time.' He brushed my words away, impatiently tapping his watch, and ignoring my questioning gaze. 'Come on. Let's get changed for dinner, otherwise there'll be a queue for the bathroom.'

Pulling open the back door, he paused. Letting it swing shut, he sat down again, his gaze fastened on a point across the yard, frowning at it almost defiantly. It startled me. This was an expression that belonged with Hans not Pieter. 'I only ever wanted one thing out of life, to make mirrors and be the best in the business, the same as Pappy. I'm determined to do that, whatever comes.' He got to his feet again and, as if reinstating his own personality, held out his hand to help me up. 'Maidy. Keep this conversation between you and me, as we always did?'

'Of course I will, Pieter.' I handed him back his handkerchief. 'You never need to ask that.'

23

Like an interlude between one act of a play and another, the welcome home dinner for Pieter passed off delightfully, as if the donning of party clothes also brought with it a determination to both give and take pleasure; the guests at our table basking in a bright glow of contentment that comes from good food, good wine, and good company.

As always, Mevrouw Kleissler talked non-stop. I noticed Pappy and Hans exchanging sly looks that included Pieter in their conspiracy. She was a kindly soul and a godsend in any difficult situation. Even Mevrouw Endelbaum had clapped her hands with delight at Pappy's jokes; the ever present spectre of their flight and capture momentarily forgotten. Yoav had been invited too. Pieter hadn't met him before and they seemed to get on well, but then Pieter always got on with everyone. I liked Yoav; he and Berthe were a good match. He was plain and she was pretty, although with his bone structure, his features would last a lifetime and change very little, whereas Berthe's prettiness would fade. Hans seemed better too. After a while, the alcohol in the wine dulled his pain and jealousy, reawakening the love he felt deep down for his brother.

We were late going to bed, Berthe and I tidying the pots away, and I fell asleep to the sound of my brother's footsteps tracking across the bridge. It reminded me of the promise I'd made and I wished he'd trusted me further. Whatever his secret, it would have been easier to bear than the weight of wondering what it could possibly be.

Next morning, I came downstairs to hear Mother berating Pappy soundly. 'You wear those old things all week – you cannot talk to customers dressed like that. They'll think you the errand boy.'

'My dear, no one could possibly mistake me for an errand boy, I am far too old.'

Pieter nodded towards the stairs, our parents' voices still ringing out. 'Some things never change.'

'Oh yes, they do.' I hurried into the kitchen to get my coffee. 'Last year,' I called through the open doorway, 'when Pappy got influenza, Mother took his work clothes away and he was forced to stay in bed.'

'He did manage to stay put for a day.' Hans reached out with the tongs and placed a roll on my plate, pushing the butter and honey across the table within easy reach. 'World record for Pappy, I should say. Next day, he donned his best suit, the one he keeps for church, and came back to work. He was really sick too.' Hans grinned, remembering. 'Mother was so angry … you know how she hates going into the city? Says it makes her head ache?'

Pieter went over to the sideboard, loading his plate with cheese and ham. 'Of course.'

'That day, she went to the tailors and ordered a new suit for Pappy. When it arrived, she made him try it on then and there to make sure it fitted, and then threatened to burn every stitch of clothing he owned if he ever did that again.'

I expected Pieter to find it amusing, as we had done. It was a good story, one that could be told time and time again, whenever a family sat together after dinner, reminiscing about the past. Those kinds of evenings were the glue that bound a family together.

As if he hadn't been paying attention, Pieter's attention was fastened on the tablecloth, tracing a pattern of curlicues on the nap with the tip of his knife. 'Can you believe they've been married almost twenty-three years and remain as happy as newlyweds; I want a marriage like that.' I sensed despair behind his words and recalled again his staring into the canal, his body bereft, little more than an empty shell. 'A girl who loves me enough to stay and grow old with me.'

I felt a sudden ice cold breeze as if winter had returned. Startled, I caught sight of Hans, his fists bunched tightly on the table top; his jokey expression replaced by anger. My fears came storming back and I bit my lip helplessly, wondering how long this antagonism on Hans' part could continue. I burst out with, 'What are you doing today?'

'Ruth and I are going to the cinema,' Pieter raised his head. Now, I saw only anticipation mirrored in his gaze and wondered if I had perhaps imagined his earlier anguish. 'And you?'

'I usually work with Pappy in the shop.'

'That's new.'

'Mevrouw Kleissler is too old to climb ladders,' I explained, endeavouring to sound cheerful. 'I dust the tops of mirrors while she has a Saturday afternoon off.'

Hans got to his feet, quickly draining his cup. 'I need to get to work, I'm late.'

'Why don't you come to the cinema with Ruth and me?' Pieter called after him. 'She says there's a good film on; a musical.'

Hans stayed looking towards the door, and I observed his back rigid with tension. 'Not for me, Pieter. I expect Maidy and I saw the same one last week.'

He headed out of the room, his feet thumping out his despair on the stairs, and I heard the yard door crash shut behind him.

After Berthe had left for work, I ran next door. Despite my disapproval of her reckless behaviour I had missed Ruth. Her lovely bubbly nature was so very different from the students I met up with daily in class.

'You live in one another's pockets,' Pappy had once said, watching us fly back and forth between one another's houses all evening. Maybe that had once been true but I had grown and now, like a newly fledged bird, I wanted to try my own wings. Nevertheless, whenever I heard the front door click open, I automatically listened for her feet on the stairs, before remembering they would stop at the first-floor sitting room and it was Pieter she had come to see, not me.

Meneer Endelbaum was tidying his shop and I tapped on the window. I didn't ring the bell, aware Mevrouw Endelbaum was probably still asleep and a sudden noise would wake her. 'Ruth's still in bed.' He waved me towards the stairs.

Little larger than a doll's house, this was how I had always imagined my prince's house to be. On the ground floor, a narrow staircase hugged the wall and an even narrower corridor led through to the kitchen and into a yard. Sheltered on all sides from the winds that blew in from the sea, there Meneer Endelbaum had created a garden for his wife to use whenever the weather permitted. Without access to the yard except via the front door, Pappy had permitted the builders to erect their scaffolding against the intervening wall in our yard, and use a bucket and hoist for their building materials. Under the eaves of the house, they had built a patio. Scarcely wide enough for two chairs and a table, there was also a tiny bubbling spring, its water tumbling down into a round, copper basin.

With room for only a single tree, Meneer Endelbaum had chosen a cherry that had white flowers in spring and red fruits in summer, and he had draped its branches with crystals that spun in the breeze, showering the house walls in rainbows of light. When the tree had first been delivered, with its roots encased in sacking to protect them, it had seemed quite dead. Meneer Endelbaum promised that it was only sleeping and, a few months later, had called me to come and see the magic unfurl; every branch smothered in tiny pinkish-brown buds.

When the garden was complete, Meneer Endelbaum took Ruth and me with him to the market to buy bulbs, eager to create a year-long display of flowers for his wife to enjoy. We returned laden with paper bags, each one carefully marked, and I had helped plant hundreds of tiny aconites and chionodoxa, that we called glory-of-the-snow, my fingers more nimble than his. In sheltered spots, these bloom even before snowdrops.

Mevrouw Endelbaum had always been nervy, never fully recovering from their ordeal. Last night at dinner, I noticed how frail she had become, even a visit to a neighbour's house tiring her. Despite the size of their house, they employed a maid to cook and clean, sending meals to their first-floor dining room on a lift – what people sometimes called a dumb waiter.

The same with Ruth's breakfast. When I arrived on the fourth floor, she was eating croissants in bed and drinking her coffee from a blue earthenware bowl with double handles. I didn't knock, why would I? We had made free with one another's houses for ever. As I opened the door, I caught her expression, before it swiftly changed to one of welcome. For a moment, she had looked almost petulant as if her lavish surroundings no longer appealed. It was an expression I had never seen before, and I was reminded of our hidden experiments with cream and powder and rouge. Once it had all been wiped off, for a brief second or two, her face would appear washed out and naked. Yet still so very beautiful, her long hair glowing golden brown in the electric light and her skin tinted ivory, with high cheek bones and a full mouth that needed very little excuse to curve into a bewitching smile.

And her surroundings were lavish. Her four-poster bed was hand carved and draped in curtains of sky blue, and her bedroom walls were covered in silk. Gold-backed brushes lay on her dressing table, matching the gold crochets and quavers Pappy had drawn on the edges of her pier glass.

'Do sit down, Maidy, I'm *so* glad to see you. It's so boring on my own, with nothing to do but stare at wallpaper.' She stretched out her arm to welcome me. 'I was thinking of having it changed just to give me something different to look at. Did you have fun last night? Pappy's stories,' she continued, not waiting for my reply, 'they grow more extravagant each time he tells them. Do remind me to send your mother some flowers to say thank you.'

'I suppose it's his way of filling in gaps for Pieter. He missed a lot of years.' I sat down in the chair I always used, tucking my feet under me. I didn't sit on the bed; Ruth complained it crumpled her bedcover. As children, whenever we had sleep-overs, she shared my bed, whereas I slept in her little guest room at the rear of the house. Her bathroom was next door. The larger of the two rooms, its mirrored walls represented the sea bed, with mermaids and sea horses. Before that, it had been a circus, with brightly clad clowns and proper horses with long, cream manes, and an acrobat performing a handstand. Adjacent to the bath, mirrored shelves held a stack of fluffy white towels.

'I was thinking how different everything has become since Pieter's return.'

Ruth took a sip of her coffee. 'Has it?'

'Haven't you noticed? Remember how we laughed at Yoav, appearing on our doorstep with flowers or chocolates every night, asking Pappy's permission to take Berthe for a walk along the canal. How boring we used to think that was.' I smiled fondly at the memory. 'Who would ever believe, a year later, you and Pieter would be doing the same.'

Ruth didn't reply, her frowning gaze focussed on her cup as if she was reading the future in it. After a moment, 'It's not the same at all.'

'Perhaps not for you and Pieter,' I shrugged and gave a heartfelt sigh. 'Our lives were so carefree back then ...'

'So come with us on our walks, why don't you?'

I spluttered with laughter. 'I don't think Pieter would approve.'

She leaned back against the pillows, wriggling her feet up and down under the covers. 'Do. Pieter wouldn't mind, not if I asked him.'

I shook my head. 'What happened to you yesterday? I didn't get a chance to ask last night, there was so much going on.'

'If I tell you, promise you won't be cross with me again? Croissant?'

'I've had breakfast but I wouldn't mind some coffee. It's cold out.'

Twisting round, Ruth picked up the little speaker tube and blew into it. After a moment, their maid answered and she ordered a fresh pot of coffee. 'I went into town with Tristan.'

'You had a date with Tristan?'

'Don't be so ridiculous. I felt sorry for him that's all. He's been begging me all week. And it wasn't a date. It's only ever been Pieter.' Her answer was out before I had even asked the question. 'I spend time with Tristan, that's all. He's in love with me.'

I caught the raucous clanking of the hoist as it arrived on the fourth floor.

'Be a dear ... I don't want to get out of bed.'

I went out onto the landing, pulling open the doors to retrieve the tray. 'Oh, Ruth, I'm so sorry.'

'What about?' Her tone changed, becoming as sharp as a knife.

'Tristan. Shall I pour?'

'Yes. What about Tristan?'

'He's so intense … I can't help wondering what will happen when you dump him?'

'Why would I need to do that?' Ruth seemed genuinely puzzled by my question. The entire Tristan-thing obviously meant little more than the bracelets and necklaces she used to wear for school to make other girls jealous, discarded next moment and never worn again; her jewellery case overflowing with unwanted items.

'Because of Pieter.'

'Oh Pieter,' she said casually as if his name had slipped her mind. 'Tristan will get over it.'

I burst out impetuously. *And Zande? Will he get over it too?'*

She flinched. 'Now you're being ridiculous, Magrit. He's the last person in the world I'd have anything to do with.'

I placed the tray on the bedside table, my hands shaking. 'Are you so sure?'

'What a horrid thing to say!' She picked up her hand mirror from the coverlet, examining her face for imaginary spots. 'What's got into you these days, you never used to be spiteful. You know perfectly well, it's always been Pieter. I've *never* wanted anyone else. And he wants to marry me.'

'It's only been a few weeks, Ruth.' I protested, wanting to bang sense into her head as I would a pillow.

'What's time got to do with falling in love?'

Remembering Yoav's unswerving and lengthy courtship, I wished I might have answered … everything. Except that would have been a falsehood. Time really had very little to do with falling in love.

'Has Pieter said anything?

Picking up a pair of tweezers, she tweaked an imaginary hair from her eyebrows. 'No, not yet. But he will. Girls know these things.'

'And you love him back?'

For a moment, I wondered if she was going to fling the mirror at me, her hand drawn back ready.

'How dare you? *Of course I do*. I told you, it's always been Pieter,' she repeated for a third time. 'He's so perfect and so gloriously handsome. We're all going to be so very happy. You'll see.'

A phrase from Hamlet came to mind and refused to depart; it lingered awkwardly like an unwelcome guest at a party. Professor Dulmes had used it to chide one of the girls in my literary class whose work was habitually late. "The lady doth *protest too much, methinks*".

She stretched out her hand, once again her long fingers fluttering in the air, her voice cajoling. 'Oh don't let's fight, Maidy. I've missed you so much. Tell you what; we're going to see that new musical this afternoon, the one we'd planned to see the other Saturday. Please, come with us? *Please do*. We can have something to eat afterwards … it'll be like old times.'

'I can't, I'm working this Saturday, remember.' I softened my refusal with a smile and tried again, 'Have you given any thought to the age difference? Pieter's twenty-two.'

'Men should be older,' she flashed back. 'There's ten years between my parents.'

'Ruth …'

'Oh, *do* stop going on.' She slid out of bed, placing her breakfast tray on the bedside table.

Her nightgowns came from Paris and were sent out to be laundered. The one she was wearing was white, its silk folds floating to the floor from a gathering of tiny pleats under the bust. Picking up a matching robe from the end of her bed, she slipped it on over her nightgown and drifted over to the window.

'Anyone would think you didn't want me to marry your brother,' she snapped. 'I hope you won't behave this way when we really are sisters.' She opened the curtains staring out at the river. It was a view I knew by heart; a handful of seagulls riding the waves, their dark grey feathers neatly folded, superciliously ignoring any small craft powering past them through the choppy waters. She tapped gently on the pane as if wanting to attract their attention. 'I never told you! Papa promised we would sell up and go to live in America. We can't now. Mama cannot travel and Papa is too old.'

Meneer Endelbaum was only a few years older than Pappy although I'd noticed he had recently taken to using a stick in the street.

'So, I am stuck. Have any idea how that feels?'

She waited for my reply. I kept silent.

'When he asks me, and he will, I will marry Pieter and we will travel the world. Papa has plenty of money. I will see all those things Pieter has seen. And I will have a family, too.' She came away from the window, the folds of her diaphanous robe clinging tightly to the lines of her body. 'You're right. It is freezing out there; I can feel it through the window.' Shivering, she hugged her arms around her chest. 'I'm going to have a bath and get dressed. Come and choose something for me to wear today. I have a new jumper – I could put that on. And perhaps my new black trousers. Pieter likes me in trousers.'

24

Telling Ruth, I needed a walk to clear my head, I ran downstairs again. Another day, I would have stayed, roaming restlessly around her dressing room, watching enviously while she tried on outfit after outfit. Ruth loved an audience and I was usually happy to oblige, despite it leaving me with a niggling discontent for the paucity of my own wardrobe.

As I passed the shop window, I waved to Meneer Endelbaum. He was a kindly man. I had grown very fond of him and felt sad that Mevrouw Endelbaum was so poorly. He had a customer, the man studying a tray of diamond rings on the counter. He wasn't particularly well dressed, although it was probably his best suit, wishing everything to be perfect for the girl he loved.

I headed for my bridge, as I always did when my thoughts jabbed at me with their rough edges. I found its old stones soothing, reminding me how fleeting life truly is, our troubles no bigger than a pin-prick in time and certainly not worth squandering precious minutes on.

The wind off the canal was raw and biting, and I was grateful for my old winter skirt, not wanting to wear my new clothes with an afternoon of dusting ahead. Under the balcony of my prince's house, tubs of tulips were in flower, their bright faces encouraging. Pulling the collar of my heavy jacket up over my ears, I leaned over the little parapet to see them better, restlessly picking at the wall and roaming back over my conversation with Ruth. A splinter of stone came loose, crumbling to dust between my fingers. Her words, so seriously spoken, had surprised me. She had never once mentioned America, although it explained a lot – especially her determination to go to college after her mother's health had prevented the family travelling abroad.

'Why have you been avoiding me?'

I jumped. Jaan was standing on the steps that led down to the canal side. He had exchanged his sandals for shoes, and was wearing a beige duffle coat, its hood up.

Without thinking, I came out with, 'You told me that Ruth liking Zande would do her no good. I applied the same logic to you.'

Taken aback, he remained silent. 'I am thrilled to learn that you do like me yet devastated you think I resemble Zande,' he said after a moment or two. 'We couldn't be more different.'

'Maybe,' I caught my voice, high-pitched and ill at ease. 'I still don't want any part of it.'

'Do you know the city possesses a bridge for every day of the year and I have seen them all?'

'You must have started early.' I said somewhat inanely, startled by the sudden change of subject.

'I started yesterday.'

'Oh!' Any idea of reading the riot act and storming off vanished. I tried to think up something clever to say. 'I don't live here,' I managed.

'I was planning to leave a note with your prince.' He pointed towards the little stone house with its shabby balcony.

'Why?'

Jaan was tall enough to perch on the edge of the parapet. He stretched out his legs, crossing them at the ankles, and I noticed he had on brown socks, embossed with some sort of bird motif. I glanced down at my feet. I had put on socks too, but had been too distracted to notice their colour.

'Because ...' His voice was slightly sing-song, his accent more marked and I realised he was nervous. 'I met this girl. She reminds ...' He wasn't wearing his glasses, the blue of his eyes bright against his brown hood. 'That bit doesn't matter.' He shrugged, 'In short, I behaved like a jackass and I needed to tell her why.'

Below me, a door opened and the little old man came out into the garden, a shawl pinned across his shoulders. He tottered down the path, scattering crumbs of bread into the water. Upstream, I heard an acknowledging squawk and a family of ducks scurried down the canal, quacking noisily. He stayed for a moment, watching them snap up their breakfast then, with a wave of his hand, went back in and closed the door.

'Why?' I said more calmly.

'Except for Zande, we don't go in much for girls.'

'You don't fancy girls?'

'I didn't say that. We care for girls all right,' he said, adding hastily, 'Waldger and me, we hope to be lucky enough someday to meet the right girl and marry. Only that will depend ...' He stopped abruptly, and reached in his pocket for his glasses case. Unaware of his action, he pulled it half out, nervously flipping its lid open and shut with his thumb.

'Depend? On what?' I said curiously.

'No! Forget all that.' Raising his head again, 'Experience has taught us that girls almost always go for Zande. In the sports hall ... I thought you were interested in ... well ... you know.' I heard him swallow. 'If we play it that way, let Zande have first pick as it were, it saves confusion and embarrassment later.'

'Pick?' I glared at him. My countenance must have resembled the scudding clouds threatening rain because Jaan flinched, his hands flying into the air in protest, his glasses case vanishing back into his pocket. '*You take the leftovers.* That's not very complimentary.'

I swung away, wanting to leave.

'Please, *please* don't go. I promise you, it's not that way at all.' His voice cracked with anxiety.

I hesitated. 'So explain which way it is. I already think of you all as cruel; you can't make it any worse.'

He flinched. I watched him take a deep breath as if inhaling courage. 'Always before, when we went to a new place, Waldger and I never mixed.' He paused as if chasing words, seeking something palatable to offer. 'We can't afford to make mistakes, you see.'

'*Mistakes?* You think befriending a girl a mistake?'

'No! No! I can't explain … it's something else … something to do with us. *Oh, God!*' Jaan thumped his fist against the palm of his other hand.

Suddenly, I felt ashamed. Maybe he wasn't making sense, nevertheless he was attempting an apology and my snide remarks were only making it worse. 'Sorry. Go on.'

'If Zande is in one of his moods, he'll go after them, and take them from us,' he said. 'He can do that quite easily, you see.'

I remembered Kirsten saying how every girl in college was in love with Zande.

'He drops them as easily, too.' Jaan walked the four paces to the far side of the bridge, staring out along the canal, the little family of ducks already drifting past, leaving a ripple of water behind them. 'I didn't want that happening to you.'

'Zande is with Elina,' I argued. 'He wouldn't be interested in me. If it's anyone, it's Ruth.'

'I understand that now. By the time I realised Zande wanted to make Ruth jealous, you had swept out.' He smiled at me. 'It was a good exit too – very dramatic. I wasn't going to do anything about it,' he shrugged. 'As you have seen to your cost, my explanations are generally so muddled I end up with my foot in my mouth. Then I decided, at the very least I should say sorry. I went to the library to find you, only it seems you don't go there anymore.' He raised his hand to stop me speaking, grimacing painfully. 'Yes, that's my fault too. However, it left me no means of contacting you. The office wouldn't give me your address and I don't even know your family name. So I decided to don sackcloth and ashes, and scour the city. A fitting punishment, wouldn't you say.' His attention was caught by an acrimonious encounter between two drakes. They pecked viciously at one another, noisily skittering across the surface of the water, their wings flapping uselessly. I saw nothing except genuine amusement in his expression. Unless, he was the greatest actor in the world, he was telling the truth as he knew it.

Delight flared at the realisation I'd been wrong. He wasn't cruel, quite the opposite, he cared enough not to want to hurt me. It was a good feeling, soft as the down on a baby bird fluttering warmly in the palm of your hand. 'You said Waldger. Isn't Tristan your friend?'

'Yes, and he's a damn fool. Apparently it hasn't sunk in not to play with fire.'

I guessed he was referring to Ruth; it was a fitting epithet.

He turned away from the bridge, waiting for me to speak, to accept or reject his comments.

I smiled instead, watching his face spring to life.

'Have you ever been to a fair?'

'I've never been anywhere outside the city.' I waved my arm nonchalantly through the air, secretly thrilled that a boy admired me enough to search an entire city, and comparing his actions with those of my imaginary heroes, who searched the whole universe to find a girl they had seen only once.

'Of course. I remember you telling me you wanted to travel.'

'Not on a day like today,' I shivered, and grabbed my handkerchief to wipe my nose, the blustery wind making it run. 'It's cold, and boats don't have central heating.'

'Are you busy?'

'Why?'

'There's a little coffee house close by. It has to be warmer than this bridge.' He took my arm. He was almost a full head taller, his grip on my elbow firm.

'What were you saying about fairs?'

'The bumper cars.' He fitted his steps with mine. 'You go there with a friend and each of you rides in a separate car. It's all about trying to knock seven bells out of your opponent before he does it to you ... in fact, treating your best friend as your worst enemy. When your time is up, all is forgotten.'

I laughed. 'I am not quite sure how that fits our friendship.'

'It's perfect. There will be knocks in plenty.'

'Knocks? That doesn't sound right.'

'Don't you ever fall out with your friends?'

'I suppose,' I said cautiously, thinking of Ruth. I might not approve of her behaviour but I still loved her. 'You don't seem the quarrelsome type. Still, perhaps it would be safer to skip coffee, just in case?' I kept my voice light.

Jaan responded by tightening his grip on my arm. 'I'm not; placid as the proverbial cow. However,' he hesitated, 'misunderstandings may well arise. If they do, I hope we can still remain friends.'

I didn't understand what he meant by misunderstandings and thought of asking, tired of all the secrets people were keeping from me. Then I decided perhaps if we were friends, the answer might well rise to the surface like flotsam, and need no explanation.

In the warmth of the little coffee shop, we talked. I can't

remember what about except that he enjoyed music and films and had gone to the theatre the previous night to see the production of Othello.

I noticed the clock on the wall over the counter, its hands pointing ominously past one o'clock and jumped to my feet. 'Oh help! I promised Pappy I'd work with him in the shop this afternoon.'

I didn't particularly want to leave. With Jaan, I felt relaxed – exactly as I used to feel at home, having breakfast or dinner with my family. Even from the outset, he'd not seemed to be a stranger, rather more someone you'd grown up with and had known for ever, as comfortable as your favourite pair of slippers. Believing him cruel and callous had challenged every instinct. While trying to convince myself of his uncaring nature, I only recalled the warmth and sincerity of his smile.

Jaan rose to his feet, fishing in his coat pocket for coins. 'I'm sorry. I've sort of hogged the conversation – spilling all my dreams. You're so easy to talk to; I knew you would be once I got past the prickles.' He smiled warmly to show he was making a joke. 'Would you like to meet up again tomorrow? I want to visit the art gallery at the old palace. I hear they have some interesting collections.'

'Is that a good idea?' We had drunk two coffees and with all that caffeine the problems of the world seemed very far distant. It was with difficulty I recalled Jaan saying we shouldn't be seen together outside of college.

He smiled down at me. It was a good smile, one that said he'd enjoyed our conversation and would like it to continue. 'I doubt if any of the others bother with museums. Let me walk you home.'

'No need, it's not far.' I gestured vaguely towards the river. 'I live by the swing bridge. My family make mirrors.'

'Baders?'

Jaan had opened the door for me to pass through first. I saw his hand on the door knob clench white.

'Yes.'

'Is Pieter Bader a relation?'

'He's my brother. Do you know him?'

I caught his glance, full of sadness and pity. 'Not really.'

25

I washed my hair before going down to breakfast, putting on my new cotton skirt with its matching turquoise blouse. I had woken early, sensing a change in the weather, the shrouds and stays on the boats tied up to the bridge no longer beating harshly against their wooden mast. I hadn't slept well despite going to bed late, thoughts rattling through my head like the clanking of a tram against its iron rails. Maybe it was the coffee; maybe it was delight at acquiring a new friend, yet it had been Zande's voice that rampaged through my dreams, not Jaan's.

Pappy, noticing I had on new clothes, rather than the black skirt I wore for church, raised his eyebrows.

'I am meeting a friend in the city,' I hastened to explain. 'We are going to the museum. I know I am missing church; I promise I'll go next week.'

'All my children seem to be flying the nest, eh Margaret.' He grasped Mother's hand, enclosing it within his own. How different she had become; no longer contained and withdrawn, simply radiating happiness. 'Pieter and Ruth are going out on their bicycles and taking a picnic.' Pappy directed his gaze through the window, the sky a patchwork of blue and white. 'It promises a dry day.'

'Where's Hans?'

'Still sleeping,' Mother frowned down at the table and Pappy gave her hand a comforting squeeze.

'Shall I …' I began.

'No, Pieter's already gone for the bread.'

I had spent most of the evening upstairs in my room, happily reading, and it hadn't registered that Hans wasn't at home. If I had thought at all, I would have assumed him to be out sketching. Thinking back, I remembered rain pattering on the roof outside and guessed from Mother's displeasure that Hans had spent the evening in an inn and drunk too much.

I hurried into speech, wanting to make my parents aware exactly how unhappy my brother was. 'Pappy? About Hans … he's …'

I stopped, hearing his feet on the stairs. They sounded heavy, stumbling down the two bottom steps. He looked awful, his skin streaked yellow, his eyes peering out from dark bruises.

'Mother, I'm sorry, I overslept. I'll go and get the rolls.'

'Pieter's already gone.'

I heard disapproval in her voice and jumped to my feet. 'I'll get you some coffee, Hans.'

The yard door opened and I caught Pieter's light tread. He came in, his face untroubled and radiating happiness, as Mother's had a moment before. Copying Hans, he carefully served Mother and Pappy, placing a roll on my plate before sitting down.

'So, what have I missed?'

'Only me getting drunk and upsetting Mother.'

Hastily pouring coffee for us both, I returned to the silence of the dining room. Hans had remained standing; frowning down at Mother's bent head.

'Mother, I'm sorry I got drunk last night.' Hans hated

apologising, finding it difficult to say sorry. Nevertheless, if he hadn't volunteered an apology, Pappy would have demanded one, before accepting him back at the table. 'I promise you, I am feeling very sorry for myself. And worse ...' He pulled the pockets of his trousers inside out, his expression sorrowful, and held them between his fingertips like a ballerina taking a curtsy. 'I am now skint and have no money till payday on Friday. Thank you, Maidy, for my coffee; I'm not sure how I would manage without you to keep me on the straight and narrow.'

Pushing the lining of his pockets in again, he pulled out a chair, stumbling in his haste to sit down.

'Ah!' Pappy cleared his throat. 'Your apology is accepted, Hans. I am not sure if this is the right moment. Yesterday, I received a letter from an old friend in Strasbourg. In case you are unaware, this is a city in northern France. He runs a business restoring stained-glass windows in churches. His foreman has broken his leg and is out of action for a couple of months and he has written to ask if I could spare someone. I thought you might like to go.'

I felt the silence, bitter and angry.

'So you want to get rid of your drunken sot of a son, do you? Sounds an excellent plan, although won't your friend be disappointed when you send him someone so obviously second-rate.'

Pappy banged the table with the flat of his hand, making us all jump. 'Enough! I will not have you upsetting your mother. It doesn't bother me your being drunk, I did equally as stupid things when I was young; Pieter too.'

Mother frowned at Pieter's sheepish grin.

'I suppose you believed you'd got away with it, Pieter. Unfortunately, you cannot disguise your inebriated state by enunciating each word carefully.' Pappy peered at him over his spectacles. 'I promise that makes it even more obvious. I tried the same ruse with my father when I was young; he saw through it too.' His whimsical mien was exchanged for something more serious. 'You children seem to forget I know everything that goes on in this house. For instance, although she hasn't said anything, I don't doubt my youngest daughter has a beau.'

'Not a beau, Pappy. He's a friend, nothing more.'

'In that case, I approve. Friendship is the right way to go about things.' Pappy said, pointedly ignoring my red face. 'What would bother me, Hans,' he continued, 'is if you make a habit of getting drunk. As you have said, you have no more money till next weekend.' Hans went to say something and Pappy held up his hand. 'It may interest you to learn that I have been writing to colleagues since last year, hoping one of them would offer you the opportunity to work with them. Your talents are wasted here. I have always been aware of that and was determined not to hold you back.'

'Pappy!' Hans exclaimed, his face ready to explode with excitement and shame.

'Yes! Yes! Let that be a lesson to you. Get drunk by all means but don't become a fool as well. That will damage you far more than a hangover. Ah, here's Berthe now.'

Berthe pushed open the door from the landing and came in; as neat as a pin, bestowing her cheerful smile on each of us in turn. She stayed in bed late on a Sunday, whereas Mother got up early to spend the day with Pappy.

'Maidy, make a fresh pot of coffee, there's a good girl. I've no doubt Hans will drink it, even if we don't. Berthe, your young sister seems to have acquired an admirer.' I felt my face growing scarlet again. 'I was just saying to her, if she takes her time to become friends first, any marriage that follows will last … don't you agree?'

Pappy eyes twinkled, aware that Berthe always insisted she had fallen in love with Yoav the moment she saw him, standing in the doorway of the little chocolate shop.

'That's quite true, Pappy,' she said calmly, ignoring his teasing.

I cycled into the city, the traffic almost non-existent on a Sunday, and headed for the main square where the old palace, aloof and majestic, stood astride a road junction. Originally surrounded by parkland, now a constant stream of motor vehicles circled it, carrying traffic south and west towards the capital. It was a pleasant spot. Last winter, Hans and I had often directed our steps there on a wet Saturday afternoon, the explosion of colour and movement within its walls capable of vanquishing even rain-soaked skies.

Jaan was already waiting, casually dressed in a light sweater and slacks in deference to a rise in temperature. As I parked my bike, pigeons burst from the hexagonal cupola on the roof, taking to the skies in a noisy flutter of wings. As a child I had believed it a dovecote, a place where fairy tales reached a happy conclusion, and had always felt disappointed not to catch sight of these magical birds. Perhaps in the deep recesses of my mind, I still hankered for it to be true.

Jaan was absorbed in watching a line of children playing leapfrog over a row of concrete bollards and, for a moment, he didn't notice me. When he did, he waved and raced down the long flight of steps two at a time.

'I always felt such sympathy for the family who were forced to live here,' I confided as we entered the museum. 'With these high ceilings and no central heating, it must have been freezing.'

'Hence their heavy garments.' He stopped beneath one of the biblical scenes that adorned the entrance-hall ceiling, tilting his head back. Close by, a workmanlike scaffold lay abandoned for the weekend; the opulent colours on a portion of the fresco not yet cleaned, still hidden beneath centuries of grime. He pointed upwards. 'I, on the other hand, feel sorry for the artists who were commissioned to paint these frescoes.

231

Imagine lying on a scaffold for months at a time; one false move and you'd get an eye-full of paint.'

I laughed, enjoying his company and pleased he'd asked me to accompany him. With the imminent departure of Hans, the arrival of a new friend was very welcome. We strolled on taking our time, a tacit understanding between us that we go at our own pace, view what we wanted. Gradually, more and more, we found ourselves standing side by side, delighting in the same canvasses, our tastes very similar, and I was somewhat surprised when Jaan ignored the gallery where some of our most famous artists were hung.

'You're not interested in the seventeenth century?' I indicated the room, its lofty ceiling reducing the canvasses on its walls to mere pinpricks.

'Another time, perhaps.' He steered me past the entrance. 'There's a painting along here I want you to see.'

Midway down a gallery of eighteenth century artists, he stopped at the portrait of a young girl. Wearing a dress of drab brown, with a white collar framing her dark hair, she was standing next to a scrubbed wood table, gazing out of the kitchen window, its leaded panes promising a view of open country beyond. Presumably she'd been preparing a meal, the table littered with different objects, all of them in shadow except for a vase of dried flowers, its glazed pottery showing dabs of bright colour, both blue and red. Dark red flagstones drew your eye across the floor towards a black-leaded range, where a single gleam of brightness from a copper saucepan lifted the overall darkness of the kitchen. It was stunning, its dark tones rich and vibrant.

'She reminds me of you,' he said.

'You mean, a woman's place is in the kitchen,' I felt comfortable enough to tease.

'No.' Jaan pointed to a line of bench seats and I dropped onto the nearest, my body reflecting my brain's exhaustion after the onslaught of so many beautiful images. 'Besides, you said you wanted to write.'

Nearby, a young couple sat together, the girl's head resting on her companion's shoulder. I saw Jaan flex his fingers as if bolstering his courage to take my hand. I wasn't sure if I wanted that. I shifted in my seat, arranging my skirt, and inconspicuously edged my fingers away. 'I do, if I'm good enough. What are you going to do when you leave college?'

'I've always wanted to be an engineer. It may not be possible now, it all depends.'

That word again.

'My brother, Hans, has a similar style,' I hastily changed the subject and pointed to a river scene, wind spilling from the sails of the barque so realistic I could almost feel it brushing against my skin. 'He taught me how to row.'

'Row?'

'Don't sound so surprised. Girls can row, you know – although it was years ago. On the spur of the moment, Hans decided he wanted to draw a group of buildings from the river. Only he refused to pitch his easel on the opposite bank, saying that wouldn't work. My brother is awkward that way,' I explained. 'My parents tried to dissuade him, reminding him he wasn't a particularly strong swimmer. Nothing any of us said made any difference.'

It never did. That was Hans; all trouble and no sense was how Pappy had once described him.

'As it was a lovely day, I went with him. He'd already selected his subject, a little group of farmhouse cottages, and had persuaded a fisherman to rent out his rowing boat. Naively, I assumed he'd already asked the man to do the rowing, forgetting what a skinflint my brother is. Sadly, he'd already decided it would be cheaper if I took the oars.'

Jaan was listening intently, his head cocked to one side, still studying the painting of the girl.

'We lasted less than an hour.' I broke into giggles. Jaan's raised his eyebrows in enquiry. 'How did my brother put it? If I couldn't do a better job, the next fisherman to pass by, he'd swap me for a week's worth of fresh fish. I couldn't keep the boat still, you see,' I explained. 'I don't know if you have ever tried it, but it's pretty difficult, especially in a tidal river. Eventually Hans lost his temper completely, threw his canvas in the water, and took the oars himself.'

Jaan joined in my laughter.

'We finished up having a picnic in the middle of the river and then Hans fell asleep, so I was forced to take the oars again.' I fell silent, recalling the day with fond nostalgia; the sun's reflection in the water almost blinding in its intensity, making me wish I had brought my sunglasses with me, the tumbledown cottages on the far bank foreshortened by distance. 'Right from being a small child, his plan was to go to college and study art.'

'Why didn't he?'

'In our family, it's traditional for the eldest son to take over the business,' I prevaricated, reluctant to explain about Hans having to take Pieter's place. I had been alarmed by Jaan's obvious concern on learning Pieter Bader was my brother. That he knew of him was evident, but why pity? 'So now my brother Hans makes mirrors for a living and dreams of visiting the south.' I got to my feet. 'If we go up to the first floor, there's a room of mirrors there made by my ancestors.'

'Your ancestors?' Jaan gazed at me in disbelief.

'That's how it all started, except I am never sure which ancestor it was. When I was little, Pappy told us almost weekly about the Prince of Orange, boasting as to how he had changed the fortunes of my family by ordering mirrors for his salon de dance. Unfortunately every time he told the story, he changed the number of greats.'

'Greats?' Jaan said with a puzzled frown.

'Grandfathers,' I explained mischievously. 'It varied from, your great-grandfather to your great, great, great, great, *great*-grandfather.'

'I see,' he chuckled. Reaching out, he patted my hand, all of a sudden serious again. 'You care a great deal for your family, don't you?'

'You mean I've talked non-stop. Sorry if it was ...'

'I didn't mean that,' Jaan said, his tone reassuring. 'In fact you talked very little about them; you talked mostly about the old city and growing up there. And it wasn't boring, quite the reverse.'

'You're right, I do care for them,' I replied, 'especially Pappy. I love him most dearly. As to my memories of the old city,' I confessed, certain Jaan wouldn't scoff at my silliness, 'they are like having my own private photograph album. Each corner and bridge holds a special memory. You see, as children we roamed far and wide, even when the city was overrun by the enemy. Then Pieter went away and the memories stopped,' I added without thinking.

I caught the sharpening of his brow as Jaan rose to his feet. 'I need to go.' Grasping my hand, he pulled me up. 'Let's see the mirrors another day. I'm late already and I want to buy a postcard or two on the way out.'

Keeping my thoughts hidden and my face expressionless, I waited while Jaan went to the shop. He emerged a few minutes later a paper bag in his hand, pulling out a picture postcard of the young girl – the one that reminded him of me.

'I don't have your childhood memories,' he explained awkwardly, 'being an only child. I decided I wanted to start making some.'

I gazed down at the postcard, reluctant to acknowledge I occupied more space in his thoughts than he did in mine.

A moment later, we were back in the entrance hall. I wished

I might have spoken more openly about Pieter; how, during the long years of occupation, he'd been the one to keep us safe, especially Hans, making sure his younger brother's recklessness didn't end in tragedy. Yet how could I, without knowing what it was that had caused Jaan such concern? Without warning, I felt the darkness of the secret Mother and Pappy shared edge closer, enfolding Jaan in its grip too, and felt the first stirrings of fear.

*

When I arrived home, Pappy was at his desk writing a letter. The news that he had been corresponding with colleagues had been a revelation. Pappy detested letter writing, grumbling that he had a brush in his hand all week; surely he could spend one day without. Mother usually sat next to him until he was finished and, to spare him further torment, she wrote the books of the business.

I draped my arms around his neck, peering over his shoulder at the elegant copperplate, each stroke as delicate as his brushwork.

He patted my arm. Picking up his sheet of writing paper, he wafted it in the air to let the ink dry. 'There, it is done. And Hans will follow in a few days.'

'To Strasbourg? Are you sure he hasn't left already and forgotten to say goodbye.'

Pappy chuckled. 'He's sleeping off his hangover.' Folding his letter in three, he slipped it into an envelope, then dipping his pen in a pot of ink, neatly printed the address. 'I hope you won't cause me as much trouble as your brother.'

'I promise.' I kissed the top of his head. Crossing to the window, I perched on the sill. Sunday afternoons were always quiet on the river, fishing vessels left in port while their owners attended church, reluctantly complying with the edict: *Six days shalt thou labour, the seventh shalt thou rest.* For such men, the sea, with its constantly changing moods, must have proved a life-long passion, greater even than the love they felt for their wives and children, otherwise they would never have survived such a solitary and hazardous existence. 'I wanted to tell you, Pappy, about Hans. I imagined it a ...' I hesitated; *betrayal* was too strong a word.

He patted me on the arm. 'Yes ... yes. It will all come right, you'll see. I am a great believer in time and distance.'

'Had you really been searching for a place for Hans?'

'Maidy! My dear child! *You doubt me?*'

'No Pappy, of course I don't.' I shook my head, my ponytail flapping against my chin.

'That letter from Strasbourg was a happy coincidence. Had it not happened, I would have found some other way to get your brother away. I made up my mind, ever since I realised his feelings for Ruth.'

'You knew?' I exclaimed. 'Hans admitted it to me a few days ago; I never imagined ...'

'Oh, he disguised it well enough.' Pappy twinkled at me. 'He didn't mope around the house like Berthe, and cry into his pillow every night.'

Yoav had taken a year to pluck up courage and ask Berthe to marry him, and the sound of her crying at night had quickly become as familiar as the distant clanking of tram wheels. The day he finally proposed, Pappy went into the city, something he rarely did, buying flowers for Mother and a bottle of champagne. Mother was so angry at him for wasting money. 'My dear,' he told her, pulling the cork with a loud pop. 'I feel like a castle under siege that's finally been liberated.'

'I was hoping Hans would have reached the end of his apprenticeship first,' Pappy explained. 'Pieter's return has brought it forward, that's all.'

'You were against it?'

Pappy put the lid back on the ink bottle, tidying away his pen. 'Hans and Ruth would never have been happy, Maidy. Your mother and I talked it over. Ruth, poor child, had such bad early years, she craves excitement and romance.' He hesitated. 'Hans couldn't give her that; his art would always have to come first. Once away, he will soon realise it. And we have so much to be thankful for; your sister's wedding and then, hopefully, Pieter and Ruth.'

Pappy and I often chatted, although never before had he been so open. I decided he'd done so on purpose, taking me into his confidence as someone now worthy. I remembered with shame how I had avoided confiding in him before, in case he believed me unchristian. How ridiculous. How could I ever think Pappy was anything other than sympathetic? He was never judgemental, not even when Hans got drunk; he always understood.

Encouraged, I lurched into speech, conscious I wouldn't have dared broach the subject had Mother been in the room, her obsession with Pieter and Ruth marrying dominating her every action. 'Pappy, I know there's a mystery—'

'Tell me about this boy you've met.' Pappy licked the envelope. Pulling open the top drawer, he ferreted among a pile of papers in search of a stamp. 'Nice is he?'

I sensed a door closing and wished I was brave enough to keep my foot against it. A lifetime of obedience stopped me. Then I remembered Kirsten, able to come out with things that were bothering her and clear the air. Hauling in a breath, I pushed hard against the door. 'Pappy, you always answer my questions, why not this time?'

Pappy tore off a stamp and licked it, 'Because there is nothing to answer. Pieter is home and we should be grateful and want for nothing more. This boy, is he local?'

Pappy never lied and hadn't done so now, he had simply skirted round the truth, leaving it lying on the ground behind him.

'He's from the south. His name is Jaan and he's an only child,' I said after the longest pause, hoping it would express my disapproval. 'He's at college, in year three. And, yes, he's very nice.' I added. 'He reminds me a little of you, Pappy,' I said, forgiving him, 'except he's much taller. And since you're my favourite person in all the world …'

'Go off with you,' Pappy roared and gave me a little push. 'Run down to the tram station and post my letter, there's a good girl. Perhaps you will bring him home one day, then I can see how much alike we are.'

I ran off down the street, the air clean and fresh without secrets, my feelings as jumbled as the contents of my school bag. A few weeks ago, I had complained how uneventful and dull my life was. Now I felt as if I were on a helter-skelter, flying down its slippery surface out of control. At the end of the ride stood a deep trough of disquiet, filled with secrets; secrets I couldn't fathom and which made no sense. In one of our lessons, Professor Dulmes had quoted from the French writer, Anatole France: "Beware, my Lord! Beware lest stern Heaven hate you enough to hear your prayers!" He had explained that it meant, *Be careful what you wish for.*

A tram was parked up ready to leave, and I slipped Pappy's letter into the box on the back, wishing problems could be as easily disposed of; carted off to the farthest corners of the earth by an obliging tram.

26

Three days later, a telegram arrived for Pappy. We waited impatiently, our conversations broken off while he read it. It was agreed that Hans would leave the following Sunday and Pappy would go with him.

'I can spare a few days, I've not set foot outside the city for fourteen years.'

Mother kissed him on the cheek as if sealing a bargain.

The week flew past. Time for me mirrored the antics of a gloriously patterned yet wayward kite, one moment almost stationary jerking along the ground, the next soaring into the air with me running after it unable to catch up. I saw nothing of Zande. Maybe at the outset I was beset by disappointment, but then I began to enjoy spending those few minutes at lunchtime with Jaan in the library. The weather reflected my mood, wisps of fluffy cloud blown about on a brisk north-east wind, interspersed with an occasional black sentinel, reminding me of the shadow that surrounded my brother's return.

It was the opposite for Hans. He came to my room and perched on the carpet with his back to the wall and his head bent, his expression darkly morose.

'I wish Sunday would hurry up and arrive. I can't wait to leave,' he muttered. 'This house, it's become a hell hole. However late I am, I can still smell her perfume in the air. It's agony ... it ... it's like ... If it wasn't for you ...'

Dropping my pen into the open pages of my book to mark my place, I sat down next to him and slipped my arm through his, my head on his shoulder. 'Let it go, Hans. I promise you, it will get better in time.'

'That's what I'm afraid of.'

I jerked upright, staring at him. '*Afraid?* Of what?'

'Forgetting her.'

'But Hans ... you just said ...'

'I know what I said.' He brought his arms up covering his head, his voice muffled. 'I almost wish I didn't have to go. Even the pain of seeing her is easier than the torment of never seeing her. I don't think I can stand that.'

I remembered Pappy's words. 'So don't go,' I said sternly. 'Tell Pappy you're not bothered about becoming an artist. Give it up. Stay here and make mirrors or get a job in the city, painting shop signs. There's always a need. Then you can see Ruth every day and be there when she marries Pieter.'

Hans obviously didn't hear the last part of the sentence. He raised his head staring blankly. 'Give it up ... you mean ... drawing?'

I shrugged. 'If that's what it will take to see Ruth.'

'But art is my life,' he protested.

I hugged him fiercely. 'Yes Hans, it is your life. You may not realise it now, Pappy said you love drawing far more than you will ever love Ruth – I agree. It will bring more excitement to your life than any girl. If you don't go, you'll never forgive yourself.'

He raised his head and smiled; that lovely little truculent, reluctant softening of his mouth. I would miss him dreadfully. It felt like a knife cutting away a tiny piece of my heart.

Everything to do with Hans was over the top: his love, his temper, and his ferocious talent.

'How will I manage without you?' he complained.

'You'll manage.' I said firmly. 'You'll bury yourself in work and when my letters arrive, you'll cast them impatiently to one side, intending to read them later. Then you'll forget all about them because you've caught a shadow on water and need to paint it before it vanishes.'

He hugged my arm. 'No, I won't. Others, perhaps, but never you, Maidy.' He kissed me gently on the cheek. 'Get some sleep.'

That was easier said than done, waking again almost immediately each time I managed to doze off. Feeling a sudden disquiet, I slipped out of bed and tiptoed out onto the landing where I curled up in a ball, listening to the soft ticking of the clock two floors below. Someone turned over in bed, making its springs creak, and I caught the gentle snuffling sound Berthe sometimes makes if she eats too much. These were the sounds I'd grown up with, unchanged throughout my entire life. Sadly, I sensed they were about to change, exactly as a placid river becomes a ferocious torrent when it flows over a weir, and I was listening to them perhaps for the very last time.

27

Then almost before I could take a breath, it was Sunday. We all went to the railway station – ten of us. Yoav with Berthe, even Lars and Hendrik, shaking Pappy's hand and promising to care for the business as if he and Hans were setting off to war. Maybe Pappy's going was as momentous. Throughout the years of my childhood, a stroll along the canal or a visit to the theatre had been the furthest he had ever strayed from home. All at once, he was leaving the country. He was concerned also. Dressed in his best suit, he constantly fingered the registration documents in his pocket, patting the bulging fabric to check he'd not lost them. Even Ruth was there, her hand in Pieter's; garnering attention with every step she took. In the drab, smoky atmosphere of the station, she resembled an exotic flower.

Mother and I returned alone to an empty house, a mountain of silence drifting up the stairwell from the empty streets; even the furnace quiet until morning, when Lars would arrive to stoke it up. Automatically, I listened for Hans, his tread on the stairs, his cheerful whistle. And already, I missed Pappy; his dependable presence at the table like a ship's anchor holding us all firmly in place.

Even the sitting room felt cavernous, the windows onto the street and river, although shut, still allowed a banquet of silence to seep through its thick panes. Shafts of sunlight stretched their inquisitive fingers towards the photographs on the wall, the images blurred and shadowy in the background, as if they no longer belonged to the present. All at once, I wanted to be on that train, viewing hills and valleys as they rolled past the carriage window, no longer comfortable in this tiny pond in which I'd been born. It might have been my home, but without Pappy and Hans, it no longer fitted.

The silence was abruptly broken by the sound of knives rasping and saucepans clattering together. Mother must have gone directly to the kitchen to start preparing our meal, yet even those sounds seemed muted with the intervening door closed. Aware she wouldn't want my help, I made to go upstairs and was surprised to hear her call my name.

I pushed open the kitchen door. 'Would you like help or company? It's so quiet, without Hans and Pappy.'

'Neither Magrit. I want to talk to you, I'm very concerned.'

'About what?' I said, genuinely puzzled, wondering what I could possibly have done to warrant her calling me Magrit.

'Pieter says there are some new students at the college.'

'Yes, there are.' I admitted cautiously, wondering how Pieter had found out. Ruth wouldn't have told him, she was always very careful to keep her swains apart, and he had only accompanied Ruth out to the lake that one time. 'They're in year three and four – three years above me.'

'No matter, I don't want you mixing with them, do you hear? They're foreign to these parts and don't follow our ways.' Mother was seated at the table scraping carrots, her head bent, and didn't once look at me. How very different my parents were one from the other; Pappy's gaze was always open and frank, delaying judgement until after he had acquired the facts. 'I have been concerned ever since your birthday,' she continued, still studying the scrubbed wooden top of the table, 'you seem to be showing a wilful lack of decorum; most unseemly in a girl your age.'

I knew instantly what she was meant; my new clothes and my new friends.

'It's this college business; I was against it right from the beginning.'

'Yes, Mother, I heard you telling Pappy.'

'You were eavesdropping?' Mother's head shot up.

'Of course not,' I retorted, shocked to discover she had such a poor opinion of me, although perhaps not surprised. She had always despaired of my make-believe world, incapable of understanding that I found more happiness in my daydreams than I did in my real life, with its hardship and deprivation; a legacy of the war.

I had written about it in my journal. At night, the distant squeal of tram wheels trundling workers to the steel mills echoed loudly across the silence of the city and it often woke me. That particular night, I'd gone down to the kitchen for some warm milk. As I passed my parents' room, I had been surprised to hear raised voices, the grandfather clock on the landing showing past midnight. Pappy opened the workshop at seven every morning and was rarely up after eleven. They were arguing about my attending college.

'What if they return? I have no worries for Berthe; her feet are planted too firmly on the ground. So very different from Magrit; her head is in the clouds. For her, I am so fearful.'

'You have no need to be. Our youngest daughter sees danger far more clearly than you give her credit. She won't fling herself headfirst into life like Hans, nor avoid it altogether as Berthe does. She will sip at it slowly, taking her time. Come now, Margaret. We must sleep and Maidy must follow Ruth.'

I never knew what she meant by the words: *and what if they return* because our enemies were long gone.

245

Mother's tone had quieted slightly, nonetheless she still sounded disparaging. 'This boy you're walking out with. I trust he's not one of them? Think of your reputation. No well-brought-up girl would ever be seen with an outsider.'

I thought of Jaan and the gentleness of his speech, nothing forward about him at all. I retorted angrily, 'Pappy says so many people were displaced by the invasion, where you come from no longer matters.'

Picking up my jacket, I fled downstairs into the street, my thoughts racing ahead of me, and I was at the canal bridge before I was even aware. Below, the dredgers stood silently, their long arms drooping in an ungainly fashion over the water, dozing away the remainder of their day off. I wished I could do the same, curl up on my bed and sleep away my anger, but I had never been able to do that.

Swinging my jacket by its label, I walked fast, thankful not to have to watch my step as I was forced to do in our ancient alleyways, where cobblestones loosened by the rain often tripped you up. Even so, like Hans, I much preferred our little enclave with its bridges and walkways, too narrow for anything other than a bicycle. Hans complained that in giving the alleyways a name and the houses in them a number, the Burghers' had all but eliminated our independence from the city proper.

Gradually, my disquiet retreated. It was a lovely afternoon, the sun offering gentle reminders as to what we might expect in July and August, when even trees drooped their leaves over pavements blasted with heat.

There were few people about. An occasional car wandered past, the dual carriageway into the city wide open, as if the flood of trams and motor cars on a weekday caused it to shrink.

On either side of the road, modern concrete buildings stood shoulder to shoulder with others of black stepped or pointed gables, their leaded windows offering a very different image of the street from one viewed through plain glass. Hans often commented that he did his best work on a Sunday, 'that's when buildings wear their best clothes, the same as us when we go to church.'

I eventually came to a halt on a bridge near the railway terminus, having walked myself to a standstill, thirsty and in desperate need of a drink. The sun had dropped and was playing hide and seek among the roof tops, before finally settling down for the night. I didn't want to go home, childishly deciding to wait for a train to pass before catching the tram. I leaned over the ledge of the parapet staring down at the tracks and felt Mother's words rise up to meet me. Replaying the scene with a cool head, I recognised fear rather than anger in her voice. But why? How could anyone be afraid of Jaan? It was like saying Pappy was an ogre.

Without warning, a brutal spasm raced through the rails, the metal struts of the bridge shuddering in protest as, with a scream of noisy energy, a train hurtled towards me and vanished under the bridge. A moment later it re-emerged, furiously belching out a column of black steam, tiny flecks of soot drifting down to settle on the dusty iron ledges of the bridge. It roared away and I watched it growing steadily smaller, until there was nothing left except the railway tracks.

Reluctant to move, I stayed where I was, absorbed in tracing the gleaming lengths of rail as they wove over and around the points, wondering where they might take me.

In the distance, I caught the clanking of a tram and broke into a run, waving at the driver to stop. I had forgotten it was Sunday and this would be the last tram until morning. Feeling a searing pain in my feet, I stumbled to a halt and glanced down, spotting blood on strap of my sandals where its leather edge had rubbed against my heels. Miserably, I watched the tram trundle away, annoyed with myself for forgetting the time. Now I would have to walk. Trying not to limp, I began to retrace my steps, hoping to find a coffee house open where I might get a drink, and was alarmed to find the streets tightly shuttered. Even the cinema was shut, its wooden T-boards advertising forthcoming films tidied away. Remembering the old inn by the canal, I headed in that direction and was rewarded by a gleam of light as its door opened and shut again.

It was a tiny place, crouched low on a spur of land where two canals met, a succession of lock gates protruding into the air, mimicking a row of exclamation marks at the end of a sentence. To avoid walking round by the road, I crossed upstream using a narrow railed footbridge over the lock gates. Built of red brick, the lock held a deep trough of water, a solitary weed with bright yellow flowers growing out of a crack in the mortar.

Mounting the steps, I timidly pushed open the inn door, recognising the taproom from Hans' drawing of it. Barrels lined the walls, its counter little more than a plank of wood on two trestles. A group of men were using it as a prop for their elbows, a tankard grasped in their fist. Seeing me, they ceased their conversation, staring in an interested yet not unkindly manner. I had never gone into a bar before and had no idea what to expect. I caught Hans' voice in my head, rebuking me. The man serving put down the glass he'd been wiping and came over. He was typical of how I'd always imagined an inn keeper to be; balding and florid, his apron made of coarse cotton. He wiped his hands on it as he walked across the floor, his feet scuffing silently through a layer of sawdust.

'Mevrouw, are you waiting for someone?'

I hesitated. 'No, I'm on my own.'

He lowered his voice, confirming my fears. 'This is no place for a respectable girl like you. We serve working men here.' He inclined his head and I looked beyond him to where another group of men were playing some sort of game with dice.

'It's just that I'm so thirsty,' I plucked up courage. 'And everywhere is closed, even the cinema.'

'As is only proper on a Sunday,' he nodded his approval then peered over his shoulder at the clock on the wall. 'We finish shortly. You should go home, Mevrouw.'

'Yes, and I will. But, please, let me have a drink,' I begged. 'Water will do. I'll sit here quietly. I promise I won't be a nuisance. I've been walking all afternoon,' I rushed on, 'and it's warm.' I hesitated again, saying haltingly, 'I think you know my brother, Hans – he's an artist.'

The barman's stern attitude lessened. 'Yes, we know Hans.' He peered at me closely in the dim light. 'You're not much like him.'

'He's fair haired.' I gave an awkward little grimace, my mouth almost too dry to conjure up a smile. 'I promise you, he really *is* my brother.'

'In that case, Mevrouw, I will make an exception and serve you …' Again that half turn, indicating the five men absorbed in their game; a fair-haired young man watching over the others' shoulders. As if the landlord had been speaking directly to him, the man raised his head, staring in my direction. 'You may sit outside. The language at this time of the evening is not suitable for a young lady's ears. I'll bring you some lemonade and …' He stopped and peered at me closely. 'Was it a row with your boyfriend or your parents that has given you that white face?'

'Neither. Hans has gone to Strasbourg to work and I miss him already.'

'How does a dish of potato soup sound? That will set you up for your walk home.' Opening the door again, he ushered me out and pointed to a bench seat under the lighted window. 'You'll be quite safe there. I'm afraid there's not much to see until morning when the locks are busy, apart from the bridge. See there!'

In the distance, I recognised the Bridge of Lights, its metal joists glowing in the light from the setting sun, as if a tiny piece of its golden orb had broken off and fallen to earth.

'It's beautiful,' I exclaimed. 'How strange, I cycle past it every day but have never once seen it from a distance.'

The bar man propped the door open with his foot. 'Worth seeing,' he nodded approvingly. 'I always think it a blessing from God there was no money to paint it. Ask any fisherman. To them, it's a beacon of hope. After a rough day fighting the waves, the sight of that light in the sky brings tears to the eyes of the strongest.'

He was back in a moment with a glass of lemonade and a large bowl of steaming soup. I realised then how hungry I was. Missing dinner, I would most likely have gone hungry to bed. Contentedly, I sat listening to the steady rumble of voices in the background, broken by an occasional bark of merriment. Slowly, the bright glow of the bridge began to fade, reminding me how late it was. I had slipped off my sandals and, aware I needed to get going, bent down to ease them over my sore heels and found it impossible, my heels screaming out in protest.

It wasn't quite dark. After the brightness of the day, twilight was still hanging on, the way a small child drags their heels disinclined to go to bed. Below me on the canal, a black swan was preening its feathers and, in the distance, scarcely visible, I recognised the silhouette of a dredger, its stork-like shape marking the sky with a dark finger. That decided me. If I cut across the city, along the canal, it would be far quicker than retracing my steps through the city streets and I could walk barefooted, and carry my sandals. Draining my glass, I dropped down onto the grass at the side of the towpath, walking silently in my bare feet. I was amused to see the swan keeping pace with me and felt envious of its effortless glide, wishing the canal had been warm enough to swim in; even with bare feet, my raw heels were painful.

I'd gone no more than a couple of hundred metres before I heard footsteps. I swung round expecting it to be the inn keeper. It wasn't; it was the blonde-haired young man, the one who'd been watching the game of dice. A few years older than me, his hair and skin were so fair he'd not yet started shaving. Unconcerned, I continued walking, and suddenly became aware that he had increased his pace, and was catching up with me.

'Mevrouw?' He called out.

Wondering what he wanted, I slowed and swung round.

His smile fumbled about as if he had forgotten how to make his lips move. 'You can't walk home alone, not a pretty girl like you. I'll take you.'

His words came out slurred and I guessed he'd been drinking heavily, his face noticeably flushed even in the dimming light. He came up close and put out a hand. I am not sure whether he meant to grasp my arm. Hastily, I backed away.

'No, thank you. I've not far to go.'

'I insist.' He gave a loud hiccough and took a second step forwards. I contemplated running, confident of outpacing his drunken stagger. Before I could move, the black swan waddled out of the water, pecking at the grass close to my feet. It made no move to hurt me; at the same time, it didn't seem overly bothered by my presence. It was big, much bigger than the white swans I had seen out on the lake, with a powerful neck and huge wing span. I regarded it warily; aware a single blow from its wing might easily shatter an arm or leg.

The young man stopped too. He eyed it cautiously then, as if the alcohol had taken control, began stepping towards me again, circling round the swan.

'Don't tease. I don't like girls who tease. I only want to hold your hand.' He grabbed my arm as I broke into a run, pulling me tight against him, his clothes reeking of tobacco. 'There, isn't that better,' his thick mouth leered at me. 'You tease! That's what you really wanted all along … isn't it? You just wanted me to beg for it. Come on, one kiss and I'll let you go.'

He fumbled his mouth towards mine, smearing my cheek with saliva.

'No!' I kicked out, feeling the vibration through my bare toes as I struck his leg. He never faltered, his hand continuing to creep upwards, pausing only to fondle my breasts, pinching and squeezing, fastening around my neck.

He panted out, 'Come on, be a good girl. One kiss and I'll let you go.' He hiccoughed in my face, the acrid smell of hops making me eyes water. Flinching, I tried to move my head away and found it impossible, his fingers tightening all the while against my throat.

'Stop it.' I beat impotently at his back with my free hand. 'Let me go.'

'One kiss and I'll let you go,' he repeated. 'Promise.'

I felt his body thrust against mine, his other hand still gripping my arm. Over his shoulder, I saw the black swan hiss aggressively, its neck stretched rigid, its partially opened wings undulating rapidly.

The noise seemed to excite him more. He pushed hard against me, his foot kicking my legs apart and pinning me tightly against him. I stumbled back, trying to keep my balance, and then I was falling. I landed awkwardly, the heavy fall taking my breath, the weight of my attacker pinning me to the ground. His face fastened greedily on mine, his breath searing my throat, his lips slobbering. I felt his fingers digging in cruelly until I had no breath left and blackness took over.

28

From a great distance, I heard my name, 'Magrit, Magrit,' repeated over and over. With great difficulty, I tried to open my eyes, feeling my lids incredibly heavy. I heard my name again and blinked them open into a forest of mist. Through its deep haze, I thought I saw Zande, water streaming from his hair, as if he had been swimming. I heard a voice, the words distorted and distant. I tried to answer but couldn't get the sound past my throat, the imprint of a hand still clutching at my neck. My arm felt heavy as I lifted it, only to find nothing there except memory cutting at my breath. I moved my head, catching sight of a dark shape lying prone on the canal bank, half in the water. Then I felt strong arms lifting me, before the hollow blackness took over once more.

When I eventually opened my eyes, it was to the friendly glow of a table lamp shining warmly. 'Where am I?'

I caught my voice; it sounded strained and I put a hand to my throat feeling it bruised. All of a sudden, I remembered the nails digging in, making it impossible to breathe. Instinctively, my arms shot up to protect me from another attack, my panicky gaze flashing round the room.

'Hush there, child! No cause for alarm. You are quite safe, I promise you. Remember your prince? You are in his castle.'

I recognised the voice. I blinked away the mist in my eyes and cautiously sat up, my pounding heart gradually slowing.

It was the old man, the one who lived in the little house next to my bridge. A little gnome of a man, up close his face resembled a wilted flower, dried and crusted with lines. He was perched on the edge of his chair, a small jar clasped tightly in his hands.

'You are surprised?' He chuckled, a tiny impish sound. 'I heard you telling your stories to that girl. Every day, I listened out for your running feet, and opened my window to hear your tales of mermaids and pirates and princes. My favourite story was about the gardener who grew flowers as beautiful as my own.' The sentence ended with another chuckle.

It felt strange hearing my own words being repeated back at me, and I sensed he was offering them in sympathy, aware I was hurt.

'And the princess ... let's not forget her; riding a different horse each day of the week, with three hundred and sixty-five dresses, one for every day of the year. I knew you longed to be that princess and wear a dress made of silver thread.' He gave me a little nod.

With his bright eyes and red waistcoat, he reminded me of the friendly robin that visited our neighbour's garden. 'Never mind all that. You are feeling better?' He bobbed his head towards the little table standing by my elbow. 'I have made you some coffee. Not too hot.'

Still dazed, I picked up the little cup and took a hesitant sip, the warm liquid soothing my bruised throat. 'That was kind,' I managed. Surreptitiously, I wriggled my shoulders to ease them, feeling pain streak down my back. 'How did I get here?' I stared down at my feet, astonished to discover a neat bandage on each heel. 'I didn't walk. So how?'

'I hope you will forgive my presumption; they looked so painful.' The old man held up the jar. 'It is a remedy my wife created and tragically, this is the last pot. Wondrous for healing though, and that is all that matters. As to how you arrived here; a young man brought you. Said he found you collapsed on the canal bank and not knowing where you lived, brought you to me.'

'You mean Zande,' I gasped in bewilderment.

'Yes. That's the lad. He visits sometimes; it helps break the monotony of my evenings.' The old man sighed wistfully, 'A nice young man; a little wild perhaps. Unfortunately his circumstances are responsible for that.'

'He carried me all that way!' I burst out, scarcely able to believe what I was hearing. So it wasn't my imagination, it had been Zande. But why was he wet? Had I fallen in the canal to escape my attacker and he had pulled me out? Cautiously I fingered my skirt, and felt it only a little damp. No, I hadn't fallen into the canal. Then how?

I sat quietly for a moment, grateful to the old man for not asking the most obvious of question; what had I been doing on the canal bank at night?

The room I was in was the opposite end of the spectrum from the one created by my imagination. I had furnished my prince's abode with tapestries and rich paintings, lavish furniture and a carpet with a pile so deep, your feet sank right into it. In reality, the windows facing onto the canal possessed only simple blinds, a shabby carpet covering the tiled flooring. Through the window I spotted the dark outline of my bridge. From this angle it appeared to be floating in the air and it would have been a simple matter to keep a watch for Ruth and me on our way home from school. For someone living alone, our daily history must have proved a welcome episode in an otherwise empty day.

Finishing my coffee, I inched slowly to my feet, careful to

255

disguise the sudden dizziness as I stood upright. 'I ought to get home; my family will be getting worried.'

'Are you sure? You are welcome to stay as long as you wish.'

'No, I must get back. I'm quite recovered. The coffee revived me.' I pointed to my empty cup, 'It was a lifesaver.' I had meant my words to sound flippant. Recalling the hands clutching my throat, they came out on a serious breath. 'Er ... Have you seen my shoes?'

'Ah yes, your shoes. The young man said he is sure you would understand that it was either you he rescued or your shoes – but not both.' He chortled gleefully at his little joke.

I smiled too, aware it sounded so exactly like something Zande would say, with that tiny twist of his lips and his eyes gently mocking.

'I have a pair of clogs here.' He pointed to a shelf where a pair of brightly patterned clogs sat next to a row of books.

He seemed to have few possessions besides books; a couple of chairs and a few photographs; nothing of any value. Much of the ground-floor was taken up by a large dresser and the flight of stairs that led up to the first floor. Through an open doorway, I saw a tiny kitchen, little bigger than a ship's galley, and remembered Pappy taking me to see that family on the river barge, their entire lives fitted into an equally small space.

'They were my wife's. You are welcome to use them. I keep them as a memento to remind me how noisy she was in the house, her voice equally as loud as her feet. Yet, these days, I would welcome the disruption.'

'That's very kind of you. I promise to return them tomorrow,' I said politely. Picking them up, I slipped them on at the front door. Outside, the canal lay sleeping, bright moonlight inviting an answering gleam from its depths. 'When I was little,' I confided, watching rivulets of silver light skip across its dark surface, 'I imagined mermaids and mermen lived in a palace at the bottom of this canal.'

'Perhaps they still do.'

I walked down the path, a dozen steps taking me up to the roadway over the little bridge, the heavy soles clacking noisily as I climbed. 'They're very comfortable,' I called down to him.

'Of course. That is why she wore them.' The old man glanced down at my feet, the bandages showing up white in the moonlight, his bright eyes belying his stern words. 'In my day, there was never any need to flaunt our feet. Goodnight, sweet princess.'

29

It was sheer willpower that got me out of bed next morning. My body was a mass of bruises where I had hit the ground, and although my heels no longer felt as painful, I debated not going into college. Almost at once I changed my mind, our house little more than an echoing shell. I listened, surprised not to hear the gentle rumbling of the furnace in the basement. Lars must have decided to service it while Pappy was away and had let it out. To me, the boiler's gentle humming was the cornerstone of our family life, providing the background on which every other noise was superimposed, like a cloth spread over a table before cups and saucers are placed on it.

Carefully keeping my heels dry, I'd had a hot bath the night before and washed my hair, putting my clothes out for the maids to wash, but I still felt grubby and very ashamed. Hans would have been furious, shouting that it was my own fault for being so stupid and going to the inn in the first place. I remembered Berthe warning always to stay on lighted streets and never use the short cut late at night. Strangely, I had slept well. Perhaps I had been both too tired and too shocked to think what might have happened if it hadn't been for the swan. It must have attacked and chased the man away.

I reminded myself to take the old man a gift to say thank you for his kindness ... and this time to ask his name. Something I had neglected to do, which was very rude of me.

Gently pulling on a pair of old socks, I wedged some cotton wool under my heels and inched my feet into my old sandals. Only Berthe and Pieter greeted me when I got downstairs. Mother frowned down at her plate, displeased by my late return. I'd been lucky, I knew that. She had already gone to bed by the time I got back and was unaware of what had happened.

When Ruth pushed open the door and came upstairs, I knew by her polite greeting that she hadn't forgotten my impertinence. It had been over a week now.

I'd thought her in a strange mood at the station, overly affectionate towards Pieter as if she was daring the world to question her feelings as I had done. There was an awkwardness about Pieter also, an impatient edge to his voice that I'd not heard before, as if he was jealous of every moment he spent apart from Ruth and I wondered if they had quarrelled.

We'd not spoken seriously since that one time in the yard, but I'd been thrilled when Pappy told us at the station that Pieter was to resume his apprenticeship. 'Meanwhile, while I am away, you can take my place, Pieter, and be responsible for the family. Work with Lars for the next couple of weeks, to get accustomed to the way we do things these days.'

Hans had not been happy with anything and ignored Pappy's words, flinging a hurried goodbye to Ruth and Pieter over his shoulder.

Drinking my coffee quickly, I headed downstairs to get my bike. I didn't bother asking Ruth if she wanted to ride in with me. Not wanting to chance my sore heels, I ignored the river walk and rode straight through the city centre past the old palace, where Jaan and I had spent last Sunday morning. It seemed weeks ago now.

I had become used to heading in early, my bike almost always among the first in the rack, although I rarely went inside, happy to remain reading on the steps instead, until I heard bicycle bells and laughter on the driveway. I disliked its echoing hallways, finding the silence of the building intimidating, and sensing a chill on the back of my neck, made worse whenever footsteps echoed along its corridors. Pappy believed the evil that men did lived after them. I wondered how many years would pass, and how many fresh coats of paint would be needed, before the air inside smelled as sweet as the garden.

Taking my school bag with me, I wandered across the lawn towards the lake, hoping Zande might be there, telling myself it was only good manners to thank my rescuer. He wasn't; the bench was quite empty. Disappointed, I continued down to the water's edge where a stream leached into the lake, its edges crowded with willows. Noticing one tree almost toppled over, I pushed aside its trailing branches and discovered its bole split open to the ground, leaving a large space inside.

Pulling out *War and Peace*, I tucked my bag inside the gap to use as a seat, the rough bark enclosing my shoulders in its friendly grip, a dense waterfall of green fronds obscuring all sight of the outside world. Content with my hidey-hole, I leaned back and started to read, as always finding the long, Russian names confusing.

'If you're trying to hide, you're doing a very bad job of it. I saw your feet from the beach.'

Hastily pulling my skirt down over my knees, I poked my fingers through the fronds and cautiously peered out. Zande stood on the bank, his eyes sparkling with amusement. It was already warm, and he had on a short-sleeved shirt, the ends tied in a knot at the waist, his feet bare. I wondered if he had been sailing.

'You remind me of a fawn peeking through all that greenery.'

'I'm glad I'm not a fawn because then I would have four painful feet instead of two,' I retorted.

'Ah, yes, your feet. How are they by the way?'

'Better, thanks to that sweet old man. Do you know his name?'

'Albert Meijer.'

'Steward of the Castle – that sounds about right.' I hesitated, 'I wanted to thank you.' I paused, adding cautiously, 'Was I alone when you found me?'

'Quite alone. To be honest, I thought you passed out drunk.'

'No, you didn't.' I frowned at him, attempting to make my voice sound irritated and cross.

Kirsten had joked that the sight of Zande was like going on a diet, losing weight, and then finding yourself locked in a cupboard full of chocolate. I had smiled at the analogy even though I agreed with her. His presence was like a powerful pulse of energy that made you feel intensely alive.

'No, I didn't.' He crouched down, touching my sock, 'May I?'

I found myself unable to breathe properly. 'There's nothing to see, I told you they're better.' I insisted, sounding inane.

'In which case I'll go fetch your sandals, I have them safe in my boat. I must warn you, I'll be demanding a forfeit.'

Startled, I let go my hold on the willow fronds. They spun against one another instantly tangling and I heard Zande laughing as I struggled to separate them. It was a joyous sound.

I took a deep breath, willing myself to speak out. 'All right, I'll pay your forfeit if you answer my questions. You weren't at that inn, I'd have seen you. So how did you come to find me? And, yes, before you say anything, I'm grateful … very grateful. You'll never know how much …'

'Won't I?' Zande parted the fronds and peered down at me, his eyes gleaming with mischief, his tone mocking.

I blushed, frowning sternly. 'Behave! Why carry me to Meneer Meijer's when the inn was a few hundred metres away.'

'I needed the exercise. And he's a nice old man. What are you reading?' Before I could move, he had picked up my book, swinging it round on my lap so he could read its title. '*War and Peace*. That's on my list too.'

'You really are impossible,' I stormed.

'So I have been told.' He regarded me steadily, all traces of mockery wiped away. 'How I came to be there doesn't really matter. And if I ever go near that inn again, it will be to burn it to the ground.' I caught his expression; he looked angry. 'There, does that answer your question?'

It didn't, it only presented me with more. 'What are you studying?' I changed the subject.

'Humanities, and I am a very bad pupil. In the past, I've had little opportunity to read and while the weather's good, I prefer the human experience to be practical, and so I go sailing.' He got to his feet. 'Which I am planning to do right this minute.' As if to make amends for his outrageous behaviour the moment before, he added, 'I will leave your sandals with your bicycle.'

Impulsively – more to keep him talking than anything else, 'You can be so nice when you try.'

It was the wrong thing to say. I saw darkness sweep in. 'Don't be fooled, Maidy. You've seen the other side of me – that's not about to change.'

He moved aside, and immediately the green fronds drifted towards one another, closing off the space he'd occupied and leaving me alone.

30

It was a week before I could wear my turquoise sandals again and even longer before my confidence returned. I'd been lucky. I knew that and, in part, Mother was right. Wandering the city on my own would do nothing for my reputation or my safety. Once upon a time, everyone knew everyone, with marriages most often taking place between families who lived next door or in the next street. With the ending of the war, strangers had flocked into our city, their families and history a secret to us all. Nervously, I made sure I left class promptly, attaching myself to the train of students cycling into the city, and wheeling my bike along the canal, where the old women sitting by the water's edge knew both my father and my grandfather. At night, I stayed at home.

I didn't tell Ruth. I didn't tell anyone, not even when Berthe came back, agog with the news that a swan had attacked a young man.

'It happened on Sunday night,' she gossiped. 'The man had been to the inn, and he was walking home along the canal minding his own business, when the swan attacked him. Broke several of his ribs and his arm.'

Pieter had gone out with Ruth, and only Berthe, Mother and I were sitting down to dinner. 'Is Pieter aware of this?' she asked. Laying down her fork, she peered about her, almost as if she was wondering where Pieter had got to.

'I've no idea, Mother. They're talking about it in town; one of our customers told me.'

'Who are?' Mother's voice had a sharp edge.

Berthe stared at her in surprise. 'Fishermen mostly. Some are saying the swans need culling, there's too many on the lake. If it had been a child that was attacked, it would have been killed.'

'Perhaps the man was tormenting it,' I interrupted, all at once feeling as guilty as if I had perpetrated the crime.

'He says not,' Berthe responded in her usual placid fashion.

'People around here have never liked swans,' I persisted, thinking of the lads I had once seen beating at a young swan with sticks.

'With good reason,' Mother said firmly, 'horrid spiteful creatures and so dangerous. That poor young man. In any case, I don't want you telling Pieter.' Berthe frowned and leant forward as if to speak. Mother hurried on, 'You would have hated anything unpleasant spoiling your courtship, dear.'

'Yes, of course, Mother; I hadn't thought.'

Leaving my dinner half-eaten and making work an excuse, I ran upstairs to my room taking my bag with me, conscious once again truth was being disguised as something else. Why the need to keep Pieter in the dark? Was Mother concerned that he might leave again if he found his home life not to his liking?

Resting my elbows on the window sill, I let my mind drift and found myself back in the bole of the willow, safely wrapped in its arms. I caught the sound of Zande's laughter, a gust of pure amusement, without dissemblance or confusion, and wished I could conjure up the magic wand of my childhood, capable of transporting me to that happy-ever-after sunset whenever I wanted. How naïve I had been to imagine Pieter's return might restore our lives to how they used to be. In six years, every one of us had grown and changed. Sighing, I picked up my bag, pulling out my history essay, childishly thinking if I went to bed early, morning might come more quickly, and I could escape and go to college.

It was a startling notion, especially since I had never been entirely at ease there, convinced I had stolen the opportunity from Hans. Naturally shy, I had also found the sheer number of boys overwhelming, almost grateful when their gaze skipped over my head in search of something more glamorous, and relying almost exclusively on Ruth for companionship. Now, with three new friends, it had become a place where I felt comfortable, sometimes cycling in with Jules and meeting up with either Kirsten or Jaan at lunchtime.

Jaan mostly spent the day doing research in the library. The previous year, some wealthy benefactor had donated their entire collection of leather bound volumes to the college. They had not yet been catalogued, stacked haphazardly on the bottom shelves of some spare units. Jaan had begun sorting through them, searching for volumes about ancient myths and legends, and I had promised to help.

'It would easier if we knew what we were searching for,' I called from my lowly position on the floor. With Jaan being so tall, it was far easier for me to perch on the floor than for him. 'Telling me you'll know it when you see it doesn't help much.'

He raked his fingers through his hair. It had become a familiar gesture, so had the twisting of his glasses between his thumb and forefinger. I had never thought before but sometimes gestures can be more revealing even than words.

'Did you get to the city library, yesterday?'

Jaan took off his glasses to smile his reply. 'And how I suffered. The assistant there explained, in great detail, how extraordinarily rich their library was, containing a wealth of literature. Apparently, the section on myths and legends had been destroyed in a fire last year.' He grimaced, inviting me to join in the joke. 'I think the assistant took the fire as a personal insult, assuring me if it hadn't been for that, I'd have definitely found something suitable. Apparently, she's worked there for thirty years, all through the occupation, and nothing untoward has ever happened before.'

I sighed. 'What a waste of time.' I picked up a book, leaving a grey dust mark on the shelf where it had stood. 'Heinrich ... er ...' I screwed up my nose, squinting at the embossed lettering on its spine, the volume so old its dark red dye had worn away. I flicked it open and read the fly sheet. 'Heinrich Hein. *The Flying Dutchman.* If I remember right, he's a long-forgotten poet. Any good?'

Jaan got to his feet and came over, perching on the edge of the table. 'What's it about?'

I passed it up. 'A man cursed to sail the world for all eternity, who is allowed into port only once every seven years.'

Jaan read the fly sheet and I saw his brow sharpen as if with pain.

The library door creaked open and a voice called out, 'So this is where you're hiding. I did wonder.'

It was Zande. I caught the edge of anger in his voice like the clash of symbols.

Patting the air to warn me to stay put, Jaan stood up.

I saw Zande's reflection in the long window, his fists clenched and hanging by his sides. I hadn't seen him since that moment in the garden but I still found my hands trembling.

'I'm not hiding, as you call it. I told you where I would be.' Jaan leant casually against the rack of books, the muscles in his back tense. 'Trawling through thousands of books ...'

'And have you found anything?' Zande's tone was haughty, belittling.

266

'Not yet.' He indicated the shelves. 'There's hundreds of books to go through and until I have checked them all, I refuse to give up hope.'

'*Hope!*' Zande sneered. 'What is there left to hope for?' The words came out on a cry of anguish. I saw the librarian frown, an admonishing finger in the air. 'Don't play games, Jaan.'

'Then come and help, instead of wasting your time trying to seduce every girl you meet.'

Zande hesitated. 'To run your fingers through hair smelling of sunshine or ...' Unfurling his fist, he peered at his fingers as if they were strangers. 'Spend the hours left to me chasing through a pile of old books. I know which I'd prefer. I was hoping to find Ruth, have you seen her?' There was a silence. I held my breath, watching him ravage the room like an animal scenting its prey.

'Zande, you can't have every girl in the world.'

'*Why not,* if it amuses me?'

He spun round on his heel and his reflection was lost.

I let the swing doors close and settle before I moved. Jaan remained leaning against the shelf. He was staring down at the book about the Flying Dutchman, his glasses slowly revolving round and round in his fingers.

'Are you all right?' I said anxiously.

I had come to cherish Jaan's rare smiles. He smiled now, a whimsical twisted smile, full of warmth and as light as the dust motes dancing in the air. I knew then, without a shadow of doubt, that he cared for me.

My only awareness of life and love had come from books, my own experiences carefully monitored by a loving family. Yet, instinctively, I understood that for girls, this would be the one moment, out of all the moments in their lives, that nothing could surpass. The realisation that someone cared ... really cared. I remembered Berthe, when Yoav slipped a ring on her finger, her face glowing and suffused with happiness. Perhaps I might have felt that same sense of joy had I not caught sight of Zande's expression; crippled by a bitterness so deep and so savage, I sensed the well into which it poured was bottomless.

'Of course.' As if waking from a trance, Jaan wandered back to the table. 'Poor Zande. Of us all, he's the one that hurts most.'

'Hurts most?' I echoed, 'I thought you hated him.'

'*Hate?* Never!' Abruptly, he shut the book and I sensed urgency behind his gesture. 'I *have to* find it, Maidy. He's depending on me. Where else can I try?'

I left him reluctantly, my head in turmoil, wishing he would confide in me. As a result I was late for my afternoon class and I was grateful it was Professor Dulmes. Since my story, he had come to regard me as one of his special finds; someone who showed promise and for whom expectations were high. Had it been Professor de Witt, I would have ended up with a five-hundred word essay.

'Have I missed anything, professor?'

'Not at all, except the role of Desdemona?' He beamed at me fondly.

'The role of Desdemona? Why?'

'We are going to act out Othello this afternoon.' A hand flew up into the air from one of the boys and he patted it down again. 'Yes, yes. I realise you are reluctant to waste your time on foreign writers, even the most famous of them. Please try to understand, while so many authors remain on the banned list, and the college has no money to buy new books, since we already have copies of Shakespeare's plays, we must continue to use them. Besides, almost half of the class have already seen the play.' He picked up a dog-eared copy, and passed it to me. 'You can share the role of Cassio.'

I groaned and sidled up to Danique, one of only four girls in our literature class. 'Did you warn him?'

'That chaos will ensue?' She winked at me. 'I figured we should let him find that out for himself.'

I felt genuine sympathy for Professor Dulmes then. Naively, it had obviously never occurred to him that students, boys especially, were more than likely to disguise embarrassment by hamming it up, conscious he would feel each mispronounced phrase as keenly as the dagger Othello used to pierce his own heart. I was right. Before we had even reached the end of act one, in which Iago obsesses about his hatred for the Moor, the play had been changed from tragedy into comedy, gales of laughter ringing out. It did me good, chasing away my gloomy introspection. Despite our scathing comments, secretly we all enjoyed the play of emotions engendered by its ancient words, and I promised myself to finish reading the script at home.

As always when I got out at the end of the afternoon, the courtyard was a bubbling cauldron of noise and energy, with students calling out to one another and wrestling with jackets, books, and bikes. I pushed through the bodies hanging around on the steps. When the Burghers took over the building to use as a college, they ripped out the statues they considered immodest, but left the original steps intact. With their wide treads, they were much in demand as staging for college photographs and plays, and had quickly become a meeting place for both friends and enemies.

Habit made me seek Ruth, although less and less I had come to expect our riding home together. I was surprised to see Zande, since seniors rarely mixed with younger students, entering and leaving by a side entrance. Dressed in casual slacks and a long-sleeved shirt, he was staring out over the milling figures in the courtyard. A little coterie of girls surrounded him, Elina among them, with both Jaan and Waldger hovering nearby. I had been surprised by Jaan's admission that neither bothered with girlfriends. Seeing the coquettish efforts of the girls to attract their attention, both he and Waldger could easily have taken their pick.

Ducking behind a group of boys, I quickly hauled my bike from its stand. When Zande burst into the library I had sensed friction, the cords of his neck tight and his fists balled as if he was battling for control, the candour that was so appealing as far distant as one side of the lake from the other. This was the Zande he'd warned me about, the one that pulled wings off insects. It was better if I kept away.

As so often happened, the weather had changed throughout the day. After the warmth of the previous few days, the light air of the early morning had been replaced by a brooding quality, as if it disapproved of the frivolous nature of mankind, leaving any lingering sunshine sour as curdled milk. Beyond the trees, a gathering army of clouds was massing over the lake and I guessed a storm was heading our way.

I swung into the saddle. That's when I saw Pieter. For the briefest of moments, I wondered if he'd come to dry my eyes, as he always did when I was child and he had found me sitting on the back step, sobbing over some imaginary hurt. Then I realised it was Ruth who filled his thoughts these days, not me. I waved anyway, glad to see him and scooted over.

'What are you doing here?'

'I've come to meet Ruth. Where is she, I can't see her anywhere?' His glance roamed possessively around the line of students exiting the doors.

'Did you warn her you were coming?' I heard my anxious tone.

'It's a surprise.' Pieter replied, continuing to sweep the courtyard.

Troubled, I bit my lip, wondering what to do. Ruth hated surprises, she always had, obsessive about looking her best. Maybe she and I might never quite recapture that deep, uncritical relationship of our childhood, even so friends don't walk away as I had done. However much you deplore someone's behaviour, you can't turn off the tap on love quite that easily.

'Honestly, Pieter, you might at least pretend to be pleased to see me,' I said gaily, my eyes flashing back and forth hoping to spot Ruth before he did.

'You're my sister. It's different.' He waved. 'There she is. *Fantastic.*'

Pushing her bike, Ruth came into view round the corner of the building. I breathed again, relieved to see her alone.

'*Ruth?*' Pieter called.

Ruth was wearing her green skirt with its waspy belt and, as always, it drew the attention of almost every boy in the courtyard. I watched eyes slyly following her swaying walk, hands circling in the air as if testing the span of her waist. She must not have heard Pieter, although Jaan did. He glanced up and saw me standing at Pieter's side, acknowledging me with a movement of his hand.

I smiled to myself. I was so lucky to have him as a friend. *Maybe something more than a friend?*

I couldn't answer that question until Zande had ceased to plague my dreams, walking casually in and out as if they belonged to him and I had them out on loan.

He was there now – watching Ruth.

Nonchalantly he raised his hand. Like Caesar, who carried the power of life and death in that tiny gesture, his vanity was overwhelming, convinced all he needed to do was crook his finger and a girl would come running. He called out. 'Come and chat. I need cheering up.'

Astonished, I saw Ruth lift her head in a smile and steer her bike towards the steps.

Waldger gave an artful grin and nudged Zande with his elbow as if to say, *why you sly dog.* Sensing his interest, Elina twisted round also, apprehension wracking her body. She was thinner than she'd been a month ago. She'd been slight before, now her jawline had become sharply etched, her eyes staring out of great hollow pits. Her gaze ravaged the courtyard, searching through the crowd before homing in on Ruth, her expression so venomous Ruth should have died on the spot. Tragically, I realised that Elina had fought her last battle; there was nothing further she could do to keep Zande at her side, her time in the sun had run its course.

'*Ruth?*' Pieter called again.

That's when everything stopped moving.

Ruth froze. I saw her bewilderment, her body still angled towards Zande. And something else, an expression I'd never seen before, genuine and unguarded—

As if she'd been struck a blow, her face emptied. Almost in slow motion, she changed direction and wheeled her bike towards us.

Disbelief swept across Zande. Grasping the hand rail, he cleared the steps with a single bound.

I had the answer to my question and it wasn't the one I wanted.

Elina shouted. 'Forget her, Zande. You're with me not her.'

Catching Ruth by the arm, he spun her round.

I heard him call out, his eyes boring into hers. '*Stay.* I'm tired of playing games with you. Let's play them together.' I might have been wrong.

With a loud thump, a bike hit the ground, hard, thrown down. For a moment, I supposed it to be mine, except I hadn't moved. It was Pieter's. He leapt across the space. Diving at Zande, he struck him forcefully on the shoulder with the heel of his hand. 'Let her go, you cur.'

'*Pieter? No!*'

I ran, hearing my bike crash to the ground behind me.

Zande stumbled backwards with the force of the blow

and tripped over a row of bikes, stacked one against the other. They tumbled to the ground with a discordant clatter; Zande sprawled out on top of them. Rubbing the heel of his hand against his thigh where he'd knocked it, he climbed slowly back on his feet. I could see the blazing anger in his eyes, the control it was taking not to retaliate. He ducked away, his head bent.

I grabbed my brother by the arm. 'Pieter, what's got into you? Let it go.'

He didn't hear me. Shaking off my hand, he darted forward. 'Come on,' he yelled, 'is that the best you can do?'

Zande spun slowly round on his heel. 'I don't want to hurt you.'

I caught Pieter's raucous outburst. 'You're chicken. *A great washbag of chicken!*'

I tried to get between them. '*Pieter! No!*'

He pushed me away so hard I stumbled and almost fell. He hurtled forward, grabbing Zande by the lapels of his jacket, their faces within spitting distance.

This afternoon, acting out Shakespeare, the boys had play-acted their ferocity and outrage. This was real, not acting. And it was my brother. My brother, the person who always slowed down, wanting to give his little sister a chance of winning the game.

'Let go.' I heard the fury in Zande's voice.

'*Make me.*'

'A fight!' I caught the gleeful sound, faint among the ringing of bicycle bells.

Students ran over, crowding round.

'Pieter! For pity's sake.' I grabbed his arm again and hung on.

I hadn't ever considered my brother as being strong but he was easily the equal of Zande. Shoving me away so hard I felt pain, he launched a ferocious blow at Zande's body, pitching down on top of him.

Throwing him off, Zande was back on his feet first. He stepped back. I saw quite plainly that it was done; he was walking away. Pieter dragged in a breath, the air hissing sharply through his teeth.

It had the desired effect.

Zande's head went down like a bull about to charge, only the forefeet scraping the earth were missing. He dived at Pieter as I tried to pull him away. I felt the vibrations all the way down my arm as his head struck my brother in the chest. Doubled up, Pieter was catapulted backwards, his breath gone, hurting, me on the ground beside him.

A moment more and he was back on his feet, panting, swaying backwards and forwards, his arms wrapped over his chest trying to recover his breath. He seemed possessed of a curious madness, his body overtaken by some outside element and out of control, the softness of his skin mottled an ugly red colour. The unpleasant hissing sound sounded again and then again.

I saw ... *I don't know what I saw.*

Waldger and Jaan dived forward. Using their elbows as battering rams, they forced a path through the enthralled onlookers. Jaan grabbed at Pieter's flailing arms, wrestling him away. I caught his voice, sharp and clear amongst the shouts of encouragement. 'Pieter, you'll betray us all. Is that what you want?'

'*You crazy!*' Waldger cried out, his voice high-pitched. He hauled on Zande's arm. I caught a glimpse of his expression. He was terrified, a world away from the mockery that was his benchmark. 'Zande, for God's sake! Calm down. Listen to me. Calm down. No girl's worth it.'

And Ruth?

She never moved. She stood there as if she was an automaton in need of winding, her expression as bewildered and lost as a child in a forest of alien trees. Then she got on her bicycle and rode off down the drive.

Slowly Waldger let his arms drop and stood back, his chest heaving with the effort of restraining his friend, the tension plainly visible. He brushed at his sleeves as if to free them of contamination.

For a moment Zande didn't react. Gradually, I saw his fists uncurl and he straightened up, staring out over the grounds, his head slowly revolving from left to right as if absorbing a scene he might never see again. That scared me even more than the fight had. I don't know why. Yes, I do. I sensed that he was no longer with us. He was deep in a world that only he knew.

Alarmed, I took a step forward. Immediately Elina was by his side tugging at his jacket.

'*Darling*, are you hurt? Tell me; *tell me you're all right!* You poor darling; that trollop, Ruth! This is all her fault.'

The girls he'd been chatting to on the steps circled around him, twittering sympathy like little birds.

Zande twisted round on them, his voice dark and bitter. 'Get away, all of you,' he snarled.

'Darling, you can't mean that.'

'That word!' He clutched at his head. 'I never want to hear it again, *especially from you*.' He spat out the indictment like a bad taste.

Elina took a step back, her face ashen. 'You can't mean that. I understand you're upset. Anyone would be.'

'Understand! Can you understand exactly how boring you are … *all of you*. There's nothing behind those pretty faces except emptiness and—'

'*Stop it Zande!*' The words flew out before I could prevent them. 'They're not to blame.'

Waldger gazed at me in astonishment and grabbed Zande by the sleeve. 'She knows? You told her?' he gabbled, all colour draining from his cheeks, leaving them chalk white.

Firmly in control again, Zande's face twisted in a scowl. 'That I'm a heel.' His eyes reached for mine, expressing what his mouth couldn't admit, the mockery and contempt he felt for his behaviour and ... something else ... defeat. He wrapped his arm around Waldger's shoulders. 'Yes, I told her. Luckily for Maidy, she knows that already,' he added more lightly. His expression changed, becoming sardonic. He bowed to Elina and the little retinue of hopeful candidates for his interest. 'My apologies, ladies,' he said, his tone as smooth as silk. You'd never have believed a moment ago he'd been fighting to control his anger.

Elina was crying. 'You told me you loved me,' she begged.

I saw his expression change and raised my hand in warning, aware that his next words would cut deeply. The movement caught his eye. He raised a finger acknowledging my rebuke, his mouth twisting in a painful grimace.

'Elina, I am more sorry than I can say. Unfortunately, the male of the species is inclined to say anything in the throes of passion. The moment passion is spent, such words become meaningless.'

'You didn't mean it?' she said helplessly, tears beginning to flood in earnest.

The door banged behind us. It was Kirsten, as always weighed down with an armful of books. By now most of the students had drifted away, only a half-dozen or so bothering to hang around once the fight had ended; mending fences of little interest to a voyeur. Dropping her books on the ground, she ran down the steps and folded Elina in her arms. 'If I were a man, I'd probably kill you.' She hurled the words at Zande and, still with her arm supporting Elina, led her away.

Zande called after her. 'The way I feel right this minute, if you were a man, Kirsten, I'd probably let you.'

It was an unusual exit line but well up to the standard I had come to expect of Zande. Had we been watching a play, it would have merited rapturous applause. I so wished it had been. In the last few minutes, I'd met up with jealous lovers, a fight, and broken hearts. Sadly, unlike a theatrical performance, the end was not yet written. I wondered what that would be, although deep down I already knew. It was a tragedy playing at this theatre.

I found Pieter crouched on the ground, his arms wrapped over his head to shield him from curious stares. I heard him muttering. 'It's never happened to me before. Why now?'

'Shush! Not here.' Jaan bent down, staring fiercely. 'Go home.'

'In a minute.' Pieter raised his head, his face white and strained. Noticing me, he burst out, 'It'll never happen again, Maidy. I promise. Put it down to jealousy.'

I hesitated, still unsure, conscious that the lovely carefree expression – once so much a part of him – had gone for good. I bent down to pick up my bicycle. 'Oh, no!'

Jaan came over immediately. 'What?'

I pointed to a long jagged scratch like forked lightning on the mudguard. 'It was new for my birthday.'

'I'll paint it out for you,' Pieter called, getting slowly to his feet. 'At least I'm good for something.' He stared round bewildered. 'Where's Ruth?'

'She went,' I said sternly. 'I don't think she approves of people fighting.'

'I don't either,' Pieter winced. '*Oof!* That hurt. I'm sure he's cracked a rib.'

'If it's any consolation, he said he was sorry.'

'Yeah! So am I. Rather stupid on my part.'

'Very,' Jaan added. 'You know how strong he is.' His smile flickered into life disappearing again as quickly.

The truth hit me. When Pieter had called out to Ruth, it was his voice Jaan had recognised, only noticing me afterwards. 'You do know each other,' I stammered.

'No!' they replied in tandem. 'We've met once or twice,' Jaan tried to reassure me.

I felt the curtain shift as if to begin the last act. Then it fell back into place.

31

Jaan walked as far as the end of the drive with us, leaving Pieter and me to cycle home in silence. His leaving took with it the last glimmer of brightness from the day. There was no comfort to be found in Pieter's expression; it resembled that of an old man, suddenly becoming aware death is waiting for him around the corner.

Beneath our feet, the waters of the lake lay unmoving under a lowering sky, sullen and bleak, the air humid and almost sticky to the touch. In the far distance, I caught the snarling of dogs and recognised thunder. Pieter rode fast, as if those same dogs were chasing him, the loose chain on Mother's old bike clanking discordantly. I struggled to keep up, finding the noise bothersome; no longer familiar and welcoming, but simply an irritant that frayed at my nerves, until they felt as jagged as the jigsaw Pappy uses for his work. I was relieved when the bridge came into sight, a tram swaying unsteadily across the intersection. I had expected Pieter to slow down and walk his bike across the bridge; bicycle tyres so often becoming trapped within the mesh of interlocking rails. Ignoring the danger, he pressed on his pedals, speeding towards the city centre, traffic building towards evening with people leaving work.

By the time we reached our street, he was way ahead and racing into the yard. I caught the slam of the back door as I lifted my bike through the little Judas gate. Lars poked his head round the workshop door, curious to discover who the caller was. Seeing me, he waved and vanished back inside, shutting the door after him. When I got upstairs, there was no one about. Below me in the shop, Mevrouw Kleissler was talking to a customer, her piercing soprano drifting up the stairwell. She was extolling the value and beauty of Bader mirrors: 'Each reflection as pure and honest as a spring morning.'

Wearily, I dropped my bag on a chair, aware that accolade no longer applied to the family who had created and built those mirrors. In less than a moment of time, not even a heart-beat in a universe that has been around for millions of years, night had become day and the world a topsy-turvy place full of lies and deceit – and I hated it.

From the kitchen came the gasp and stutter of the kettle, its lid rattling impotently whenever it boiled unchecked. I ran in to find steam flooding everywhere and hastily removed it from the hot plate. Above my head, footsteps paced across the floor of Pieter's bedroom and I heard Mother's voice soothing and calming. A pile of half-peeled potatoes lay by the sink. Whatever it was that Pieter had told her, it had been serious enough for Mother to drop everything and run.

Helplessly, I peered into the larder, wondering what Mother had planned for us to eat, wishing I had paid more attention when she had tried to teach me to cook, my efforts with the potato peeler painfully slow and clumsy. Berthe would be home shortly and expect a meal on the table. Mother always timed our dinner so that it was ready to serve the moment she got in.

Overhead, the muted voices ranged on, sometimes raised in

anger before fading away again; first one, then the other, then both together. I wondered what explanation Pieter was offering for his outburst and wished he could explain it to me. Not for the first time, I yearned for Pappy to be back with us. He had promised he knew everything that went on in this house. Was he aware somewhere along his travels, his eldest son had acquired a murderous temper which, for a second or two, had threatened to spiral out of control? Deep down, the impression lingered that I'd seen something carnal, from the dawn of civilisation. Had Jaan not struggled to pull him away, Pieter would have gone on and on, oblivious to hurt, until either he or Zande lay dead or dying.

I had washed the potatoes ready for cooking before I heard Berthe's tread on the stairs, as measured and solid as she was. She pushed open the kitchen door, her friendly open countenance enquiring,

'Where's Mother?'

'Upstairs with Pieter,' I tried to keep my tone normal. 'I've done the potatoes ...' I frowned helplessly, feeling tears behind my eyelids.

'Maidy, you goose. I know you hate cooking,' Berthe patted my arm, 'but surely you aren't crying over a little thing like potatoes.' She dropped her bag on the table. 'Let me put my things away and I'll do dinner. Make me a cup of coffee. You're good at that.'

I wiped my eyes and put the kettle back on the stove.

'What's wrong with Pieter?'

I hesitated. 'I'm not sure,' I said slowly.

Slipping off her jacket, Berthe went out into the hall, hanging it on a peg before making her way upstairs. Dear Berthe. I doubted the word hurry ever entered her vocabulary. Calm and measured was how she led her life. Pausing on the landing, I heard her knock on Pieter's bedroom door.

Mother called out, 'That you, Berthe?'

I listened for the door opening. 'Oh dear, is it that time already?'

Then Berthe's calm tones. 'Maidy said Pieter is poorly.'

'It's nothing,' Pieter's voice.

I'd been right to show caution. Obviously Berthe was not to be party to Pieter's fight.

We ate an hour later but only my sister tasted the food. Mother and Pieter pushed it around their plates and I had little appetite, the scene in the college forecourt still grating. As a child, Mother used to rap the table with her knuckles to remind me to eat. I was silent too – except that was little different from always – leaving it to Mother and Berthe to keep up a desultory conversation concerning Berthe's employer, who was planning to open another shop and appoint Berthe manager of the one she worked in.

I spent the evening in my room writing, only to discover on re-reading my lines I had generated more questions than answers. Had it been Hans, I would have understood and forgiven, his outbursts unpredictable and as suddenly over; Pieter had always been the placid one, able to diffuse emotions with a calming word. What made it worse was his outburst had scared him as much as it had me. I saw it in his face when he was talking with Jaan; resembling a frightened child, his loss of control had shocked him badly.

I thought then of sending Pappy a telegram, begging him to return. I had seen Mother's face when she came down for dinner. She looked old.

32

I didn't sleep much. When I did finally drop into an exhausted sleep, I was back in my dream, searching the winding streets for Pieter again, grateful for the daylight that woke me a few minutes later.

Wearily, I climbed out of bed and stared out of the window, surprised to find the pavements dry. The promised storm had failed to materialise, although the brooding quality persisted, the early morning light streaked an ugly brown colour, with swollen and puffy fingers of cloud pointing across the sky. Below, the river drifted sluggishly as if it too had had bad dreams. It was still early. Finding sleep had passed me by, I tiptoed downstairs to take a shower and wash my hair, hoping hot water might slough away my fatigue.

When I got down, only Pieter was there.

The weight of lies and secrets spiralling through the air had taken my breath and my appetite with them, beset by the absurd notion that I was somehow responsible for unleashing this mayhem on my family. Those words I had written in my journal; *nothing ever happens, my life as uneventful as a blank sheet of paper* ... Maybe the gods had thought I was challenging them.

I sat down opposite him, scarcely knowing how to start a conversation or indeed if I should, rehearsing the phrases I wanted to use and jettisoning them the next minute: *What happened? What did Mother say? Have you seen Ruth? Has she forgiven you?*

I took a sip of the hot coffee, swallowing it down. 'Have you spoken to Ruth?'

Like me, Pieter appeared weary, and I knew he hadn't slept, although strangely peaceful, as if some life-changing decision had been made. He picked up a roll, piling ham and cheese onto it. With so few of us, the little bread basket, with its red-checked lining poking through the wicker, seemed suddenly over capacious, the few rolls Pieter had bought lying awkwardly in the bottom.

'Yes. We're going out especially this evening.'

I heard the clock on the landing strike the quarter hour. Without Pappy and Hans at the table expanding the conversation into a lengthy technical discussion concerning polishing and silvering or chatting about the day's work ahead, breakfast was over in minutes. 'Are you walking with Ruth or shall I wait?' My words sounded stilted and polite, miles away from the confident tones of the day before.

'No, I'll take her.' As appalled as I was by my brother's behaviour the previous afternoon, I still wanted to weep for him; his countenance awash with anguish that matched the deep shadows ringing his eyes. 'Once we're married, I don't expect Ruth will want to bother with college.'

'Pieter, why are you so set on rushing things?' The words burst out before I could stop them 'There's plenty of time. You've got your apprenticeship to finish first.'

Maybe they had talked it through and Ruth had reassured him. Yet, after winding back to the fight, I felt no such reassurance, only a grave concern. That moment in the college forecourt, the truth had flashed before Ruth like some half-remembered words of a poem and I had seen her shocked awakening. Next moment it was gone, buried out of sight, and she had walked towards Pieter.

I added more quietly. 'Wouldn't it be more sensible to spend the summer getting better acquainted?'

'I can't wait, Maidy.' Pieter crumpled the roll in his hand, scattering crumbs on the cloth. 'I was telling Mother last evening ... I need to get it settled, then I can begin to live my life again.'

'But Ruth ...'

'Maidy. I know what I'm doing.'

Quickly draining my coffee cup, I reached for my bag on the chair. 'In which case, I'll go in early, I've got work to do. I didn't get it all finished last night.'

'My fault, I think.' he said, his tone remorseful. His hand reached out to me across the table. 'Maidy, I'm sorry. I didn't mean to snap. It's just so ...'

For a moment I thought he was going to break down, the eyes raised to mine full of pain. If only time could pedal backwards as easily as it did forwards. Maybe I would never have met Zande or Jaan or acquired new friends, and I would still be wearing my hair in those despicable plaits. Nevertheless, I would have willingly sacrificed any or all of these changes to restore the even tempo of our lives.

I tried to reassure him. 'Remember when I was little – you and Hans quarrelling. You were always rebuking me for being a pokey-nose and sticking my oar in.'

'It was different in those days.'

I heard Mother's bedroom door creak open and leapt to my feet. Calling a hasty goodbye, I ran downstairs. I didn't want to meet up with her. Last night, that hidden conversation behind closed doors – she was Pieter's confidant and fully aware of his intentions. She could easily have stopped him, told him to wait before saying anything to Ruth. Pappy would have done that; he always urged caution and sleeping on a decision.

Lars was on his way up, carrying coal for the kitchen range. He hesitated, smiling his greeting.

'You're early, Magrit. Forgotten to do your homework again?'

'I miss Hans.' I said impulsively.

Lars rested the heavy bucket on the step. 'Aye, he did his work well enough but his heart was never in it. Different from Pieter. Making mirrors was all he ever wanted to do. Hans, now … well, he's young, he'll find his way.'

'I think he wants to paint.'

'Maybe.' Grasping the banister, he edged up a step. He found the steepness of the stairs troublesome with his artificial leg.

'Where's Hendrik?'

'Decided I'd get started a bit early today,' Lars nodded his explanation and continued up the stairs. As I closed the back door behind me I caught the clank of the fire door and our ancient iron poker rattled noisily as it cleared away the ashes, coaxing any unburned coal into flame.

Pushing my bike, I crossed the road onto the river path. There was no one about, the air clammy, and from the opposite bank of the river, the long line of houses regarded me warily. In my dream, they had warned me to stay away, not to follow Pieter. All at once I didn't want to be alone, jumping at shadows, my nerves jangling as discordantly as the silver charms on a bracelet. Retracing my steps, I mounted my bike and cycled down the street.

Ahead of me, a tram pulled out from the terminus, its wheels squealing against the metal tracks. I followed behind, watching its loosely hinged compartments sway from side to side, the normality of it somehow restoring a sense of order and balance to the day. The bridge was quiet also, too early for students to gather. On the canal below, the dredgers were equally silent, their shovels drooping over the water like herons patiently waiting for a fish to surface. At college, not even the director had arrived, the empty courtyard offering a rebuke for disturbing its final few moments of peace, before the start of yet another frenetic day.

I parked next to the steps, and wandered across the lawn to my hidey hole. The extreme humidity had scooped up all the air, making it difficult to breathe, a heavy pall of cloud hovering over the lake. Blotched and mired, it resembled the fleece of a sheep before it's washed and dipped in bleach. Idly, I wondered if the gods created cloud formations to mirror their emotions. If so, they weren't happy with mankind this morning. Even the daisies seemed downcast, their white petals drooping.

I was surprised to see Zande standing by the edge of the lake, scattering bread crumbs for the moorhens, their tiny black heads never still. They reminded me of the jerky movement of the staple gun Hans uses, when fixing hangings to the back of a mirror.

I hesitated, aware I had nothing to say to him. I had spent the night tossing and turning, wondering if the character I had bestowed on him was as much a fiction as my celluloid heroes with their dashing sword fights, who wooed a beautiful damsel with a cutlass in one hand and flowers in the other. Most likely, he was no more than a handsome boy with a huge ego, as shallow as the waves trickling onto shore.

He was dressed differently in a sleeveless red jersey that clung to his body, his trousers cropped to mid-calf, their cuffs frayed and bleached by water and sun. It suited him. Perhaps, in another life, he really had been a pirate.

I ducked sideways, meaning to skirt around and slip into the garden. I swear I made no noise.

Keeping his back to me, he called out, 'I was waiting for you.'

'You can't run to me every time you need absolution for your sins.' I retorted, my eyebrows set in a tight line of anger. Even so, I felt my body quiver in response to the liquid music in his voice.

'Please don't set about me, Maidy.' He shrugged. 'As for Elina … I did her a favour.'

'I don't imagine she thinks of it like that. You broke her heart.'

Impatiently, Zande tossed away the rest of the crumbs, the balls of fluff at his feet jostling together, trying to nudge one another out of the way. 'I'm not responsible for her heart. Only my own.' He came over, standing close, his glance soft and intimate.

Automatically, I stepped back.

'Surgeons removed your heart the day you were born,' I snapped, trying hard to keep my voice from trembling. 'However you try to justify your behaviour, Zande, you can't. It was callous.'

To my surprise, he laughed, his teeth flashing brightly against his dark skin. It was exuberant and totally out of place. He should have been suffering a bad conscience and scowling the day away. 'Not quite at birth. It was later than that. Still, anything that runs contrary to my father's wishes makes me more human, I'm delighted to say.'

He grabbed my hand, pulling me across to the seat. 'Don't let's fall out. You're the one good thing in my life. I wish the rest could be like you.'

I stayed silent, perched uncomfortably on the edge of the slats.

'They see what they want to see. A heavenly being.' His voice mocked the words. 'They never notice the twisted, stunted creature beneath, then feign shock and dismay when I hit out at them.' He shifted in his seat, his gaze resting on the lake. 'You see the wreck beneath and still believe I can be better. I can't, you know.' I heard his voice empty of hope and felt a surge of fear. No one so young should sound that way; despair belonged to the old who have become embittered by life, not to the young with all their life ahead.

'Sometimes, I can't tell when you're acting or if you really mean what you say. It's so frustrating.'

He gave a sly grin. 'There's an easy cure for that.' He circled the tip of his finger around my palm. 'I'm surprised ...' his eyes gleamed, 'a nice girl like you.'

I snatched my hand back. 'You're impossible. That's *exactly* what I mean.' My words came out as hot as our furnace and I made to rise. 'Why can't you be serious for once?'

He caught at my arm. 'Don't go, please. I promise I'll behave.' His eyes sparkled as if at a hidden joke. 'I saw you in the library. Had you forgotten that windows reflect both ways? Do you care for him?'

'Jaan?'

'Who else?' He slid back down and sat sideways facing me. Pulling his knees up, he rested his chin on them; his bare feet pushed into rope-soled shoes, their heels worn smooth on the outer edges.

When I first saw him, his bold gaze had stripped my clothes away, but on that bench by the lake, I read in it only pity. 'Waldger told me Pieter is your brother. I'd never have guessed; you're not a bit alike. If I had been thinking at all, I would have assumed him to be a boyfriend. You're so very different, with your violet eyes and dark hair.'

His eyes met mine, deeply serious and filled with a gentleness I had not imagined to be part of his make-up. I felt strangely breathless, as if I had run the ten kilometres from the city. I was reminded of the first time I saw him swimming naked in the lake, and had felt a powerful urge to smooth my hand down the elegant planes of his body, his muscles long and rounded, yet both graceful and powerful, his form carrying not an ounce of extra flesh.

'Believe me, had I known, I would have tried harder to walk away.'

'You did try,' I gave him the absolution he wanted. 'Doesn't it bother you at all that Pieter is in love with Ruth? That's what started the fight – or had you forgotten.'

'Why would it bother me? Every boy in college is in love with her, including Tristan.' He shrugged, 'She's not interested in any of them.'

'You can't have every girl,' I exclaimed, repeating Jaan's words.

'Why not?' His face darkened, covered with that bitter sneer. 'It's the role I've been cast in this theatrical farce we call life. Why not play it to the full?'

'You sound almost proud of it,' I accused.

'Isn't it something to be proud of?' Below our feet, like some monstrous slug, the water slid monotonously forwards and backwards across the little beach. 'That you can get any girl you want just by crooking your finger? Girls and me, it's like walking down a road. Every house has a "to let" sign.'

'Not my house.' I kept my tone sharp.

'No, not your house,' he echoed. 'You walk away from me.' He stopped, adding musingly, 'Ruth now, she's the real challenge because it has to be on her terms.'

'No different from you.'

He shrugged. 'I agree. Unfortunately, if she and I are to get together, one of us has to give in gracefully. It would be a crime to waste such beauty,' he added. 'I remember the first time I ever drank wine. You grasp the glass as a lover would, holding back from that first sip, wondering if it will taste as good as it looks.'

Why was I even listening to this? All at once, I wanted to be on my sailing ship, the wind sweeping over me clean and honest. Heading for some far distant land where I might leave behind this jealous muddle of who admired whom and secrets as dark as night; uncaring that Zande was as fickle as the weather, simply another work of art with a beautiful frame and a botched canvas inside.

As if he had sensed my anger, he shifted round in his seat, regarding me intently. His mouth trembled, all trace of boasting gone. 'Maybe the thought of that one person walking away is enough to keep my feet firmly on the ground. Promise me, Maidy ...'

'What?' Once again I felt my breath desert me.

'Nothing much. Stay as you are. Never change. Weren't we talking about Jaan before we got side-tracked? What sort of friend is he?'

'Honestly, Zande. No wonder I get mad with you! Can't we ever have a sensible conversation?'

His mouth quivered with amusement. 'I'm being sensible right now. I am asking you, politely, what sort of friend Jaan is.'

'A good friend. Satisfied?'

'Nothing more?' Idly, he picked up my hand again, tracing the lines on its palm.

'No! Nothing more,' I repeated the words firmly and once again, although hesitantly this time, removed my hand.

'Good. You know I can't stand competition, it brings out the worst in me.' I saw the sneer was back, this time directed at himself.

I didn't approve the direction our conversation was heading, conscious Zande derived an almost sadistic enjoyment in condemning his own actions, making him sound far worse than anyone had a right to be.

'I had a dream the other night.' I interrupted his soul searching.

Zande started back, his expression wary. 'Do I want to hear this?'

'You were in it.' I said.

'Girls often dream about me,' his tone once again airy and trouble free.

I tried not to smile, finding it impossible to stay angry with him for long. His mercurial changes of mood left you running breathlessly trying to catch up. He would never be boring – maddening perhaps, but never boring. I felt doubly sorry for Elina suddenly aware how much she must hurt.

'It's a regular pastime of mine. I hear from all sides that I am a prince among men, a knight, a glorious vision, the perfect specimen—'

'Mine was a nightmare,' I said tartly, cutting him down to size, delighted to turn the tables and make him uncomfortable for a change.

Zande roared, a great gust of amusement. Like a sudden wind in the sails of a barque, blowing freely. He rubbed his hand over the lower half of his face, clasping his chin. 'Ah! I really led with my chin that time. I suppose if I wait, you will tell me that I'm not a perfect specimen – far from it. Let me save you the trouble, Maidy.' He stretched his right arm along the back of the bench, the tip of his fingers level with my shoulder. 'I know I'm not perfect. I broke the bone in my arm some eight years ago.' He pointed to the bony callous which destroyed the perfect symmetry of his right arm and yet, in some ways, only added to it. 'And your dream?'

'I was following Pieter. He'd crossed the bridge opposite our house that leads to the fishing port on the lake. You know how it is with dreams; everything is both the same and very different. In my dream, the streets refused to remain still, changing to water beneath my feet.'

The moorhens, having eaten their fill, had drifted back into the water, zigzagging directionless across the water. Their watery gait was unsteady, as if Zande had fed them bread soaked in wine, and their tiny black heads, topped with red-crested beaks and bright eyes, lurched raggedly.

291

'When I caught up with my brother, he was already on the island, feeding the swans. He called to me to follow him.'

Tension tore through Zande, his gaiety wiped out as quickly as spring flowers torn to shreds by a bitter east wind. 'And did you?' he said, his voice strained and harsh.

'No. Maybe it's silly,' I hesitated, pushing the words out before I changed my mind, 'but the streets frighten me.'

Somehow I expected him to ask why. I so hoped he would, wanting release from the secret I'd kept hidden so long, the shadow in the mirror on my thirteenth birthday, convinced with the complications he brought to his own life, he would understand mine.

Keeping his expression hidden, he began lacing my fingers one on top of the other. I wondered if he was thinking about the conquerors, firstly sweeping the island bare of both birds and people, before filling it with their prisoners for whom hope no longer existed.

'It used to be called Swan Island. Of course other birds live there too, gannets and kittiwakes, even terns go there to breed, despite it being surrounded by fresh water. If you are a bird, the ocean's right on your doorstep.'

'Is that where you live?'

'Sometimes. The man who owns it ...'

'You mean Meneer Van Vliet?'

He flinched. 'Bad news *does* travel fast,' he said in a surprised tone. 'Van Vliet, yes, that's exactly who I mean. A most unpleasant man who, unfortunately, happens to be both my employer and my father.'

'Your father,' I exclaimed. 'How ...'

'How do fathers get to be fathers?' I caught the slight shudder, 'Except he never married my mother.'

'Is that where you and Pieter met, when he was working for your father?'

He shrugged. 'Work is the wrong word. No one simply

works for my father. They serve him; they do his bidding, always at his beck and call … and I hate him.' I caught the final words, softly spoken yet as sharp as a splinter of wood embedded in your finger.

'If Van Vliet is your father, you must be aware of the secret Pieter is keeping from us.'

'Secret?'

I felt the words ticking away inside my head like an unexploded bomb, 'One that involves you all.'

Zande got to his feet in one graceful move. 'Oh, that secret.'

'You don't play fair, Zande,' I burst out.

'Why would I possibly change the habit of a lifetime and play fair?' I watched his face; grim, his eyes hooded.

'Because we're friends.'

'So be satisfied with that.'

'You are the most infuriating person I have ever come across.' I pointed to the little beach. 'You're devious and vacillating and shallow, exactly like that water. Why do I even bother with you?'

'Ah! One day you will know the answer to that question.'

I blushed.

He bent down and, raising one finger, lightly touched the tip of my nose.

I leapt to my feet, breathing heavily. 'Is that your way of telling me to keep my nose out of your business?' He moved his feet and then we were facing one another, our faces inches apart. To my surprise he leaned forward and touched his lips gently to mine before stepping away again.

'No! Yes! Perhaps!' He shrugged. 'I made my father a promise … one I'd happily break, except I couldn't bear to see your face change when I told you.'

'What's the matter with my face?' I faltered.

'Nothing. You may not be as beautiful as Ruth yet there's a trust in your eyes which, as callous and treacherous as I am, I have no intention of destroying. Now, before I say something I regret, I must go. I am going sailing.'

'Don't you have a lecture?'

'Naturally, I do.' His eyes sparkled with energy. 'However, I much prefer to go sailing.'

'My dear fellow,' a voice called out. 'What excuse are you using this time? I saw that kiss.'

'Goodbye kisses are different, Waldger.'

'Goodbye!' I faltered.

A bitter, mocking expression swept over Zande's face. 'You're not good for me, Maidy, because you wreak havoc with my worst intentions. My father would hate you. He expects me to take after him. No doubt, he'll be proved right.'

I caught the discordant clanging of the bell, warning us that classes were about to begin and, closer now, an ominous rumble of thunder.

Waldger glanced up at the sky. He'd heard the thunder also, except for him it was unimportant, simply another storm. For me, it signalled the end of the world. 'If I warned you never to take anything Zande says seriously, would you believe me?' he asked, with a sly grin.

'Probably.'

'And if I told you he's actually the best of fellows. Would you believe that too?'

What was it Jaan had said? *Of us all he is the one that hurts most.*

Zande picked up my bag from the bench and handed it to me. 'Don't say yes to that, Maidy, I promise, you'll be disappointed.'

33

I didn't bother going to class. The comedy of Moliere's Tartuffe clashed discordantly with my troubled thoughts, while any discussion about Don Juan, who is portrayed as a villainous libertine and ends up cursed and in hell, would only have reignited my anger with Zande. If anyone was heading for the fires of hell, it was him.

I ran into the garden, hiding away in the bole of my willow tree, its scarred and ragged edges reminding me of the stones on my bridge. They'd both been around a long time and must have witnessed aeons of grief and heartbreak. I had failed miserably to make sense of our conversation. Resembling the hidden depths of the lake, there was more below the surface than above. The kiss had been an adlib thrown in to soften what was to happen next. I had no doubt it would be something beyond understanding or forgiveness, and Zande was warning me in advance that he was sorry.

My tears ran freely, grieving for Zande, whose torment was so deep I felt it like a bleeding wound. At some time in his life, something devastating had befallen him; something so unspeakable it had transformed him into an emotional cripple.

I recalled one of the fairy tales *Beauty and the Beast*. Zande reminded me of that beast, obstinately acting out the role fate had allotted him.

My skirt was covered in bits of green leaf where I had stripped the long strands of the willow bare. I stared down at them, inconsolable that neither Pieter nor Zande had trusted me with their secret. However bad it was, it had to be better than this turmoil that left me imagining something quite heinous.

I eventually dragged myself into class for second period and found my lecture tedious and of little consequence, relieved to reach the shelter of the lunchtime bell without attracting any further demerits. My essay on the gods of time and inevitability had taxed my mind to the limit and Professor De Witt had shown his displeasure by awarding it a poor grade. At the time I thought it unfair. How can a sixteen year old possibly understand about inevitability? After this week, if I had to write it again, I would do a far better job.

As always I headed for the library and was surprised not to find Jaan in his accustomed seat. However tedious my morning, his gentle concern, dismissing my grumbling with a friendly word, always set me back on my feet ready to cope with even the most tedious of afternoons. Although, if I was honest, my encounter with Zande had left me so confused and uncertain, I was almost grateful he wasn't about. I sat down, pulling out a book to read, and caught sight of a piece of paper poking out of the volume of legends Jaan had been diligently scouring, recognising a page from his notebook.

It had my name on it.

'*Maidy, I am heading out to the capital to try the library there. With luck, the section on myths won't have burned down. Back Friday sometime.*'

All at once I felt abandoned. Ruth no longer bothered to meet up at lunchtime, Kirsten was away, and now Jaan. Once again, the college had become an alien place, the air of permanence that possessing friends had given me expunged. Pappy had always said the college building should have been razed to the ground and built afresh. You can do that with walls but not lives, however off-course they might seem. Whatever happened, the past could not be changed or forgotten.

I rode home alone. The threat of thunder still lurked, the air oppressive and continuing humid; something that rarely happened except in the height of summer after a long, dry spell. A blanket of dense cloud obscured the sun and I felt its penetrating heat, sweat trickling between my breasts. Pedestrians walked sluggishly, the same cloud pressing down on their shoulders. Nothing moved; the breeze too feeble even to stir the ropes of the fishing boats.

As I pushed my bike along the canal, I saw the benches deserted; even the old people who had taken such delight in spring's arrival were hiding indoors behind their thick stone walls, like molluscs seeking the cool of the ocean floor.

When I reached my bridge, Meneer Meijer was sitting on the bench-seat under his balcony, pots of bright flowers gathered around him as if they were children listening to a story. I had already taken back his wife's clogs. Finding the little house tightly shuttered, I'd left them on the doorstep with a thank-you note. Wishing to express my appreciation more appropriately, I had asked Berthe to bring home one of the pottery clogs from her shop that were filled with chocolate, telling her it was for a friend's birthday.

Leaning my bike against the balustrade, I ran down the steps. 'You were out the other day when I called with your wife's shoes. Did you find them?'

'I am glad they were of use.' Struggling upright he bowed his head, presenting me with a bunch of anemones, their delicate green sepals gripping the closed buds like cupped fingers.

'Oh, how kind. I have a gift for you too,' I murmured. Rummaging in my school bag, I pulled out a miniature pottery clog, seeing his face light up as he espied the trio of tiny chocolate clogs beneath their cellophane wrapping.

'I am no better than a child in my love of chocolate.' His bright eyes glowed with pleasure. 'All my adult life I have been the same. While rationing lasted, my wife made honey sweets …' He gave me one of his pixie smiles. 'A poor substitute. These days, I save up my money and on my wife's birthday, I buy a piece from this very shop.' He pointed to the label.

'My sister works there.'

'How very fortunate she is. Does she get to eat the stock?'

'No!' I protested laughing. 'And thank you again for the flowers; it was so very kind of you, and quite unnecessary.'

'Those aren't from me. No, a young man left them for you.'

'A young man?' I exclaimed, checking the white wrapping paper for a card. 'How do you know they're for me? There's no name.'

The prince of my childhood dreams glowed with delight and I wondered if, once upon a time, his wife had truly considered him a prince. 'He told me they were for the little girl who was all grown up, yet still looked like a flower.' I blushed. 'That girl, your friend, she always reminded me of the sun. You are more like my children …' He indicated the pots under his balcony, 'you needed care to flower and become beautiful.'

He peeked up at me, his eyes bright with pleasure and curiosity. 'One day you will be asked to choose.'

'Choose?' I echoed.

He pointed to the flowers.

'It won't come to that,' I said remembering Zande's farewell kiss. Impulsively, I added, 'May I visit you sometimes?'

'I remember being young,' he reminisced. 'You are so busy drinking in life, there's no time for visiting old folks.'

'I'll make time,' I tugged one of the little flowers loose, a hint of dark blue showing under the green, and handed it to him. 'That's my promise.'

I placed the little green buds in a vase on my dressing table and by the time I came upstairs after dinner, they were already taking on colour. In a very few hours petals of blood red and dark blue, with centres black as coal dust, would shrug off their green overcoats.

Pulling out my journal, I re-read everything I had written, curious as to why the old man considered me in a position to choose between Jaan and Zande, hoping my words would offer an alternative outcome to the one I expected. After all, it was only a kiss, yet attaching it to the word *farewell* had left me totally adrift, like flotsam washed away on an outgoing tide. I found myself back at that first meeting in the garden, the little daisy lying withered inside the pages of my journal. The lines I had written since revealed quite clearly that in Jaan, I had truly found everything I could ever want. With him at my side, I would be as happy as Mother and Pappy had been. And I wished, *I so wished*, that all feeling for Zande had withered with that daisy.

34

Like an interval between one act of a play and another, when audiences recover their emotions with a glass of wine, and gird their loins ready for another helping of tragedy or comedy, we were in the middle of breakfast when our front door bell rang. Pieter, not bothering with the speaker tube, ran downstairs, reappearing almost instantly, clutching a letter for Mother in his hand. It was from Pappy, his distinctive handwriting instantly recognisable.

For the past week, I had been watching out for the telegraph boy, hoping Pappy had sent a telegram announcing his date of return. A handwritten letter was a missive of bad news, the same as black-edged mourning cards.

I missed him so much, his absence reinforcing what I had always believed, that Pappy was the fulcrum around which this family revolved. Without him, we were like marionettes with no one there to work our strings. We took for granted his patience in the face of Mother's impatience, with limitless time for our woes and grievances.

'Pappy says Hans has settled down well and is finding the work challenging. Pappy wishes to stay a little while longer, to view the whole process,' Mother read out.

She seemed better, the grey tinge on her skin gone. We still rattled about and I dreaded the day when Berthe would move out and leave us.

I heard the door open again, Ruth's feet on the stairs. As she came in, Pieter leapt to his feet, hugging her to him. I saw his expression, the same proud, almost boastful demonstration of possession that young men wore at church, when they promenaded down the aisle arm in arm with their intended. I felt delighted for him but didn't say anything. This was the sort of news only the two people concerned should break. I glanced out of the window, wishing the skies might celebrate too. The promised storm continued to linger, the sky grey and dolorous, reminding me of a technicolour film played out in black and white.

Ruth broke away, pirouetting out of reach. 'Mevrouw Bader, will you please teach your son not to mess a girl's clothes.'

Mother reached up and tapped Pieter on the shoulder. 'She's right, Pieter. I am always complaining to Pappy that he messes my hair. We spend so much time making ourselves beautiful, men need to observe and not touch. Ruth, dear, we had a letter from Pappy ...'

'When's he back?' I caught an anxious note in her voice. Of course, if Pieter and she were engaged to be married, they couldn't possibly announce it until Pappy was back.

'Sadly, my dear, not for another few days. I am pleased for his sake; it's all of fourteen years since we returned to the city. Not once in all that time has he left it.'

I expected Ruth to say something reassuring. She didn't. Instead, relief flicked over her, as if the delay was an unexpected bonus. She took Pieter's hand, swinging it lightly to and fro.

'Would you mind terribly if Maidy and I cycle to college together today and leave you behind? I've neglected her shamefully and if she is ever to be my friend again, I need to start making amends.' Pieter's cheerful expression faded. I thought of bright colours in a room that vanish when someone switches off the overhead light. 'Pieter,' she squeezed his hand. 'Stop being a grouch. Go and do some work. Before you realise the day will be over and I'll be back.' She trilled her best smile. 'Come on, Maidy. You don't need to finish your breakfast, I will be eating humble pie all the way to college.'

Mother nodded as if to say, *and so you should*. Her attention immediately shifted back to Pappy's letter, re-reading its fine copper plate.

'At least let me walk your bicycles out. Then I will go and ask Lars to provide me with some suitably dull task to keep me occupied till you get home.' Pieter's words tugged at my heart strings and I thought how lucky he was to have achieved everything he ever wanted from life.

Mother wasn't listening, busily scanning the lines of Pappy's letter as if they were the train tracks that would carry him back to her side.

Ruth seemed quite different also. Her face sparkled with energy, even more glorious than usual. I was no longer in the dog house; all that was forgotten. She was wearing a sleeveless summer dress in her favourite colour – green – and sprinkled with tiny pink roses like a wedding bouquet. Tight at the waist, the skirt danced along the street in her wake, almost all the men we passed swinging round for a second look. Her gaiety was infectious, leaving people smiling. It was rare for me to get a second glance. Today I did, dressed in my colourful skirt and turquoise blouse. Passers-by allowed their eyes to drift slowly from Ruth to me, taking delight in the gaiety of two young girls on the cusp of life, without a care in the world.

'I heard you were seeing Jaan.'

'Who told you that?'

Ruth shrugged. 'I can't remember. I talk to so many people.'

Her words didn't ring true. Gossip went on between

friends, with an unspoken agreement existing between them that prejudice and mean thoughts would never be repeated. Kirsten had said girls were jealous of Ruth and didn't speak to her, and it wouldn't have been any of the boys, very few even knew my name.

'He's not a boyfriend,' I kept my words casual. 'We're friends who enjoy spending time together.'

'That's perfect. I'm so glad for you. Perhaps you can understand how happy I am.'

'Of course, and I'm thrilled.'

'Oh Maidy, dear, I've been so rotten to you. I'll make it up to you, I promise and I'll never neglect you again.'

She did a twirl. Her skirt flew up, briefly exposing the top of her legs. Noticing, a passing cyclist swung around for a second look and promptly steered into the kerb. Hastily righting his bike, with one last glance he cycled off.

'I wish you didn't have quite such an effect on them.'

'Who? Men? It's fantastic to possess such power, I absolutely love it.' She stopped talking for a moment, adding, 'I really am like the princess in your fairy tales. And you can be my bridesmaid.'

'Has he asked you to marry him?'

'He will. They all do.' Ruth's tone rang with confidence. 'Oh, Maidy, I am so happy. You cannot believe how wonderful it is to be in love. I hope one day you will be. Perhaps not with Jaan; he doesn't seem to approve of me.' Her tone changed. 'I can't really blame him. I was such a fool.'

'What about?'

'Tristan.'

'Yes, you were.' I manhandled my bike over the kerb. 'At least now you can set it right.'

'I was thinking …'

'Y-yes?' I answered cautiously.

We had passed the bookshop, two men in overalls already

hard at work repainting the wood surround on its windows. Opposite, the door of the little cake shop had been propped open in search of a breeze, its ovens spilling their heat into the passageway.

'You know me … I'm not very good … I was wondering if you would tell Tristan for me.' Her tone changed again, cajoling.

Shocked, I stopped dead.

Ruth twisted round, her smile uncertain. 'I wouldn't ask only I hate hurting boys. They wander around with such long faces, it makes me feel like a criminal and I haven't done anything wrong,' she pleaded. 'It's not my fault if they fall in love with me.'

'Isn't it about time you grew up, Ruth?'

I hurled the words at her. Surprise and alarm swept across her face. Maybe she couldn't help being beautiful. Isn't that what all girls wanted? Nevertheless, young as I was, I was old enough to recognise that with beauty comes responsibility.

'What do you mean? *Grow up?* I'm older than you, *and wiser*. Everyone says so, even Pappy and Mevrouw Bader.' She spat the words at me. Her tone changed, wheedling, 'But Maidy, you always do as I ask,'

'Doesn't everyone?' I echoed sadly. 'Not this time. You have to speak to Tristan. You owe him that.'

'I don't understand what you mean by *owe*.'

I caught the phantom stamp of her foot on the cobbles. Ruth had never needed to understand the feelings of those around her.

'Nothing too difficult. You thank him kindly for his friendship and hope he will understand that you love someone else.'

Her face cleared. 'Is that all? All right, I'll try. But if it goes wrong, it's your fault.'

We started off again, the silence between us awkward. Ruth

hadn't used those words to me since we were little children. She said them a lot then to keep me in line but with children, love is always unconditional. Now, I simply felt irritated and angry that she could ask such a favour.

Miserably, I trailed into class. This time my inattention did bestow on me a demerit, plus the threat of a visit to the director. 'Your birthday aside, Magrit,' Professor De Witt stormed, his glare intended to reduce me to dust. It swept over my head. Nothing he said could make me feel any worse, nervously wondering if Ruth had seen Tristan and had managed to recite the words that would sound to his ears like a death knell.

'There are plenty of young people wanting to study here. If your work doesn't improve, I suggest you change places with one of them.'

I felt almost sorry for the Professor then and wished I could have explained. He must have found my inattention so frustrating; the first six months, I had listened to his lectures with sparkling eyes and rapt attention. Today, instead of setting out a timeline of events leading to the overthrow of Napoleon, I had been drawing up a different timeline in my head.

I was running upstairs to my afternoon class when I caught sight of Kirsten.

'Thank goodness for a friendly face.' I gasped out. 'How's Elina?'

'She's asleep, thank heavens. In the last couple of days, she's not stopped crying for more than a minute or two. He was very generous, always buying her trinkets.'

'I'm sorry.' Kirsten had lost weight, the waistband on her skirt looser than it had been. 'You'll make yourself ill.'

Grinning cheerfully, she inspected herself from top to toe. 'Don't worry; it'll all go back on once she's better. Food and I are far too good friends to give one another up. Jules phoned.' She saw my astonishment. 'You don't have a phone?' I shook my head. 'Oh, I guess Pa needs it for his work. Anyway … what was I saying?'

'About Jules?'

'He says you tried to stop it happening. Thank you.'

'Zande was simply lashing out and Elina happened to be standing in the firing line.'

'He did her a favour.' Kirsten sighed again. 'Except it's no good telling her that. She's reached the stage of accusing herself. I almost had to sit on her, to stop her coming into college to find him. She thinks if she promises not to do it again, whatever it is, he'll give her another chance. *Stupid girl,*' she added scornfully. 'He was gorgeous, though,' she sighed regretfully. 'Anyone else will be second best.'

'For what it's worth, and I know I've said it before, Elina is lucky to have you as a friend. I wish I did.'

'I *am* your friend,' she replied, her cheeks pinking up with indignation.

'I didn't mean you, I meant Ruth. I don't think she likes me much, anymore.'

'Oh Ruth, of course, I'm way down on the list.' She grinned good-naturedly, her countenance wide open, nothing concealed or hidden. 'So, anything to report?'

'Ruth's out of the running.' Kirsten raised an enquiring eyebrow. 'I told you she and Pieter were going steady. He's asked …' I thought of the scene this morning, that air of possession on Pieter's part and then Ruth's insistence that he hadn't yet asked. 'He's going to ask her to marry him and I know she's intending to say yes. She's telling Tristan this morning that she can't see him again, so it's all fine.' Kirsten went to interrupt and I hurried on. 'It's not official yet. Please don't tell anyone till my father is back and it's announced formally … I don't know who I'm more pleased for … my brother or Ruth.'

As I said the words, I realised they were true, I *was* happy for her.

Kirsten's mouth opened but no sound came out.

Alarmed I grabbed her arm. '*What?*'

I heard her swallow. 'Come with me. Now!' Even when Kirsten was speaking normally, her voice was loud enough to elicit attention. The 'now' boomed down the stairwell. Passing students paused, their faces foraging around ours in the hope of gleaning some juicy titbit to pass on.

'W-Why?' I stuttered.

She dragged me down the stairs and into the girls' cloakroom. 'If I tell you, you've got to promise not to shoot the messenger.'

I wondered what on earth she was going to say.

She went over to the tap and ran some water into a mug, 'Just in case.'

Impatiently I knocked it away. 'Kirsten!' I threatened.

'Okay! Jules told me that Ruth has skipped classes the last two days to go sailing with Zande.'

'She can't!'

My words echoed back at me from the bare brick of the wall. *She can't … she can't … she can't.*

In the distance I heard someone muttering, '*She never said who; I swear she didn't. She never said who.*'

It was me.

Then Kirsten was holding the mug up to my mouth. 'Water. Drink!'

Shakily, I put the cup to my lips only to find my teeth chattering, suddenly cold. So that was the reason for the goodbye kiss. 'I feel sick.' I muttered.

'What did you mean by, she never said who?'

'Did I say that?'

'Several times.'

'It was this morning …' I grabbed at my head, wanting to burst into tears. *And I had believed her.* 'When we set out, Ruth was saying h-how m-much she loved him.' Hot tears

307

scalded the back of my throat as I stammered out the words that spelled disaster. I took another sip of water trying to swallow them away.

'Maidy, I'm so sorry.'

'It's not me you should feel sorry for,' I wiped my eyes. 'I thought she was talking about Pieter. I was convinced of it. So was Pieter. I never imagined she meant Zande ... Of all the nerve, she even asked me to tell Tristan, because she felt too scared to do it. I almost fell for it.' My voice settled; the anger in it no longer predominant. 'Sorry about that. It was the shock. I love my brother and it will break his heart.'

'Yeah, sure.'

'Honestly, Kirsten. I promise.'

'You can promise till the cows come home. You didn't see your face.'

I ignored her. 'I was scared as to how Tristan might react when Ruth told him, that's all. I never heard a word of my lectures all morning. My history teacher, Professor De Witt, was almost apoplectic, poor man. It wouldn't have been so bad if it had been Waldger or Jaan ...'

'You mean you don't mind if Ruth falls in love with Jaan?'

'*No*! I meant Jaan and Waldger have a pact, never to ask a girl out before Zande has made his choice.'

'Eww! How disgusting is that?'

'Not really. It makes good sense. You said yourself practically every girl in college is in love with him.' I paused. 'Poor Pieter, at breakfast, he literally radiated happiness. This will break his heart.'

'You said that before too.' Kirsten sat down beside me and took my hands in hers. 'First thing's first; forget school.' She checked her watch. 'We're late, anyway. Pull yourself together and go down to the lake. Find out if it's true. I'll lend you a gun and you can shoot whichever one of them has upset you the most.'

My laughter sounded shaky. 'Honestly Kirsten. I was being silly, making such a fuss. I was only thinking of Pieter.'

'Oh God, Maidy, you've not much of a liar.'

Tears began to run again in earnest, 'It's not what you think, I promise. He accepts I'm with Jaan.'

'He does?' She goggled at me. 'That's doesn't sound like the Zande I know.'

I said sadly, 'I don't actually think he's much like the Zande anyone knows.' Kirsten's mouth opened and I could see a hundred questions lining up on the tip of her tongue. 'He told me …' I sighed again. 'He told me goodbye, although not in so many words.'

Kirsten sat up straighter. 'They're going. So soon? I thought not before the end of the summer.'

'Not that sort of goodbye. He was warning me, what he was about to do would make me so angry and disappointed, I would never want to see him again. He meant Ruth. He knew about Pieter – and Tristan – and he didn't care. Boasted he could have any girl he wanted.' I stared down at my hands, still shaking as badly as if I suffered from a palsy. 'How do you do it?' I muttered.

'What?'

'Keep so calm?'

'Easy, get yourself landed with two rapscallions for brothers and all your finer feelings escape out of the door. All you're left with is an intense desire to throttle them.'

I made an effort to smile. 'My brothers were older. When they fell in love with the same girl, I wanted to make it all better …'

'Well, look on the bright side, Maidy. You never wanted Ruth to marry Pieter.'

She'd said those same words to me before. Perhaps they weren't true then, but they were now. 'It will do more than break his heart. It will break up our families and we live next door to one another,' I argued, trying to convince myself as much as Kirsten. I shrugged. 'If I'm totally honest, I recognised it that very first day. Zande wanted Ruth and she him.'

'*Oh heavens!*' I went to stand up, and felt my legs still trembling and fell back in my seat. 'I just had the most terrible thought. What if they marry and come to live next door, I'll have to move away. *We'll all have to move away*. Pappy might forgive her. Mother certainly won't.'

'Sweetheart, stop crossing bridges. Go and find out. Demand the truth and don't budge till you get it.' Kirsten got to her feet and just as suddenly chuckled. 'How I'd love to be present when you tell Zande that Ruth's been ... what ... two ... no ... three-timing him! For two cents I'd come with you, except I'd better make sure first Elina hasn't woken up and escaped. My God! Can you imagine if she turned up here too?' She grinned gleefully. 'It would be pistols at dawn between her and Ruth. Oh Magrit, come on. It's almost funny. We'll laugh one day and wonder why we took it all so seriously. So why not now?'

35

Not bothering about my afternoon classes, I stowed my books in my bicycle and wandered down the driveway towards the lake, the busy hum of a building hard at work gradually falling silent behind me. In the last week, the driveway had changed, taking on the appearance of a Can-Can dancer's skirt, with layers of pink and white ruffles. I didn't hurry, trailing my fingers over their velvety softness, full of wonderment at the myriad shades of pink in a single petal.

Where the lane emerged onto the highway, steps had been cut in the side of the embankment for easy access to the lakeside. I dropped down onto the narrow beach and wandered in the direction of the bridge, little larger than a dark smudge on the horizon as if it were smoke escaping from a chimney. Within a very few minutes, sandy grit had found the gaps in my sandals lodging uncomfortably between my toes. Removing them, I was drawn to the water dipping a toe, the shallows still icy despite the warmth of the day. All at once, my mind flashed to those naked figures gambolling in the water, so light-hearted and carefree it was easy to imagine their lives being the same. How wrong that had been. Yet, even they might have remained untroubled, if Ruth had not been a student here.

Gradually, the gentle sound of water lapping against the shore began to soothe away my distress at Ruth's duplicity. If it all came right, maybe the humour Kirsten promised could well take over. The weather shared the dullness of my thoughts. Under its gloom, the lake lay black and still, and as solid as iron. Patches of rusty sunshine had broken through, like a prisoner struggling to loose his bonds, and the sticky heat bore down on my shoulders and arms. It was days since we'd glimpsed fresh blue skies and light winds. In the city, friendly smiles welcoming the spring had changed to ragged frowns, even tram drivers impatient of cyclists who approached too closely, loudly tolling their warning bell. A storm would clear the air, hotter even than the day before, as if an extra blanket had been dumped on the bed of sky.

I don't know how long I walked. Now my temper had cooled, I felt unsure about confronting Zande and Ruth. All at once, a vein of sunlight caught at the edges of a sail, its triangular silhouette too distant to identify.

It made up my mind for me.

This was wrong.

It was not my place to decide the fate of others. I wasn't some deity, an arbiter of good and evil, able to alter people's minds and desires with a frown or flick of the hand. By now, I should have accepted my part in this play. I wasn't the leading lady, however much I wished to have been offered the part. That role belonged to Ruth. Mine was simply a walk on role, the obligatory maid in an opera who tends her mistress's toilette. Always present on stage, she witnesses the action, seen but not seen, and unspoken.

Heading back, I chased up the steps, brushing off any lingering grit from the soles of my feet before slipping on my sandals again. The grounds were deserted, my bike standing dwarfed and solitary in the middle of the courtyard.

Then, out of the corner of my eye, I spotted Tristan, his hair damp and clinging to his collar, his beaky profile proudly etched. He was carrying a bag and had obviously been at the sports centre. He didn't see me, the canopy of blossom too dense. Shocked, I read into his expression a deadly intent. He devoured the ground with his eyes, his gaze fixed implacably on some point that only he could see.

Alarmed, I ran after him.

I didn't call out.

Maybe I should have?

Brushing aside the trailing strands of willow, he dropped his bag on the ground and leapt down over the bank. Zande was on the beach, his boat pulled into the shallows. At first, he didn't see Tristan powering towards him. He had taken down the sail and was busy furling it, packing its red folds into a sailcloth bag. There was no sign of Ruth. I took that in, even I grasped that the sail I had detected out in the bay was innocent of any crime; most likely a fisherman trying to eke out a living.

Like Jaan, Tristan was wearing new clothes, his slacks and shirt matching the smoky depths of his eyes. I saw them flash with lightning. My head flew up to the sky, imagining the storm to be upon us.

It was.

Before I could take a breath and shout a warning, he had dived at Zande, cannoning into him with such force that Zande was knocked off his feet, the two figures hitting the water with a crack like ice breaking.

I gasped in shock, recalling once again the light-hearted gambolling of the four friends. This was as different as summer is from winter. And had Tristan been carrying a knife, the water would have been blood-soaked and Zande dead.

Regaining his feet, Zande shouted out, water cascading off his body in a torrent of spray. He reached out a placatory hand.

Bellowing a reply, Tristan knocked it away. I didn't hear what he said … the splashing of water drowned his words even as he was trying to drown Zande, forcing his head down under the water. I moved then, trying to run on the soft shale, lurching to a stop as Zande struggled free and stood up. I caught his gasp for air like a cry for help. Launching himself at Tristan, he tried to wrap his arms around him. He shouted out, his words snapped in two as Tristan struck them away with his fists, the force of the blows taking them down below the surface again.

This time, it was Tristan who came up first.

I cried out, 'Tristan, no.' But there was no wind to carry my words and they lay there, unheard. He was panting, swinging first one way and then another, his fists beating at the water as if it too was guilty of a crime.

Relieved, I saw Zande emerge. Unsteadily, he staggered to his feet breathless, noisily sucking in enough air to fill his lungs twice over. Again, he tried to restrain Tristan's flailing fists. He grabbed him around the waist, taking the beating on his shoulders and back. I saw his mouth open, shouting without sound. The water panicked by Tristan's violence leapt into the air, like cymbals being struck together. I caught a solitary word, *calm* before Tristan dived at Zande yet again. With both hands pressed flat against his chest, he shoved him once … twice … deeper and deeper into the water, the waves displaying their anger by lashing wrathfully at the two bodies.

I could see Zande struggling to avoid being pushed out of his depth. He came up again, and took a step towards the beach. Tristan leapt onto his back, pinning Zande's arms to his chest.

I didn't understand how all of a sudden Tristan could be the stronger. Yet he was. Then I remembered how swifts recklessly skimmed rooftops, using their skill as fliers to outdo another male and attract a female. Tristan at the sports centre had behaved in an identical fashion, determinedly outplaying all his team mates. Once again, he was acting out the role of the dominant male animal, crowding out an intruder who had dared stray into his territory.

They disappeared again, their flailing feet threshing at the water like harvesters separating ripened ears of corn from chaff. The water became swamped with darkness as silt rose to the surface, changing it into a cesspool of mud.

I should have moved, gone for help. I dared not. I felt frozen into place my limbs as rigid as any statue, convinced if I moved something beyond terrible would happen. My nails dug into the palms of my hands as the two figures struggled up into the air, Tristan, his arm around Zande's neck, trying to choke his friend.

Breaking his stranglehold, Zande threw him off and down they went again, bursting up next moment, their chests heaving. Zande clutched at Tristan, struggling to keep a grip, the two figures clasped in a dance that stumbled forwards and backwards as they tried to retain their balance on the shifting lakebed. Tristan's shirt was ripped from neck to waist and protruding from his back and shoulders and arms – steel barbs.

I heard him cry out ... once ... twice ... the sound unrecognisable.

Overbalancing, he took Zande back down under the water, flailing blows at his head. Zande emerged first. His clothes were also in tatters, like the bark of a tree shredded by marauding animals. I saw his dark skin as black as night and covered in spines, resembling fletched arrows.

Changing!

Changing!

Changing!

Into what?

I knew what; I had caught a glimpse the other day in the courtyard.

Tristan raised his arms and I saw the skin of his underarms

sagging down in a loose web. As I watched, it became pitted then covered in a soft white down.

Once again, he dived headfirst into Zande. They vanished beneath the surface; the water around them boiling, erupting upwards towards the sky. Bits and pieces drifted to the surface and I saw feathers, a mixture of white and black, like tarnished silver that has lain uncleaned in a cupboard too long. Then out of the water rose two swans, hissing and wailing, their long necks and vicious mouths plucking savagely at the feathers of the other.

Down again, uppermost a tangle of human limbs, long and elegant, white and coffee coloured. A moment later ... long necks and vicious, brutish mouths.

I screamed.

Somehow Jaan was at my side. For a moment he couldn't see the fight taking place in the shallows, the prow of the little sailing dinghy obscuring the foreshortened figures. 'I came back early and saw your bike. I was hoping—'

His gaze followed the horror in my eyes.

'*God! No!*' he cried and leapt into the water. '*Maniacs, the both of you. Stop!*'

I watched my hand over my mouth, to keep the sound of my scream walled up, as he was felled by the panicky movement of their wings. He staggered to his feet and reached out with his arms. With its massive wing span, the black swan was driving up water, harried by the white swan, its long neck streaking forwards to strike that fatal blow.

I screamed again, terrified, and the black swan swooped back out of range.

As if the gesture might make them pause, arms akimbo, Jaan tried again and again to get between the warring creatures. I saw blood on his shirt where he'd been pecked, and found both my hands pressed tightly against my mouth, to stop myself shrieking out again.

He shouted, shifting from side to side, moving slowly through water that dragged at his limbs. It made no difference, the white swan lashing out with its beak to stab at the eyes of its rival. Buffeting Jaan with its powerful wings, it knocked him backwards. Waves of water crashed into the little dinghy toppling it over, seeping over the gunwale as if in search of a place to hide away from the flailing wings. Shifting under the weight of water, the little boat began to slide slowly down the shoreline. Jaan, staggering backwards in an attempt to keep his balance, tripped over its floating mast and vanished from view. A moment later, he was again on his feet, plunging back into the fray.

A momentary lapse of time … That's all, I'd swear. Not even a breath in time … I was counting. Yet that was all it took.

With its feet skittering over the agitated water, the white swan rose to its full height, the air quivering with the speed of its movement. Furiously driving its wings as if taking to the air, I caught again the hissing sound I'd heard Pieter make. Even as Jaan staggered forwards again, his arms raised in protest, the long white neck began to move in a blur of speed.

My hands fluttered from my mouth and I heard my scream. I saw the black swan thrust its wings forwards as if in protest; the concussion as they met thunderous and echoing loudly. The white swan lurched sideways and toppled headlong into the boat, the force of the assault thrusting the little craft out into deep water.

As if wanting to stop the boat escaping and bring it back to shore, the black swan, with a hiss of defiance, turned its back and paddled after it.

I felt my heart lurch and stop, my eyes fixed on the creature in the shallows. Jaan didn't move either, his gaze riveted on the white swan, its long willowy neck no match for the iron strip of the keel. It lay limply like a flower thrown haphazardly into a river, lifting slightly as the settling waves rocked it. Gradually, as if they had been fashioned out of smoke, its white wing feathers faded away, their feathery barbs lost amongst scraps of tattered grey cotton – and Tristan floated to the shore, his body as still as that of a broken doll.

I screamed again and again, instinct telling me to run. I heard water lashing behind me. Jaan grabbed me and pulled me back, holding me as Zande had tried to hold Tristan. I fought him, striking out with my nails, only to have him tighten his grip, pinning my arms to my side. Overbalancing, we collapsed down onto the grass. I stared at him with terrified eyes that could only recognise him as something inhuman.

'You don't understand,' I gasped out. 'I have to tell the authorities.'

'No! You can't do that.'

'I have to,' I begged. 'Let me go. Don't you understand? He's dead. Zande…' I struggled to get free, tears blotching my face. 'He killed him. You have to let me go. I can't stay here.'

Silence.

'Oh please, Jaan! *Please let me go.*'

I pulled against his arms, trying to get my hands free, feeling them bound tightly against my chest. Finally, I lay still, his body holding mine, as tired as death itself. Slowly, I raised my head in defeat, staring out over the lake. A little way out, the boat drifted aimlessly, as devoid of life as I felt.

I felt Jaan shift round, and the pressure on my arms eased. 'If you promise not to move, I'll go and check.'

I nodded wearily.

Cautiously releasing me, he got to his feet and crossed the sand and I watched him go. Tall and willowy with a natural elegance, in that regard very different from Pappy; in every other way, very much the same. I'd acquired the same belief in him as I had in Pappy, instinctively aware he would never willingly cause hurt to a soul.

How wrong I'd been.

He was not like Pappy, not in the slightest. He was a monster, something alien; as different from Pappy as it was possible to get.

I tasted bile in my throat. Ducking behind a bush, I vomited up the sandwich I'd eaten for lunch. My head pounded mercilessly and I remembered Kirsten's light-hearted suggestion that we would one day laugh about all this.

Jaan bent down and touched the gently floating figure. Removing his hand, he stood up, staring out over the horizon. That's when I knew for definite that Tristan was dead and he was making his own farewell.

Keeping his head bent, he walked slowly back to my side.

I scuttled backwards. 'Don't touch me,' I whispered.

Monster that he was, I still couldn't bear the pain that flooded across his face at my words.

'I wasn't intending to.' He handed me a handkerchief to wipe my mouth. 'Here.'

I was cold, despite the blanket of warmth coating the earth, and hugged my arms to my chest. 'What are you? Mutants?'

The agony in his smile vanished my breath. 'Mutants or cursed – does it really matter which? Come – sit down here where it's fresh and pleasant.' He pointed to the little arbour of willows. 'Nothing's changed, Maidy. You may think me some terrible creature and for that I don't blame you in the least. That's what I am. Beyond all that, I'm still Jaan. I would never hurt you. That's my sacred promise to you.'

I didn't move, staring long and hard at the delicate stems trailing across the ground, wondering if everything in nature carried a secret malignant armoury with which to rip your heart and your flesh.

Gradually, I realised they hadn't changed, no different from when I first saw them, their long fronds compliant and gently parting when you pushed them aside. The sky hadn't changed either, covered in an endless forest of black cloud. Nearby, tiny rivulets of water still tiptoed across the shore line, as delicate as the feet of the waders that I had watched from our living room window. The only thing different was me and the way I now viewed a world, in which a person could be alive one minute and dead the next.

Sadly, I watched Tristan's body nudge up against the shore, strands of his long brown hair floating in the shallow water.

'You've seen some of the story. I need to tell you the rest.'

'I don't want to hear it,' I replied, my voice weary, defeated. 'Zande killed him. He's a murderer and I have to tell the authorities,' I repeated.

'You can't believe that. Zande would never kill anyone.'

His words gave me hope. 'Why not?'

'Because death and he have recently become good friends.'

'I don't understand,' I whispered.

'It was an accident, Maidy. Didn't you see? Zande turned his back the moment he could and walked away. Except the word *walk* isn't appropriate.' Jaan fell silent, staring over towards the island. 'I must go, inform Van Vliet what's happened. Zande'll be distraught.' He shifted restlessly, getting to his feet. Then, as if his words had outstripped his thinking, subsided onto the sand again. 'Not yet … in a moment. First, I must explain to you. Sit down. *Please*,' he begged, 'then I know you won't run away.' His face was a mask of confusion, unsure of my reaction. 'Believe me, I can't let that happen. Once you understand … it won't matter.'

I sat down with my back against the willow. Perhaps the same willow I had sheltered under and used so light-heartedly as my dressing room, its lime green fronds gradually darkening towards summer.

Jaan pulled out his wallet, his hand shaking out of control, and handed me a coloured postcard of a painting by Peter Paul Rubens. It was entitled *Leda and the Swan,* and depicted a nude woman, a white swan on her breast. 'When I met you,

I hoped the time would never come when you needed to see this. If you remember at the museum, I avoided the salon of work by artists earlier than the seventeenth century. The original hangs there.'

'Yes, I've seen it many times. It's the legend of Zeus who comes down to earth in the form of a swan. I don't understand,' I said, trying to block out the images crowding my eyes; the human forms of Tristan and Zande swept away and replaced by mythical creatures, equally – if not more – beautiful. 'You saying it's true? It can't be. It's a legend, *a legend.*' I repeated the word as if it was a mantra and if repeated often enough would prove true.

'Maybe. Whatever it is, it's a curse on mankind, not just some fable about the gods of old. What did you call it? A story drummed up by our ancestors to explain the world around them. If only it had been, Maidy. A fable ... a charming little tale to tell our children. It's not. It never was, although for centuries that's what our people have believed. It has taken a world war to teach us differently. Nevertheless, whatever the truth, it's real and it exists. Despite the war that ignited a whole world and destroyed almost half of it, it hasn't gone away.' He paused and gave a sigh, as if taking stock of the scene in front of us, the water lapping the shore, the long slim form of Tristan resting gently on the sand as if asleep, his body swaying slightly as a wave lifted it. In that sigh, I heard wretchedness, fear, and acceptance. 'Although mostly to boys or so I am reliably informed.'

I wanted to ask why not girls, but felt too exhausted to form the words.

'They change as teenagers, leaving the family they were born into. I was almost sixteen, too young to understand why me, why not my friends as well.' Jaan was silent for a moment remembering no doubt his home in the south of the country. 'They call us carinatae, children of Zeus, devils, monsters, sometimes even angels. The history books tell us we have existed since the gods walked the Earth. Although why we are not extinct when we've been persecuted to death, and driven from one country to another, I don't rightly know. Once changed, our human lives are on fast-forward.' I shuddered at the anger in his voice. 'The most foolhardy return home, hoping to live a normal life and hide their abnormality ... as we have tried to do.' Silence fell again.

In the far distance, unaware and uninvolved, I heard the friendly chirp of a robin which, satisfied with its place in the evolutionary wheel, was busy searching out food for its young.

'It rarely succeeds; this world doesn't encourage freaks. And so, we live apart until we are once again discovered and forced to flee. We have one chance ...'

He stopped and looked directly at me. I felt his pain brim over, exactly as the water in the little rowing boat had done. 'If we succeed in finding a loving partner, who will stay with us always, then the curse will be lifted. We will gradually change back, becoming completely human again. Even more amazing – any children we have will also be untainted. How or why, again no one knows. Perhaps after all Zeus did once exist? Can you see where this is leading, Maidy, how it explains why Waldger and I rarely if ever get involved with girls?'

Jaan was watching me, his voice steady again, full of compassion. From somewhere deep down I found the courage to look back, noticing his blue eyes filled with a boundless hurt.

'Because the stakes are too high.' I whispered, finding my voice.

He wasn't a monster. I should never have doubted. If he wasn't, neither were Zande and Tristan. I sensed the disquiet in my words ... they simply didn't ring true. I closed my eyes, watching again the bestial frenzy displayed by Tristan; unyielding even until death in his desire for dominance.

'No one can say where it began; a malignant gene perhaps.'

He frowned down at the painting of Leda. 'I don't believe in Zeus, none of us do, not those of us who have lived through the war. I read the story you gave me of the Flying Dutchman, cursed to sail the seas. It might easily have been written about us. Wherever we go, as soon as people learn what we are, we are persecuted. Klüsta …' Jaan broke off, pointing out over the lake. 'For generations, it has been a place where we can live in peace, returning to it year after year. Yet even here we have been hounded. Last time, it was war. If anything unusual happens: abnormal weather, an epidemic in the city, anything at all …' He hesitated, 'Perhaps a girl … we are blamed and driven out, slaughtered even, and our homes burned …'

'Why did you return this time?'

'Because Van Vliet hoped the authorities might allow us to stay permanently. The world is changing and after the horrors of the war, all we want is to be left in peace. Remember me telling you the outside of the shutters isn't always worth seeing. I have seen the world twice over, Maidy. Yet, I would willingly give up everything I have seen or will ever see to be free.'

'That's why you're searching …'

'Not especially for me. For Zande. Tris …' his attention fastened momentarily on the silent form in the water. 'Waldger and me,' he amended his words, 'we still have a chance. Like Pieter, Zande is older than the rest of us. He married young in the hope of escaping his fate. It was to a girl he had met as a child. She lived on a farm where he'd been sent with his brother and sister … again fleeing persecution. A couple of months after they were married, she ran away. She left him a note saying she didn't want to be a farmer's wife and asked for a divorce. Even though it was not his fault, his one chance was gone.' He stared down at the ground, shaking his head as if the words he was planning to say ought never to see the light of day. 'We learned later it was his father, Van Vliet, who paid her passage to America.'

323

'His father?' I could not believe what I was hearing. 'You mean his own father took away his opportunity to become …' I hesitated, hearing the word *normal* sound out in my head. 'Well again?' I shivered, my words faint. 'What happens to him now?'

'Swans generally live for twenty years, sometimes more. Those of us that are cursed, we get thirty, maybe thirty-five if we're lucky. Less if we're not. Only the Black gets more.'

You didn't say what happens to Zande.

I didn't speak the words aloud. Jaan's sigh had told me everything I needed to know. Marriage for them was the Holy Grail, the elixir of life and hope. What had happened to Zande, the shock of losing his one chance … his own father condemning him to a half-life … it was eating into him. Eventually, it would destroy him. That's why Jaan had said he was dying.

'So you see Zande would never willingly let anyone suffer as he is doing.'

'Does it hurt … the changing?'

'Not if you accept and let it happen. Most of us have done that. Tragically, Pieter couldn't accept what had happened to him. He has fought and fought. Doubtless he will continue to do so until the bitter end, suffering greatly as a consequence.' He stared out over the lake. 'Surprisingly, I always felt sorrier for Pieter than for any of us. We all did. He shut his mind, hiding away, refusing to make friends in case he was contaminated further. He was so lonely.'

Pieter!

I found myself on my feet. 'I have to get home.'

'You won't …'

'Tell?' My laughter resembled the cackle of a crazy woman. 'Who would ever believe me? Besides, someone has to report Tristan dead.'

'I'll do that.' Jaan stood up, his wet clothes clinging to him as if overcome by fear. 'I'll go straight to the island …'

Somewhere in a far distant memory, I recollected that Zande had called it Swan Island. He would have found the name amusing, taking sadistic pleasure in sailing so close to the wind.

'I'll warn Van Vliet. He'll deal with it. Can we meet up as planned tomorrow?'

'*No!*' The word flew out, astonishing me with its violence. 'Don't you understand, I can never see you again.'

'I can see how upset you are, Maidy. Anyone would be. It's a terrible story. However, once you've slept on it, thought it through, maybe you will change your mind ... We're friends, aren't we? Just friends.'

It was a lie. He knew it as I did. I tasted blood on the inside of my mouth where I'd bitten my cheek, watching Zande's dark curly head being hurled down into the bowels of the lake, fearing I would never see it emerge. I wasn't in love with Jaan. It was unfair to let him think otherwise, especially when that person's life hung in the balance.

'It's not the same anymore.'

'Maidy ...'

I swung away, running – fleeing – escaping across the lawn to my bike. My entire being felt torn apart, ripped down the middle like a sheet of paper; part of me wishing Jaan had told me earlier, the rest that he'd never told me at all.

36

I've no idea how I got back to the city. Perhaps it was the winds of fate that blew me there, the air silent as if holding its breath.

I vaguely remembered swinging out onto the highway. Had a car been driving along at that moment, I wouldn't have seen it, tears blinding my eyes. My head bent, the asphalt surface of the road flowed beneath my tyres like a roll of celluloid film, imprinted with the black and white images of a newsreel that conveys news from around the world to its audience. I saw again the feathery barbs, mirroring the spines on a porcupine, where once smooth skin had existed; the firm skin of young men at their most beautiful, their most seductive, with all their lives ahead of them, treacherously replaced by bright plumage that glistens in water, and long necks as graceful and sinuous as weeds drifting on a river current.

Was it folly to dismiss all legends as the wild imaginings of an untutored race? Maybe they did exist, those ancient gods for whom cruelty carried no more significance than a new robe or sandals. Athena, who had found it amusing to change Arachne into a spider, when her only crime had been to win a weaving contest; Artemis who transformed the hunter Actaeon into a stag because he was foolish enough to spy on her graceful form, encouraging his own dogs to tear him to pieces. This was little different. Was this curse simply another snatched moment of drollery, a fleeting entertainment for one or other of the deities, Zeus himself, perhaps? To change something glorious into something equally as beautiful yet doomed.

And Tristan? When I saw him first, I had been captivated by his imperious profile which spoke of history past and the glory of the Caesars, finding it difficult to take my eyes off him. Had the gods also found it amusing to watch him drown in the lake of Ruth's beauty?

My mind spun haphazardly, exactly as pedals do on a bike when its gear chain falls off, spewing out isolated words and phrases as useless as droplets of oil. First, I had to find Ruth and discover if Pieter had gone ahead and asked her to marry him. If he hadn't, I needed to stop him. Then I had to find him a wife. That bit would be easy. Anyone would love Pieter.

Except Ruth, the words reverberated round my head as did the words ... *if he has asked her and she has accepted ... what then?* I shied away from the answer.

Should I tell her about the swans? Should I beg or plead with her to honour her promise and marry Pieter. She had always wanted to belong to a real family, maybe it would be enough ...

Somehow I doubted it.

As I left the lakeshore behind, I caught a sound of distant drumming like an alarm call. It faded while the sky, forewarned of what was about to happen, held its breath. A moment later, the horizon flashed a rapid semaphore of bright zigzags and a dozen shafts of lightning streaked across it, the cables supporting the bridge pulsating with light.

I felt the strengthening wind, my pedals all at once heavy and difficult to push round. I was cold too, the temperature nose-diving piteously, consigning the heat of the last few days to memory.

I had to find Ruth.

I had to save Pieter.

In the gathering gloom of the approaching storm, motorists switched on their headlights. Unused to the glare, I kept my head buried, watching the ground fly past. Enormous shadows loomed over me like monsters from the deep, except somewhere in the back of my mind I accepted them as cars, waiting for a chance to overtake. Blindly I rode on, the heavy evening traffic pressing in on all sides, making it impossible to breathe. A horn sounded, startling me and automatically I swerved, my thin tyres skidding on the slippery iron ridges of the tram tracks. A hand shot out and grabbed my handlebars, pulling me upright.

'Are you all right, Mevrouw? That was close. Nearly had you off that time.'

I couldn't make out the face or take in the words so kindly meant.

Ahead I noticed cars driving into the city had slowed to a stop, horns sounding, the long line impatient to get moving again.

'What's happened, an accident?' I murmured still out of breath.

'Protest.' The man waved his arm vaguely in the direction of City Hall. 'Couldn't say what about. Last time it was the farmers complaining about the high cost of diesel for their tractors. Once it was teachers about their salaries … Always something.' He listened intently, thunder resonating in the distance. 'This weather, it'll be fishermen; they're always belly-aching, if you'll excuse the expression, Mevrouw.' He glanced back at the stationary traffic. 'You in a hurry?' I nodded. 'You'd be better off walking; this little lot won't be moving in a hurry.'

Thanking him, I ran my bike along the pavements, twisting through the backstreets to avoid the city centre, conscious of time ticking remorselessly. Pictures rampaged through my mind of four children playing their youthful games, helpless with laughter as they pelted up and down the many staircases in our house. I chased down the narrow pathway heading for the canal, seeing it awash with a simmering darkness.

'Good evening, Magrit.'

I jumped and twisted round, recognising the old boatman, Pappy's friend. Sat in the stern of his boat, I must have walked straight past him. He used to moor his boat on the canal near our house and of an evening, Pappy would go for a stroll as far as the canal and share a pipe with him.

Removing his pipe, he drew its stem through the air as if measuring me. 'Or perhaps I should say Mevrouw, now you are all grown-up.'

Impatiently, I searched for a polite reply, frantic at yet more delay.

Somewhere in the back of my mind, I wondered if the same ancient gods that had once cursed mankind were trifling with me and blocking my route home. 'You have always known me as Magrit.'

Across the canal, a dozen or more fishing boats were tied up alongside the helmeted bridge. 'Did you come in early to avoid the storm?'

'I am too old to battle the seas, Mevrouw Magrit.' I saw he spoke only the truth, his once strong body diminished with age. He indicated the small sailing vessel, its silken sides polished and glowing with bright colour. 'My son suggested we moored it on the canal here, where I might find more people willing to stop and chat. He'll be along in a minute and will help me back to the house. That lot,' he pointed to a crowd of men on the towpath, 'they never bothered going out today. They say the fish aren't biting.'

'How strange! I thought fishermen found their catches improved in stormy weather?'

'Aye, mostly they do but no one's had as much as a nibble this past week and fishermen are a superstitious lot. One marker is considered a challenge, a double is an omen. Fish not biting and a storm?' He eyed the clouds in their unbroken overcoat of greyish brown, yellow streaks cutting through as if the sun had melted. 'Fishermen never disregard omens – not if they want to raise their grandkids, they don't.'

'I never understand how they can reconcile superstition with a belief in God?' I asked, genuinely interested in his answer.

'You have a lot to learn, Mevrouw Magrit.' Pappy's old friend stirred, shifting in his seat, and I caught sight of his right hand knotted into a claw with rheumatism. 'Superstition predates religion. Something you are born with. Religion you acquire.'

Through a gap in the crowd of men, I noticed a line had been rigged across the towpath. A motley collection of small birds hung from it, mostly larks and rooks. At one end were three white swans, their plumage limp and bedraggled.

The ground shifted beneath my feet, heaving up as if alive. Trying to keep from fainting, I clung to the handlebars of my bicycle, my knuckles blanched white with strain. 'Why are they killing swans?' I whispered, my voice a stranger.

'They're hungry and swans make good eating, not fiddly to pluck like larks. Without fish, their kids'll go hungry,' the old man swept on, delighted to have an audience. 'Besides, fishermen think it's them what's causing this.'

'I must go.' I made to get on my bike.

'Did you hear about that lad what got attacked?' he continued relentlessly, determined to hold onto his audience. 'That's him, there.' He pointed with his pipe across the canal. I recognised the blond young man, a plaster cast over his arm.

'That's not happened before neither.' He spat into the water. 'A third marker.'

I lurched into movement sick with fear, terrified the youth might look up and recognise me, my throat burning at the memory. 'Meneer, forgive my rudeness but I'm so late,' I called over my shoulder. 'I'll tell Pappy I saw you.'

Instinct took me home. I fell into the yard, clumsily tripping over the little ridge of wood framing the Judas gate. Leaving my bike leaning against the garage door, I fumbled open the back door and chased upstairs, stopping halfway to regain control of my breath.

Faint sounds came from the kitchen. I glanced at the grandfather clock sonorously tick-tocking its way through the hours, surprised to find its hands pointing to a quarter past five. Mother would be cooking dinner.

If Pappy were here, I could confide in him. Maybe I was still little enough to perch on his knee as I did as a child, my head burrowing into his chest, seeking warmth and comfort after a tumble. 'It will be better in a moment,' he would say. And it always was.

I couldn't share my thoughts with Mother. I never had.

I turned to go downstairs again. In my panic, I must have neglected to close the yard door properly. The blustery wind caught the edge and flung it open. Before I could get down the stairs to catch it, it had bounced hard against the wall, immediately slamming shut. Mother opened the kitchen door onto the landing and peered round to see who had come in.

'Magrit? Your skirt's wet? Whatever's happened?'

I heard her tone, rebuking me.

Reluctantly, I slid my hand up the banister, trailing up the rest of the flight. Where the material in my skirt had stayed dry, its colour remained light and carefree, much the same as me when I had set out this morning, its bright colour attracting smiles of admiration. The remainder looked dark and stained as if by blood. Somewhere I'd caught the hem, and it drooped down like some bedraggled halfwit. My sandals were ruined too; the narrow turquoise straps that I'd so admired in my mirror, twisting my feet one way and another, mired by water and their soles caked with grit.

'I fell off my bicycle.'

Mother's eyes bore into my face as if it was a map and she was reading from it. I've no idea what she saw there. I imagined it blank and without feeling; the experiences of that afternoon wearing away all emotion, leaving no room for anything further. She reeled back, her hand clasped to her mouth. 'Oh, Magrit, Magrit! *Not you too?*'

Not me, what? I opened my mouth to voice my words aloud but the lies sat deep in my chest and refused to be spoken. And the truth, the secret Jaan had passed on to me, becoming too heavy to bear, I felt the ground rising up to meet me and then … nothing.

37

I regained consciousness to find myself lying on the sofa in the study covered with a blanket, a cold, wet towel on my forehead. Mother was sitting in our old rocking chair, the one grandmother used; the pattern of its wicker seat and back as expertly crafted as the stiches she had conjured up with her crochet needle.

'How did I get here?' My voice sounded scratchy as if I had a bad cold.

'Lars. I called him to carry you. He was ready to leave and came to stoke up the range and say goodnight.'

'What did you say to him?' Concerned I sat up, gazing with questioning eyes.

'Nothing.' She reached across with her hand, touching her fingers to my wrist. 'That feels better,' she said, taking my pulse. It was a rare gesture. I had always felt I was a disappointment to her. Since my ninth birthday, I had become more used to rebukes than caresses. She laid her hand on mine. 'All these long years, Maidy …'

That's when I remembered.

I didn't remove her hand. I left it lying there inert, unwilling to pretend a tenderness towards her I didn't feel. A week ago, I might have been overjoyed at her approach. Not now. On my journey home, driven by the pounding of my feet, I'd worked out what she had done to Pappy all those years ago.

She began talking. 'You and I have never been close. Nevertheless, I think you should hear my story. It's not a pretty one. Maybe …'

She didn't complete the sentence, and I realised she was nervous, fearing condemnation.

That was only fair. I had grown up experiencing bushels of it.

'I was a fisherman's daughter, growing up in one of those little houses near the old port. It was all I knew, the view over the bay and the road to our little primary school. The same one you attended.'

She removed her hand, brushing a loose strand of hair from her neck. She didn't replace it, perhaps sensing my antagonism, clasping her hands together on her lap. 'School was the one occasion I was allowed out alone. I was told that strangers had come to the old city and the streets were unfit for decent women. If the Burghers hadn't made it compulsory, girls would not even have been allowed to attend school. At fourteen, they were taught a trade; lace making, sewing, anything that could be carried out in the home. I was taught sewing. Then at sixteen, they were married off to someone chosen by their parents.

'Pappy …' She gave a little whimsical smile. 'He was always Pappy from the moment Pieter was born; no one ever used his name apart from me. *Gerard* …' She said the word slowly, repeating it again as if it was newly discovered. 'Gerard and Pieter … Do you remember your uncle?'

'No, only his photograph.'

'We were at the same primary school. Whereas I was poor, their family – the Baders – were rich. Despite that,

Pappy and me, we were friends. After school ended, we didn't meet again. Like every other girl in our community, I found my confinement irksome and was always seeking to escape it. I didn't learn why girls were treated in this way until later. All I knew was that it was wrong to be so guarded. One day, I strayed across the bridge, aware if my father found out he would beat me. That's the day I met Pappy again, standing behind me as I peered into a mirror.' She paused. 'By then, I was in love with someone else, slipping out to meet him while my father was at sea. His name was Robert.' Mother leant over and tucked the blanket more closely round my shoulders.

'To a young and impressionable girl, he was beautiful, like some god. I knew he came from Klüsta. As closely guarded as I was, I had heard rumours about the menfolk of Klüsta; that they were wild, foreigners from outside our community and the reason we were so closely confined. I heard my father say on many occasions, they should be forced to leave – never to return.

'One day, Pappy called at the house asking my father's permission to marry me.' She brushed an imaginary wisp of hair impatiently away. 'In love with Robert, I refused and ran away to the island. Robert wanted me to stay with him, although he never offered marriage. After that, I couldn't go home. Pappy came after me and took me away and we were married the following week. Shortly after, I knew I was pregnant.'

'And you waited fifteen years to tell Pappy the child wasn't his,' I rebuked, my tone scathing.

'You heard?' The words came out on a gasp of painful breath.

'Yes, but I didn't understand until now.'

'He forgave me, Magrit.'

Maybe I would eventually. Not today. Not when this particular truth had waited so long in the wings.

'I love Pappy dearly. I grew to love him,' she corrected her words. 'In all these years, he's never broken a promise, the most caring and honourable man you could ever want to meet. He's given me a good life and ...' I caught the hesitation, '*four* beautiful children.'

'Why are you telling me this?'

She seemed surprised. 'Isn't it obvious, Magrit. I wanted to tell you that I will stand by you. I won't turn my back as my family did.'

I wanted to laugh, to cry ... maybe both at the same time. My own mother knew me so little, she would more readily believe the worst and jump to the wrong conclusion, than seek out a more rational explanation for my fainting fit.

The physical characteristics we shared, the ones Pappy had once remarked on, were a family resemblance, nothing more. No more significant than the similarities Berthe and Hans shared. Their characters were polls apart, as was mine from Mother's. She and I had nothing in common beyond being tall and slight with long dark hair. Nevertheless, that resemblance had been sufficient to create in her a belief that her youngest daughter would doubtless tread down the same ruinous path she had taken.

It explained so much. Already critical of the fantasy world in which I lived, she had withdrawn from me more and more as I grew up, curbing my freedoms with a dull uniform of navy blue ... exactly as her father had tried to restrict her freedom. If it had been left to my mother, no doubt her relentless criticism would have sent me down that same treacherous path. It was Pieter who had reaped my share of Mother's affection. I had always wondered why. Now I knew. He reminded her of someone she had once cared deeply for.

It was Pappy who had rescued me. He knew me to be very different from his wife; someone who saw life clearly through eyes of a different hue. He had asked to meet Jaan, reassured when I said that Jaan resembled him, my favourite person in the entire world.

I took the cold compress off my head and sat up. 'You don't have to worry; I'm not in any trouble.'

Relief spread across my mother's face so quickly, I was shocked. How could she so easily assume her own daughter to be as ruined as she had once been?

I threw off the blanket and stood up. 'I have to go.'

'You're not in a fit state to go anywhere.'

'Why should it matter what state I'm in, Mother?' I heard my voice, as cold as ice. 'Where's Pieter? I need to find him.'

All around me the house was clothed in silence, the giant furnace in the basement workshop sleeping. I listened intently, hoping to hear Pieter's footsteps overhead. Nearby, a horn sounded out from a passing fishing boat, a desolate wail announcing its safe arrival at its river anchorage. It was late, most boats would have been back by mid-afternoon, their crew already at home with their feet on the fender, taking their ease, if they had bothered to go out at all. I recalled Pappy's old friend saying the fish weren't biting. 'He can't be at work. You said Lars had already left.'

'Why are you asking about Pieter?'

I relented. 'Because I know what happened to him.'

'What are you talking about?'

Anger swept through me. I wanted to rail at her, tell her to stop lying. To shout out, *Because of you, Mother, Pieter is cursed.* I wanted to find words to hurt her as much as Pieter had been hurt. A lifetime of speaking respectfully stopped me. Just as suddenly my anger was gone, replaced by an overwhelming sense of pity. All those birthdays when she'd been sad, I had always wondered if something was waiting up ahead – something she dreaded. For the crime of falling in love, she had been punished every day since.

'Some boys came to the college. Now Tristan, one of the four, is dead. All because of Ruth. They fought ...'

My mother's expression changed and the hand that had clutched mine sped to her chest, as if needing to hold her heart in place. 'Pieter?' she gasped out. She grabbed my hand with her other one, her grip fierce. 'I warned him ...'

'It wasn't Pieter.' I reassured her, seeing relief spread through her body. 'It wouldn't have made any difference if it had been. The two boys became angry and changed. That's why Pieter was so frightened when it happened to him. That's right, isn't it, Mother?'

She dropped into grandmother's chair setting it rocking violently forwards and backwards as if trying to escape from the room. 'The belligerence is the start, Maidy,' she burst out, tears falling onto her hands. 'Swans are like that ...' The truth caught at the back of her throat, making it difficult to speak and she panted out the words. 'He was so afraid. He didn't want to wait another week, until Pappy came home. I told him to leave work early, go to the island, and ask his employer for permission to marry.'

I laughed.

Not because what Mother said was funny but because it was so unbelievable. The ugly sound vibrated against my eardrums. Hans had once compared my laugh to a corncrake. He'd been teasing. But that's exactly how it sounded; harsh and discordant, merriment as far distant from my voice as peace and harmony were from our home. 'Mother, do you honestly believe he hasn't worked out that Van Vliet is his father? After all, he's had six years to brood on it.' Then I said something unforgiveable, something worthy only of the gutter. Something so out of character that even as the words flew out of my mouth I was ashamed for them. 'What price did you have to pay, to win him those extra months till he was sixteen?'

Mother struck me, my cheek stinging with the sharpness

of the blow. I staggered back and my hand knocked against a pile of papers, sweeping them to the ground in a waterfall of pencil and ink letters. Bits of stories that in another life I had arranged so neatly.

Concern for Pieter swept me downstairs and into the street. A light was on in Meneer Endelbaum's shop. In the far corner, where a fireplace had once been, he had installed a tiny workbench, a lamp shining down onto it. He was bent over it, his back to the window, a jeweller's glass to his eye.

He had always cut his own diamonds, telling me that's where the skill and money lay. 'Anyone can sell them,' he had once said holding up the stone he was cutting. 'This comes from the great continent of Africa.'

He had placed the stone in my cupped hand. I remember it being as large as a pigeon's egg with rough edges, too young to appreciate why all the fuss. 'It's dull and there's no sparkle to it,' I had complained, disillusioned by the film of blue in which the stone was wrapped.

'Of course; that's where the magic comes in.' Meneer Endelbaum had given me the jeweller's glass, showing me the line of tiny marks he had drawn with a special pen. 'Imagine them as fault lines in the earth's crust. If you make a clean cut at that point, the sparkle will be revealed. Two or three cuts and I promise you this stone will rival the stars.' He had smiled, chucking me under the chin, 'Although never as beautiful as my Ruth or you, Maidy.'

He waved and, removing his eye glass, crossed the shop floor to unlatch the door. 'Ruth isn't here.' Noticing my dishevelled appearance, 'No bones broken, I hope,' he chuckled.

'No, no bones. Not even a bruise. Where is she?'

He seemed astonished. 'If you don't know ...' He hesitated and I saw a whimsical sadness seep over him. 'But then everything is different now, isn't it, my child.' I nodded, aware he had already accepted the loss of his daughter to marriage. 'I expect Ruth's out somewhere with Pieter. They've become very close. I'm glad.' he reassured me. He made to shut the door and hesitated, 'If you've nothing better to do, you may stay and watch me work.'

Without Ruth, his life would be so lonely; Mevrouw Endelbaum was now too frail to be cheerful company. Once Ruth married and moved out, there would be nothing apart from his diamonds to keep him company; beautiful maybe, and attracting admiration from every quarter, yet cold, proud, and unfeeling.

'Another day. It's almost dinner time and I daren't be late,' I smiled my lie. 'Mother fusses.'

I didn't know where Ruth was, although I could make a pretty good guess.

In the space of a few minutes, the wind had increased, howling reproachfully as if I had personally upset it. Spitefully, it blew me across the bridge, my feet echoing hollowly against its planking. Surprised, I caught sight of a figure walking ahead and recognised Meneer Meijer. He was using a stick and alarmed for his obvious frailty in the blustery wind, I ran to catch him.

'Meneer Meijer,' I shouted as I reached him, 'what are you doing out?' I grasped his arm, feeling the bones close to the skin brittle, as easily snapped as a twig.

'I need to get to the island ...' he gasped out, a gust of wind blowing away the end of his sentence.

'What?' I bent close.

'The island. I must get there.'

'The island? Why?'

I searched around for shelter, the area poorly lit and shadowy. Its lamp posts widely spaced and few in number offered little reprieve from the encroaching darkness. Noticing a passageway between two houses, I helped him across the road. 'I can't hear a thing in this wind.' I explained. 'What's so urgent, you would risk getting caught in the storm?'

My childhood prince grabbed my hands in his. 'The fishermen are going to the lakeside tonight to cull the swans. They are angry about the boy being attacked.'

'But he …'

'Deserved it?' The bright eyes regarded me with compassion.

I flushed. 'You know?'

'About the swan people. Yes.'

'How?'

'I was one of them.' He clutched his shawl more closely across his chest. Pictures of four boys light-heartedly frolicking in the lake flashed through my mind. 'Almost fifty years ago now, I met a girl. She gave me a gift.'

'Gift,' I echoed stupidly. Then I remembered Jaan's words. 'She gave you your life back?'

'Indeed she did. I never asked her for another, for anything else would have paled into insignificance beside that.' He gave a tiny half-smile, lost in his memories of his wife. 'We had over forty years of marriage, perfect years, and then she left me. I still feel it unfair. It should have been me who died not her.' He nodded his head at me, as if the gesture might encourage his feet into action again. 'Now, I must reach the swan people, and warn them of the threat.'

'I'll go.' I swallowed painfully, instantly wanting to withdraw my offer, afraid of the streets that had featured so vividly in my nightmares. 'But let me walk you home first.'

'No need.' He gave a little laugh. 'My former life did have some advantages. I can still tell when the weather is about to change. There is time enough to get home; the storm is not quite ready to unleash its fury on our streets.'

What was it Zande had said? *The human condition can be so restrictive.*

'Tell them if it happens, it will be at night while the swans are supposedly roosting.'

He noticed my puzzlement. 'That is when they celebrate

their lives child, in the darkest hours. Did you not know?'

'My brother Pieter,' I whispered, 'I wondered why he never slept at home.'

'Oh, my poor child,' his bright eyes focussed on my face. 'Once upon a time, even I would have celebrated his good fortune. No longer; not since Zande.'

'Zande!' My heart leapt. 'You know him well?'

'I brought him up. He was the loveliest, the most gentle of beings until … Still, now is not the time. Your brother, does he still have a chance?'

I felt tears sweep the back of my throat. 'Yes, if I hurry.'

He didn't say any more, pointing down the street. 'Take a left at the end of this street; it's quicker than the main road and more sheltered.'

I left him then, walking quickly away into the dark streets. Concerned that he might have misread the speed of the storm, I swung round to check. He had crossed the river safely, his small figure illuminated in the lights on the swing bridge. I saw our house, with its cream awning stowed away for the night. It stood as strong and unyielding as Pappy, easily able to withstand the fury of storm or tempest.

I hesitated, nervously eyeing the darkness ahead, with its rows of stubby houses shorn off at the second floor. Dark and forbidding, they had been cobbled together from rough timber planking, their buckled doorways and warped lintels revealing shoddy workmanship. An overwhelming silence had invaded the air, the familiar fluttering of shrouds against a pine mast missing, and as I walked on, I came upon cobbled pathways criss-crossed by narrow waterways, like the warp and waft of a weaver's frame. Most were little wider than a puddle and easy enough to leap across. Only those too broad to jump had been given a plank bridge, railed on one side. And everywhere the stink of refuse and rotting fish, the narrow streets too close-set for the wind to blow through and sweep away the noxious odours.

Shocked, I realised I was back in my dream, the streets little wider than rat runs, dark and twisting in a labyrinth of nightmares. Then, exactly as I did in my dream, I began to run, conscious of a need to find Pieter, aware of shadows watching from upstairs windows, listening to the thunder approach.

Without warning, the streets opened into the square, made familiar by Hans' sketches. At its furthermost edge lay the long wooden jetty that fishing boats thought of as home, with its steps leading down to the lakeside. It had not occurred to me until that moment that I might need a boat. I ran over to the jetty, relieved to see a rowing boat moored at the bottom of the steps, although, in all honesty, I hadn't banked on rowing out to the island. Somewhere in the back of my mind, I still hoped I might find Zande and tell him.

Across the bay, the island shone with light from a dozen lanterns. They spilled across the shoreline, creating orbs of gold in the water. Huddled close to shore were a family of swans, almost spectral in the gloom, their paddling feet breaking the bright circles of light into a thousand gold pieces. Above, cliffs rose in steps like a ladder built for giant feet, their dark silhouette cutting sharply into the evening sky.

The little square seemed deserted, its boutiques, stacked with paintings and objets d'art for visitors to buy, shut for the night. On the far side stood the inn that Hans once told me served good beer. Old, and battered by age and weather, it hugged the ground, its upper storey within easy reach of a tall man's fingertips. Its doorway stood open, so low, the landlord had tacked a notice to the lintel, light from its many windows fastening on a single word: *Beware* ...

38

I didn't notice Ruth at first, although it was by no means fully dark. On a normal day, the sun would not yet have set, but with the approaching storm, objects had lost their colour fusing together in shades of grey. She was sitting at one of the outside tables and must have moved slightly because all at once, I caught sight of her in the light from the window. It shone down onto her head, bestowing a halo around it. She had once told me that photographers who worked for Vogue frequently wasted reels of film searching for that one elusive shot. With her hair loose and cascading down her back, it defied even the dark clouds with its radiance.

'I was waiting for someone.' I caught an edge of defiance in her tone as if she needed to justify her actions.

She had changed out of her summer dress and was wearing her black trousers under her tan jacket, with a matching blouse.

'I would never have thought to find you here.' Conscious how dishevelled I must appear, I attempted to smooth the creases in my skirt, hoping its damp patches weren't as noticeable in the subdued light.

'It's a nice place on a sunny day.'

I recalled her first outing with Pieter. They would have passed through the square on their way to the ferry.

Ruth smiled cautiously, waving her hand at the skies. 'However, if you insist on waiting for a fine day, you'd never leave home. Besides, the cooking's good. Our maid does everything well except cook. Sit down, do. I'm glad to see you. We spend too little time together.'

She sounded nervous as if we were strangers who had just met, her voice contained and polite. 'I saw Tristan. He wasn't pleased, but he'll get over it. How we used to laugh at them, Maidy, those silly boys drooping about as if the end of the world had come.'

I flinched away from the thought of Tristan lying dead. I couldn't tell her. Not when something far more important was at stake; my brother's life.

She obviously caught my change of expression and misread it as censure. 'Please don't be angry with me, Maidy,' she said timidly. 'I know you disapproved. Please tell me what I can do to make it right?' She gave a cautious smile, a tiny dimple appearing briefly before vanishing again, like a gas lamp guttering out.

'Right now, I couldn't care less about that.'

I hurriedly sat down, perching on the edge of the seat, conscious Zande might appear at any second. 'I want to know if Pieter has asked you to marry him.'

'Why?'

'It doesn't matter why,' I retorted sharply. 'Sorry,' I dredged up an apologetic smile. 'I didn't mean to sound cross.' I shrugged, 'But it's sort of important to say one way or the other.'

'Maidy, dear, it's not strictly any of your business,' her laughter was self-conscious. 'Still, as it's you, and you always keep my secrets …' She leaned over the table patting my hand, as much to say, *well you do, don't you.* 'Perhaps.'

'And you refused him?'

'*What is this, Maidy?* Twenty questions?' She took a sip of her orange juice, her gaze directed at the little island. I glanced over my shoulder, making out the long, dark silhouette of a boat tied up against the island jetty. 'What you said ... you were right. It was simply a childish infatuation. I've grown up so much since.'

Relief swept over me. She had listened after all. And Pieter was saved. It no longer mattered who she married, *he was safe*.

'I was going to tell you that Zande and I ... Of course, he hasn't asked me to marry him yet. But he will, any day now,' she said her smile confident.

Strange how a single sentence, a few words even, and everything falls into place – even a farewell kiss.

I recognised the question in her eyes even before Ruth confirmed it with her words.

'I wondered if you ...' Ruth reached up to unclasp a little silver chain from her neck. I hadn't noticed it this morning, hidden by the high collar of her summer dress. At its lowest point, a tiny ring dangled down, its diamond reflecting a gleaming rainbow of light.

I rocked back on my heels as if I'd been struck. 'Who gave you that ring?' My eyes were glued to the little silver object, unable to move away.

'Pieter did. He asked me to keep it for him.'

'Keep? You mean wear?'

Ruth flinched back in her seat, her hands raised in protest at my tone as if I was about to strike her.

'You told me you refused him,' I said, praying for the tiny circlet of silver in the palm of her hand to vanish, for it not to be real.

'No, I didn't,' she cried out.

'You ...' I took a deep breath, my pulse rocketing. She was right. She hadn't. Perhaps doesn't mean yes or no. No different from a skilful boxer sidestepping his opponent, she had danced around the question.

'Maidy. I am saying that I agree with you. *It was a mistake* – exactly as you said. Remember, what you told me I should say to Tristan ...' She trilled a laugh. 'I looked for Pieter earlier. I searched everywhere. I promise; I really did. When you get home, please ... *please* Maidy ... give this to him.'

A storm of noise roared through my head, leaving me dizzy, and I clutched the edge of the table to stop myself blacking out.

Noticing my silence, she frowned, her lips tightening. 'It's the very least you can do, Maidy. After all, it was you who kept on at me, insisting it was simply a childish fantasy. And it would be so unkind to have carried on with it when I love someone else.'

She was blaming me!

From a long way off, I heard my voice. It sounded as if I was reading from a book. 'A ring infers a betrothal; a contract to marry. You don't break a betrothal.'

'Don't be so old-fashioned, Magrit,' she retorted, spitting out my name. 'People get divorced all the time. What about film stars; they marry a dozen times over. What does one little-old ring matter? Besides, I only wore it for a day. I took it off next morning. It's been on a chain around my neck since.'

'Why did you say yes if you were going to change your mind later?'

'It was a mistake, Maidy. You're *always* making mistakes and I never say anything, however much they hurt.'

What mistakes? What was she talking about? How could I make mistakes when I always danced to her tune? I remembered her birthday gift and her telling me afterwards it was a mistake.

'Pieter wanted me to marry him so very much. He kept pestering me to say yes. Begged. *How could I say no?* I didn't want to hurt him. He's your brother.'

Unbelieving, I listened to her twist the truth round and round, like the silver chain she was grasping between her fingers.

347

I might have stuttered and stumbled my way through life and speech, never Ruth. She had always reminded me of the river that flowed past our doorway, languidly heading out to sea, calm and confident, always in control. Now, her words spilled out. I heard them as lies … half-truths even. Only they weren't. This was the truth according to Ruth; the child who had concealed her traumatic past behind a smokescreen of beautiful clothes and lavish bed hangings, her imagination locked away to avoid revisiting the traumas of her past. She had loosened the chains that bound it one time only … for a single story … one that had a happy ending. Now, she was facing a situation not of her choosing and had no clue how to deal with it.

'All the time I was in love with someone else and didn't know it. It happens that way – it's no one's fault.' She gave a tiny shrug. 'It would have been wicked to continue. Please don't be angry, Maidy. You can explain to Pieter, you told me what to say to Tristan. Remember? Thank him kindly and tell him I love someone else. He'll understand.'

All at once I was angry – my anger so deep it reached down to the bedrock of the lake. I couldn't let her get away with hurting the people I loved any more. 'I don't care who you love,' I stormed. 'It's life that matters. You can easily learn to love again, Ruth. You get one chance at life.'

I don't know where my strength came from. Dragging Ruth to her feet, I ran her across the square. Surprised, she had no time to retaliate. Uncaring if she broke her neck, I pushed her viciously down the steps and into the boat. She gave a frightened scream, falling to her knees and making the little craft sky wildly. I jumped in after her, tugging savagely at the rope anchoring the boat to a ring on the harbour wall.

'Stop playing games, Magrit.' Clinging to the edge of the hull, she crawled back up onto her feet and clamped her fingers round the gaps in the planking, holding the little craft tight against the wall. Stretching out her foot to the steps, she made to climb out again.

I couldn't let her escape. I couldn't. Not until I had the answer I needed. Seizing an oar from the bottom of the boat, I pushed it hard against the dockside, making the little craft lurch violently. Overbalancing, Ruth teetered on the edge, her leg outstretched and reaching for the step, forced to choose between tumbling into the water and letting go of the dockside.

She collapsed down onto the little plank seat across the stern, holding on with both hands. '*Have you lost your mind?*' she yelled.

I shrugged. Maybe I had. I wanted to shout back at her, and wipe that beautiful expression of polite enquiry off her face, leaving her as scared and helpless as I was. I raged with hatred, feeling her injury to my family as a festering wound.

Quickly fitting the oars into their rowlocks, I dipped their blades into the water and pulled back, my left arm fumbling and awkward, slicing across the surface. As I raised them out of the water, light from the jetty caught at the tip of the blades, drops of water shining like tiny pearls.

'Maidy, this is not the weather for a boat ride. What are trying to do, kidnap me? Let's go back.' Strands of anxiety mired her voice. '*Please.*'

I'd always done as I was told. She knew that and banked on her smiles and favours winning the day.

Not this time.

Grasping the oars more firmly, I leant into the stroke as Hans had taught me that summer after Pieter had vanished, taking me with him whenever he went out on a Sunday. In his own clumsy way, trying to help me recover from the loss of a favourite brother.

'I'm sorry.' My voice bounced back from the stone wall of the dock, hollow and colourless. It bore no resemblance to the hopeful cadences of that sixteen year-old who had strolled along the street earlier in the day. I sounded old and defeated by life. 'I need you to promise me something first, then I'll take you back.'

Wanting to make certain we didn't drift back to the jetty, I dipped the blades again and again. Slowly, I pulled away from the wall.

'Is that all? *Of course I promise*. Honestly, Maidy, and you made me break a fingernail just for that. Let's go back before I ruin my clothes.' She brushed fruitlessly at her black trousers. 'Does lake water stain? Salt water does.'

With all that was happening, how could she even think about clothes? I felt my anger ignite again and swallowed it down. 'I have to tell you what I want first.'

'Hurry up then.' Ruth inspected her nail and pulling a file out of her bag began smoothing its broken edges.

I paused, unsure how to begin, telling myself over and over again that it was a good bargain and if she had any sense she would snap it up. 'It's to do with Pieter when he vanished.'

She glanced up, little interested, staring over my shoulder at the island.

'He only vanished because he was sick.'

She shrugged. 'What a fibber. He said he'd been travelling and I believed him.'

'He was travelling,' I flew to his defence. 'And he doesn't tell lies. He's like Pappy. Totally genuine.' Except he wasn't, none of us were. 'Besides, it wasn't that sort of sickness.'

All round us the wind gusted noisily, complaining that it wanted to hurry the storm along and get it over with, rocking the little boat from stem to stern and blowing it back towards land. Lightning flared, its brightness quenched by a massive crack of thunder almost overhead.

'Maidy, I'm scared. *Please, let's go back.*'

I ignored her. 'This is an illness that can only be cured if he marries.'

The words sounded ludicrous even to me.

Ruth's reply confirmed it. 'You want me to marry Pieter because he's ill,' she said, her tone scornful. 'And you say that will make him better. How silly. Stop playing stupid games and take me back.'

'No! Not before you swear to honour your promise and marry him.' I felt myself a beggar pleading for food for her young. 'And, yes!' I was shouting, the wind drowning out my voice. 'He will be cured. Mother and Pappy, they want you to be part of our family.' I began throwing in a bushel of words, hoping she would cling on to a few. 'Only the other week, Mother told me Pappy had always thought of you as a daughter. And you'll be so happy. I know you will.' I felt the wind drying my tears even as they spilled over. 'With Pieter at your side, you can travel the world. That's what you told me you wanted. And your children, they will be so beautiful – you said as much yourself.'

'That was yesterday, Maidy,' her words battled with the wind to be heard. 'Why would I need any of those things now? Have you a clue how love makes you feel? It's …' She paused for a moment, studying the dark water as if it held the answer. 'It's like being able to fly,' she finished up. The word *fly* flew back and forth keeping pace with the blades of the oars. 'Please take me back,' she smiled winningly, 'and I'll forgive you my nail and we'll still be best friends.'

Away from the shelter of the harbour, the wind had become stronger, gusting fiercely. Long swells began to lift the boat, rolling smoothly under it before breaking against the harbour wall. I worked the oars, trying to keep us steady, unconcerned that the gap between the rowing boat and the jetty had widened. The harbour was still the closer, and the swell would take us back in.

'Don't you care if he dies?'

'*Your stupid childish imagination, Magrit,*' she snapped.

'Why on earth would Pieter die? There's nothing wrong with him. If anyone's going to die, it's my mother. For goodness sake, grow up. People don't die of love.'

Wind swept across my face, screaming out its fury like a banshee.

'Tristan did.' I shouted into it.

'What did you say?'

Suddenly, as if the wind wanted to eavesdrop on our conversation, it died away, the silence so loud it was almost deafening. The waves, exhausted by their battering, fell silent too. The boat settled, rocking gently in the swell.

I spoke more quietly, needing to get my message across before the wind started up again. 'Tristan's dead, Ruth.'

'I don't believe you. You're making it up.'

'It's the truth. It was an accident, but that doesn't make him any less dead. And Pieter will die too if you don't keep your promise to marry him.'

I stared back towards the shoreline, my thoughts drifting as was our little dinghy, wondering how many secrets it had been party to. Perhaps on another night, when it was warm and the moon was full, a boy would row his sweetheart into the bay, stopping at this precise spot to say how much he loved her and ask her to marry him. 'We're staying right here until I get your promise – and this time I'll make you swear it by everything you consider holy.'

As if playing a duet, a second flash of lightning lit up the bay. Ruth jumped, nervously awaiting another crash of thunder. 'Stop it!' she shouted. I saw her fists clenched tight in her lap. 'I won't listen to your nonsense anymore. What do I care anyway? In a moment, Zande will come. He'll take me back, so don't bother.'

As the lightning left its vivid mark on the sky, I glanced over my shoulder, somehow expecting to see Zande rowing out towards us. For the briefest of seconds, the empty shoreline with its little dock remained as clear as a lighted stage. Then darkness drew a curtain over it. All around, the wind began to howl with renewed vigour.

'*Of course* ...' She pointed her finger accusingly. 'That's it! You're *jealous*. You want him for yourself and with me out of the way, you think you'll get him. Well, you won't, Magrit, *because it's me he wants.*'

I felt the inside of my cheek sore and rough where I'd bitten it. I had to say the words, to acknowledge what I knew to be true. 'I know he does.'

I dug the oars in, taking out my anger and frustration on the water. 'I'm not jealous, Ruth. I promise you, it wouldn't matter at all. I'd even dance at your wedding. Only, you already accepted Pieter's ring. You can't go back on your word.'

I expected her to laugh, to rail at me for being a bad friend … anything … but not sheer, blind terror.

It swept through her as quickly as fire burns through paper. Her eyes a moment before had flashed with anger. Now they were huge and terrified, fixed on something behind us.

'*Oh my God, no!*' She screamed. '*Maidy!*'

From overhead came a furious rumble of sound, as if the hounds of hell had been set loose. Lightning streaked across the sky like a comet burning up. I twisted in my seat, seeing the rock illuminated as bright as day. This was how I had imagined the end of the world would happen for our little land with its streets and houses below sea level … a vast wall of water. Crashing against the rock base of the island, waves leapt high into the air, roaring out their hurt and displeasure. Above them, pale fingers pointed at the sky and I recognised the legendary Devil's Hand. Partially submerged in a torrent of fume and spray, it resembled the last gasp of a drowning man clutching at the air.

Swinging my legs over the seat, I grabbed the oars and pulled back on them, sensing what I should have felt minutes ago – the current inexorably drawing us in like a fish on a hook. I felt the little boat speed up, closing in on that wall of water.

Lightning flashed again, the water boiling, exploding up the cliff in a torrent of spray as if wanting to drown out those five pale fingers of death, so close now I could make out ridges on the tip of the rocks that so closely resembled long jagged nails. Buffeted by the wind, the rowing boat began to buck and rear. Water cascaded over the side as if it too was trying to escape the wind's fearful temper. It fled out the far side, dragging an oar with it.

I noticed the water already up to my ankles and shouted out, 'Use the bailer.'

'I can't move, Maidy. Please, please, you've got to do something. *I don't want to die.*'

I reached for the bailer floating in the water under my seat and tossed it her. 'Start bailing,' I bellowed against the thunderous echo.

Grabbing the boathook from under my seat, I crawled into the bow. Kneeling up, I thrust it hard into the rock. Using all my strength, I forced the little dinghy away from the rocks, prodding at the broken surface like a crab walking. All at once, we were surrounded by swans. They were sheltering in those same rocks that were trying to crush our boat, waiting out the storm. I pushed against the rocks again … and then again … the muscles of my back and arms hurting with the strain. Then we were through and drifting quietly into shore.

39

Protected on all sides from the ferocity of the storm, the little cove might have been a million miles away from the enmity we had just witnessed; its lanterns brightly cheerful, offering a warm welcome. On either side, cliffs rose vertically, with waves crashing endlessly against the rock face. Perhaps as long ago as the creation of earth, some force of nature had severed the cliffs in two, as easily as fabric cut by scissors, creating this smidgeon of land where boats could find sanctuary.

Beyond the reach of the angry water, two men were talking; the sandy surface churned up by the webbed feet of swans wandering restlessly in and out of the water.

They glanced up as the keel crunched the shingle. I recognised Jaan. The other man was older, but somehow still youthful looking, tall and elegant and very handsome, his fair hair thick and smoothed back.

'What the devil?' He strode into the water, ignoring the waves trying to knock him off his feet. Casually lifting Ruth from the boat, he carried her to shore.

This had to be Van Vliet, Zande's father.

Jaan waded in after him, pulling the little boat further

up the beach and helped me out onto dry land. Behind him, the water in the bay moved more peacefully now, seemingly resigned to losing its prey. Across the divide, the roof tops belonging to the inn and cottages bordering the wharf, lay banded in shadow from a street lamp.

'Maidy, whatever are you doing here? This is no place for you. And why bring Ruth?'

'I didn't intend coming here quite like this. The wind sort of took charge.' I kept my head lowered, unwilling to meet his gaze. 'Ruth had no choice in the matter. I'm sorry about earlier, I owe you an explanation.'

'You owe me nothing, unless you're a harpy, in which case an explanation might be required.' Surprised, I glanced up as he knew I would. He was smiling at me, the misty blue of his eyes unchanged, as warmly steadfast as they had always been. He took my hand, helping me across the loose shingle. 'Whatever comes, Maidy, I will never regret our friendship.'

A few hours before, I had told Jaan we could never meet again. What a pathetic lie. I wanted to smile, to say how relieved I was to see him. 'That's the second time today, you've got wet trying to rescue someone.' My voice rang out awkward and uncomfortable. 'You must be running out of clothes.'

Van Vliet broke the silence. 'To what do we owe this pleasure?' He was addressing Ruth. Of course; why would anything change? 'On such a wild night too.' I listened to his voice, recognising Zande's sarcastic overtones.

'Can you believe I was kidnapped?' Ruth had recovered her composure and was in control again, basking in the flattering attention of the man standing next to her. She smiled up at him.

Without thinking, I put out a hand to Jaan. 'Is that Van Vliet?

'Yes.'

'You told me swan people can only live to thirty or thirty-five,' I whispered. 'He has to be older than that.'

'He's the Black. Remember, I told you they were different.'

'The Black?'

I tried to think back, recall what he had said, remembering little apart from Tristan's body floating in the shallows.

'They are the princes of our ... er ... family.' I remembered Pieter saying that he worked for a prince. Jaan hesitated, his smile bitter. 'Their duty is to maintain the continuation of our species. For that, they change earlier and live longer.'

Swivelling on his heel, Van Vliet finally noticed me. 'Margaret?' He took a step back, the smooth mask of his visage as disturbed as the waters of the lake. 'No, it can't be.' He dredged up a haughty smile.

I recognised that too.

'You have to be Margaret's daughter. Your name?'

'It's Magrit. She and Ruth are students at the college.' Jaan answered for me.

'The fabled Ruth.' Van Vliet stepped to her side and placed a finger under her chin, smiling invitingly. 'I have heard much of you. Welcome.' Stepping away, he called across to me. 'Your mother is well?'

'Yes, Meneer.'

'She doesn't know you're here?'

'No. Our coming here was an unfortunate accident, it wasn't meant. *And no,* she wouldn't approve.' I tried to keep my words from trembling, determined not to be overwhelmed by the power in his voice that rivalled anything a storm could produce. 'I was stupidly rowing in the bay and our boat was caught by the current. It wasn't intentional ... Oh no!' I stopped. In the emotional battle of the past half-hour, I had completely forgotten my promise to Meneer Meijer. 'I'm so sorry.' I heard the fear in my voice, its tone rising shrilly. I swung on my heel half-expecting to see boats filled with angry men approaching the island. 'I promised Meneer Meijer I would warn you only I—'

'Meijer! What has happened to him?'

'Nothing. He's fine. He wanted to come himself.' I put my hands to my ears to block out the wailing of a wind that sounded like souls in torment. 'He told me there's going to be a cull.'

All at once, as if the storm in my own body had subsided, I felt calm again. At least my lapse of memory wouldn't prove mortal. I had reached the swans in time and the proposed cull would never happen.

Van Vliet's expression changed, anger and mockery battling for supremacy. 'So much for the promise the City Fathers made me. It cannot be Tristan. Then why?'

I shook my head feigning ignorance.

'When?'

'Meneer Meijer says after midnight when the birds are roosting. He said to take the ...' I swallowed down the words *swan children*. 'Your people and leave.'

I saw fury sweep across his face. Nodding abruptly, his eyes flicked to Ruth and back again. Understanding, I shook my head.

'You obviously possess both sense and a silent mouth. Thank you.'

'My brother, Pieter. Is he here?'

Beyond the narrow stretch of shingle beach was a wooden landing stage, buttressed with solid timbers fixed into the rock and, beyond that, a stepped path, furnished with a handrail and lights. Presumably it led to the village. There had to be one, people couldn't build their homes on ledges like birds.

Lightning flashed, and a movement at the top of the path caught my eye, although there was no sound, everything drowned out by Thor, beating out his paean of war. Across the bay, the fishing port had been swallowed up by the lowering sky. Only the island remained. Zande came into view, the faithful Waldger by his side. With them were two boys, perhaps sixteen, no more. I thought back to those exquisite feathered bodies that had flown over the city on my birthday and with what joy I had greeted them. I wondered how many of that flock carried the same terrible gene as Pieter. Catching sight of strangers, the two boys instantly vanished back up the path.

Up until now, Ruth had said little. Standing alone, she seemed lost and misplaced in a scene not of her choosing. When Pieter and Zande fought in the yard at college, she had simply mounted her bicycle and headed home. Stranded on an island, she couldn't do that. Maybe she had persuaded herself that if she stood still, she wouldn't be there – not really. At the sight of Zande, it was as if someone had flicked a switch. Her face lit up, illuminated with beauty.

For some reason Zande didn't spot her, at least not right away, the lanterns on the nearby jetty illuminating her feet and legs and leaving her head in shadow. It was me he saw. And he wasn't pleased.

Instantly, I schooled my face into a roadmap of nothingness, reluctant to show emotion of any kind, but was unable to prevent my fingers tracing the faintest shadow of a greeting.

'I warned you not to come here?' he shouted harshly. 'Why on earth did you ignore me? On a night like this too. You might have been killed.' He ran on down the slope, Waldger strolling behind. Catching sight of Ruth, he pulled to a stop, examining the scene with frowning brows. 'What *is* going on? I thought we'd planned to meet at the inn, Ruth.'

'We did,' Ruth bubbled over with happiness. 'It's all Maidy's fault. I told her, only she wouldn't listen and now she's trying to make out that Tristan's dead. That's so silly. Tell her Zande—'

'I gather you are unaware you killed Tristan.' Van Vliet cut in and Ruth's remaining words were lost to the wind.

'*Killed?* What rot. He nearly killed me,' Zande flashed a retort. 'I've got the bruises to show for it.' He spun round. 'Jaan? You tell him.'

Jaan slowly shook his head. 'He's dead, Zande.'

'*He can't be.*'

'He is, blast you.' Van Vliet stormed. 'Jaan brought me the news. Didn't I warn you, we wanted no truck with the authorities? No trouble they said. You can live here peaceably or you can leave. *And what do you do?* Two minutes later, you get into a fight and kill someone. You damn us all, boy.'

'It was an accident.' I flew to his defence.

'How do you know that, girl?' he said contemptuously, anger uppermost in his voice. In our country we use the polite form *Mevrouw,* not girl. 'Are you one of those silly creatures that follow him around, unaware of his real intent, to increase the numbers of our little community. We've become rather too few in recent years.' He swept his arm in the direction of the swans sheltering among the rocks, their white feathers gleaming in the light of the lanterns. 'They no longer count.' Again thunder sounded but more distant now; the storm clouds clearing the lake and heading towards the city. 'For some admittedly it was a brief life; nonetheless, a merry one.'

'I was there,' I retorted, refusing to be cowed. 'I watched the fight. It was an accident. And, no! I am not like my mother.'

Van Vliet mocked me with his eyes then his gaze changed, becoming speculative. 'I agree; you are not like your mother. I wonder what you are like? It would be so interesting to find out.'

I felt Jaan tense up, his fists curling into tight balls of anger. 'Maidy is right.' He spoke quietly, his voice well under control. 'You weren't to blame, Zande. Tristan broke his neck when he fell against the iron keel of the sailing boat.'

It was too dark to read the expression in Zande's eyes, although I recognised the mocking smile. Deep down he might well be shocked and grieving but he would never let on. His pride wouldn't let him. Instead, he would punish himself the only way he knew, by killing off everything good in his life.

Wiping away all traces of emotion, he schooled his voice in mimicry of his father's – harsh and controlling, 'Another day when I live up to your expectations, Father. You must be overjoyed. I apologise for bringing more shame and dishonour upon our happy band of brothers.'

'*Drat you, boy.* You should have brought him back with you,' Van Vliet lurched at Jaan.

'How? I told you I saw the porter heading for the beach. He'll have found Tristan's body by now.'

I heard footsteps on the stone path. It was Pieter.

'Ruth,' he called, 'Oh, how wonderful.' With a warm smile, he raised his fingers in a kiss, and ran on down the path, his joyous outburst at odds with the tension swirling about the little jetty.

Waldger eyed him smilingly, a twist of sardonic humour in his expression, already anticipating the scene to come and relishing the discomfort it would bring. Even being party to the truth, I deplored the streak of cruelty that had wedded itself to his character, although I understood why it had happened and no longer despised him. How would I have dealt with such a blow on my sixteenth birthday? My birthday had been full of bright sunshine. His would have ended in the darkness of despair. Confronted with an obliteration of hope, maybe for him cruel humour had proved a more effective antidote than anything else.

I clutched at Jaan's arm.

He covered my hand with his. 'What?'

I pointed with my free hand. 'Pieter,' I whispered, 'he has asked Ruth to marry him and now …'

I didn't finish my sentence.

I had expected Pieter to go straight towards Ruth. 'Maidy!'

He stopped by me. 'Didn't I warn you … *you know?*' he said, reading the ready sympathy in my expression. 'How long?'

'Only today. I witnessed the fight between Tristan and Zande and saw them change, so Jaan was forced to explain it to me.'

Pieter frowned at Zande as if my words had just penetrated him. 'Why on earth were you and Tristan fighting?' He sounded bewildered. 'You're good friends. You and I; we never got on.' Awareness hit me then. Pieter and Zande were half-brothers, with the same father. Pieter must have known, although I doubted Zande had. 'Even so, I regret being so stupid. But Tristan? *Why?*'

Waldger broke in. 'It was over Ruth,' he leered. 'Tristan thought she loved him. Naturally, Zande had to prove him wrong.'

'Let it go, Waldger.' Zande snapped at his friend.

None of players in this final scene were standing far apart. The beach head and the little wooden dock were the stage, lit from behind by a row of lanterns. A whisper could as easily have travelled from one player to another, drifting out over the orchestra pit to the stalls where an audience of swans milled about. Yet I felt as if each one of us had been placed on a mountain peak, miles from the next, and needed to shout our words.

Like Pieter.

He took a step forward his gaze troubled. 'Ruth, what did Waldger mean?' A shade too loudly.

'That was just a silly mix up.'

I have rarely, if ever, seen Ruth look nervous. She did now and her chin came up in a challenge: *Don't dare to question me. I am above that.*

I saw the dagger flash through the air, Waldger wielding it. Except he thought it to be papier-mâché, perfect for the farce he was taking part in. 'Some mix up,' he spoke his lines clearly. 'Like one of those dances where you constantly change partners. Ruth fancied Tristan then dropped him to take up with Zande. Now he's dead.'

I caught his jealous tone. Maybe their future did depend on a cautious approach to girls; nevertheless, it didn't prevent feelings of desire and envy from welling up.

'Dead? He can't be. I was chatting with him only this morning.'

Pieter didn't need a reply; one glance at Zande's bitter expression showed him the truth, the pain carving dark hollows below his eyes.

It stripped the happiness from Pieter, leaving him uncertain and questioning. 'You must be mistaken. Ruth wouldn't do that. She and I are going to be married.'

Too late, Waldger realised he was in the wrong play. He flashed a look of appeal at Zande. He didn't even notice, standing in shocked silence.

Remembering her lines, Ruth dug into her shoulder bag, pulling out the little diamond ring. She held it out. 'I'm sorry, Pieter. Maidy told me I'd made a mistake. Kept on about it. And I had.' She stepped forward. 'You'll find someone else, of course you will, and you will be so happy. Only it won't be me. I'm in love with Zande. Please understand, I couldn't help it, I did try.' She threw in the final words, genuinely believing that made it all right, oblivious to the shock in Pieter's face.

Then she gave him the diamond ring.

A little way away, I caught the sound of waves beating against the Devil's Hand like applause from an audience.

Van Vliet laughed; a mirthless sound that echoed around the rocks.

Zande was shouting. Leaping across the sand, he grabbed Ruth by the arm. 'He asked you to marry him. *He gave you a ring. And you said yes?*'

'Yes ... No ... It was all a mistake. I was mixed up. Ask

Maidy. She'll tell you. She knows. She told me right from the beginning I was in love with you. I should have listened. You know me. I'm so giddy, I never pay attention.'

Ignoring her, Zande switched his attention to Pieter. Unmoving, his gaze was riveted on the bright object nestling in the palm of his hand. Racing across the little clearing, Zande grabbed him by the shoulders, their faces on a level, exactly as they had been once before, when they fought.

'*Pieter, I promise I never knew*. I would never ... I asked. *I did ask*,' he repeated plaintively. 'She never told me you were courting and were going to be married. *Do you think I am so lost as to ... Oh God!*'

His cry hurtled into the storm clouds. The rock echoed it, changing his heartfelt plea into a protracted lament. Gradually it died away, diminishing into a sob. He shook his fists at the sky. 'Curse you! *Curse you!*' he bellowed. A roar of thunder replied.

I hated Van Vliet. I hated his amusement at other people's agony. Yet at this moment I needed him. 'Please, Meneer. *Don't do this*. It's your son you are condemning. Please, save Pieter. I'm sure you can. Please, for the woman you loved.'

'Yes, I loved her.'

'Please.' Twisting round I reached out a hand towards the mainland, wishing like the anchor rope on our little rowing boat, I could as easily pull on it and draw this rocky atoll back across the bay. 'I told you, she doesn't know I'm here. I'll run and tell her ... Please. She'll come. I know she'll come. I know. I promise.'

His laughter mocked me. 'I warned her I would win in the end. Remind her of that when you see her next. Yet, even if it was Margaret on her knees before me, there is nothing I can do.'

'Please, *you can't*. He's my brother and I love him.'

'*Father, for God's sake!* Listen to her. There has to be

something you can do. Pieter doesn't deserve this. His feelings for Ruth were sincere and honourable. Don't let him be punished for a crime he's innocent of.'

Pieter didn't move. As if he had been turned into a pillar of salt, like Lot's wife after the destruction of Sodom and Gomorrah, he stared into the darkness, his face devoid of all expression.

I knew what he was seeing, the pits of hell opening up.

Ruth plucked at Zande's sleeve, her face plaintive yet still exquisite. It was as if a tiny droplet of sun had emerged through the warring clouds. 'Please can we go, I don't understand what's happening and I don't like it.' She began to cry.

'*You don't like it.* Oh my God, Ruth.' I caught the torment in Zande's voice. 'Have you any idea what we've done?'

'I haven't done anything except fall in love. We are going to be married, aren't we?'

'Married?' he snarled out before I could stop him. As if a touchpaper had been lit inside him, I watched his anger and bitterness against the wretched injustice of the situation flood out. 'I never wanted to marry you. I lusted after you, as all men would do and if that had to be the price, yes, I would have married you, heartless wretch that you are. There was only ever one woman I took to my heart,' he spat out the words, '*and it wasn't you.*'

'But Zande, I promise, it meant nothing, I keep telling you that. And you love me, you told me so. Everyone loves me.'

He took a step back, as people do in an art gallery, desirous of viewing a painting from another perspective. 'You really don't understand, do you?' His anger had gone, his words emerging on a note of surprise.

'No, I don't and I never will! Have you any idea what you have lost?'

'I have lost? Do you even have a clue what Pieter has lost?' He said the words quietly, not expecting an answer.

'If you don't want to marry me, *I'll marry Pieter*,' she challenged. I was shocked to hear genuine emotion in Ruth's voice, her loss of control something quite new. 'Then he'll have lost nothing. *You will.*'

Zande turned his back.

I saw her hand reach out and drop slowly to her side.

Like a camera shutter clicking, her expression changed, the glow of a minute ago drained away. She stumbled over to where I stood, searching for a handkerchief to wipe away my tears.

'Maidy, don't beg to that man. He's horrid. If you want me to marry Pieter, I will.'

As if we were in a film studio and she had been told we were moving on to a different scene, she dusted off her jacket, brushing away any problems as easily as a grain of sand. 'You'd like that. And Pieter.' She smiled at him, her hand reaching out. 'We'll all be so happy. I just know it.'

I remembered that first day, the moment she came into the sitting room. Pieter saw her and never looked away.

'I'll be such a good wife, you'll see. We can travel; do anything we want.'

She stretched out her hand. I held my breath, aware she was asking for the ring back. Did she really believe she could get away with it? That beauty alone was powerful enough to wipe out her wrong-doing? I remembered the fairy stories I had made up, in which the main character was a heartless princess. She had always lived happily ever after. Why not Ruth?

Pieter stared down at the little ring in his palm. As he made to hand it back, he gave a great cry.

I knew that sound – it had disturbed my dreams often enough.

Like a corkscrew piercing a cork in a bottle, his body twisted, struck by a mountain of pain, and his knees buckled. He collapsed down and the little ring dropped to the sand unnoticed. At once swans surged onto land. With their vast wings extended into a feathered whirlwind, they camouflaged the descent of man into beast, leaving wisps of white down floating in the air. When they drew back, the tattered remains of Pieter's clothing lay scattered around a white swan. It staggered to its feet, teasing its feathers smooth with its beak.

For a moment, I didn't move ... I couldn't, my body frozen, my thoughts colliding, crashing together. Strangely I was reminded of those great gods ... Kronos and Ananke ... time and inevitability. A single thought eventually found its mark. Pieter had only ever possessed one ambition, to continue the Bader tradition and make mirrors with Pappy. I had no doubt it would have proved far more enduring than even his love for Ruth, but neither would now be realised.

Then as if those self-same gods had decided to rein in their mischief-making, my thoughts came back to life and I remembered something else ... all those years ago ... the young swan ... the one those boys had tormented with sticks and stones. It had done exactly that, with its wing broken and jutting awkwardly, it had teased its feathers smooth.

Zande!

The words I said came flooding back. 'I'm sorry, I can't mend your wing, but please go away it's not safe. People are afraid of swans, and you may get hurt again.'

It had held my gaze, memorising my face – seeing it again some seven or eight years later, dressed in that same dreary navy. That was the connection I'd struggled to make. Why Zande had always thought of me differently. Found his way to my side whenever he was hurt; saved me when I was.

He couldn't tell me before, because of the secret. 'Oh, that secret,' he had said dismissively.

As I raised my eyes from my brother, I saw Zande watching me. He gave me a little whimsical half-smile as much to say: *there, I didn't need to explain it after all, you knew all along.*

Suddenly, Jaan pointed back across the bay. Wanting to close my eyes on my brother's torment, I spun on my heel, noticing the door of the inn wide open, and figures surging out onto the quayside.

'I had hoped to wait until the end of the summer,' Van Vliet called out. 'Apparently not. Get those girls out of here.' The storm over, thunder and lightning were now unleashing their violence on some other part of the country. 'And tell them to keep their mouths shut. We don't want our business voiced abroad.'

Swinging on his heel, Van Vliet strolled up the path. I stared after him, mindful how much Zande hated him, his own father, and how desperately he wanted not to be like him. Sobbing, I ran to Pieter and embraced the long neck, 'Please come back to us, if you can.' I whispered.

'Pieter …' Ruth gasped. Then, closing her eyes to the truth, quietly faded down onto the ground.

Zande picked her up, as if she weighed no more than the handful of stray feathers floating on the current. He carried her over to the little rowing boat, leaving Jaan to retrieve the missing oar that had floated into the shallows.

'I didn't mean it, Maidy.'

Zande touched his fingers to Ruth's forehead, gently brushing back a strand of loose hair. She stirred and opened her eyes.

'I'm so sorry, Ruth. You are right. Everyone would love you. For a moment, I even thought I might. Sadly, with two deaths on my conscience, we would never have stood a chance.'

'Pieter's not dead, Zande.' I reminded him.

Zande raised his eyes to mine, seeking solace and forgiveness. I understood and I forgave. 'This is not how it should have been.' He spoke his words with a simple sincerity foreign to his nature. I stared at him, desperate to memorise every nuance and gesture before they vanished forever; his mouth with that tiny twist at its corner, his gaze awash with a terrible sadness as if all those malevolent traits had been peeled away, leaving only his essence behind.

I forced myself to say the words. 'I know it isn't. And Ruth would have made you happy, I can see that now.'

'I wasn't talking of Ruth, Maidy! With Ruth, I was simply about my father's business. I was talking about you.'

My breath failed as he raised my hand to his lips, gently brushing the tips of my fingers.

Van Vliet called down from the top of the path, his voice blistering with contempt. 'Zande, to me please, *now*.'

Zande shrugged and vanished into the darkness.

'Waldger, give me a hand.' Jaan came over carrying an oar. He indicated the lantern fixed to the end of the wooden jetty, 'If you keep that light in line with the central one on the harbour wall, you won't have any problems getting back.' He pointed back across the bay, 'We will have to leave before the men come, they will burn us out otherwise. You'll be quite safe though, they won't hurt you.'

I glanced back at the harbour, the lights on the wall illuminating the milling shapes that I had once seen in my mirror, swept away by the wing of a swan.

Together, Jaan and Waldger ran the little craft into the water. It floated quietly, the huge swells gone as if they had never been. Keeping his head buried, Waldger hurried up the path after Zande.

I called after him. 'It wasn't your fault, Waldger. Tell him, Jaan. It wasn't anybody's fault – not really.'

I bit down on the words, *not even Ruth's*. Even though I was too tired now for anger, I couldn't find it in my heart to say them. Not today. Not when I had to go back to an empty house and walk past a flight of steps where, as a child, I had so often sat with my brother.

The smile Jaan gave me was full of understanding. Feeling

369

a brisk wind begin to pick up, he tilted his face to the sky. High up, a distant star cast its faint light through millions of miles of blackness. 'Remember how you once told me you enjoyed reading about the gods because they weren't perfect. How like us, they usually made a mess of things and an even bigger mess when they tried to set it right?'

'I said a lot of silly things. You never were a monster, Jaan.'

He swung round, and for a moment he didn't continue. I heard him sigh. 'We're not gods either, Maidy. As mortals, all we can do is try our best.'

He was right. Somehow, but not tonight, I would need to be strong and help Pappy piece together the broken strings of our family. Of us all, only Berthe might remain unchanged.

Jaan stood back waiting while I fitted the oars into their rowlocks. Grasping their handles I began to row, the swan that had once been my brother still raking its feathers into order.

*

I couldn't speak. Even if I could have, what was there to say? Ruth didn't speak either. Trailing her hand in the water, she looked beyond me to the dockside, her gaze quite calm. By tomorrow, all of this would have been buried out of sight – in a large box with the rest of her painful memories.

I stared back at the island and saw Zande on the cliff top. I thought he raised his hand in a farewell but it was too dark to be sure. Feathering the blades over the water, I dipped them in, moving the little craft forwards. As if apologising for its temper earlier, the waters of the lake lay quietly, scarcely stirring, and in less than a heart-beat, we were halfway across.

I caught a glimpse of moonlight. Like a timid maiden, it slowly edged out from behind a cloud, bestowing a tiny nugget of silver on the water. A moment later, a great Armada led by two black swans sailed out into the bay. With a great, raucous cry they took to the air. I waited till the beating of their wings, so similar to the rasping sound made by the sails and halyards of a yacht, blown back and forth in a strong wind, had faded into silence.

And a drop of rain pattered softly down onto the palm of my hand.

Is the end also the beginning?

The Children of Zeus - Book 1

The Click of a Pebble

Yöst listened to the darkness unsure what had woken him. In the distance surf stirred restlessly and wind soughed through the tops of pine trees. Yet that wasn't it. Those were sounds he heard every night since he'd come to live on the island, five years previously. This was more the click of a pebble against a glass window. He and his mother had had glass windows in their tiny house on the mainland. Once he had broken a pane throwing a stone against its brittle surface. He stared into the darkness listening to the quiet breathing of his five companions. Older than him, two were from the great continent of Africa, their skins the colour of aubergines ripening in the sun. Geography was good, Yöst decided, grateful that his mother and grandmother had insisted he attend school, crossing the narrow gap between the island and mainland by boat.

'Learning will take you places,' his grandmother's voice chided him, invading his thoughts as she did almost every night, her voice ringing out as plainly as if she were still alive. That had been her speciality, nagging, when all he wanted was to play with the other boys. Going on and on about learning how to gut a rabbit and build a fire, 'so that you can care for yourself when I am no longer about.'

'Why should I bother?' he had retorted impatiently. 'None of the cobs do that sort of work.'

'That's no excuse. Just because someone else is lazy and

374

stupid. If they stuck their arm into a fire, would you do that too?' she countered. 'I want you to do more than read and write.'

'Why?'

'Because the world is changing and when you are fully grown, you may not wish to live this life.'

'Not wish?' Yöst echoed. 'How can there be anything more wondrous than our lives? I cannot wait to fledge; it is the most exciting thing ever.'

'Yöst!' The old woman had frowned, his name on her lips a rebuke. To her grandson, she was as old as Methuselah, even though her dark hair had little grey in it. Fifty was very old – too old. She had to be old to die from something as trivial as a cough. 'Listen to me. This is no longer a world in which we belong—'

'Grandmother, I'm not listening.' He had laughed then and run outside to watch the young cobs.

A few days before she died, she had suddenly renewed her attack; warning him to be wary of people on the mainland and making him promise never to speak out about his heritage.

'Why not?' he asked, resting her head against his shoulder so she could sip a drop of water.

'It's only my usual winter cough,' she had told him in the April. 'It will be gone soon.' Except it hadn't; her cough worsening each day.

'Because people fear anything different.'

'Fear us!' Yöst laughed in protest. 'We are too few to fear.'

'It makes no difference. We are descendants of Zeus, magical creatures—'

'You aren't,' Yöst retorted.

She chuckled, her amusement quickly evaporating, her thin shoulders humped over her chest as she fought for air. 'No, but I loved a man who was,' she said, her words spoken on an outward breath, fast and shallow. 'Your father was also special, and you will be too. All I can hope is that you heed my words … and learn to listen. Only then may you experience the wondrous life that Zeus promises.'

Yöst listened now, his hearing acquainted with every sound on the island. Still perturbed, he raised himself up on one elbow staring down at Willem, fast asleep on the pallet next to his. That was the first thing new arrivals learned; how to build a bed, although they weren't expected to make its cover. Weaving was women's work. When his mother was alive, each spring they had gone out into the fields above the town, scouring hedges for sheep's wool. She had woven the blanket he was using now. Once Willem fledged, he would move in with the rest of the cobs and leave his blanket behind for a newcomer, not needing it again except in the bitterest of winters.

Yöst closed his eyes, whispering the prayer his mother had taught him when he was little. 'It will help you fall asleep,' she had said.

'Why?'

'If you thank Zeus for all the good things in your life, the list will be endless and you will fall asleep long before you reach the end,' she had replied laughing, changing the serious moment into an unforgettable one. 'And don't forget to say thank you for supplying water to wash your dirty knees and for your argumentative nature, which has left all donkeys hereabouts balancing on three legs. Also, for finally learning how to tie your shoe laces.'

Later, after his mother died, Yöst had made his own list: thanking his god for a mother who had taken such good care of him, and a grandmother who was equally wise and caring; for his sharp hearing and the swiftness of his feet which enabled him to outrun other boys – even Willem who was three years older. Sometimes, if he managed to stay awake until the end of the list, he included his skill with a slingshot and arrow, and—

He caught the sharp crack of stone and sat up, every sense alert. This was not the bare feet of cobs returning from the skies or women rising early to fetch water. This was a shod foot.

He waited to be sure.

Then he heard it. Not a sound, more an absence of sound, as if all the air had been sucked out of a container leaving a vacuum. Close by, he sensed the presence of wild animals standing motionless, awaiting a signal to attack.

Leaping off his pallet, he shook Willem and Tast awake. '*Danger!*'

A lantern flashed, followed by raucous shouting. The door to their hut was flung open and a burning brand flew through the air landing on his pallet. The coarse blanket caught, filling the air with a dense cloud of acrid smoke, tiny flames leapfrogging over the wooden slats to reach the hut's walls.

'Cover your heads,' Willem roared tossing Yöst his own blanket. Grabbing up his pallet, he ran with it towards the back of the hut, pushing the terrified boys in front of him. 'Help me out here, Yöst. Which way out? Where is it safe?'

Yöst spun slowly round, sensing variations in temperature, the dry tinder of the thatch roof already ablaze, with flames spiralling voluptuously red and gold and black, and waves of smoke clogging the air. Covering his nose and mouth, he listened, hoping to pick out an area of quiet, hearing instead the sound of cudgels landing on bone and breaking it in two. Shrieks pierced the sky scarcely recognisable as human, flames crackling and sparking eager to consume life. Another sound added to the layers already besieging his eardrums; birds flocking upwards in panic, and then another, as nets meant for trapping fish swirled through the air to catch at the flailing wings.

'There!' He pointed to a spot where a little pocket of air and space still remained quiet; the ferocity of the storm not yet overwhelming it. He heard a groan and swung round to find Tast collapsed on the ground overcome by smoke, flames nibbling at his hand, searing patches on his already dark skin.

'Hurry.'